PALACE

of

LOVE

and

HATE

OLIVIA WILDENSTEIN

A PACK OF LOVE AND HATE
Book 3 of *THE BOULDER WOLVES* series

Cover design by *Ampersand Book Covers*
Art design by *@elionhardt*
Editing by *Krystal Dehaba*

To finding your true mate.

PROLOGUE

Minutes ago, I volunteered to be my ex's Second in his duel against the ruthless Creek Alpha. In other words, I signed up to referee a fight-to-the-death between the two most powerful werewolves in Colorado.

Both my heart and stomach were a mess of nerves, but not for the same reasons. Where my heart pounded with dread, my stomach clenched from my mate's heightened pulse.

I craned my neck and squinted into the bright midday sun until I located August standing on the deck overlooking the lawn, light-brown skin a shade paler than usual, and the spray of freckles across his nose and cheekbones a shade darker.

I bit my lower lip. He was about to get a lot angrier once he learned the extent of my deal with Liam. Even though I itched to touch my navel that was fluttering with August's fury, I didn't want to draw attention to our bond, so I clenched my fingers into fists and locked them against the frayed hem of my cut-offs.

Liam strode ahead of me onto the sun-soaked lawn of the inn. "Set Alex Morgan free!" he bellowed to the males of my pack holding Everest's murderer.

Blue eyes flashing with confusion, my uncle leaned over the wooden railing of the inn's deck. "Free? He murdered my son, Liam!"

Releasing the enemy Alpha's son was a risky move, but it was the only one that gave us leverage on this godforsaken duel. By cutting Alex loose, Liam and I were buying time to figure out how Cassandra Morgan defeated the Pine Pack Alpha. Even though Liam wasn't convinced she'd cheated, I was. Julian had thrown up after biting her. A throatful of fur and blood shouldn't have upset a werewolf's stomach. My theory was that she'd rubbed a toxic but odorless lotion into her skin, odorless because Julian's Second inspected the Creek Alpha's body before the duel and didn't notice anything amiss.

Cole freed Alex's arm and stepped aside.

"Watt, let Alex go!" Liam repeated, voice clapping the air.

Color darkening his jaw, August all but tossed Alex's arm, making the Creek shifter stumble. The boy steadied himself against the railing, then pushed his blond hair off his bruised face—the Boulders who'd held him captive had done on a number on him—and started down the deck's staircase, a small limp in his gait, probably a result of my pack's roughness. The limp didn't damage his self-assurance, though. His confidence was as potent as the scent of day-old sweat and caked blood that wafted from his body. I backed away as he passed me, then backed away some more when his gaze zipped over me.

The boy might've resembled a Renaissance cherub with his golden curls and arresting violet eyes, but as far as I was concerned, he was the devil.

Liam stepped in front of me. "Eyes off my wolf."

I cringed. Technically, Liam *was* my Alpha, so I *was* his wolf, but I sensed that wasn't how he'd meant it. And from the heightened pounding inside my abdomen, I took it August sensed the insinuation too.

I looked over my shoulder, imploring him with my eyes to calm down. After a moment, the pulsing quieted. Not to say it became quiet. Oh no. My navel still ticked like a time bomb, but the sensation stopped overwhelming all my other senses. I returned my attention to Cassandra Morgan, who'd finally cloaked her naked body in a white sheath that made her look more wraith than werewolf.

"Alexander Morgan." Tipping her face down toward her son, Cassandra ran her knuckles over his cheek.

Alex wasn't short—he had a good three or four inches on my five-seven stature—yet the top of his head only reached Cassandra's chin.

Suddenly, the same hand that had caressed him slapped him. Hard.

Alex jerked in surprise. "What was that for?"

"Scarin' your poor old ma. Now"—she turned the full force of her tapered blue eyes on Liam—"state your terms, Kolane."

I sidled up to Liam. What sort of message did cowering behind my Alpha like a frightened pup send? Definitely not the right one. I didn't think I could ever inspire fear in someone, but I hoped to come across as a worthy enemy.

I was so close to Liam that I could feel the steady beat of his heart. Would it still be drumming had I not raised my hand to be his Second? The memory of Cassandra eating Julian Matz's heart to acquire his link to the Pine Pack had my gaze drifting over the field, toward the sheet-shrouded body of the fallen Alpha. Bile surged up my throat at the sight of the ruby stains that had bloomed over the white cotton. I gritted my teeth.

"As discussed, Ness and I will set the date and location for the venue, and we don't need to give you more than a half-day's notice," Liam said.

"I'm not at your beck-and-call."

"Then we don't have a deal."

Cassandra pursed her lips. "I agree to the twelve-hour notice, but we duel before summer's end."

"We duel when my Second and I decide," Liam answered.

"Be sensible, Kolane. We have packs to govern and care for. It's not fair to them to drag it out. Let's get this over with as soon as possible. I'm sure it's in your best interest, too."

Was it in our best interest, or simply in hers?

Liam peered down at me. "Ness?"

Summer would end in a little over a month. Would that be long enough?

Even though I hated giving Cassandra an inch, I nodded.

Liam focused on the Creek Alpha again. "Before summer ends it is. But, Morgan, if your son, or any other Creek for that matter" —Liam's brown gaze surfed over the field dotted with shifters in skin before returning to Cassandra—"if any of them so much as harm my wolves or their families, your son *and* cousin will be executed without trial and without contest."

Cassandra's cousin, who'd posed as a werewolf-hating hunter for decades in order to gather information on our pack, eyed Liam and me through the wire-rimmed bifocals propped on the bridge of his nose while thumbing his earlobe.

"Alex will behave, just like I said he would." Cassandra wrapped a hand around her son's wrist.

The duel had blunted her nails that, last night, had looked sharp enough to gouge out an eye, but somehow hadn't chipped her burgundy polish. Or had it? As I squinted at her fingers, she released her son's wrist and curled them into her palm.

"This goes both ways, though, Kolane. If any harm comes to my son or to Aidan before the duel, the choice of time and date reverts back to us."

A warm breeze blew tendrils of my blonde hair into my eyes. I wrenched the strands back, but they escaped a moment later. "Alex and Aidan are living on borrowed time, so you have no right to make demands."

"Ness is right," Liam said. "You're lucky they're even alive, and that we've returned Alex."

A crooked smile touched her blood-stained lips. "Careful, Kolane," she said, taking a step closer to Liam, "you're grossly outnumbered."

The Creek pack had swelled by a hundred today, making my pack, with its forty wolves, an even tinier blip on the shifter map.

"Is that a threat?" Liam growled.

"It's a warning."

"I thought you came in peace," I said.

"We offered peace," she snapped. "Your Alpha turned it down."

My jaw set tight. She was right. She had offered, but Liam insisted on dueling her.

"My request that you not harm my son or my cousin is far from outrageous."

"They won't be killed," Liam said after a beat. "Satisfied?"

"Or tortured," she added.

Liam crossed his arms.

As she waited for Liam's answer, Morgan's eyes became incandescent, as though her wolf were fighting to surge out.

"My people will stay away from them," Liam finally relented.

Her eyes lost their inhuman glow. "Good. Do you have any more demands, Kolane?"

Should I ask her to take her pack and leave Boulder until the duel? Liam's voice tickled my mind.

Since I couldn't communicate the same way my Alpha could, I shook my head.

As much as I didn't want Creeks wandering our woods, I also didn't want to banish my best friend and her family from their hometown. I couldn't do that to Sarah. She might be a Creek now that her uncle had been defeated, but at heart, she'd always be a Pine.

Besides, there was a reason the saying *keep your friends close and your enemies closer* had endured through the ages. We'd have an easier time of finding out how Cassandra had cheated by observing her and her pack.

"We have no further demands," Liam finally announced.

"Then it's settled." Morgan started to lift her hand, probably to shake on their deal.

"Who will you choose as your Second, Mrs. Morgan?"

Cassandra's hand halted in midair. I still had trouble reconciling that this woman was the same one who'd set me up on dates through a fake escort agency. The same way I had trouble coming to terms that my cousin had allied himself with her and pinned Liam's father's murder on me.

"I was gonna pick my daughter Lori . . ."

The thin woman, who bore the same narrow facial structure as Cassandra, seemed to stand a little taller.

"But I'm tempted to go with one of my new wolves." The Creek Alpha raised her gaze to the deck where Sarah stood, her straightened blonde hair gusting around her taut shoulders.

As much as I wanted to spare Sarah the perils of being involved in a duel, if she became Cassandra's Second—

"Better not pick me," my friend yelled. "I'd let them kill you."

Hand coming back down to her side, Cassandra grinned. "Dear

Miss Matz, I don't believe you'd let them kill me. I believe you'd do it yourself."

"You're right. I would."

Liam's best friend loomed closer to Sarah. I wasn't sure when it had happened, but Lucas, who'd always abhorred the pack that shared our land, had decided Sarah wasn't hateful, or at least, not *as* hateful as non-Boulders.

"Are there any volunteers who'd care to duel at my side?" Was this her way of testing her new wolves' allegiance?

For a long moment, no one spoke.

But then, a voice I despised more than the Creek Alpha's rang across the blue summer air. "I'll do it, Alpha Morgan." Justin Summix stepped away from his two buddies, his white wifebeater and the skin around his nostrils still speckled with blood from the beating August had delivered after the creep insulted me.

As he approached, Cassandra sized him up. "And you are?"

And here I thought she'd done her homework on all foreign packs . . . Justin Summix must not have been of much interest to her. He *was* a petty and vile shifter who'd insinuated more than once that being the pack's only "bitch"—however biologically correct, I hated the term—meant I was a Boulder slut. He'd touted this barely an hour ago when I strolled up to the inn in August's company.

"Justin Summix, ma'am." He palmed his brown scruff that was the same length and shade as his buzzed hair.

Her gaze halted on the blood splatter before rising to his pulsing nostrils. "Why do you want to duel at my side, Justin?"

"'Cause I know how the Boulders operate." One side of his mouth curled in a sneer. "And I'd really enjoy bringing these two to their knees."

All three Morgans surveyed Justin.

I glanced up at my Alpha, whose lips had arched into a smile. I sensed the turn of events pleased him. Was it because he felt like he knew how Justin operated?

"What happened to your nose?" Cassandra asked.

Justin locked eyes with me. "Like I said, I know how the Boulders operate."

Did you do that?

I didn't answer Liam's question, busy pondering what Justin was hinting at. Was he saying he knew about the mating link? That he would go after August to get to me? My navel tightened from this conclusion, or maybe my navel tightened because August was contemplating wringing Justin's thick neck.

Cassandra licked her lips, removing some of Julian Matz's blood. "Mr. Summix, a duel isn't a settlin' of scores."

I blinked. Was she turning him down?

Justin's yellow-brown eyes widened.

"However," she continued, "I'm willin' to accept your candidature."

Of course she was.

"Are we good, Kolane?"

Liam nodded.

She extended her hand again.

Liam looked at it, then looked back up at her.

"Keep your phone on, Morgan." And then he whirled around and yelled into our minds with such authority that my forehead spasmed. *We're done here!* On our way back toward the deck's staircase, he added, *Ness, you're coming home with me.*

I stumbled, just managing to catch myself on the handrail. He'd said those exact words to me a month ago.

Our work starts today.

I swallowed.

August started down the stairs, but Liam stepped into his path and said, "I said we were done here."

"Get out of my way, Liam."

Liam must've spoken directly into August's mind, because my intended's jaw turned as hard as bark, and then his gaze fell on me, *narrowed* on me. He backed away, before stalking into the inn, stretching the tether so violently that, for a second, I feared it would snap.

But it didn't.

It simply thinned and weakened until all that was left behind was a dull hollowness.

To spare Liam's heart, I'd maimed August's.

CHAPTER 1

I didn't speak to Liam during the ride over to his house, because I was angry at how he'd dealt with August. I was also mad at myself for not having put up more of a fight. Then again, I'd been trying to get Liam to calm down and leave the inn with his heart still locked in his chest.

I propped my elbow on the door handle and my forehead on my fingertips. A headache was blooming against my temples. Too much stress and too little sleep. I didn't regret the too little sleep part, though.

Spending the night with August had been . . . well, it had been something I would never regret. My lips still tingled from the heat of his mouth, and my heart still pounded from the memory of his beating against mine.

Would I ever get another night with him? What if he left Boulder until the Winter Solstice? Or what if he stayed but shunned my existence?

That made my heart start twisting.

Before being my intended mate, he was my friend, the boy who'd taught me to climb trees and read stars, the boy who'd picked me up from school when my parents couldn't, the boy who'd sat in my darkened room so the monsters under my bed couldn't reach out and harm me.

When the mating link clicked into place between us on the

night of Liam's swearing-in as Alpha, I'd been desperate to break it. After all, Liam was still my boyfriend then. But that relationship lasted a whopping four days. The rain-soaked afternoon Liam called me a traitor was the end of him and me. However much he'd groveled once he figured out I hadn't backstabbed my own pack, I couldn't bring myself to forgive him for his rushed and erroneous judgment. And then last week, he'd slept with his gorgeous, redheaded ex, Tamara, which hurt, but the pain of losing him was nothing compared to the fear of losing August.

The black Mercedes SUV bumped along the short dirt driveway, jostling me out of my morose deliberations. Once we were parked, I reached for the door handle.

"I know you hate my guts right now, but I didn't force you and August apart to annoy you, Ness. My life's on the line, and I need a hundred percent of your attention."

I side-eyed my Alpha. Like I would believe that. He'd been willing to give up his life minutes ago.

"Do you have any food?" I asked, forcing the topic away from August.

Liam's tense expression stuttered. "Yeah. Matt's mom sent me lots of stuff a couple days ago."

"Good. Because I'm starving."

I got out of the car and walked to the front door of his sleek one-storied cabin with the glassed-in living room. I didn't tap my foot as I waited for him, even though he was taking his grand old time. He checked his phone and typed out a message before finally making his way to me. He unlocked the door and gestured for me to go ahead of him. My nostrils flared at the scent of mint lacing the air, which had once felt like silk against my senses, but now felt like sandpaper.

"Why don't you take a seat? I'll get the food."

I crossed over the cowhide rug and sank into his brown leather couch. As he banged around in his kitchen, I checked my phone for messages. I had plenty, but none from August.

I opened one of Sarah's. The first read: *WTF?*

The second: *You volunteered to be his Second! Are you insane?!*

The third: *Why did you leave with Liam?*

The third: *Call me.*

The fourth: *I'm worried. Please call.*

I was touched she was concerned considering she'd lost her uncle today. I should've been the furthest thing from her mind. I pressed on her phone number, then held the phone to my ear.

Big mistake.

Her voice poured out of the receiver so shrilly I winced. "What the hell, Ness? You're going to duel Cassandra Morgan? *And* Justin? Did you see how he was looking at you? Like he wants to kill you, that's how he was looking at you! And knowing him, he'll try! I know I said I wanted Liam to take over the packs, but—"

"Sarah!" I spoke her name sharply to make her stop yelling. "Your mom was Julian's Second, and she's fine."

"But Julian's not! He's not fine! He's . . ." A sob lurched out of her. "He's dead. Julian is dead." Another sob. "Oh, God . . . I think I'm going to puke again." Her words were muffled, as though she'd clapped a hand over her mouth.

"Is someone with you?"

"Yeah. Robbie and Margaux. We're going to the . . ." She sniffled. "To our old headquarters." She blew her nose. "We're holding a vigil for Julian."

"Oh, sweetie."

"I can't believe he's dead. I can't—"

A thought occurred to me. "Sarah, did your pack have a stock of Sillin?" The word tasted bitter, because the anti-shifting drug had caused so much harm.

First at the Alpha trials, when Everest blackmailed me into entering the last duel so he could steal the Boulder's stock from HQ. Then, when he'd reneged on his deal to sell the pills to the Creeks, and Alex Morgan drove my cousin's Jeep off the road.

The night I decrypted his last voicemail and found the Boulder's stock—minus one packet—under the loose floorboard of my childhood home, I hadn't felt any pride or relief. Just despondency, because it had been too late . . . my cousin was already gone forever.

Werewolves possessed magic, but resurrecting the dead wasn't part of our arsenal.

Unless the fable Liam had told me of the wolf resurrecting her mate with a love bite was true, but I doubted fangs sinking into flesh could do much else than stop a heart. It was a pretty legend, nonetheless.

"Robbie says we have some," Sarah answered just as Liam walked out of his kitchen, toting two plates and silverware.

He set everything down on his wrought-iron coffee table, then took the two bottles of water he'd secured underneath his arm and placed them on top of a huge glossy tome.

"Before you go to the wake, can you grab them and hide them?" I asked Sarah.

As he sat in the armchair across from me, he lifted an eyebrow.

"We'll go get them now," Sarah said.

"Thank you."

"If you need anything else, Ness, anything at all, call me."

I smiled in spite of the hellish day I'd had. In spite of the hellish days to come. "Is the wake open to other packs?"

"If Cassandra shows up—" Sarah started.

"I was asking because *I'd* like to come."

"Oh." She paused. "You don't need to, Ness."

"I never do anything I don't want to do."

"You signed up to be Liam's Second," she said.

The tendons in Liam's neck strained against his tanned throat. Even though Sarah wasn't on speakerphone, his hearing was sharp enough to hear her.

"As crazy as it may sound, I wasn't ready to see him die," I replied softly.

Liam rested his forearms on his knees, linked his fingers, and stared so hard at his knuckles that a vertical groove appeared between his eyebrows.

After hanging up, I placed my phone face down on the coffee table. "I think it would be in good form for you to attend Julian's wake, too."

His gaze jerked to mine. "You do realize they're all Creeks now."

"They're also human. *Part* human. Anyway, it was just a suggestion. Not an order."

Slowly, he nodded. "You're right. I'll accompany you."

"Good."

"So, Sillin, huh? You're really convinced that's how she defeated Julian?"

I looked around the bright, clean room with all of its sharp angles and muted colors. Dust motes sparkled in a streak of sunlight. "Any chance your house is bugged?"

"Cole did a sweep of it the other day. No listening devices or hidden cameras."

"I'm not convinced of *how* she cheated, just that she did."

"Then why didn't Nora Matz signal foul play?"

"Sillin is odorless. If Sandra ground it up into her body lotion—"

"Cassandra." When I frowned, he added, "You just called her Sandra."

Right. "Sandra's what she called herself when she posed as a Red Creek Escort pimp." I ran my lower lip between my teeth. Three little letters that had hidden her identity from me. I couldn't figure out if she'd chosen the moniker for lack of creativity or in the hopes that I'd figure out who she was.

"Your theory?"

I picked at the frayed hem of my cutoffs. "She rubbed it into her skin, and when Julian bit her, it made him weaker."

"But Sillin doesn't make us throw up."

He was right, but maybe mixed with lotion . . .

"Besides, wouldn't it have penetrated her bloodstream?"

"Eventually." I sighed. "I'd like to test my theory. Is the Sillin here?"

"No."

"Where did you put it?"

"Somewhere safe."

"Which is?"

"Somewhere safe," he repeated as though I hadn't heard him the first time.

I crossed my arms. "Which you're going to keep me in the dark about?"

"It's better that I do."

"Because you still don't trust me?"

"I trust you."

"Then why won't you tell me?"

"Because the Creeks killed Everest over this drug."

"They killed him because he defaulted on his deal to sell it to them."

"The Creeks have more money than they could ever use. Especially if you factor in Aidan's real estate contribution. I may hate the man, but he's smart at business and has built an empire." Liam unlinked his fingers and set his palms on his denim-clad knees. "They didn't off your cousin because of a monetary loss."

A chill swept over me. *So they really need Sillin . . .* "And yet you were willing to fight her."

"I was ready to fight her because I know how the drug works."

"And I don't?"

He made a growly sound that had my shoulders squaring.

"I took it for weeks, Liam. When I moved to LA, Mom forced me to ingest it every day to make my werewolf gene dormant."

"Then you know that once the pills are popped out of their packaging and exposed to air and heat, their effect wears off. That's why we kept ours in a padlocked fridge."

I raised an eyebrow.

"So *if*—and this is a huge if—Sillin was in Morgan's bloodstream or on her skin, its effect would've diminished by the time I got around to fighting her."

I took in this information, filed it away.

He tilted his head to the side. "You know what baffles me most about all of this? You're always the first to proclaim that women are equal to men, yet a female Alpha defeats a male, and you're convinced she cheated? Why is that?"

My arms went lax, but since they were still knotted in front of my chest, they didn't plummet against the couch. "Julian threw up."

"Yet his Second—who has absolutely no love for the Creek Alpha—didn't signal foul play? Either Nora Matz is dumb as shit or you're smart as fuck."

I watched his expression, watched it closely to know what his conclusion was.

"Don't look at me like that."

"Like what?" I asked.

"Like you don't know what I'm thinking."

"I don't know what you're thinking."

His haggard face softened. "You always know what I'm thinking." He looked down at his long fingers as he rubbed his knees. Back and forth. Back and forth. When he raised his gaze back to mine, he said, "If you were dumb as shit, I wouldn't have accepted you as my Second . . . however enthralling you might be." A heavy breath puffed out of him. "I know I suggested killing your father, Ness, but I'm the first person to admit how wrong it was. I sincerely hope that, someday, I'll be half the man he was."

Liam hadn't moved off the armchair, yet it felt as though he were kneeling beside me, repeatedly flicking my heart.

"If *you* think I'm worth fighting for, then fuck, I'll fight. Alongside you, I'll fight. I'll become a worthy Alpha. One that you will never"—his eyes bore into mine—"want to run from again. One who would never let you run again."

Silence settled between us.

"I want your admiration, Ness. I might never get anything else from you, but I hope I'll earn that much back."

Tears slickened my eyes.

Because he'd brought up my father, I told myself. That was the reason for my tears. The *only* reason for them.

Big fat lie. If that had been the only reason, I would've been able to keep my gaze on his, and I couldn't.

I studied the cowhide rug, discreetly running a knuckle along my cheeks, then took a fortifying breath and lifted my gaze. "How much are you going to pay me?"

His piercing stare swept over my face. For a moment, he neither answered nor moved. Then he leaned back in the chair, crossed one foot over the other, and bounced his legs as though annoyed I'd brought up payment. "How much do you want?"

"Five grand."

"Per week?"

I blinked, whipping my gaze to his. "No. In total."

He stilled his legs. "I'll give you five grand today and the sum of *my* choice when we win the duel."

"Liam, I don't need—"

"Without wanting to sound cocky, I have more money than I could ever spend already. If I win, well those zeroes are going to add up."

"Good for you and for the pack, but that's not why I'm doing this."

The steadiness of his gaze was unnerving. "Why are you doing this?"

"I already told you why."

"Tell me again."

I raked my hand through my hair. "Because I don't want you to die."

"Why don't you want me to die? Don't I deserve it?"

"Don't worry. I've tortured you plenty in my thoughts for calling me a traitor."

He snorted, and crazy as it sounded, I smiled.

How far we'd come, him and me.

How far we still had to go, though.

I took my plate of food and balanced it on my knees. "Can we be clear about one thing? This isn't a game to me. I want to save your life, and the reason I want to save it is because you don't seem to care what happens to it."

That sobered him up.

I bit into a chunk of cheese. "I have some leftover Sillin from LA. I haven't refrigerated it, but it's still in the packaging. You think it's still effective?"

He picked up his plate and cut into his steak. "If it's from the same batch you slipped my father, then yes, it's still effective."

Guilt spread through me. Heath hadn't deserved to live, yet I regretted having a hand in his death. "You think Morgan will release Julian's body to his family?"

"Not if she poisoned him." He uncapped his water bottle and took a swig. "Unless she was certain the Sillin was no longer in his blood."

"How long would that take?"

"Depends on the dose."

"I guess it doesn't actually matter," I ended up saying. "Once we test the Sillin out ourselves, we'll know whether she used it or not."

CHAPTER 2

After discussing other ways Cassandra Morgan might've won the duel—Sillin-free ways—Liam dropped me off in front of the apartment I shared with Jeb on the top floor of a two-story house.

Before I could shut the car door, Liam said, "Matt will be over in the morning. Probably around 6:30."

I frowned.

"I want you to start building muscle and stamina."

"Why do I need Matt for that?"

Liam draped his hand over the back of the seat I'd just vacated. "He's going to take you running."

"I can take myself running."

He smirked. "I'm sure you can. But in case you've forgotten, we have a lot more wolves in town."

"You think they might attack me?"

His eyes blackened. "No. I don't think they'd risk such a *tactless* move, but you're not running around in the woods alone. Come to think of it, Lucas should move back in with you, or you could"—he ran his hand through his hair—"stay at my place."

However much Lucas had grown on me, he was not moving into my two-bedroom apartment. "I have Jeb. Besides, what sort of message would me needing a babysitter send out?" I didn't even bother bringing up Liam's other suggestion. "They already don't take me very seriously. Don't add to it."

"Who's *they*?"

"Pretty much everyone." When he opened his mouth, I tossed in, "I'll be going to Pine HQ around seven."

He scrutinized my face a long moment before saying, "Okay. I'll pick you up at six."

"I have my license now." I flashed him a smile that he didn't reciprocate. "I'll get myself there."

His eyes clouded, as though he wasn't pleased with my budding independence. Or was my arrangement of getting there on my own not to his liking?

THE LAST AND ONLY TIME I'D GONE TO THE PINES' headquarters was for Margaux and Robbie Matz's engagement, and it hadn't been to celebrate them. I'd gone to secure an alliance with Julian because my cousin had convinced me I'd killed Heath and that the pack would avenge their Alpha's death by ending my life.

I'd gotten so much more than Julian's help that day. I'd gotten a confession which had overturned my world: the name of the man who'd murdered my father . . . a man who was still very much alive even though my pack had claimed otherwise.

My heels clicked on the stone staircase that was bare of rose petals and votive candles tonight. Steeling my spine, I stepped past the open doors. The high-ceilinged atrium lined with French windows on one end and dark, wainscoted walls on the other was filled with black-clad grievers. Even the orchid arrangement by the propped picture of Julian was a shade of purple so dark it looked black.

I tried to replace the last image I had of Julian with the blown-up tanned and expressive face staring back at me from within the gilt frame. He would've loved that frame, so golden and ornately carved. The man had such a weakness for expensive things.

My gaze surfed over the room until I spotted Sarah. She was opening one of the French windows overlooking the labyrinthian hedges that separated HQ from the deceased's pale-stone mansion.

As I forded through the copse of wary wolves, I offered condolences to the mourners. From the scrunched brows and skeptic looks, I surmised few believed I was being genuine.

Oh well. I wasn't here to convince them; I was here for Sarah.

When I finally reached her, I tapped her shoulder, and she spun around, puffy brown eyes growing wide in surprise. Apparently, she hadn't put much stock into me coming. She hooked her arms around my neck and hugged me tight.

"Twice in a day. What's the world coming to?" I said into her blonde mane.

She pressed away from me. "Wh-what?"

"You hugging me. That's twice."

Her lips quirked up in a smile. "Don't get used to it."

"I wouldn't dream of getting used to anything around here. Everything's always shifting: alliances, hearts, Alphas . . . people."

She cocked an eyebrow. "Did you just make a joke?"

"Maybe. But don't get used to it," I said, using her own words. "I'm not a very funny person."

Her smile grew a little wider, and then it froze as her gaze locked on a place over my shoulder. She tilted her head toward the entrance.

I turned and saw Lucas and Liam making their way toward us. Both wore black—where Liam had donned a button-down over dark slacks, Lucas sported a T-shirt over jeans.

"Are a lot more of you coming?" Sarah asked after they reached us.

"Why?" Lucas waggled his eyebrow, the one slashed by a white scar. "Afraid of running out of finger food, blondie?"

Liam coughed, probably trying to signal that Lucas's joke was in poor taste, but Sarah laughed, which won her many scowls.

"I don't know if more of us are coming." Liam scanned the room, which from his vantage point, was way easier than from mine. Not quite as tall as August's six-and-a-half foot frame, Liam was still up there. "Did they release Julian's body?"

Sarah shook her head. "I doubt they will." She took a small step toward me, almost as though she were about to drop a kiss on my cheek. "I got all the packets out."

I squeezed her wrist in gratitude.

"What packets?" Lucas asked, ever so subtle.

Liam must've answered Lucas through the mind-link, because the latter blinked.

Sarah nodded. "I put them somewhere safe and cool."

"Not in your house, I hope," Lucas said.

Her cheeks pinked. "No."

"Remind me to play poker with you. You're a shit liar."

She flushed a little more.

"Lucas . . ." Liam started, a warning in his voice.

"She shouldn't keep that shit anywhere near her," Lucas growled.

Panic tightened my throat. "He's right, Sarah. Look at what they did to my cousin."

"Oh." Even though Sarah's lids were bloated with tears, they lifted a little higher. "Where should I put them then?"

"You could give them to us," Lucas offered.

I could tell from the way her head jerked back that she wasn't fond of the idea. "I don't think Robbie will go for that."

Lucas puffed out a breath. "Your brother knows?"

"He helped me get them out," she murmured.

A nerve ticked in his jaw. "And he let you keep the stash?"

Sarah splayed her hands on her hips. "He trusts me, Lucas."

I didn't think trust was the issue.

Before I could say anything, a hush fell over the room, disturbed only by the swish of fabric and the clink of jewelry.

"Don't stop talkin' on our account," came a voice that was becoming familiar all too quickly.

I whirled toward the sweeping staircase. At the top of it stood Cassandra Morgan, barefoot and sheathed in a tunic that resembled a burlap sack.

Sarah hissed before clapping her hands over her ears.

"What did she say?" I whispered.

"She called us her little Creeks," Sarah muttered.

Cassandra gestured behind her. "I've come barin' a gift."

Two men with bulging muscles entered the room, hefting a stretcher. On top rested Julian's naked body. No sheet covered it. No blood or dirt either. The Creeks had cleaned him up and sewed his thorax shut with thick black thread. Considering how waxen his flesh was, I assumed they'd syphoned away his blood. Unless they'd left him in the field until he'd bled out completely.

Gasps thundered through the crowd, and then a jarring sob ripped across the room, louder than all the gasps.

"Justin urged me to return your fallen Alpha. So here I am, returnin' him. Consider it a peace offerin'."

The men behind her crouched, depositing the stretcher beside the framed picture; then they backed up and remained standing shoulder to shoulder by the front door.

A raucous voice swam through the bewildered crowd. "Cover. Cover," it said, and then heels clicked on the stone stairs as a gray-haired woman tottered up to the landing. She vanished through a small door, before returning with an armful of lavender hand towels monogrammed with golden Ps. Complexion almost as pallid as her dead Alpha's, she kneeled and gently covered him, strip by cottony strip.

Once Julian was mummified in terrycloth, Casandra started down the stairs. "Aidan said Boulders weren't empathetic, but I see my cousin was wrong. I thank you"—she inclined her head toward us—"for showin' my people such kindness."

"We are *not* your people!" Sarah's voice pinged against the buffed stone floors.

Cassandra narrowed her eyes, and Sarah clutched her head, shrinking into herself.

"You can hear my voice in your head, can you not, Miss Matz?" the Creek Alpha asked pleasantly.

Sarah didn't say anything, but her spine tautened.

"If you can hear me, then you are mine." As Cassandra strolled through the room, shadows played across her features, staining her eyes. "Just as I am yours." She stopped when she reached Sarah's brother, who'd gathered his shoulder-length blond hair into a pony-tail. "You were next in line if I'm not mistaken."

Robbie nodded cautiously, his hair glinting gold in the dim lighting.

"I'd like you to tell me about your pack so that I may lead it well. Shall we take a walk in the gardens?"

Before he acquiesced, Robbie's eyes flashed to his sister's. I moved in front of Sarah as though I could somehow deflect his glance, but Cassandra trailed his line of sight, and although her gaze paused on me, she tilted her face, which told me she hadn't missed the true object of Robbie's attention.

Dread pooled in my stomach. Robbie probably hadn't considered the repercussion of looking his sister's way, but I did, and I didn't like it one bit, the same way I didn't like that he'd left the Sillin in her care. If he didn't have all the answers Cassandra wanted, she'd come looking for Sarah, and I didn't want the Creek Alpha sniffing around my friend.

Cassandra claimed she'd come in peace, but if that were true, she wouldn't have brought her shifter army with her . . . she wouldn't have created an escort agency to spy on other packs.

We should leave. Liam's silent command startled the air out of my lungs.

I sucked in a breath before nodding and turning toward my friend. "Ready to go?"

Sarah's dark eyebrows quirked. "Go?"

I spread open my eyes to drive my intent home; I wasn't leaving without her. "My car's right outside."

Maybe Cassandra wasn't after the Pine's stock of Sillin, but what if she was?

As understanding crept over Sarah, color leached from her skin. "Let me say goodbye to Mom."

"Of course."

She wound around her pack toward her mother, who was slumped on a couch, pallid cheeks shiny with tears.

"Ness?" Liam nodded to the entrance.

I set off alongside him and Lucas. As we took the stairs, my gaze wandered to the lavender shroud atop Julian's still form.

"If anyone ever buries me in fucking tea towels, I'm going to haunt their ass," Lucas huffed under his breath.

Laughter burst out of me. Even Liam's lips quirked up. I pressed the back of my hand against my mouth to stifle the sound that was so incredibly inappropriate that even Cassandra's bodyguards gave me a hard stare, and I doubted they had any love for Julian and his pack.

I elbowed Lucas as we exited. "They're all going to think I'm heartless now."

Lucas dragged his hand through his shaggy black hair, grinning. "You should always keep your enemies guessing."

"The Pines aren't my enemies."

"They're no longer Pines," Lucas said just as Sarah surged out of the building.

She must not have heard him, because she didn't react to his comment. She hooked her arm through mine and all but dragged me down the stairs. "I've changed my mind. I'd like you guys to take the stuff."

It took me a second to compute what *the stuff* was. When I did, I turned and exchanged a quick glance with Liam.

"Lucas"—he tossed him the car keys—"take Sarah home."

Lucas frowned at first, but Liam must've elaborated, because he nodded. "How're you getting home? Running?"

"Ness has a car."

I clutched my keys tight enough to leave an imprint. "I think it's better if you go with them, Liam."

A dark lock of hair fell into his eyes.

"I'd feel better if Sarah had both of you with her," I added.

A half-truth.

The other half of that truth was that the drive took a little more than a half hour, and I felt like Liam and I had spent enough time together for one day.

And I might not have trusted his intentions concerning me yet.

It took a couple minutes—maybe seconds—for Liam to unglue the soles of his black boots from the flagstone path. Shoulders wrenched back, he strode to his car.

Lucas looked between us before going after our Alpha.

Sarah bit her lip. "I'll call you tomorrow, hun." And then she was gone too.

And I was finally alone.

The drive home took me straight past the Watts' warehouse. Even though it wasn't late, August's apartment, which flanked the warehouse, was pitch-black.

I tried to feel him through the tether, but my stomach was a giant jumble of emotions. I parked on the side of the road, grabbed my phone, and typed out a text: *Don't leave Boulder, ok?*

In the starlit darkness, under a moon that was almost full, I waited for August to reply.

No reply came.

CHAPTER 3

At 6:15 a.m. the following day, I peeled my body out of my warm bedsheets and got ready for my early morning run with Matt. I was lacing my sneakers when he messaged me that he was downstairs. Stuffing my key and phone in the zippered pocket of my track jacket, I tiptoed past my sleeping uncle's room, opened and shut our front door discreetly, then bounded down the porch stairs.

"Sorry you got saddled with me."

He pushed away from his silver Dodge sedan, palming his cropped blond hair. "Don't sweat it, Little Wolf. I owe you."

"What do you owe me for?"

"Stopping Liam from dueling Morgan without backup."

I tightened my ponytail, sighing. "If only he'd taken her deal."

"You're telling me." Matt Rogers was a big guy but as gentle as a puppy. "Should we get going? I need to be at work in an hour."

I stretched out my calves. "I'm ready."

Thirty minutes into our ridiculously strenuous workout—Matt had picked a trail that wound up the flank of the mountain—I wheezed, "I don't get . . . why I have to train. Your brother said . . . Seconds rarely get . . . dragged into the fight." I gulped in some much needed oxygen, then puffed it out. "Look at Nora . . ." My heart rate became so frenzied I had to take a minute off from speaking.

"If Julian's sister had gotten involved, he might still be alive today." Perspiration beaded on Matt's forehead, but unlike me, he wasn't panting like a bull in a pen.

I came to an abrupt halt, which forced Matt to stop, then bent at the waist and pressed my palms into my thighs. "The poison was already . . . in his system."

His gaze swept over the fence of evergreens on our left, as though he were expecting to see furred creatures with perked ears and glowing eyes. "I heard about your theory, but Morgan could shift. If she'd been jacked up on Sillin, there's no way she could've transformed."

"I don't think it was . . . in her blood." I sucked in a lungful of hot, dry air. The sun was peaking, brightening the pink hue of the mountain lupines lining the steep path. "I think it was . . . on her skin."

"Stuff on your skin penetrates your bloodstream."

I straightened, crossing my arms in front of my still-heaving chest. "Don't tell me you think . . . she won fair and square."

"Nora Matz seems to think so."

I wasn't in wolf form, yet I growled at my friend. "That's impossible."

A slow smile lit up his ruddy face. "I agree. I mean, she *is* female—"

"Prick." I slugged his huge bicep, which just increased his smirking.

"You know I don't actually think your gender is feeble, right?" His smirk turned back into a smile.

"Yeah. I know." It had taken me months to prove that a female could hold her own in a pack of all-male wolves. Did I regret entering the Alpha trials at the start of summer?

No.

Okay . . . Maybe a little.

After all, I'd almost lost my life during a landslide and then again during the final duel, which thankfully had been aborted when my crafty cousin had his mother kidnap Evelyn.

As Matt and I started down the mountain, I asked him about work, which was merely a roundabout way of getting to August since he was Matt's boss.

He told me they were putting up the walls on some luxury lodge on Valmont Road. "Place is wicked."

"Is August . . . Does he help with the building part?"

"Yeah. He gets his hands dirty."

"Is he on site every day?"

Matt cast me a sideways glance. "What exactly do you want to know?"

I bit my lip but released it to gather some oxygen. "Did he stay?"

"You seriously think he up and left? He got the girl. He's never going to leave. At least not without you."

A flush creeped up my neck. Hopefully Matt would attribute it to our strenuous exercising. "Liam's making me keep away from him."

"What do you mean, *making you keep away?*"

"He told me that since he's entrusting me with his life, he wants my entire focus to be on him. He said that until the duel, I couldn't hang out with August. That if I did, he'd duel Cassandra on his own terms."

Matt didn't say anything, just focused on the dust puffing under his sneakers.

"You think he's really worried about August being a distraction, or do you think it's his way of getting me back?"

Without breaking stride, he said, "What do you think?"

"I don't know what to think, Matt. I don't know Liam like you do."

"He's not over you, Ness."

Even though my limbs felt on fire from running, a chill crept into my bones. "You think he'd really face Cassandra without my help if something happened between August and me?"

"I'd hope he wouldn't do something so dumb, but he was ready to challenge her without a Second, so yeah, I think he'd really schedule a showdown without you. Men will do stupid shit to impress girls."

"It wouldn't impress me, though. It would just piss me off."

"It'll get your attention."

I sighed.

"Look, I'm not sure I'd take my own advice, but if you can rein in your urges, then do it."

I snorted. "Rein in my urges? I'm not some animal."

Matt grinned. "Beg to differ, Little Wolf." After a beat, he added, "At least, try to repress your lustfulness."

The flush, which had started on my neck, engulfed my entire face.

"Did I just make Ness Clark blush?"

"Shut up," I grumbled, breathing hard again. "And I'm not blushing . . . I'm just overheated from this stupid . . . run."

"Uh-huh." He simpered all the way to his car. "Look, if anyone can tame their urges, it's you."

Hand pressed on the hood of his car, I pulled my ankle into my hamstring to loosen my thigh.

"Besides, we're talking days, right? Not weeks?" Matt asked, muscles bunching in his arms and thighs as he stretched.

"I don't know how long it'll take." I kicked a stray cigarette butt off the sidewalk and into the gutter. "Perhaps it'll take the full five weeks we have."

As he got into his car, he said, "Well, I'm sure August'll understand."

Yeah, I wasn't sure about that at all. He still hadn't answered the text I'd sent him last night.

"Same time tomorrow?"

I whipped my gaze off the squashed death-stick. "We're running tomorrow?"

"Every day until the duel. I'll plan a different route, though."

"What the hell did I sign up for?" I grumbled.

"You signed up to save your Alpha's ass."

"I don't need muscle for that, Matt; I need a working brain and time to think."

"Little Wolf, if the fighting gets dirty, you'll want the muscle."

Matt's comment eclipsed all my residual annoyance.

Before taking off, he added, "We can't make you unbreakable, but we can make you strong enough to break Justin Summix."

When he put it that way . . .

He shot me a quick grin and a wave as he drove off.

I watched his taillights become mere pinpricks and then vanish altogether. Before heading inside, I checked my phone, hoping I'd gotten a text message.

I sighed when I saw that I had, but not from the right wolf.

Liam had sent me the address of a gym I was to meet him at after lunch. At least I had the morning off. It would give me time to deposit his check and pay Evelyn a visit. Two things that made me happy.

I'd have to find a lot more to keep myself sane in the coming weeks.

CHAPTER 4

After a delicious homemade breakfast at Evelyn's and plenty of bone-crushing hugs to last me throughout the day, Frank McNamara insisted on walking me out to the Boulder Inn minivan.

"I didn't tell her about the duel," he said as I set the container filled with cinnamon rolls on the passenger seat. "I suggest you don't either."

"I don't plan to, Frank. She's already so worried about . . . *everything*." Evelyn had only recently learned of the existence of werewolves. I'd been so afraid she would stop loving me and start fearing me, but she hadn't. "Did you tell her about Aidan? About what he is?"

"I did." He rubbed the white stubble coating his jaw. "Said she wasn't surprised."

"Really?"

"Apparently he had this room in the basement that locks from the inside. A bunker of sorts. And it had all these scratch marks on the walls. When she asked him about it, he said it was where he kept the dogs that weren't housebroken yet. She didn't believe him of course—I mean the lock was on the inside of the room—but back then, she thought he used it as a torture chamber."

My heart clenched with horror. "You think"—I lowered my voice—"he tortures people?"

Frank shook his head, and his mass of white hair fluttered around his face. "I think he used that room when he needed to shift. Even with Sillin in his system, in his prime, the full moon would've brought on a change. Perhaps not a complete shift, but parts of his body would've taken on a different form or texture."

"When I was in LA, full moons didn't affect me."

"You were a thousand miles away. His pack was only a hundred miles away. He'd have felt their influence. Anyway"—he tapped the hood of the car—"I'm sure you have places to be."

I drew my door open, but before climbing in, I asked, "You think I'm right, Frank? About Cassandra cheating?"

"I hope you are. But if you aren't, I hope Liam will have the strength to defeat her, because the alternative—" He shuddered. "I'd rather not consider the alternative."

AFTER LIAM CHALLENGED CASSANDRA, I'D TOLD HIM HE WAS impulsive and insane, but wasn't I the same? Thinking I could save him was insane. Truth was, I didn't even wish Cassandra Morgan dead, but since only one leader could walk out of the duel with their heart intact, I'd do everything in my power for that person to be Liam.

I turned the volume of the car stereo louder to drown out the incessant chatter in my brain. Not to mention my stomach was cramping from the stress of all the thinking I was doing.

I pressed a hand against my navel as I stopped at a red traffic light, then scanned the street for a parking spot, but then I forgot all about parking and all about the cramping and all about Cassandra Morgan. Stopped opposite me at the intersection was a black pickup, and at its wheel was the man who still hadn't answered my text message.

His gaze banged into mine. The impact was so tremendous it knocked the breath from my lungs and made my heart rattle.

Only a day had gone by since I'd seen him, and yet the hours we'd spent apart stretched further than all the years we'd been separated.

I watched him watch me, wondering what he was thinking,

wondering if he'd pull over so we could talk. I imagined myself getting out of the van and striding over to his car. I imagined myself knocking on his window—

A loud honk had me jerking on the gas pedal. I lurched into the intersection before even checking if the light had turned green, and then I was driving past him, and he wasn't looking at me anymore. He was staring straight ahead as though I wasn't even there. I swerved a little, and the car behind August's honked. I spun my steering wheel and gunned the van back into its rightful lane before turning on my blinker and sidling in next to the curb to catch my breath.

Breaths tinted with the fragrance of Old Spice and sawdust that always clung to his skin.

Surely I was imagining his smell—my windows were shut. Nonetheless, I inhaled long and deep, as though if I managed to pull his scent into my lungs, I could reel in the man.

Didn't work like that unfortunately.

The only thing I could potentially reel in was the tether, but the last and only time I'd tried, it had tickled August's abdomen. When he'd done it to me, though, he'd moved my entire body.

Some things simply weren't fair.

Matt said August would understand, but Matt was wrong.

I clutched my phone and typed: *Turn back. Let me explain.*

My thumb hovered over the send icon. Before I could chicken out, I stamped the screen. Phone rattling in my hands, I waited for August to answer, but he sent no words back. How was I supposed to make him understand if he wouldn't give me the time of day? I slapped my steering wheel so hard I blasted the horn.

"Goddammit, August, I didn't do it to spite you!"

At least Liam has nothing to worry about, I thought morosely.

I gripped my head between both hands until my skull stopped throbbing and my eyesight cleared. My track record with boys was so pitiful—four days with Liam, one night with August. Was there something wrong with me? Before pulling back into the light morning traffic, I picked up my phone and texted my question to Sarah on the off-chance she'd gotten out of bed before noon.

By the time I found a parking spot, my hands were still shaking. I thought of Mom's silver-lining theory, that if you looked long enough at one, it would outshine everything else. The silver lining of today: solicitors would stop hounding me to inform me of rising interest fees.

As I entered the bank, I took the check out of my wallet and smoothed the crinkles to make sure the ink hadn't faded overnight, but all three zeroes were still there. I got in line behind an old woman hunched over a walker, the knobs of her curved spine pressing against her flowered blouse. She glanced over her sunken shoulder at me and smiled. I smiled but then wondered if she'd meant to smile at someone else.

"You're the girl from the inn, aren't you?"

The trembling subsided then, replaced by surprise that made me go rigid. And mute . . .

"You served me a lovely brunch a couple weeks ago. I called to make a reservation, but they told me the inn was closing indefinitely. Is that right?"

"It changed"—I cleared my voice—"ownership."

"What a shame. What a shame. And just when the food was getting good. You wouldn't happen to know what happened to the chef?"

I cocked an eyebrow. "She's still in Boulder."

"Oh. How wonderful. My son and his wife run a restaurant in town. You might've heard about it? The Silver Bowl?"

"I don't go out much."

"Next," a bank teller called.

The hunched woman paid her no mind. "Anyway, she used to do the cooking, but she came down with something called algeria or agora, and it made her very fatigued. So they're on the market for a new chef. You wouldn't happen to know if the one from the inn would be interested?"

"I could ask her."

"Next!" the teller called out louder.

"Great. Let me get you my phone number." As she dug through her bag, its contents spilled onto the floor.

I gathered everything up for her, then hooked it on the walker.

"Ladies, I don't have all day," the teller said, exasperated.

"You know what, why don't I just tell her to call the restaurant?" I asked.

The old woman nodded, and her wispy gray hair frolicked around her face. "Tell her to say Charlotte sent her."

The teller cleared her throat.

"The young are always in such a hurry," Charlotte huffed as she hobbled forward, her walker scraping the floor.

For a second, I thought she was talking about me because the teller was well past her prime, but Charlotte didn't know me, so she couldn't know at what speed I lived my life.

But it was true. I was in a hurry.

In a hurry to get to the bottom of Cassandra Morgan's feat.

In a hurry for the duel to be over.

In a hurry to get back in August's good graces.

A moment later, another teller called out, "Next."

I smoothed out the check again before handing it over, along with my debit card and a picture ID.

The employee squinted at my ID, then at my card, then flipped the check over. "Sign at the back, please." She tapped a long acrylic nail against the check.

I signed it nervously, my name looping off the faint line. This felt too good to be true. I expected the check to bounce and security guards to escort me away for questioning. I moistened my lips with the tip of my tongue and waited as the teller clicked and clicked her computer keypad with those long nails of hers.

Finally, she printed out a sheet of paper and handed it over. "Your balance."

I snatched it, and my heart stuttered to a stop when I saw the new number. "Um. I think there's a mistake."

"A mistake?"

"Are you sure this is my account?"

"Are you Ness Marianne Clark?"

"Yes."

She leveled her gaze on her monitor, clicked on her keyboard again. "Then there's no mistake."

My heart hurtled around my ribcage now.

"Were you expecting a higher balance?" she asked when I still hadn't moved. As I read the number over—and over—she added, "We have some great investment opportunities. I'd be more than happy to set up an appointment."

I licked my lips again. Was there any other way of depositing money into someone's account? "Can you give me a printout of the latest activity? Wire transfers or checks or . . ."

"Sure thing."

Her printer burst to life and spat out another sheet of paper, which I all but ripped from her fingers this time. When I saw the name on the check that had been deposited into my account barely an hour ago, my hands started shaking anew. Or maybe they'd never stopped shaking.

"Thank you," I whispered hoarsely.

"Everything all right, honey?" Charlotte asked from her teller's window.

I nodded even though nothing was really all right. It was all wrong. "I'll . . . I'll—Um. I'll tell Evelyn to call." I waved, then slipped my phone out of my bag and, fingers stumbling over the slick screen, I dialed August.

It went to voicemail.

Ugh!

ME: *I just stopped by the bank. What did you do?*

I tried calling him again. Again, he didn't pick up.

ME: *If you don't answer me, I'm going to hunt you down.*

A dropped pin on a map appeared in my messages.

CHAPTER 5

The address August sent me took me to the construction site Matt had mentioned during our run.

I shut the car door so hard it lifted the hem of my white eyelet dress. So many emotions whirred inside me as I stomped toward the site that I didn't feel the ground beneath my feet or the sun in my hair. I felt like a livewire, jumpy and ready to electrocute anyone who came in between me and my target: August Watt.

I walked around the work site until I located him.

The man who'd looked at a traffic light instead of at me and yet who'd deposited an ungodly amount of money into my bank account.

The man who hadn't taken any of my calls and yet had sent me his location.

The man who was wearing a hard hat even though he'd crashed in a helicopter and survived.

The man who made my heart sprint and my navel burn and yet who was no longer mine to hold.

"August Watt!" I yelled.

I must've called out his name *really* loudly because every single worker swiveled around.

August looked up from a blueprint stretched over a work table.

Unhurriedly, he exchanged a few words with one of his men before strolling toward me, hands in the pockets of a pair of faded jeans.

His body ate up the sun and the land and the sky and all of the ambient noise.

Once he stood in front of me, I craned my neck.

"Yes?" His husky voice brushed over the tip of my nose.

I swallowed because my mind had gone blank, and I couldn't remember why I'd come. And why I was mad. Was I even mad?

Oh, yes. I was *livid*.

I narrowed my eyes. "What the hell's gotten into you?"

"Funny." He crossed his arms, making all of his muscles pop. "I could ask you the same thing."

"I didn't deposit"—I dropped my voice to a hiss—*"five hundred thousand* dollars into your account."

"No, you put your life on the line for your ex. Your fucking ex who then proceeded to tell me to fuck off. So let me turn that question on you; what the hell's gotten into *you*?" His jaw clenched so hard it sapped all the curves from his face. Even his full lips looked etched in steel instead of skin.

"I hope you didn't give me all your money, because you're going to owe your mom a whole bunch for all the cursing."

His mouth didn't even twitch, which alerted me to the fact that he was well and truly mad.

I sighed. "Why?"

"Why did I give you that money? Because it was owed to you."

"Owed to me? What are you talking about?"

"When we bought your family's business, we got it at a bargain price. Dad never felt right for paying your mother such a pittance."

My jaw slackened but then snapped shut. "Mom never thought you guys underpaid, August."

"But the fact is we did."

"No you didn't. You paid the amount it was worth at the time."

"Why does it matter?"

"Because it's half a million dollars," I whisper-shouted. "You can't just go around gifting that much money to people."

"You're not people," he said, a tad more softly.

"What am I?"

"I was hoping you could help me define that."

Even though I stood in his shadow, heat still pricked my skin. I suspected it had little to do with the sun and everything to do with the looming male.

"Why did Liam tell me to fuck off, Ness? What exactly happened back at the inn? What did you promise him?"

I pushed my hair off my face. "I promised him that I would stop . . . whatever it is we'd started . . . to prep him for his duel."

His dark eyebrows dipped. "Why would you have to stop seeing me to prep him for his duel?"

I averted my gaze, studied a dusty clump of grass next to August's heavy-duty work boots. "He wants a hundred percent of my attention."

August snorted. After a stretch of silence, he muttered, "You forgot to flick me."

I returned my gaze to his. Every time he'd grunted in the past, I'd flicked him to show him how often he resorted to making that caveman noise instead of using words. "If I touch you, your scent" —spice, wood, earth, heat, home—"it'll rub off on me, and he'll know I saw you."

A muscle flexed in his forearm. "So what?"

"So he'll fight Cassandra without my input." I rolled the hem of my dress between my fingers.

"I'm not sure whether to be offended or fucking jealous that he wants you back so badly he'd lure you away with blackmail." His warm breath fanned against my forehead. "Look at me, Dimples."

I raised my gaze to his, but not because he'd asked. Because he'd called me that nickname that made me feel knee-high to a ladybug. "August, you know I can't stand that nickname."

"And I can't stand that my girlfriend is breaking up with me over her ex's bruised ego. So I'll call you what I want to from now on, the same way you did what you wanted yesterday."

I sucked in a breath that burst right back out of my mouth. "August, I didn't *want* this. His confidence was going to get him killed!"

His green gaze flared so brightly it became almost phosphorescent. And then my stomach acted up, performed a slow roll that had me pressing my palm against it. The warm wind blew August's intoxicating scent into me. Instead of easing the tension, it increased it, made my skin desire the long fingers that gripped his bent elbows to brush over *my* elbows, *my* arms, *my* wrists.

This was *so* not the right time to concoct racy scenarios.

I shifted from one foot to the other, hoping he couldn't guess all that was going through my mind.

"I need to know something." His voice was so rough it spurred my smutty contemplations. "Am I going to lose you?"

"Lose me?" I snapped out of my trance.

"To him? Am I going to lose you to him?" His words whispered over my nose. "You're worth fighting for, but I need to know if it's a fight I have a chance of winning."

My heart climbed into my throat.

"I'll step back, Dimples"—the nickname didn't sound very childish suddenly—"even if it goes against everything I want, I'll step back, but you have to ask me. Do you want me to step back?"

"No," I blurted.

His stance softened, which wasn't to say he slumped or unwound his arms. He was just more timber than steel. "But I can't step forward, can I?"

I gulped and shook my head.

He bobbed his head as though he was filing the rules away. After a beat, he said, "I don't share what's mine."

Those words were like lighter fluid poured right into my core, igniting something fierce and deep. "Good, because I don't share either."

A smile ghosted over his lips, bumped straight into my heart, made it beat faster.

"I've got some terms of my own."

"Oh?" I swallowed, trying to moisten my throat that felt as dry as plaster. "I'm listening."

"I won't touch you, but there's no way I'm not seeing you every day, and *not* from the nosebleed section."

"Okay."

"I want to know what you're up to, and where, and not through the mating link. This isn't me being a stalker, but there are Creeks in Boulder, and I trust those bastards even less than I trust Liam, which is saying a fucking lot."

I'd never heard August curse so much. Then again, he was no longer the soft boy I'd had a crush on but a man weathered by human wars and pack skirmishes.

"And before you make a comment about my unhinged swearing, know that I'll drop a hundred dollar bill in Mom's curse jar, and you're going to witness me doing it, because I'll deposit it tomorrow night during dinner at their place, dinner to which you are coming. And to which you can bring Jeb."

I jutted my hip to one side and planted my hand on it. "What if I don't want to go to dinner at your parents' house tomorrow night?" I did, but I didn't appreciate the form of his invitation.

His gaze turned challenging. "You don't have to come, but that'll break Mom's heart."

My hand skidded off my hip. "That's a low-blow. How am I supposed to *not come* now?"

His smile grew a little wider and a little more roguish too. He was enjoying riling me up.

"You know, if you'd just asked me, I would've said yes."

"Just wanted to see your face light up, Dimples. Just wanted to see your eyes turn that spectacular shade of blue they get when you're emotional. Even though I'd much rather make them bluer using . . . *other* methods."

I was pretty certain my eyes had just gotten a *lot* bluer.

He raised his hand to my face, but before he could touch me, he curled his fingers into his palm. "Fuck the convalescence period after the helicopter crash. This is going to be so much worse." His hand plummeted to his side.

"Maybe"—I wet my lips—"maybe we shouldn't spend too much time together. It'll make it harder."

He snorted. "That part's not negotiable."

I flicked him, then snatched my hand away, shocked I'd broken the rule first.

He stared at my hand. "Never thought I'd crave getting flicked, but if that's the extent of our physical contact, then flick away."

"I shouldn't even have done that," I said, tugging my lip into my mouth.

"That thing you're doing to your lips. Try not to do that when we're together." He took a step back as though it would somehow ease the tension jostling the tether between us.

I freed my lip. "Sorry."

"Don't be sorry, sweetheart. It's not your fault I'm so darn attracted to you."

A thrill shot up the entire length of my body. "I should probably go, huh?"

He palmed his dark, cropped hair, then looked over his shoulder at the construction site. We were far enough away that our conversation hadn't carried but close enough for the men to watch us. When he looked at me again, his eyelids had thinned. "Yeah. You probably should because I'm about to fire a whole bunch of people."

I frowned.

"And if you ever come back to visit, wear a muumuu or something *bigger*."

He wanted to fire people because they'd looked at me a little too long? "A muumuu? I don't even know what that is."

"A shapeless dress. Grams used to wear them."

I smirked. "I don't own any *muumuus*."

"Well, buy some."

"With your money?"

"It's *your* money. All of it. I've already paid taxes on it."

"August, I can't accept—"

"If you don't want it, give it to charity."

"August . . ." I all but growled.

"Dimples . . ."

Ugh.

He smiled.

"You're impossible," I muttered.

"Pot calling the kettle black, sweetheart."

I shook my head, but a smile made its way to my lips. "Shouldn't you be working?"

"Shouldn't you be leaving?"

My smiled increased; his, too.

I started toward the van, glancing over my shoulder as I left. His posture had straightened again, and his eyes blazed with renewed assurance.

The future was uncertain, and not just because we were were-wolves fighting for our land and pack, but because we weren't diviners. Yet I sensed August would stand by me even if he couldn't hold my hand.

The only certainty I possessed in this uncertain world.

CHAPTER 6

I remembered feeling beat-up after the first contest in my pack's Alpha trials, but two hours into training with Liam and I felt like I'd been fed through a trash compactor and dumped in a landfill.

When my back hit the sweat-slicked mats for the hundredth time, I didn't get up. I just lay there, gaping at the exposed metal tubing on the ceiling with great fascination until Liam's barely perspiring face appeared in my line of sight.

I closed my eyes so that maybe he'd leave me alone, but no such luck.

"Up, Ness. We're not done."

"You might not be, but I am," I muttered.

"Is that what you'll tell Justin if you end up having to fight? Up!"

I snapped my lids open and glared, even though I wasn't truly mad at him. I knew he was pushing me because he had my best interests at heart.

"Chicks are so fragile." Lucas's voice made me lurch up.

I sent him a chilling look that made him simper. He winked at me at the same time as Sarah smacked his chest so hard the sound echoed against the brick walls.

"Geez, blondie, I was just motivating her," he said.

I'd invited Sarah along for moral support. At least, that's how I'd presented the invite. In truth, I was worried about leaving her alone after the phone call I'd had with her on my way back from August's construction site.

Last night, her brother called her to tell her that, sure enough, Cassandra inquired about the Pine's stock of Sillin. After he told her they'd run out of the drug a couple months back, the Alpha apparently lapped it up. I doubted Cassandra Morgan *lapped* anything up.

On the plus side, it assured me the Sillin was important to her.

Now if I could just fig—

Liam swiped my ankle with his foot, sending me flailing backward. Air whooshed out of my lungs with an audible, "Oomphf," and little stars spangled my vision.

I blinked. The stars glittered less fiercely, but they were still there, brightening the maze of metal tubes crisscrossing the ceiling.

I was *never* getting back up.

Ever.

Liam brushed his brow with his forearm, pushing back the locks of dark-brown hair plastered to his forehead, before extending his arm. Even though my hand felt attached to a massive dumbbell, I heaved my fingers off the mats and latched onto Liam's. He hauled me up so fast I stumbled against him. The contact had me pitching backward. Thankfully I stayed upright, but that had little to do with my footwork and everything to do with his solid grip.

Averting my gaze from his piercing one, I slid my hand out of his and rubbed the back of my hot neck. "I'm beat, Liam. I'm not even sure I'll be able to run tomorrow morning with Matt."

He observed me slowly and silently, his musky, minty scent ribboning off his gleaming skin and filling the air, stirring many conflicting emotions within me.

After an entire minute, he nodded. "Okay."

"Okay, we're done?"

When he nodded, I contemplated fist-pumping the air, but the effort that would take felt remarkable.

"And okay to canceling your run. You'll do enough running on Sunday night."

It took my frazzled brain a second to remember that Sunday night was the full moon—the entire pack's night out in fur. After a certain age, werewolves could only shift during the full moon.

Last month, I'd run with the pack for the first time in my life. I'd experienced another first that night too. I wondered if Liam was also remembering our kiss. Even though so much had happened since then, I'd forever cherish that night.

As we walked over to the bench where Sarah was trying to convince Lucas to cut his hair or jump on the manbun-trend wagon, I said, "Shouldn't we be training in fur?"

"We'll get to that," Liam said.

"And shouldn't we be practicing with Sillin?"

"We'll get to that too."

"When?"

"You visit the Watts' construction site, and suddenly, you're in a hurry?"

So he knew . . . Had he smelled August on my fingertip, or had Matt informed him?

"Why are you suddenly so *un*hurried?" I volleyed back.

His expression, which had been far from open, shuttered up. He snatched a bottle of water from the bench and tipped the rim to his lips, squashing the plastic between his fingers.

Concern edged Sarah's features.

"You told me I wasn't allowed to date him or hang out alone with him. I wasn't alone, and we're not sneaking around, so I don't get why you're giving me attitude about this." Suddenly, I wasn't exhausted anymore.

"Hey, Lucas, can you show me where the water fountain is again?" Sarah asked, springing off the bench.

Lucas pointed to the back of the gigantic room. Rolling her eyes, she grabbed his outstretched finger and heaved him up, letting go as soon as he was on his feet. If I wasn't seething, I might've laughed at his stunned expression.

She jutted her head, and he followed suit, even though he seemed reluctant to leave Liam and me alone. What did Lucas think I would do? Claw up Liam's pretty face?

"Subtlety's not your forte, huh?" I heard Sarah ask. Whatever Lucas answered made her bellow, "Oh my God, get over yourself."

I uncapped another bottle of water and downed half of it in one gulp. "I'll be going to dinner at his parents' house tomorrow night. He'll be there too, as well as Jeb. I'm telling you this so you don't get your information from another source and misconstrue a family dinner for a hot date." I screwed the cap back onto my bottle slowly.

Liam's gaze narrowed on the steel bench. "Family? Did you get engaged?"

"No. I did not get engaged. I'm seventeen." I squared my shoulders and crossed my arms. "The Watts have always been like a second family to me. When I was growing up, I spent almost as much time with them as I spent with my own parents."

Liam still didn't say anything.

"And just so you stop assuming this, I'm not going to let a mating link drive me into a marriage. No amount of magic will dictate the course of my life. August and I go way back, but maybe we're all wrong for each other." We hadn't felt all wrong for each other the night at his place, but Liam hadn't felt wrong for me either.

Liam glanced at me, and even though his gaze was still hardened, it sparked, and that spark felt dangerous. I hadn't planned on giving him hope . . . I'd planned on setting him straight.

"But I won't know that until I actually date him, which I plan on doing once this duel is over." My words dimmed the spark but didn't extinguish it.

"You know, it would've been in your best interest to let me duel Morgan yesterday," Liam said.

"Why?"

"If I'd lost, I would've been gone. For good."

My arms fell alongside my body, the half-empty bottle clapping against my thigh. "Don't say stupid shit like that."

He balked at my sharp words.

"I'll see you tomorrow. Bring Sillin. Or I'll bring what I have left." I turned to go, but Liam's voice stopped me.

"I have to take care of some things tomorrow, so I won't have time to meet you. But I'll pick you up on Sunday morning at seven. Pack an overnight bag."

"Overnight? What about the pack run?"

"We'll be running, but not with the Boulders."

My pulse picked up speed. "Who will we be running with?"

"The Rivers."

"The Rivers? One of the Eastern packs?"

Liam nodded, then tipped his head to the side, his gaze hunting mine.

I wasn't sure if it was the sweat drying on my skin or the idea of running with lots of foreign wolves or traveling out of state with Liam, but I suddenly felt incredibly cold. "And it'll be just the two of us going out there?"

An emotion crossed his face. Hurt, maybe? He shrugged his shoulders that seemed to have gotten a little broader since he'd become Alpha. "I can ask Matt to fly out with us if it makes you feel more comfortable."

I didn't need a chaperone, or did I? "I trust you to keep this professional, Liam."

This would be the first time I would be physically far enough from August for it to affect the link. What if . . . what if my attraction to him faded? Why was I scared of this? I'd told Liam that wasn't the reason I wanted August in the first place. I stretched my neck from side to side, finding a little solace when it cracked.

"You seem nervous?"

Instead of confessing the true reason I was jumpy, I said, "I've never flown before. What should I pack?"

"Nothing fancy. The Rivers are denim-and-tees sort of people."

"Okay." I rubbed one clammy palm against my workout leggings.

"The Rivers, huh?" Sarah said. I hadn't even noticed her return. "I heard they hate the Creeks because Morgan killed the Alpha's daughter. The girl was visiting the Aspens the night Morgan demanded to duel the Alpha." I supposed she added that last part for my benefit, since I imagined Liam and Lucas were well-versed in pack facts.

Liam stared at her as though her presence had slipped his mind. "If my trip gets back to Morgan, I'll know where she got her information."

Sarah's gaze turned incendiary. "You should stop confusing allies for traitors. Didn't work out so well for you last time," she added under her breath.

Liam's posture locked up.

"Anyway, I need to get home. Ness, you done here?"

"I'm done," I said, lifting my bag off the bench.

I didn't look back at the boys as I left the gym with Sarah. The second we stepped out of the brick loft-like building that housed the gym, she muttered, "I can't believe he thinks I'd tell Morgan anything." Her blonde hair was starting to frizz, as though her kinky curls were desperate to bend her straightened locks into their original shape.

"I don't think he fully trusts *me*, Sarah."

She side-eyed me as she unlocked the door of her red Mini. "Do *you* trust him?

"What do you mean?"

"You're going on an overnight trip with him. Do you trust he's not going to try anything on you?"

I bit my lip, which made Sarah raise an eyebrow.

"I don't think he'll try anything," I said a little hoarsely.

She gave a me a tight-lipped smile. "I wish I could come along."

"I wish you could, too."

But Sarah was a Creek. There was no way she could come with us. First, because Liam wouldn't allow it, and second, because then Cassandra, who was able to track her wolves through her Alpha blood-link, would know Sarah was double-crossing her pack.

CHAPTER 7

Jeb couldn't make dinner at the Watts, so I ended up going alone. Since he'd needed the car, I took a cab. During the entire ride, I alternated between crinkling the brown paper wrapped around the bouquet of black parrot tulips resting on the seat next to me and smoothing the fabric of my red silk dress—the one that had belonged to Mom and that I'd worn only once before, for my "date" with Aidan Michaels. If it had been any other dress, I would've burned it, but it had belonged to Mom.

"That's a mighty nice house," the cab driver said as he pulled up in front of the Watts' high-ceilinged log cabin.

The wood façade glowed amber in the setting sun, and the beveled windows gleamed like diamonds.

August's pickup was parked up front, which meant he was already here.

"Nine dollars, please," the driver said.

I dug through my wallet for a ten dollar bill, handed it to the man, then touched the door handle but couldn't bring myself to pump it. This felt like a meet-the-parents, even though I'd met the parents at the same time I'd met August—in the hospital room where Mom birthed me. In one of their photo albums, there was a picture of me cradled in August's arms. My stomach churned like the cinnamon chocolate ice-cream Evelyn made this summer in the inn's fancy ice-cream maker.

God, this was wrong.

How could I want someone a decade older?

Someone who'd felt like a brother my entire childhood?

Maybe Liam's ban was a good thing.

Maybe I should wait for the Winter Solstice to arrive so the mating link vanished and put an end to my scandalous attraction.

Would it put an end to it, though?

"Is this not the right address?" The cabby spun around in his seat.

"No, it's . . . um . . . I think I forgot—"

The Watts' front door opened and filled with August's hulking shape.

My heart beat bruisingly hard.

When I still hadn't gotten out of the cab, August strode over. He opened the car door, and since I hadn't released the handle, drew me right out of the taxi. I stumbled, my bouquet toppling onto the black pebbles lining the driveway.

He caught one of my wrists and steadied me. I think he asked the cabby if I'd paid, and I think the cabby answered, but maybe I was imagining them having a conversation. All I could hear was my thundering pulse. All I could feel was August's thumb pressing lightly into my vein.

Was I too young to have a heart attack?

August smiled a little wider. "Shifters don't get those, sweetheart."

Shoot . . . I'd voiced my pathetic deliberation out loud.

His thumb stroked the inside of my wrist, and my skin broke out in goose bumps.

Remembering I wasn't supposed to make contact with any part of August, I wrenched my arm out of his grip. Where he'd touched tingled and burned. A lot like my navel. Did his navel feel as though it was forever tumbling through a dryer set on the fastest and hottest setting? I would've asked but then thought better of it. If his abdomen didn't feel that way, then I'd just be confessing to being one intensely hormonal girl.

August crouched to retrieve my fallen bouquet. I took it without touching his fingers and nestled it against my heaving chest. As he straightened, he returned his hands to the pockets of his gray jeans.

"I'm sorry." He tipped his head to my wrist. "I didn't mean to break the rule."

I tucked the bouquet closer, probably injuring the petals. "It's okay."

"You look beautiful tonight," he said huskily. "But if you could avoid wearing dresses and the color red while I'm banned to touch you, I'd be really appreciative."

My lips bent with what I hoped looked like a smirk and not an *I'm-about-to-melt-at-your-scuffed-boots* look. "We're back to discussing muumuus, huh?" A gentle breeze twisted the hair I'd spent a long time blow-drying straight. "I haven't forgotten your advice."

A firefly buzzed around August's stubble-coated jaw. "It wasn't advice."

The vibrations of his deep voice had the goose bumps, which had started receding, make a brusque second appearance. I seriously needed to calm down before entering his parents' home. Which reminded me . . .

"How much do your parents know about . . . *everything?*"

"Everything."

I almost choked on my own saliva. "They know I spent the night at your place?" I whispered, praying my voice wouldn't carry to Nelson's lupine eardrums.

"No. But they know about the mating link, and they know how I feel about it."

Heat wrapped around my collarbone and neck like a rampant vine. "Are they horrified?"

He stared at the sprinting pulse point in my neck. "Why would they be horrified?"

"Because I'm so much younger, and like a little sister to you, and you held me in the maternity ward." I said all of this in one breath.

"Hey . . ." He stepped closer, and his heady heat scent enveloped me. "First off, age doesn't matter. You're not a kid anymore, Ness. You're a woman and I'm a man, and that's all that matters. All that *should* matter. And if anyone ever makes a derogatory comment to you about our age gap, then send them my way, and I'll set them straight. Secondly, you are *not* related to me, therefore you *aren't* my little sister. And yeah, I held you in the maternity ward, and yeah, back then I didn't think I was holding my mate, but apparently I was. How many people can claim they saw the person meant for them come into this world? Not many. So I'll always cherish that, and no, it doesn't color the way I think of you today." His words were so quiet they tangled with his exhale.

His exhale which I tasted on my parted lips.

"*Fuck*." His pupils bled into his gold-green irises. "How long are we supposed to stay away from each other?"

I smiled, even though my pulse felt like it had hitched a ride on a fighter jet. "You give your mom that hundred dollar bill yet?"

His pupils retracted. "Not yet. I was waiting for you to witness the donation." He tipped his head to the house. "We better go inside before I break all the rules and take you back to *my* house."

A breathy gasp escaped me, and that little sound made August's gaze flick to my mouth.

He shook his head as though trying to clear it of any dirty thoughts. I assumed that's what his jerky movement was about since I had my fair share of brand-new steamy scenarios scrolling through my mind.

We didn't speak the whole way up the path. He gestured for me to go ahead of him inside the house. The scent of simmering tomato sauce and caramelized onions hit my nostrils, awakening my hunger for something other than August.

Isobel smiled at me from where she stood at the stove top. "We finally managed to get you to come over." She set down the wooden spoon and approached me, arms extended. I wasn't sure if she wanted to hug me or take the flowers from my arms, so I remained statue-still.

Her arms wrapped around me and pulled me in.

"It smells so good in here," I said into Isobel's dark-brown hair.

Even though the strands were real, they weren't hers. They had this chemical keratin smell to them like all wigs. I remembered visiting a shop for one with Mom before she'd decided she wouldn't need a wig. The reminder of her cancer had me pressing away and inspecting Isobel's face for signs of the disease.

"How are you feeling?" I asked.

"Alive. Very much alive." She smiled that bright smile of hers that could burn away the densest of fogs.

I gave her the bouquet, examining her for a noticeable slump or another mark of fatigue. She ran a knuckle over my cheek. "Don't you start worrying now, too, sweet girl. I promise I'm fine."

I nodded.

"August, honey, can you get one of the vases down from the shelf?"

August strode past me and opened one of the kitchen cabinets. Barely straining, he reached the top shelf and took down a fluted crystal recipient just as his father came in through the open doors that gave onto the paved terrace.

"Hi, Ness."

"Hi, Nelson."

Holding a pair of tongs out so that the charred greasy bits didn't transfer onto my dress, he leaned in for a one-armed hug. I suddenly wished August hadn't told them anything. Then they'd just be Nelson and Isobel, my parents' best friends instead of a set of parents whom I felt like I needed to impress. My nervousness was so violent that the air probably shimmied with it.

"We probably shouldn't be offering you alcohol, but would you like a glass of wine?" Nelson asked. "I opened one of the bottles from our wedding. It's matured as beautifully as my bride."

Smiling, Isobel shook her head. "I've matured, huh?"

"You've gotten more ravishing, which was a feat considering how beautiful you were thirty years ago."

When he dropped a kiss on his wife's glowing cheek, I became misty-eyed. They reminded me so much of my parents. My parents who'd loved each other so fiercely and completely that they'd resisted a mating link to stay together.

My eyes bumped into August's worried ones, before vaulting to the serrated egg-shaped heads of the purple tulips.

"So, wine?" Nelson asked me, even though his gaze was on August. "Or is my son going to give you a hard time about underage drinking again?"

August raised his palms. "She didn't drive here, so I'm not passing any judgment."

I suspected that even if I *had* driven here, he wouldn't have objected to me imbibing alcohol since the one and only time he'd made a fuss about it was back at Frank's when August had been annoyed with me over Liam.

Nelson gestured to the terrace.

Before I walked out, I put my bag down on the speckled granite. "Can I bring anything out?"

"You can grab the pitcher of water from the fridge," Isobel said, stirring her tomato sauce before removing the pan from the burner.

I pulled the water from the fridge and headed to the terrace where I set the pitcher between two giant candles flickering in glass hurricane holders.

I gazed around the paved veranda where nothing had changed: the stacked firepit was still surrounded by five burgundy Adirondacks; and the low stone wall, from which sprouted little purple blooms, still girdled the deck.

When I was younger, I used to skip atop the wall with my arms stretched out like a tightrope walker picturing a pit of hungry alligators beneath me. I had a vivid imagination back then. Not that it had changed. My imagination was still plenty vivid, except it ran on a very different frequency these days.

"You okay?" August asked, coming up behind me.

"Your parents . . . They just remind me so much of Mom and Dad."

He draped his arm around my shoulders and tucked me into his side, and although we weren't supposed to touch, I didn't fight his embrace. Even though his fingers only connected to my bicep, it felt like they were resting on my heart, towing one ripped segment toward the other.

After a while, he whispered a quick, "Sorry," against my hairline before releasing me.

I wasn't sorry.

That hand might've left a trace on my body, but it had also left one on my heart.

I thought of Mom again, of her claim that the right man could fix a broken heart. August could touch mine, and this was as thrilling as it was terrifying because that meant he could mend it just as he could break it.

CHAPTER 8

Dinner was delicious and laid-back. Neither Isobel nor Nelson brought up the mating link, and neither of them asked questions about my intentions toward their son or his intentions toward me.

But after dinner . . . Well, after dinner was a different story.

While the men cleaned up the vestiges of our meal, Isobel brewed a pot of chamomile tea before leading me to the firepit. Flames snapped in between the circle of stones and warmed the cooling night air, casting shadows over her haggard face.

She'd promised me she was well, but the deep creases around her eyes and lips worried me nonetheless. As she reclined in the burgundy Adirondack, I prayed her fatigue wasn't a symptom that her double-mastectomy had failed its purpose.

"August spoke to us before you arrived," she said, jouncing me out of my pessimistic musings.

Clutching my mug, I focused on the dancing blaze.

"Nelson and I, we don't want to meddle, but your parents are no longer here, and well, we feel a responsibility toward them to discuss it with you. This . . . *link*, it's momentous and not without consequence, for you and for our son."

How I wished the fire could leap out of the pit and incinerate something, anything, just to drag the focus away from me.

"I don't know if you're aware of this, but your mother, she was intended for—"

"Heath. I heard."

"Oh." There was a pregnant pause, then, "The reason I'm bringing up your mom is because I want to remind you that you have a choice in the matter. You and my son might have a connection—you always had a connection—but I guess, what I'm trying to say, is that this connection has grown into something . . . *more*."

At this point, if the flames decided to incinerate me, I wouldn't have truly minded.

"August feels strongly toward you, but you're so young, so if you don't reciprocate his feelings, he'll understand. Maybe not right away, but in time, he will."

She touched my forearm, and I jumped, spilling tea all over my lap.

"Oh, I'm sorry."

"It's okay." The tea seeped into the red silk, darkening it.

"A mother wants only one thing in life, and that's her child's happiness. You've always contributed to August's, but now you've become the pivotal object of it. And although he claims it's not because of the link, the link doubtlessly enhances what he feels. Doubtlessly enhances what you feel, too."

Although I wanted to melt through the planks of my chair, I finally looked at Isobel. Her green eyes were gentle instead of reproachful like I'd feared.

"I want what's best for *both* of you, and maybe that's each other. But you're only seventeen."

I'd be eighteen in two weeks, but then August would be twenty-eight in March, so we'd always have this nine-years-and-some-months gap.

Over the husky notes of the jazz song pouring from the outdoor speakers, Isobel said, "Nelson and I, we met when I was sixteen and he was twenty-two. And Maggie, she was—"

"Thirteen. And Dad was three years older, which had made a lot of people balk."

She smiled. "How I remember. But Maggie was so spirited and strong-willed that whenever anyone mentioned the age difference, she'd get all up in their faces." Isobel turned her gaze to the flames and sighed. "I guess age doesn't really matter in the end." She removed her hand from my arm. "What does matter, though, is making an informed decision. You have options. August is one of them, but the Winter Solstice is another."

I cast a glance over my shoulder to make sure the men were still out of earshot. August was drying a plate by the sink while Nelson was stacking the glasses inside a cupboard. They seemed deep into their own conversation.

"Isobel, would you and Nelson be disgusted if I chose August?"

She whipped her gaze to me. "Disgusted? No! Absolutely not. Ness, we love you. We've always loved you and we will *always* love you. *Whatever* you decide. The only reason I brought this up is because we care so much about you, and we don't want you to feel pressured into something you're not ready for."

I twirled my mug, wishing it could leak warmth into more than just my fingers. "I understand my options, and I'm not going to rush into anything that's indelible."

"Good."

"What's good?"

I glanced up at August. "The tea," I lied, raising it to my lips.

He eyed me suspiciously. *Yeah* . . . he hadn't bought that.

"I brought you girls some covers." He handed one to his mother, who draped it over her lap, then gave me the other folded rectangle that felt like spun clouds. I set my mug on the rim of the firepit to tuck the soft blanket around my shoulders.

August sank into the chair beside mine, and then Nelson arrived with a glass brimming with wine and sat next to him.

"Look at that sky," he mused.

We all raised our gazes to the glittering darkness overhead. Magical. Simply magical.

August leaned a little toward me. "Did you find Cassiopeia?"

I stared at the dark freckles beneath his left eye where a thin pale scar lingered—a remnant of when my wolf claw had scraped across his face. How I longed to drag my finger over the freckles shaped like the constellation. Instead, I burrowed my fingers into the cashmere wrap. "I always find Cassiopeia."

His gaze blazed as bright as the fire.

57

But then the heat in his eyes turned cold as a voice entered our minds.

There will be no full moon run this month. I apologize to the elders, but I urge you all to stay in skin.

Liam's voice dragged me away from the starlit evening that had been a welcomed parenthesis in my tumultuous life.

I will be leaving to meet with the Rivers tomorrow morning, and I'll return the following day. Please clear Monday evening for a debriefing.

I waited for him to mention I would be accompanying him. When a full minute passed and nothing more was uttered, I let out a quiet breath.

"The Rivers, huh?" Nelson said.

"What about the Rivers?" Isobel asked.

August studied my face as he said, "Liam's going to meet with them."

"The pack that commissioned you to build their meeting hall?" Isobel said. "I thought Heath had given you grief for working with them."

Nelson swirled his wine. "He did. Liam must be desperate for a new ally now that we lost the Pines."

"Did you know he was traveling East?" August asked me.

I nodded. Informing him that I was accompanying Liam hung on the tip of my tongue, but I couldn't propel the words out of my mouth. I was afraid my confession would stoke August's jealousy.

Besides, if Liam hadn't mentioned me, then maybe he wasn't taking me with him in the end. I held on to that possibility as the night wore on. But of course, right as I was about to call a cab, Liam's voice resonated inside my head: *I'll be at your place at 7:00 a.m.*

August nodded to my phone. "You weren't actually going to call a cab, were you?"

I forced my features to smooth out. "I don't want to get you in trouble."

Sitting together in a confined space was against Liam's rules.

"You don't want to get *me* in trouble, or *him*?" he asked slowly.

I swallowed. "Both of you. *Either* of you. I don't want to get either of you in trouble."

Nelson and Isobel were still outside on the patio, speaking quietly. Was it about us? Even though she'd given me her blessing, her anguish was palpable.

"It's a short ride."

I sighed and put my phone away. "Okay."

I prayed Liam wouldn't find out and challenge Cassandra to punish me for disobeying.

As we made our way to the pickup, August kept casting concerned glances my way.

Only when I was settled in the car did he ask, "What did my mother say? Did she try to talk you out of being with me?"

I fingered the hem of my dress, not quite daring to look at him. "She reminded me that I had options."

"Options?" His voice was low and rough.

"She told me I could let the Winter Solstice go by before deciding." I raised my gaze back to his. "That you'd understand."

Would he, though?

His lips parted a little, then pressed tight. I sensed he didn't want me to choose that option. I sensed he feared that the disappearance of the bond would lead to the disappearance of my feelings for him.

I guessed neither of us could be sure it wouldn't.

Perhaps tomorrow's trip wouldn't be so unwelcomed after all. At least it would shed light on how I really felt about him since the bond would vanish.

When we arrived in front of my apartment, I didn't linger in the car, afraid someone would spot us and report to Liam.

"What are you doing tomorrow?" August asked after I'd hopped out.

My heart, which had been beating double-time since we'd left his parents' place, stilled.

Should I tell him?

"I wanted to show you something," he said.

I opened my mouth.

To lie.

Or at least that had been my intent, but he would sense I was out of Boulder. Besides, I didn't want to lie to him. "I'm going with Liam."

His Adam's apple seemed suddenly spikier. "If I hadn't asked, would you have told me?"

"No."

He dropped his gaze to his illuminated dashboard, features tightening.

"I was afraid you'd torture yourself with what I could be doing with him in a place where the bond doesn't affect my body."

His wolf must've been close to the surface because his eyes shone like emeralds. Jaw barely budging, he muttered something that sounded like, *If Cassandra doesn't kill him, I might.* "I know the Rivers. I'll come too, then."

My heart twitched back to life. "August—"

"Unless you don't want me there."

I pressed my lips together. I wanted him there, but I also wanted him to trust me. Besides, I needed to know what distance did to us. If not now, then later, but later might hurt more.

His pupils gushed darkness into his irises. "You don't want me there."

"What I want is for you to trust me."

"You, I trust."

I gripped the edge of the car door. "Then trust that I can handle Liam."

"Sweetheart"—his nostrils flared—"you're asking a very human man to be superhuman. I'm not sure I'm capable of that."

My lips bent with a smile. "Says a werewolf."

My humor defused some of his anger. Not all of it, though. The tether was so stiff it seemed made of metal instead of magic.

"Let's hope the Rivers know something we don't," he said.

It took my hazy mind a second to understand he was talking about Morgan's tricks. "Yeah. Let's hope they do."

We stared at each other for another endless beat. I sensed him tugging on the tether, trying to reel me to him. I had to clutch the door harder to avoid stumbling.

"August," I chided gently.

"What?"

"You're going to make me fall."

The pressure on my abdomen decreased so suddenly I almost tumbled backward.

"I'm sorry," he said.

It was late, and Liam would be here early, and the longer I remained next to August, the more chances we had of being caught. "I should really go. . ."

As I rounded the bumper, August powered his window down. "Come back to me, okay?"

Pleasure and trepidation dripped in equal parts inside my veins. Because his affection for me was so absolute that I was suddenly afraid of what tomorrow would bring.

Turning away, I said, "I'll come back." I climbed up my stairs fast, then went inside my home even faster.

The tether vibrated with his hurt.

Hurt I'd put there by not telling him I would come back *to him*.

Because what if the absence of magic affected the strength of my attraction?

CHAPTER 9

I was already sitting on the bottom step when Liam arrived the next morning. I slung the backpack I'd borrowed from Jeb, and which I'd filled with the bare necessities, over my shoulder, then walked to the passenger side.

After I settled in, Liam asked, "Had a fun night?" He wore dark sunglasses that made it impossible to read his expression.

"I did."

He started driving. "I have a half a mind to cancel the trip and phone up Morgan. You reek of him."

Trying to keep as calm as lycanthropically possible, I said, "He gave me a ride back from his parents. Nothing happened."

He didn't pick up his phone or do a U-turn to drop me back off. I wasn't sure if it was because he realized the only one who would get hurt would be him or because my tone had been so flat. I wore my emotions on my vocal cords. Guilt would've heightened my pitch. I didn't feel guilty about last night. At least not in the way Liam was insinuating.

But I did feel guilt. I'd been so torn up I'd barely slept. I rested my elbow on the armrest, cradled my throbbing forehead, and shut my eyes.

A brassy whooshing sound jerked me awake. I'd meant to rest, not sleep. How long had I been out?

I rubbed my lids and stared at the gated airstrip. "We're flying private?"

Nodding, Liam lowered his window to press on an intercom. The gate clanged open, and we glided right through toward a gleaming silver jet.

I gaped at it.

"It was Dad's, but it's at the disposal of the entire pack. If you ever need to use it, all you have to do is ask."

My enchantment withered. I'd despised Liam's father so much that my hatred extended to anything he'd touched or owned.

A man in a navy suit drew open my car door. "Morning, Miss."

"Good morning," I said, grabbing my backpack and scooting out of the SUV.

"Morning, Captain," Liam said, rounding the bumper of his car.

He sported jeans—like me—and a black V-neck, which reassured me that my white tank and zip-up hoodie weren't too dire.

The man in the suit nodded at Liam. "Morning, Mr. Kolane. We're ready to go when you are."

Liam gestured to the staircase that led into the belly of the sleek, winged beast. I moved toward it, my wolf bristling under my skin, as though trying to stick her claws into the tarmac to avoid taking to the skies.

We were land animals after all.

I battled through her reluctance and climbed the stairs. The air smelled of leather and flowery air freshener, which did little to appease my pacing wolf. My nails began to lengthen. I stopped in the narrow hallway, focusing on pushing her back. I doubted the captain or the flight attendant smiling at me from the galley in the back of the plane knew what we were.

"It's safe," Liam whispered behind me, his words blowing through the hairs thickening on the nape of my neck.

He set his hand on the small of my back and guided me onto one of the buttery beige armchairs.

After taking the seat across from me, he said, "I've never much enjoyed flying either."

We weren't even airborne yet. How would I react then? The pilot pulled in the retractable staircase, and the door shut with a suction noise.

"Let me know if you feel like you're losing control," Liam said, studying my face.

I nodded and swallowed.

The air hostess strutted over toward us, her lips a shade of fuchsia so bright they were almost blinding. "I'll set out breakfast after takeoff. Would you like coffee or tea?"

"Coffee," I said.

She didn't wait for Liam's answer. She must've known his order already.

She flitted back to the galley, leaving behind a pungent cloud of rose-scented perfume that reminded me of my aunt and her prized rosebushes.

"Do you have any news about Lucy?"

"Lucy?" Liam frowned.

"You know, my two-timing aunt?"

Liam's lips curved into a crooked smile. "Oh . . . *that* Lucy."

I rolled my eyes.

The engine turned on, and the entire plane began to rattle. Or maybe I was the one rattling. I gripped the armrests.

Breathe. Liam's command shocked the tremor right out of me. Then, out loud, he said, "Last I heard she's still working at the inn."

"Why would she work for Aidan? After what she said at Everest's funeral—about hating what we were—why would she willingly work for the Creeks?"

"Grieving people say and do uncharacteristic things. It might be a way of getting back at us."

"But we didn't kill Everest."

Liam was supposed to, but Alex beat him to it.

"She still believes it's our fault. Like I said, grief screws with people's minds."

The plane started to roll past other shiny aircrafts varying in size. I wondered if one of them belonged to the Creeks. Maybe more than one. And then I wondered if the Watts owned a plane too.

"I heard August and his father did business with the Rivers two years ago," I said, mostly to distract myself from the long dotted strip in front of us. The plane bumped to a stop, and then it made a U-turn and hurtled so fast it pinned my heart to my spine.

Shh.

When my claws dented the buttery leather, I ripped my hands off the armrests and cinched my thighs. I pulled in a long breath, then let it out. I did this over and over until the plane's nose lifted and the wheels left the ground.

"You're okay, Ness. Everything's going to be okay."

"*Don't* say that," I snapped, "because nothing ever goes right when people say that."

His head jerked back a little. "Where did that come from?"

I shut my eyes, air pulsing through my nostrils. "Dad said that to me, and then he was shot. You said that to me, and then you turned on me. I hate that sentence."

After a beat, he said, "I'm sorry."

I laid my head back, eyes still clenched.

"I have something that'll cheer you up."

When paper rustled, I raised my lids. A large white envelope dropped into my lap. On the top left corner was an intertwined C and U.

"Your college packet," Liam explained, mistaking my surprise for confusion. "Classes start in a week. Do you know what you're going to study?"

"Business."

"Practical."

I stared at the envelope, feeling both fraudulent and lucky. The pack's money and connections had gotten me in, not my exceptional transcript.

"There's a course catalogue in there. I was a business major too, so I can help you figure out the best classes to take."

The flight attendant came back then, a white tablecloth draped over her arm. She pulled out a hidden table from the wall between our seats, then smoothed the crisp cloth before returning to the galley. As she set up breakfast in real porcelain and silverware, I opened the envelope and read over my welcome letter, then flipped through the catalogue while Liam told me stories of his college days, about his initiation into the frat house run by generations of Boulder wolves. Even though it was open to all male students — human or supernatural—a shifter was always in charge, and that shifter made sure the hazing was "eventful."

"What did they make you do?" I asked.

He got this far away smile. "Fight in a ring lined with dog excrement. Loser got tossed in the shit."

"Bet you didn't lose."

He turned that smile on me. "I didn't lose."

Gratitude and excitement drifted up in me. As I ate flaky pastries and drank bitter coffee, I pored over every sheet of material on my lap. "Thank you so much for this."

Liam raised a palm. "Please. It's nothing."

"It's *not* nothing. It's my future."

"No, your future is saving my ass, remember?"

A smile tugged at my lips, and I closed the catalogue. "So tell me about the Rivers."

I learned they were the largest of the Eastern packs and the most influential. They'd done their share of dueling in the East but weren't interested in expanding to the West or to the North—the territory of the igloo-dwelling Glacier Pack, descendants of the Inuits.

"I'm surprised August didn't tell you about them. He knew the Alpha's daughter quite intimately." My sudden intake of air had Liam dip his chin into his neck. "You didn't think he was a choir boy, now did you?"

"Of course not," I said a little too abruptly. And I truly hadn't, but that didn't mean I wanted to know about all the beds August had warmed and all the bodies he'd stroked.

Jealousy reared its petty head, and I turned my attention to the ocean of sky surrounding us. Just as brusquely as the jealousy appeared, the realization that my navel didn't tingle—not even a little—hit me.

The link was gone.

CHAPTER 10

B etween talk of the Rivers and petty jealous musings, I barely realized the plane had started its descent toward an airstrip at the base of the Smoky Mountains. When the wheels jounced against the tarmac, though, I became wholly centered on the aircraft. And then the pilot braked, and the lap belt dug into my stomach, sending what I'd eaten back up my throat. I mashed my lips together and swallowed so hard I almost choked on my spit, but that beat hurling all over Liam.

Liam, whose eyes glinted as though amused by my predicament.

The pilot's voice crackled over a loudspeaker, announcing we'd touched down, as if we'd somehow missed it.

"You can leave the college packet on board," Liam said, getting up. "We're taking the same plane home."

As I unbuckled myself, the door with the retractable staircase popped open, letting in a burst of hot, humid air. I followed Liam out of the jet, and when my white sneakers met solid earth, I almost purred. Liam tossed me another amused look, but then his features hardened into his Alpha mask.

Two open-roofed SUVs fit for a safari were snaking past the few parked private aircrafts. Laughter and chatter floated from the bodies crowding the vehicles.

"Did the entire pack come to greet us?" I murmured over the drone of the approaching cars.

"They're close to three hundred, so no."

I'd been joking, but Liam was too concentrated to pick up on my intended humor. When the fenders all but butted against our thighs, the vehicles stopped and the passengers jumped over the sides. A man with a thick auburn-brown beard pushed through the tight web of shifters circling us.

"Liam!" he boomed, clapping my Alpha on the back as though they were old pals.

Even though Liam was as stiff as an ironing board, he offered the large male a tense smile.

And then the man moved toward me and extended his hand. "Zachary. But everyone calls me Zack."

I shook his gargantuan palm.

"So you're the Boulder female everyone's been yappin' about, huh?" He hadn't released me yet.

"The one and only," I said, eyeing him and his pack.

"Well, welcome to the East," he boomed again.

I tugged my fingers loose. "Thank you."

He nodded before turning to Liam. "Shall we run for the hills?" A slash of white teeth appeared between the coarse brown hairs of his beard.

Some of his wolves chuckled, stances slack, exhibiting no signs of aggression.

"I'm kidding. We'll do enough running tonight. Liam, you're ridin' with me, son," Zack barked.

Liam nodded, but before going off, he signaled for me to follow.

"My son Samuel can give her a lift," the River Alpha offered.

A man, who had the same sturdy build as Zack and the same reddish-brown hair, lifted his hand in a wave.

"My Second rides with us," Liam said.

I sensed from the weighted look father and son exchanged that they weren't too pleased with Liam interfering in their plans.

"All right," Zack said, his voice a little less loud, which wasn't to say it was at a normal pitch. It was most definitely louder than any voice I'd ever heard.

Although they all climbed in the way they'd poured out of the vehicles, Liam opened the door. He gestured for me to go ahead of him before hopping in, and then we were off, warm wind scraping through my hair and pounding against my eardrums.

At some point during the drive, the girl sitting beside me introduced herself. "Jane." She looked to be around my age, perhaps a year or two younger, with a round face dusted in freckles and sweeping lashes that looked red in the sunlight.

"Ness."

"I know." She pushed a bluntly cut piece of auburn hair out of her dark-blue eyes. "Are you and your Alpha a thing?"

When I shook my head, she scrutinized Liam a little more boldly.

"Why the heck not?" she asked after a long beat.

"It's a long story." One I didn't see myself sharing with her.

"It's a long ride."

Was she really expecting me to confide in her? I didn't know her, plus Liam was sitting right there. Not that I would've felt comfortable had he been in the other car.

"The males in your pack are so hot," she said with a breathy sigh. "Makes me want to visit Colorado."

I frowned. "How do you know if you've never been to Colorado?"

"I attended the pack summit a couple years ago."

Oh. Right.

"After what happened to my older sister, though, Daddy doesn't want us straying too far off our land."

I was glad Sarah had told me about the Alpha's daughter, the one who'd been killed by Morgan. "You're Zack's daughter then?"

"One of them. We're seven. Two boys, five girls. Well, only four now." Her gaze turned a little misty, but she blinked, and her eyes dried.

I wondered which of her sisters had been the one to sleep with August, because Jane was far too young to be the girl in question.

Thinking about August made me acutely aware of his absence.

And of the emptiness inside my stomach.

I pressed my hand to my navel as though my touch could somehow reactivate the link.

Liam's gaze drifted to my hand. Thankfully, he didn't ask me how I was feeling . . . or rather *what* I was feeling.

As we drove over miles of concrete roads that turned into rough terrain, I wondered what August was doing.

What he was feeling.

My blood turned to ice as a thought collided into me. What if August had been wrong about liking me before the link formed? What if he felt relieved by its absence?

I dug my phone out of the front pocket of my backpack and powered it on to send him a message that I'd arrived safely.

That I was thinking of him.

As my carrier searched for network, Jane said, "You won't get any reception 'round these parts. Dad put up a bunch of jammers. He's not a fan of technology."

· And suddenly my concern of what August was feeling was superseded by a new one—that of being disconnected from the entire world. The Rivers suddenly felt more oppressing than welcoming.

Liam leaned over me. "Will you have Wi-Fi at the compound?"

"We have a computer connected to dial-up."

I gaped at Liam.

They hate the Creeks, not us, he said through the mind-link.

I tried to let his words reassure me, but I wasn't reassured.

What had we gotten ourselves into?

CHAPTER 11

A ugust and Nelson had come out to Tennessee and returned to tell the tale.

The Rivers weren't going to make Liam and me vanish.

I repeated this to myself as we drove down a dusty road lined with identical one-storied stone and log cabins. The only building that was different was the one at the very end. It was built in the same style—rough gray stone, tawny slats, grids of windows—but it was long like horse stables with a thatched roof.

The car came to an abrupt halt right in front of it.

"Lunchtime," Zack bellowed, stretching himself up to his full height before vaulting over the side of the car.

This time, Liam jumped over too, then held out his hand to me. When in Tennessee, do as the Tennesseans, I supposed. I sat on the edge, swung my legs over, then placed my hand in his and hopped down. As soon as my feet touched the ground, I let go.

This trip wouldn't change the fact that I was Liam's Second and not his girlfriend. Not even his friend for that matter.

Business partners.

A petite and shapely woman with crinkly blue eyes was stationed by the entrance of the thatched structure. As we approached, she extended both her hands. First to me, then to Liam, and then she stepped close to Zack.

"My mate, Eileen."

The word *mate* made my heart pinch. Even though werewolves called their spouses this way, I couldn't help but think of August.

"Nice to meet y'all," she said.

Zack pointed to the two women standing around a young boy. "Three more of my flesh and blood: Poppy, Penny, and Jack."

I committed all of their names to memory. Where Jack waved to us, his sisters—who looked identical—observed me and Liam with quiet caution. They had the same auburn hair as Jane, but their eyes were different, dark, almost black, like the bitter coffee I'd drunk on the plane.

Zack rubbed his palms. "Lunch ready?"

Eileen nodded.

He kissed the top of her head before striding through the open doorway.

Eileen tipped her head for us to go ahead of her inside the giant structure. Clutching the strap of my backpack, I walked alongside Liam, gaze zipping over every inch of the building. I'd expected it to be dark, but the entire back wall was made of glass. A river rushed beyond the picture window, and beyond that stretched a copse of evergreens so dense the trees looked welded together.

"A Watt original," Zack bellowed. "Ain't it strikin'?"

I pulled Mom's ring out of my tank top and speared my finger through the warmed band, twirling it at the same time as I rotated to take in my surroundings. The building *was* spectacular. When I stopped spinning, I came face to face with one of the twins. I wasn't sure which one she was.

The girl observed me quietly, like most of her pack.

I stood my ground even though I wanted to back up a little. "Poppy or Penny?"

"Poppy. Penny's the ugly one."

Her twin sister smacked her arm. "Bitch."

Poppy grinned.

"You're twins, right?" I asked, even though it seemed obvious.

"Yup."

I wondered how old they were. Nineteen, maybe?

"Just call them Pee. They both answer to that," their older brother said, ruffling Penny's hair.

"So not funny, Sam," she said.

Their familiarity slackened some of the tension in my body.

"We don't respond to Pee. Or Pee-wee. Or any derivative of that nickname," Poppy added.

"Yeah, they do." A girl with brown hair down to her waist came up to us. "I'm the last Burley child. Or rather the first. Ingrid." She extended her hand, and I shook it.

"Now that you've met the whole clan, it's time to take your seats and dig in." Zack gestured to the table that stretched the length of the structure and that was heaped with bowls of creamed corn, crisp salads, barbecued meat, and pitchers of fresh juice.

In a rush of excessive affability, Jane hooked her arm through mine and towed me toward one of the benches propped under the table, chattering on about how hungry she always was. I looked over my shoulder toward Liam, wondering where he would be sitting.

You okay? he asked.

I didn't need him to hold my hand, or want him to, for that matter, so I nodded.

"So, how come you're the only female in your pack?" Ingrid asked, taking a seat across the table from me.

Lowering my backpack to the ground, I bit my lip, wondering if I was allowed to disclose this. I supposed it was no longer a secret. "Because of a fossilized tree root concoction they had the males in my pack ingest. It destroyed female sperm."

Her eyes grew as round as the burger patty she'd put on her plate. Her sisters' gazes widened too.

"Whoa," Samuel said, ladling some creamed corn onto his plate and then onto mine without asking if I wanted any.

"We're not going to have any females for another decade or so, since Liam's generation took it," I added.

"Unless you absorb the Creeks," Ingrid pointed out.

"Unless that."

"I hate those bastards," Samuel said, adding three skewers of cubed meat to his plate. He deposited one on my plate too. "Well, not the whole pack. Just the OCs. You eat meat, right?"

"Yes." I cocked an eyebrow. "Who are the OCs?"

"The Original Creeks," Jane said.

"What about the Aspens?" I asked, spearing some corn onto my fork tines.

"The Aspens are chill—*were* chill," one of the twins said.

I still couldn't believe the Burleys were seven kids. No family in my pack had more than two sons. Was that because Boulder wives were all human? As I pondered this, I studied the other Rivers seated at the long table. Most of the people I looked at looked right back with just as much unabashed curiosity.

"But who knows what they've become. No one's impervious to a bad influence," Ingrid was saying.

"Do all of you live on the compound?" I asked.

"Yep, but we're not all here," Jane said.

"We'll all be here tonight though. The Wolf Moon brings all the pack together." Ingrid chewed on a bite of salad, then chased it down with a sip of something that smelled like sweet tea.

Samuel, who couldn't seem to help himself from taking care of me, had poured me a tall glass of the iced brown beverage.

"Too bad more of you couldn't make it down here," Ingrid said.

One of the twins smiled brashly. "She's just sorry *August* couldn't make it down here."

My vertebrae jammed together.

Ingrid shoved her shoulder into her sister's. "Shut up, Poppy. Besides, he's probably off in Iraq. I heard he enlisted again."

August had never told me where he'd been stationed, but he'd told her?

I was clutching my fork so hard that I was probably bending it. I set it down before anyone could notice. "He did, but he came back early."

Jane plopped both her elbows on the table. "Daddy wants to commission another building from them, so you'll see him soon enough."

"She's totes whipped," the youngest brother, Jack, said.

Jealousy sharpened my senses, or maybe it was the approach of the full moon.

"He probably has a girlfriend," the other twin told Ingrid. "Dudes like him don't stay single for long. Dudes in general. Seriously, men are like incapable of bein' alone. Why is that, Sam?"

Samuel set down the skewer he'd picked clean. "Why you asking me? I'm on a break."

"Since last week, and you're already fillin' up *her* plate."

Sam flushed. "I'm bein' a good host, is all," he muttered around a bite of meat.

"So? Does August have a girlfriend?" Jane asked.

"Yeah," I said slowly, hoping my voice wasn't giving away all I was feeling.

Ingrid blinked in surprise. "It's that girl Sienna, isn't it?"

Had he cheated on Sienna with Ingrid, or had he slept with Ingrid before hooking up with Sienna? The chronology of August's girlfriends was foreign to me, not that I had any desire to familiarize myself with his string of conquests.

"You guys know Sienna?" I asked in a wooden voice.

"We know *of* her. He mentioned her. They were casually seein' each other the summer he came to install this building." Ingrid tipped her head to the roof. "They weren't serious or nothing." After a beat, she asked, "Are they serious now?"

"No."

"Is he dating anyone else?"

I wasn't sure why, but instead of setting her straight, I said, "No." And then I focused on my food even though my appetite had vanished.

CHAPTER 12

After lunch, Jane led Liam and me to a cottage. She gave us a tour of the simply decorated space: one leather couch, two armchairs, a wooden coffee table, a stone chimney blackened by use.

In the bedroom, there was a queen-sized bed and a gray-tiled bathroom. Everything was clean and functional. There were no paintings on the wall, no books atop the mantle, no pictures on any of the side tables, no chemical smells, just the scent of sun-warmed animal hide and scrubbed pine.

"You guys can rest up." She pulled open the front door. "We'll come fetch you before the run."

I spun around. "Wait, where's the second bedroom?"

"We were told you'd be sharing . . ."

Did she honestly think I'd share a bed with a guy I wasn't dating? "By whom?"

Liam placed a hand on my forearm. "We are sharing. Thanks, Jane."

She gave him a dazzlingly bright smile.

Once she'd shut the door, I muttered, "I suppose you could stay with *her*. I bet she wouldn't mind."

"I suppose I could, but unlike some people, I didn't come here to screw girls. Plus she's a little young for my taste."

I inhaled sharply. "You shouldn't attack people when they aren't here to defend themselves, Liam."

"That wasn't an attack. It was a remark."

"It was a very judgmental remark for someone who had sex with a girl while his buddies were playing poker in his living room."

A beat of silence descended over us.

After almost a full minute, Liam asked, "Why didn't you tell Ingrid she had it wrong about Sienna?"

I'd been sitting halfway across the dining hall, yet he'd heard the conversation? I wasn't sure whether to be impressed or annoyed. "Because it's none of her business. None of anyone's business. Besides, thanks to you, I'm not his girlfriend, am I?"

"If I'm supposed to feel bad about that—"

"It was just a remark," I said.

"Uh-huh."

"Anyway, we're not sharing a bed."

His eyebrows lowered, darkening his chocolate eyes. "Don't worry. I'll take the couch. But I'll have to go through the bedroom to use the bathroom. Just in case you were planning on sleeping in the buff." His gaze locked on mine.

I hoisted my backpack higher on my shoulder and then headed toward the bedroom. "If you need the toilet, it's now or never."

A crooked grin settled over his lips. "Anyone ever tell you that you have a bossy streak?"

"I've heard it said, but usually behind my back."

Liam chuckled. "Might be because we'd like to keep our balls attached to the rest of our bodies."

As I entered the bedroom, my anger dissipated a little. I set down my bag on a wicker chair propped in the corner of the small room, underneath a window that gave right onto the living room of the cottage next to ours. I closed the blinds, then pulled out my phone, but like Jane had said, there was no reception, so I put it away and took out the rest of my clothes, setting everything neatly atop the dresser.

The toilet flushed and then water ran, and then it shut off and Liam strode out of the bathroom, running his wet hand through his dark locks. "Have a nice nap." He offered me a smile before shutting the bedroom door.

I contemplated locking it, but there was no lock. Hoping he wouldn't barge inside, I stripped down to my underwear and tank top and slid underneath the comforter.

I WOKE UP TO LOUD BANGING. "NESS!"

I blinked, disoriented for a moment. When the room swam into focus, I all but lurched out of bed. "I'm awake!" I said before Liam could enter.

I tugged on my jeans, then alternately dragged my hand through my hair and rubbed sleep out of my eyes.

I opened the door. Liam stood there barefoot in an unbuttoned plaid shirt and a pair of unbelted, low-slung jeans. "Moon's up."

The mention of Earth's satellite had my skin strumming.

When we reached the door, I bent to put on my sneakers.

He drew the front door open. "You won't be needing shoes."

Right...

"Stay close to me during the run, okay?"

I nodded. Outside, a steady stream of Rivers were exiting their respective cabins and making their way toward a field filled with long, swaying grass that tickled my calves.

"My Rivers. May the Wolf Moon light up your paths tonight and for the rest of your lives. Be wild. Be free. Be merry," Zack hollered, yanking off his T-shirt before tugging down his jeans.

I averted my gaze as the sound of zippers and rustling fabric filled the air.

"Consider this training," Liam said, chucking his shirt on the ground.

"Training?"

"For the duel. You'll have to strip in front of everyone."

I bit the inside of my cheek.

He pulled down his jeans in one quick swoop. When I realized he wasn't sporting anything underneath them, I looked down at my toes poking through the long grass.

"I'd offer my assistance, but you'd probably bite my head off."

Ugh. I really didn't want to get naked in front of Liam, or anyone else for that matter.

Sighing, I pulled off my tank top and then rolled my jeans down. Liam's gaze struck my bare collarbone and the swell of my breasts. I turned so I had my back to him, and then I crouched, unclipped my bra and shimmied out of my underwear. Finally, I removed the leather strand speared through with my mother's wedding band, which I always wore around my neck, and stuffed it inside the pocket of my jeans.

Screened off by the long grass, I let the change sweep through me.

CHAPTER 13

We ran long and hard, trampling miles and miles of moonlit grass, clay-rich soil, and fresh mountain streams. My tight muscles stretched and coiled as I raced parallel to Liam and Zack through the Rivers' domain.

It dawned on me that, for all my talk of leaving Boulder, I was unwilling to give up my ability to travel the earth as a wolf.

Twigs cracked, and leaves drifted over me like fuzzy down. I halted and raised my head. Hanging mere feet above me was a black beast with gleaming eyes. At first I thought it was another wolf, but wolves didn't climb trees. I eyed the creature, and it eyed me back. A black bear.

Liam's muzzle bumped into my haunch. **He won't come down. Too many wolves,** he said through the mind-link.

Some Rivers had stopped beside me and were pawing the ground, alternatively snarling and yapping at the creature hanging for dear life on a branch that seemed too flimsy for its massive weight.

One of the Rivers got on his hind paws and batted the branch with his front leg. The bear bobbed and then let out a blood-curling sound of his own. Emboldened, other wolves lurched up and punched the branch, howling at the bear that skittered backward toward the trunk.

A sharp crack sounded over the pack's garish attack, and then the smell of warm blood wafted through the air, tantalizing, intoxicating. Stiff, horizontal tails poked out of frenzied bodies. My own tail came up in anticipation.

Ness, move! Liam yelled.

Even though I wanted to leap onto the bowed branch and help bring our prey down, Liam's order had me backing up. I whimpered, not understanding why he was making me step back from the kill. I tried to poke back toward the tree, but Liam growled, and my body sank lower to the ground.

I'm hungry, I yelped.

And you'll eat, but let them do the kill. We're on their land. That bear's theirs to kill.

His explanation didn't smother my hunger, but at least I understood why he was making me recede. I shot my gaze up to the creature that had reached the trunk. One of the wolves leaped and latched onto the bear's back paw. The bear released a guttural yap and kicked at the wolf's head, sending the ball of brown fur tumbling and rolling. Another brown wolf scampered toward the collapsed wolf, licking at a weeping gash on her packmate's head.

The wolf whined, and even though the growls and howls had grown in volume in the forest, I heard the wolf tending to the fallen one whimper, *Poppy.*

Poppy didn't stir.

The other wolf—I imagined one of her sisters . . . her twin perhaps?—yelped, and Zack snapped his attention off his ravenous pack.

The River Alpha bounded toward his daughter, and then he headbutted the thin brown wolf aside to have access to the immobile one. I strained to catch the beat of her pulse over the thundering hearts surrounding me.

She had to be alive. Werewolves didn't die so easily. When she still hadn't moved, I peered into Liam's alarmed face.

That could've been you, he said through the mind-link.

My stomach contracted with a mix of dread and hunger brought on by the bear's fatty flesh.

After releasing a raspy bark, Zack whipped his face toward his pack. He must've spoken into their minds, because his wolves halted their attack, reluctantly turning away from the cornered bear.

The animal huffed warily as it scrambled higher.

It wasn't my place to go to Poppy, so I stayed shoulder to shoulder—or rather shoulder to belly—with Liam.

Zack nudged the lump of brown fur at his paws.

Can we die of an animal attack? I enquired.

If the bear sectioned her artery, yes, he answered.

After a minute of terrible stillness, the brown lump emitted a whimper as faint as the patter of rain, so faint I wondered if I'd made it up, but then, through the trellis of furred legs, I saw Poppy lift her head. It glistened with dark blood which Zack and another wolf began to lick animatedly.

The River Alpha let out a keening howl, which every wolf in his pack reciprocated. A branch snapped overhead. I craned my neck and locked eyes on the creature that had almost stolen another daughter from the Rivers. My wolf longed to lunge up at it and devour its flesh for the pain it had caused my kind, but the human in me rooted for it to climb higher, because we'd lashed out first.

I'd never considered myself a predator before tonight, but the combination of wolf and human made us the most lethal kind.

Poppy rose to her feet like a newborn foal, struggling to stay upright.

I'll take her back, the wolf who'd cleaned her said. I recognized her mother's voice.

My heart pinched at the sight of the two females. Not only did Poppy still have her mother, but her mother was a shifter. I envied what they shared. How I wished my mother had been a wolf too. Cancer wouldn't have taken her from me if she had been.

As I stared at them, I imagined myself standing protectively next to my own pup someday, and a maternal instinct I didn't even know I possessed rose within me.

Looming larger than the other wolves in his pack, Zack waded toward Liam and me. *Alpha, you desire an alliance? Kill the bear that attacked my daughter, and for as long as you lead your pack, the Rivers will be your allies.*

You want Liam to bring down the bear? I yelped, wanting to add that the bear hadn't even attacked his daughter, that *she'd* attacked *it*, but I bit back my observation.

You may help him. You are his Second after all.

No. I'll do it alone, Liam said.

Liam—

He fixed me with his glowing yellow eyes, and through the mind-link, he added, **Not risking your life over a bear.** To Zack, he said, *Order your shifters back.*

While Zack bellowed for his pack to retreat, I turned on Liam and hissed, *You're not a squirrel, Liam. You can't climb trees.*

He snorted in amusement, or maybe it was annoyance, then flicked his ears. *Get back, too.*

Like I was going to let him face off with a bear on his own.

When I still hadn't moved, he growled at me and shoved his head into my belly.

Don't you dare growl at me, you overgrown furball. I'm your Second, so I'm staying. Now, tell me your plan.

He blinked at me.

What's your plan? Besides biting my head off for trying to help you? When he still hadn't said anything, I added, *You do have a plan, don't you?*

He looked at me, then at the bear, then back at me. **My plan was not involving you.**

Then you need a new plan.

He blew out a long, annoyed breath that ruffled the fur atop my ears. *Squirrel . . .*

I smirked, even though the situation was far from funny. Zack's test may not have been an impossible one, but it held its fair share of risk.

Liam's eyes flashed with an idea. *When the bear hits the ground, corral him, okay?*

My brow felt as though it was puckering—maybe it was. *Are you planning on gnawing on the trunk until it tips the bear out?*

He smiled, and then his rubbery lips retracted and his teeth shortened and the fur on his body became fine hair.

I yipped, *Are you crazy?* He wouldn't understand me now that he was back in skin. I shoved my head into his shins to make him back up.

He was going to face off with a bear in skin?

I shouldered him again.

Ness! Stop.

I froze, momentarily baffled by the fact that he could speak into my mind even though we were in different forms. Taking advantage of my bewilderment, he stalked around me toward the trunk under the watchful gaze of the River pack, which had retreated so far back all I could see were lambent eyes and moonlit forms.

The sound of bark scraping had me gaping back at the tree. Muscles twisted underneath Liam's dirt-flecked thighs. He proved agile, and soon, he'd reached the first large branch. He balanced on it, then reached over and broke off a smaller one. The bear barked.

Because he'd apparently not read the same nature guides I had, Liam decided it would be a good idea to poke the massive animal. The bear's bark turned into a blood-curdling growl. Liam poked him again. This time the bear flipped around and caught the branch between his fangs before shaking his head until he'd ripped the stick from Liam's grasp.

Liam reached for another branch at the same time as the bear unhooked his paws from the trunk and launched himself on Liam, sharp teeth bared.

Liam swung down to the ground just as the bear hit the branch. It broke free, and the bear fell, hitting the forest floor with a heavy thump. Instead of stunning him, the creature sprang up. Liam started to shift back into fur, but the bear charged. I blinked out of my daze and raced toward the bear before it could jump my Alpha.

Heart pinioned to my spine, I crouched and leaped, my claws finding purchase in the bear's back. The animal growled and climbed onto its hind paws, swiping at me as though I was a pesky flea. I ducked my head and slid down the long expanse of black fur, gouging his flesh.

He let out a feral bellow and landed on his front paws so hard it knocked my claws right out of his skin and sent me flailing to the ground. I blinked up at the sky that seemed brighter and whiter, as though the moon had bloated and spread.

The sound of battle had me blinking again.

Liam!

I rolled onto my stomach and jolted onto all fours, the world spinning and fragmenting. I shook my head to clear my vision. Two black shapes collided right in front of me. I backed up, and they crashed in a heap right at my paws. For a terrible moment, I thought the bear had Liam pinned underneath him, but then my eyesight finally cleared, and I saw the distinctive yellow eyes of my Alpha staring down at the bulky beast.

Heaving with rushed breaths, Liam sank his fangs into the bear's neck. A wet pop sounded, followed by the thump of the bear's lifeless head banging against the rich soil. Muzzle dripping with blood, Liam picked his head up, leveled his victorious gaze on me, then jutted his neck heavenward and howled his triumph.

CHAPTER 14

"I still can't believe you poked a bear," I told Liam after I'd wormed myself into my clothes.

Dried bear blood was smeared on one corner of his tipped mouth. The kill, or maybe the fight, had buoyed my Alpha. His neck was straighter, his shoulders broader, and his gaze brighter. He radiated adrenaline and pride.

It had been thrilling and terrifying. I was actually slightly terrified of how thrilling it had felt to bring down the beast.

"Says the girl who threw herself on his back."

"He was charging you!"

Liam's eyes sparked as he lifted his thumb to my jaw. When I jerked, his smile blunted. "You had blood."

I rubbed at the spot he'd touched to get rid of the blood, and to get rid of the tingling left behind by his fingers. August's face flashed behind my pupils. I backed up a step, not trusting myself to be so close to a man who'd once held the same gravitational pull over me as the moon held over the magic in our blood.

Two Rivers in skin passed next to us. "Nice hunt, Alpha." They inclined their heads toward Liam and then toward me.

My fingers stilled on my jaw. Had they just bowed to me?

More Rivers trickled past, chattering excitedly and dipping their heads when they caught our eye.

Zack and one of his twin girls approached. Considering she

didn't have a claw mark anywhere on her body, I assumed it was Penny.

"Kolane"—the River Alpha extended his hand that was streaked in dirt and blood—"in fur and in skin, you have our backin'."

Liam clasped the extended hand. "Thank you."

Zack seemed to wait for Liam to reciprocate his declaration, but what had the Rivers done for us? If they helped us defeat Cassandra, then they'd earn Boulder backing.

After a pregnant pause, Zack nodded toward the meeting house. "Beverages and dessert will be served in the meetin' house shortly. Shall we? I believe we still got much to discuss."

Liam nodded.

Zack let go of Liam's hand, then grabbed a hold of my shoulder and squeezed it so hard I thought the bone might pop out of the socket. "For a little thing, you did good out there."

"Thank you."

"I get why you picked her as your Second," Zack said, lowering his hand. "She's brave and easily underestimated."

The Alpha's compliment warmed my blood even though I wasn't sure what I'd done to deserve it. I didn't think leaping on a bear was brave; in my opinion, my actions had been a little impulsive and a lot reckless.

"Ness picked me, actually," Liam said.

I fixed my gaze on the long blades of grass swaying against my jean-clad thighs. I stroked the dried tips with my palm.

I *had* picked him, and yet, I also hadn't.

Not in the way he'd wanted.

"Is your sister okay?" I asked to change the subject.

"Yeah," Penny said.

"Thank the God of all wolves," Zack added. And then he gestured to the meeting house, and we all started toward it.

Liam fell in step with his fellow Alpha, and I fell in step with his daughter, not walking nearly as fast as both pack leaders. How were they not exhausted? My muscles spasmed with fatigue. If it hadn't been for Zack's mention of having much to discuss, I would've backpedaled straight to my cottage, sloughed my skin clean in a hot shower, and stuffed my bruised body between the crisp sheets.

Nostrils working the air, Penny said, "He's not your mate, and he's not your boyfriend."

Even though they weren't quite questions, I answered, "Just my Alpha."

"But he wants more."

Again, it wasn't a question. "We had a brief . . . *fling*. It didn't end so well."

"And yet, you're his Second."

"And yet, I'm his Second," I repeated. "What about you? Do you have a boyfriend?"

"I have a fated mate. Dad expects us to get together before the Winter Solstice, but I don't know"—she tugged a lock of hair behind her ear—"he's two years younger and *real* immature. I'm havin' trouble wrapping my head around the fact that I'm going to be spending the rest of my life with him." She smiled. "But it could be worse. My sister, the one who died, her fated mate was almost Daddy's age. It was real weird for everyone at first."

I peered at her through my lashes.

She shrugged. "But then people got used to it."

"So she consolidated the link?"

"No. She chose not to. She had a crush on an Aspen. She was trying to get Daddy to allow her to marry him. That's why she was in their territory when"—she bit her lip—"when the Creeks came."

"But . . . We can't change packs."

"Technically, we can't, 'cause we can never be looped into another pack's mind-link without the same blood. Unless there's a duel, but I guess you know that considerin' what happened to the Pines."

I nodded.

"But we can marry into another pack. Usually though, it causes a rift at some point, that point being when we pop out kids. Mixed pups have to pledge themselves to an Alpha. They can't pledge themselves to two. And once they pick one, they can never pick the other."

We'd arrived in front of the meeting house that was vibrating with animated conversations and the clink of utensils. She pushed open the door, revealing a dining hall dripping in candlelight and moonlight.

Penny's smile increased. "Want to meet my mate?" She tipped her head toward a boy with a mop of black hair and lashes so long I could see them clear across the room. "Hey, Isaac!"

The boy looked up from the long table topped with plates heaped with fruit—cut and whole—and bottles of every drink imaginable. A giant smile overtook his fuzzy jaw.

Penny leaned in toward me and whispered, "I told him that if he managed to catch me a squirrel, we'd be doin' the dirty tonight." With a grin, she added, "He caught five."

I smiled, but then I frowned. "You're consolidating the link tonight?"

"Are you crazy? I'm not ready for that."

"But I thought—if you have sex, doesn't it—"

She grinned. "Um, hello. Ever heard of condoms? Got to test the goods before you buy them."

"Oh."

Before she could lead me toward Isaac, Liam spoke in my mind, *I didn't bring you along for a sex ed class.*

Hackles raised, I scanned the room, spotting him standing with Zack by the picture window. I bet that if my mate had been Liam instead of August, my Alpha wouldn't have had such a problem with my conversation.

Please come. We're about to discuss Morgan.

For a moment, I didn't move, didn't *want* to move. At least not toward him. When I took a step back, he repeated my name through the mind-link, and it halted my retreat. He was using his alpha*ness* to manipulate my body.

How I wished *I* could speak into his mind. I'd tell him exactly what I was thinking.

Unless you don't care to find out what the Rivers know about the Creeks.

"Ness, you all right?" Penny asked.

"I need to"—*punch Liam*—"talk with the Alphas."

Liam had his back to me, so I glared at his shoulder blades as I wound my way around the boisterous shifters.

"Nice of you to join us," Liam said out loud.

I squeezed my fingers into fists that knocked against my thighs.

"So, let me recap what I've just learned," Liam said. "Morgan's never lost a fight nor a duel before, and the Aspen werewolves who tried to run after their Alpha lost were picked off one by one."

"Picked off?" I asked, setting aside my annoyance. *For now.*

"Killed," Zack said. "My daughter . . . the one who was . . ." His voice trailed off as he cast his gaze on the glimmering river beyond the window.

My heart pitched because I recognized the look of loss all too well.

He returned his attention to us. "She and Will were trying to get back here. They were caught before they crossed the Colorado state line." Pain deepened the network of fine wrinkles over his sunbaked face. "Stupid blood-link made tracking them so friggin' easy. If my baby hadn't traveled with Will . . ." His voice caught.

Because she wasn't linked to Morgan, but he was.

He cleared his throat. "But she wouldn't leave him behind." His deep-seated hatred told me we would've gotten his alliance had we slain the bear or not.

"Being noble comes at a cost." Liam's voice was soft yet carried over the rumble of talk around us. ***I'm sorry for snapping at you,*** he added.

I kept my gaze riveted to Zack. Liam and I would discuss his mood swings later, in the privacy of our shared hut. If he wanted to keep me at his side, he needed to change his attitude. He pushed as hard as he pulled. At some point, he'd shove too hard, and there would be no luring me back in.

He'd be on his own against Cassandra.

I thought of August then, of how calm he was, how he contained his temper even in moments of great stress. Thinking of him deepened the hollowness behind my navel. A hollowness that had annexed my entire chest.

". . . all taken Sillin," Zack was saying.

I shook my head to dispel the fog of my thoughts. I needed to focus.

"And I never heard of anyone able to shift with Sillin in their blood. It nulls our werewolf power."

"Ness was thinking Morgan could've rubbed it into her skin," Liam said.

"Like an ointment?" Zack hiked a thick eyebrow. "Hey, Sam,

come over here a sec." As Samuel made his way over, the Creek Alpha explained that his son was studying to be the pack doctor. "We got a question for you. What would happen if we applied Sillin to our skin? Would it get into our bloodstream?"

"Apply Sillin?"

"If it's mixed into a cream," I clarified.

"As soon as it's exposed to air and heat, it loses most of its effect."

"Most is not all," I said.

He took a swig of the drink in his hand—a fizzy transparent concoction that smelled incredibly bitter. "If there *is* a residual effect, it would penetrate the bloodstream. Not to depress y'all, but I wouldn't put too much stock in that theory."

"She had nail polish," I blurted out.

All three men's foreheads grooved.

"She doesn't seem the type to wear nail polish. I mean, she wears no other makeup."

The men were still doling out confused stares.

"Maybe she puts the Sillin in her nail polish. If she brushes it on her nails right before a fight, then manages to claw through a wolf's body, perhaps some of it gets into her opponent's bloodstream." When still no one spoke, I added, "Is my theory that inane?"

Sam sighed, swirling the ice cubes in his glass. "Not inane, Ness."

"It's an interesting theory," Zack said. "But the effect would still wear off fast."

"Maybe nail polish locks in the drug's properties," Liam said.

"Maybe." Sam's hesitant tone trampled most of my hope.

"Could she"—I swallowed—"could she have won without cheating?"

I didn't dare look at Liam as I said this, too afraid of the *I-told-you-so* expression that was surely written all over his face. If she had won without help from any substance, then I'd ruined his chances of defeating her by forcing him to wait.

"Everything's possible with that woman. The best advice I can give you two is to watch your backs around Morgan. Watch your fronts and sides too for that matter. I wouldn't it put it past her to strike from any direction."

I felt my eyes widening. "You think she'd attack us before the duel?"

"If she senses her chances of winning aren't that great, then yeah. She wouldn't do it herself, of course. She'd get someone else to do her dirty work."

"Like she sent her son to kill my cousin," I said.

"We heard." Zack exchanged a look with Sam. "Got anyone in the Creek Pack you trust, Ness? Nothin' like an insider to get a clearer picture."

"I do, but she was a Pine before, so I doubt the Creeks will trust her with anything."

"Yeah." Zack rubbed his beard, picking a twig out of it. "I doubt her new wolves will be given any classified information."

Sam's eyes widened. "Will's brother. He could help 'em. I can email him tonight."

Zack's dirt–and–blood flecked hand stilled on his beard. "Avery hates Morgan, son. I doubt he's privy to pack intel."

"It's been four years. He must've learned something in four years."

"Have you two kept in contact?" Zack asked.

"I think Ingrid did."

"Ask her to message him to see what his thoughts are on his Alpha."

Samuel turned and scanned the room.

"I believe she's with Poppy and your ma."

Once his son stalked away, Zack said, "Hopefully he'll be able to help us."

It was strange to hear him say us and not you. Strange, but oddly comforting. I liked that our small pack wasn't quite as alone, that we had allies. Sure, they were halfway across the country, but that didn't mean their influence and backing couldn't stretch over the thousands of miles.

"Ness, you mind if I take Liam aside for a bit? He and I need to discuss some personal matters."

"Of course not." My gaze skipped between the two Alphas. "I'll see you back at the cabin, Liam."

"I'm not kicking you out of the grub hall, Ness."

"I know, but it's been a long and eventful night. Plus, I'm pretty sure I'm still covered in bear gore."

Zack grinned. "'Kay then. See you in a couple hours for brunch."

As I strode through the long building, I wondered what he and Liam were going to discuss—the selection stick, perhaps? I couldn't imagine Zack, father of so many girls, wanted that thing anywhere near his pack.

A brief moonlit walk later, I was back at the guest cottage. I took a long shower, then put on my sleep shorts and a clean tank top. Before getting into bed, I checked my phone for a signal, but found none. I went into the living room and held up the device; I wasn't sure why I thought elevating it could help snag a network.

The front door opened then, and Liam came in.

I yanked my arm back, hoping he hadn't seen me acting like a human antenna. "What did Zack want?"

He eyed my phone. "He wanted to know my stance on inter-pack marriage."

I frowned. "He wanted to marry you off to one of his daughters?"

"Not exactly."

"Who then?"

Liam's gaze climbed up to my face.

"Me?" I squawked.

"No. Not you either, Ness."

Relief crept over me, but then it crept away, because Liam's expression remained serious.

"He'd only be interested if we won the duel, though."

"Just spit it out, Liam."

"He said Ingrid expressed interest in seeing August again."

The missing tether felt like a phantom limb—absent but forever there. "Did you tell him August wasn't on the market?"

"I didn't tell him anything."

"Why not?"

"Because I don't think it's a good idea that people know my Second has a fated mate. I wouldn't want anyone to use him against you."

"Oh." I dragged the fingers that weren't clutching my cell phone through my damp hair.

"And because a lot can change between now and the Winter Solstice. Look at how fast it changed between us."

"Whose fault was that?"

"Mine. It was entirely *my* fault. I let Aidan Michaels put doubt in my head. I regret every second of what happened, but were-wolves can't time-travel, so besides apologizing, there isn't much else I can do to fix the past." Several breaths later, he added, "Do you miss him?"

I bit my lower lip. I did, but I didn't want to discuss August with Liam, so I kept quiet.

"Forget it. I don't want to know." He walked toward the bedroom. "I'll grab a shower, and then I'll be out of your hair for the night."

"Will you tell August about the proposal?"

He stopped in the doorway and turned sideways but kept his gaze on the fireplace mantle. "I promised Zack I'd pass on the message, but I won't force August to marry someone." His gaze scaled up the bare wall. "You two have a history, I get that, but he's a decade older than you. Doesn't it bother you?"

My fingers squeezed around my phone. "Does it bother you?"

His mouth pressed into a sullen line. "You kept telling me he was like a brother to you, so yeah, I find your attraction . . . *incongruous*, but you guys have a mating link, and apparently, they blind people to what's wrong or right."

"So you think it's wrong?"

"Does it matter what I think?"

I assumed that what Liam thought was shared by the rest of the pack. Perhaps not the entire pack. Frank had been all for it. "I didn't ask for this mating link."

Before stepping inside the bedroom, Liam sighed. "I don't know if you remember, but August thought I killed my own father, so he's not really up there on the list of people I trust or like. Plus, he got you. And I'd be lying if I said that didn't play into what I thought of the guy. But I'll also admit that from an outside perspective, a twenty-seven-year-old guy preying on an eighteen-year-old will raise some eyebrows. No one will judge *you*, but August will definitely incur judgment. Anyway, thanks to me"—he tapped the doorway—"you have some time to think about it."

The implications of what he was saying hit me.

Really hit me.

I didn't want August to be crucified because of me. And yes, in a week from now, I would no longer be a minor, but I'd still be nine years younger.

I'd *always* be nine years younger.

In my twenties, that difference wouldn't be so horrendous, but until then, what he and I had was taboo.

Perhaps Liam's condition was a blessing in disguise.

CHAPTER 15

Pounding.

It echoed around me, driving needles of adrenaline through my legs.

I twisted around to find a black bear on my heels. I pushed my breathless body harder until every footfall felt like I was shattering a bone.

The beast jumped and sank its claws inside my human spine, and I screamed.

"Ness!" a voice yelled.

Two paws slammed into my shoulders, and I lurched into a sitting position, shoving the creature's paws off me.

Not a creature, and not paws.

Just Liam.

Blood battered my veins as I scrubbed my hands along the sides of my face to dispel the nightmarish chase.

"Bad dream?" he asked.

"Yeah."

"Want to tell me about it?"

I shuddered at the memory. "The bear we killed, it was running after me. And it caught me."

Concern pinched his brow. "My first big kill haunted me for weeks."

"It's not my first big kill, Liam."

He frowned.

"*You* killed it, not me." I scooted higher on the bed. "But it was definitely the largest animal I've ever gone up against."

"*Our* first big kill together." He smiled wistfully. "We made a good tag team out there." His expression undid more of our snarled past.

"Hope we make as good of a tag team during the duel."

"I have no doubt we will." His gaze lingered on my face a moment, but then he shook his head, got off my tangled bedsheets, and rubbed his palms over his jean-clad thighs. "Pack your bag. We'll stop by the dining hall for brunch, and then we'll head straight to the airport."

After he closed the door, I exchanged my sleep shorts and tank top for a pair of white denim shorts and a black T-shirt. I made a pit stop at the bathroom and attempted to smooth out my long tresses. Sleeping on wet hair had created movement and volume. Too much of both. I brushed my teeth, then packed everything away in my backpack. As I shouldered it, excitement at returning home steamed away the remnants of the sticky nightmare.

I would see August and Evelyn and—

My breaths spiked as I remembered last night's conversation. In the light of day, being with the ex-marine didn't seem as sinister. Just thinking of him had my navel pulsing, even though he was hundreds of miles away.

I looked out the window at the long grass that shivered in a light breeze. *What would you have done, Mom?*

I would ask Evelyn. If anyone was going to be a hundred percent unbiased about this, it would be her.

When I left the bedroom, Liam was already gone, and so were his things. I walked to the dining hall, passing a couple Rivers on the way. They waved, and I waved back.

Our allies . . .

At least, the trip proved a success for the Boulder Pack.

When I entered the gussied-up barn, I beelined straight for the head of the table where Zack sat surrounded by Liam, Ingrid, and Samuel.

"Mornin'. How'd you sleep?" Zack asked as I took my seat next to Liam.

"Great. Thank you. How's Poppy?" I asked.

"She's recuperating with her mother. I reckon it'll take both my girls a couple days to recover from the attack." The crumbs of bread caught in his beard peppered the table as he spoke. "I was telling Liam 'bout the experiment Sam carried out last night—he mixed crushed Sillin into Ingrid's body lotion and rubbed it into her skin, and then he shifted into fur and licked her arm."

I grabbed a pitcher of orange juice and poured myself a glass.

"He changed back into skin a couple minutes later."

"Which was what happened to Julian," I said excitedly.

"Except I didn't throw up," Sam said.

Julian had thrown up. A lot.

"*And* although Ingrid was able to shift into fur, she was incapable of keeping her form. When she tried to shift again an hour later, she wasn't able to."

"I tried again this mornin', and I still can't shift," Ingrid said. "So it does penetrate the bloodstream, and perhaps it's still on my skin, but if Cassandra Morgan could shift from fur to skin and back to fur, then she didn't slather herself in Sillin-lotion."

I wondered if we could trust their experimenting or if we should carry out our own.

Ingrid pushed her thick, waist-length braid behind her shoulder. "I got an email from Avery this morning. He said he didn't want to get involved, because he's about to become a father and worries for the safety of his child and mate. He hopes you understand that it isn't to spite you guys but to protect his loved ones. He wishes Liam luck, though. Says many, *many* Creeks are hoping for Liam to win." She eyed her father. When he nodded, she added, "He did tell us one thing that might help. 'Parently, Morgan's often bedridden. Word circulating around the Creek Pack is that she's got a sensitive constitution."

Liam set his half-drunk glass of juice on the thick wooden table. "Werewolves can eat carrion without getting sick."

"Exactly," Sam said, buttering a slice of sourdough. "We think it might be a symptom of whatever she's doing to keep up her edge."

I rubbed the satiny finish of the wooden tabletop. "Would taking tiny doses of Sillin for years create a habituation? Meaning, could her body shift in spite of having a minimal amount of the drug in her system?"

"I highly doubt it," Sam said.

"She doesn't heal fast," I interjected. "I forgot to mention that last night, but for a shifter, her wounds bleed longer than they should. You noticed that too, Liam, right?"

"I did, but wounds caused by an Alpha take longer to heal, so I didn't think it was particularly odd."

"Oh. I didn't know that." I bit my lip, feeling a little foolish, but then I thought of her lips, and the bluish tinge. "Does extended use of Sillin cause skin discoloration?"

Sam frowned.

"Her lips are a bit . . . *blue*." I grabbed a berry muffin from the basket in front of me and bit into the cakey treat, the tart sweetness of the fruit bursting on my tongue.

"They've always been like that," Zack said. "It's a birthmark or nevus or somethin'."

"Samuel, you mind if I put you in contact with our pack doctor? He's not a shifter but has been taking care of the Boulders for years now. We trust him completely," Liam said.

"Sure. I'll communicate my findings."

Liam stood up. "I need to get back to my wolves. Are you coming with us to the airport, Zack?"

"No. I need to be with my little girl, but Ingrid and Sam will accompany you."

"And me!" came a chirpy voice: Jane's. "Sorry I'm late. I was with Poppy."

"That's all right, darlin'," Zack said, getting up. He shook my hand. "Pleasure to make your acquaintance, Ness. We wish you great strength for the coming duel." Then he shook Liam's. "We'll be in touch. And don't forget about . . ." He flicked his gaze toward Ingrid whose cheeks instantly turned crimson.

"Dad," she muttered.

He gave her a wolfish grin before heading out of the dining hall, patting backs and leaning in to wish his shifters a good morning.

From the laughter and smiles, I took it that Zack was a well-liked leader. Nostalgia for something I'd never had, a pack where everyone belonged, hit me square in the chest.

Liam touched my forearm. "Let's go."

Flanked by Zack's kids, we left the compound.

Liam sat up front with Sam, and I sat in the back with the sisters. While the men talked about setting up a lab to create a new type of Sillin, I zoned out.

"Did he answer you?" Jane asked her sister at some point. Her voice was hushed, but the urgency made it carry to me.

"He did."

"And?"

Were they talking about August? *He* could really be anyone. I was just being paranoid.

"I didn't talk to him about *that*," Ingrid murmured. "I just asked how he was doing and told him we might have a new project for him."

Jane giggled and chirped, "Project *marry-Ingrid*," but then she blurted out, "Ouch. What was that for?"

Ingrid must've made her reason clear with a look, because there was a long stretch of silence.

"I bet Ness would love not being the only she-wolf in her pack," Jane said. "Right, Ness?"

I untaped my gaze from the landscape and turned to look at the two Burley sisters. I almost told them that August wasn't on the market for a wife but bit my tongue. When their expectant gazes turned to frowns, I said, "It would be nice to have other females."

But not Ingrid.

At least, not as August's mate.

There were about ten other eligible guys to pick from within the Boulder pack. "You should meet the other Boulder bachelors before you settle."

The back of Liam's neck clenched. Of course he was listening.

"I did meet the others at the pack summit," Ingrid said. "They were . . . *nice*. But I can't picture myself with any of them. August, though"—her dreamy expression made me want to stab her eyeballs with toothpicks—"I can totally picture myself with him."

Well, stop doing it. I jerked my gaze to the road before she could pick up on my rampant jealousy.

If I wasn't able to let him go when the mating link was absent, how was I supposed to let him go once the link clicked back into place?

CHAPTER 16

The plane ride back was nerve-wracking. I spent most of it gouging new scratches into the poor leather armrest. Liam didn't make me feel bad about the damage. He barely seemed to notice, contemplative as he was. He alternated between staring out the hatch window and studying his phone screen.

I'd looked at mine and found a message from August that dated to the previous night: *I wish you were sleeping next to me*. The words created a resonating pang inside my chest that echoed in my heart.

"What did you take away from our trip?" Liam asked, dragging me out of my reveries.

"That I should start taking micro-doses of Sillin."

"What?" Clearly not what he was expecting.

"Greg can figure out a dose that doesn't affect me more than a couple hours at a time, right?"

Liam's lips thinned in disapproval. "Not you. I'll get Matt or someone else—"

"You're paying me to help you, Liam. Let me be worth what you're paying."

His nostrils flared a few times before he finally conceded. "Fine." He bobbed his head. "Fine. What's your height and weight?"

"Five-seven. I haven't weighed myself in months, though."

"Approximately? One-forty?" he asked, typing out an email.

"Last time I checked, one-thirty." I contemplated the cottony clouds fraying and assembling into new shapes outside the window. "You think Aidan Michaels can still shift? He must've taken more than Morgan to hide in plain sight."

Liam looked up from the screen, amber eyes shaded by a swooping curl of black hair.

His cheek dimpled as though he were worrying the inside of it. "It'd be interesting to know."

"Maybe we can invite him for a run? Like a ceasefire before the war . . ."

"Ceasefires happen after wars, Ness."

I wasn't trying to be literal. "Like the calm before the storm then."

"Even though I'd rather fight another bear than extend an invitation to run with that man, you might be onto something."

After the flight attendant removed our empty glasses to prepare for landing, I asked, "I've been thinking a lot about something recently. Why didn't you tell me your father wanted to kill mine?"

Liam's head jerked in surprise. Had he thought I wouldn't pick at the scab? That I'd just let the truth of my father's death slide into the tide of things past and unchangeable? "What made you think of that?"

"Aidan."

He bobbed his head twice. Then, "Telling you meant confessing I knew your father was going to die . . . that I'd done nothing to stop it."

That he'd been all for it.

"I didn't know Callum well, Ness, but Mom used to say he was a good man. She would tell my father that she wished he would be more like yours." He stopped talking and directed his gaze to the tiny rooftops and blue spots that were swimming pools gleaming below us. "You can imagine what that did to him." He pressed his lips together for a long, *long* moment. "To me."

"I'm sorry you suffered because you didn't have the right role model, Liam. I'm sorry Heath gave you all these inner demons. That he made you lose faith in people. But I've also seen what sort of man you can be when you fight those demons, and that's the sort of man I want as my Alpha."

He swept his gaze back to me. "But only as your Alpha?"

"Liam, you just want me"—my eyes drifted to his black V-neck that quivered with breaths—"because you can't have me."

"That's not true."

"I'm the girl who got away."

He crossed one ankle over his opposite knee. "You challenge me. You're the only girl who's ever dared challenge me. How am I supposed to become a better man if all I get are pats on the back and strokes to my ego?"

I raised a small smile. "I don't need to date you in order to challenge you."

"But it would make the challenges and criticism a lot more palatable," he said, just as the wheels of the plane bumped into the tarmac.

The lap belt dug into my waist, slamming my navel into my spine. "How about we try to be friends? According to Sarah, I'm pretty good at friendship."

The vein in his neck throbbed and throbbed. "Fine. But I draw the line at mani-pedis."

I snorted. "Is that really what you think we do?"

"I also think you discuss shoes and tampon sizes."

"Tampon sizes?"

He smirked.

I took the balled napkin in my cupholder and lobbed it at him. "Ass."

He batted it away, then picked it up and stuffed it inside his cupholder.

"Besides, according to you, dating and sex interfere with concentration, so you should really swear both off until after the duel." I smiled, finding a little pleasure in tossing his words back at him.

"Done."

The smile skittered off my lips.

"How about we grab dinner this week?"

"Liam . . ."

"Friends have dinner together, don't they?"

"They do, but—"

"But we can't?" He got up, gripping his overnight bag so tight his knuckles whitened.

"I'll have dinner, but not just with you." I stood and swung my backpack onto my shoulder. "We can go out as a group."

"Does that group include August?"

"I would hope so."

His pupils pulsed with annoyance. "Fine, but don't expect me to make small talk with him."

"I'm not expecting you to talk to him at all."

"I'll ask Matt and Lucas. Some of the girls might come too then. Hope that's okay."

"As long as I'm not expected to discuss tampon sizes with them, the more the merrier."

He smiled, but it didn't reach his eyes. It barely creased the corners of his mouth.

CHAPTER 17

After landing, I asked Liam to drop me off at Frank's.

I realized I hadn't even phoned ahead to know if Evelyn was home. I assumed she'd be there. I always assumed Evelyn would be there when I needed her.

Sure enough, when I rang the doorbell a little after three, she was the one to sweep the door open, dispersing her familiar scent of menthol and cooking oil.

"*Querida!*" Her solid arms came around me, and she drew me into her soft chest. "What a beautiful surprise."

After thoroughly kissing my forehead and cheeks, surely smearing her red lipstick all over my face, she pressed me away and looked me over. Seemed like since we'd moved to Colorado, she was always checking for new bruises or cuts or other signs that I'd been hurt.

When her gaze alighted on my backpack, she asked, "What did Jeb do now?"

"Jeb?"

"You have a backpack."

"Oh." She thought I was coming to stay the night. I smiled. "I'm actually just returning from an overnight trip."

"Overnight?" She cocked one of her thin black eyebrows. "Do I need to sit down for this story?"

My smile increased. "Probably." The bear hunt returned to me. "Actually, yes. Unless you want me to spare you certain details."

She paled.

Yeah. She probably didn't need to hear about the bear.

I took her hand and led her to the couch, and we both took a seat.

"Before you begin telling me, have you had lunch?"

"I'm not hungry."

"I am not asking you if you are hungry. I am asking if you had lunch."

"I ate a sandwich on the plane."

"The plane? You took *un avión*? Where did you go?"

Clasping her lotion-softened hands in between mine, I started from the beginning but left out the midnight battle. Just as I was about to speak to her about August, the front door opened, and Frank traipsed in, forehead glossy with sweat, which he mopped with his forearm.

"Hi, Ness. Heard the trip went well."

Evelyn spun in her seat. "You knew about the trip and did not tell me?"

"Evelyn, you know I can't share all the happenings in the pack. And not because I don't trust you, but because I don't trust that someone won't try to get that information out of you."

Her intake of breath was so turbulent I squeezed her hands.

Frank walked over to the sink and poured himself a glass of water before returning to the living room. "Heard about that hunt of yours," he said, sinking into one of the armchairs. "Proud of you, kid."

"What hunt?" Evelyn asked.

I shot Frank a look, which made his gaze widen before dropping to his glass. "Um. The deer. Ness caught a deer."

"I have never seen you so fascinated by a glass of water, Frank," Evelyn said.

He tipped up his face, shooting her a rueful look from beneath his bushy white eyebrows.

"It was no *ciervo* that she hunted, was it?"

Frank tugged at the collar of his sweat-soaked undershirt. "It's mighty hot out today. I'm going to go shower. You girls probably don't even want me around."

Oh, I wanted him around.

I sent tiny imaginary daggers into his back as he walked away.

"Why do I feel like I am going to have an attack to the heart?"

I clutched her fingers a little tighter. "Let me preface this by saying that I'm a hundred percent fine."

"What. Did. You. Hunt?"

I winced from the brittleness of her tone. "A bear." I said this really fast and really quietly.

Her black eyes went so wide they looked like eight-balls. "A bear? You hunted *un oso*?"

"Not all by myself."

"Is that supposed to reduce my worries?" she asked. "Why?"

"To secure the Rivers' backing."

Her lips thinned, vanished. "They made you hunt down a bear? Please tell me you were sitting in a vehicle with a very big *pistola*."

I grimaced.

She clapped a hand over her heart. "As *un lobo*?" she whispered.

"Yes."

"I believe even the dye I put on my hair will turn white."

I grinned, but then realized she wasn't joking, so I swallowed back my smile. "Evelyn, I completely forgot to tell you this, but I ran into a woman at the bank the other day. She asked me if you were looking for work."

"I do not think I have the energy to clean—"

"Not a housekeeping job. She asked if you'd be interested in becoming the chef in her son's restaurant."

Evelyn's dark eyes grew wider, rounder. "A chef? Me? I am no chef."

"Are you kidding? You're the best cook I know."

A smile played on her red lips. "Do you know many cooks, *querida*?"

"I know enough of them to appreciate how talented you are."

Her hand rose to my face and cupped my cheek affectionately.

"Will you at least interview for them?"

"Perhaps." She lowered her hand. "I will talk about it with Frank. What is the name of the restaurant?"

After I gave her all the details, I steeled my spine and said, "Oh, and I need to talk to you about something else." I eyed the bedroom door that Frank had closed behind him. "It's nothing dangerous or worrisome. I just need advice. About boys."

"Oh." Surprise drove the fear off her face, and then her reddened lips bent into a smile. "What would you like to know about boys?" she asked, settling against one of the flowered throw pillows.

"I, um . . . I don't know if you heard but, uh . . ." I loosed a deep breath. "Our kind sometimes develop something called a mating link."

When the smile drifted off her lips, I understood Frank hadn't touched upon the subject.

I dragged my hands through my hair. "It's basically some sort of link that pushes two people to be together. For the continuation of our . . . species." Her slowly thinning gaze made me suck in a breath. "It doesn't mean the two people end up together. Mom had one, but she resisted its pull until it vanished. Anyway, I have a link, which will vanish after the Winter Solstice as long as I don't act upon it."

Her brow wrinkled. "Act upon it?"

My face became exceedingly warm. "Have sex with the person."

Her neck seemed to grow a little longer. "Go on."

I dragged a pillow into my lap and hugged it to me as though it could somehow prevent my navel from pulsing. Because, God, was it pulsing. Was August on his way here? Or was he angry I hadn't returned his call yet? Or was it just nerves from discussing boys with Evelyn?

"Who are you linked to?"

"August Watt."

"Isobel's son?" Her voice went a little high-pitched.

I clutched the pillow tighter.

"But he is almost thirty."

"Twenty-seven," I blurted out.

"And you are not even eighteen."

"I'll be eighteen next week."

"Do not get me wrong, August is a fine young man, but you cannot entertain thoughts about dating him, *querida*. You two are not at all at the same place in your life. You are starting college next week. He has been out of college for years. He has traveled the world. Fought for his country. He surely has had many girlfriends, which means he will expect things from you. He will pressure you—"

"He hasn't pressured me into anything," I mumbled,

"Yet. But it will come." She patted one of my hands. "If you came to ask for my blessing, I cannot give it to you. And it is not because I want to hurt you, but because I want to protect you."

My bottom lip started wobbling.

"Oh, Ness. Love is not an easy thing, and I cannot imagine a magical link makes it any easier, but you are still so young. The link will fade this winter, and then you will be free."

The heat in my cheeks filtered into my eyes.

She sighed. "You like him very deeply, don't you?"

I swallowed. "I do. I've always liked him."

"Then wait a few years. If you still feel this strongly about him once you are done with college, you two will reconnect."

"That's in four years. He'll be thirty-one. What if he gets married?" Ingrid's face flashed in front of my eyes. I blinked her away.

"If he feels the same way for you as you do for him, he will wait. The same way I waited for Frank, and Frank waited for me after his wife passed away." She dipped her chin into her neck. "Besides, have you considered what reputation he will have?"

There it was again . . . his reputation.

When a tiny whimper broke out of me, she leaned forward, tugged the pillow out of my hands, and gathered me against her, her palm stroking my hair.

"Think of what people will say about him when they learn he seduced an underage girl. That is not a reputation any man wants to have. He will be judged harshly, and that judgment will cause both of you pain." As I attempted to stifle my sobs against her slowly rising chest, she added, "Please, Ness, do not be mad at me," she said this softly, as though her tone might mitigate my pain. "I cannot encourage this relationship—however magical—because you are too precious to me."

Moment after moment passed in interminable silence.

Hands coasting over my hair, she finally added, "But in the end, it is your decision, not mine. I can only advise you. And whatever you decide, you will always have my love."

And here I'd come for her blessing.

As I shed tears against her shoulder, I rehashed all that she'd just said.

I'd never much cared about what people thought of me, but I didn't want the world to turn against August.

Which left me with only one thing to do.

Wade back toward shore before I got in too deep.

CHAPTER 18

I got home a little before dinnertime, having moped away the afternoon with Evelyn who tried her best to cheer me up with episodes of her favorite TV show and homemade brownies.

An uncharacteristically quiet Frank drove me home. Not that I felt very chatty myself, so the silence was welcomed. I didn't ask if he'd heard our conversation, because it wouldn't change much if he had.

I did a load of laundry, then turned on the oven and set the casserole Evelyn had prepared for me and Jeb inside. As I waited for it to bake, I took out my college course catalogue and circled the classes that held my interest, but my mind kept wandering back to August.

I needed to call him, but I didn't want to break up with him over the phone.

Maybe I would stop by after dinner.

I took out my phone to read the message he'd sent me when I was at Frank's: *Heard you were back. Want to grab dinner? Cole will be there. So no rule-breaking.* :)

I'd answered him that I was with Evelyn and that I'd call as soon as I left her house. I hadn't called yet, and I'd left over an hour ago. Guilt was making my stomach throb and pulse. I massaged it as I tried to focus on the catalogue.

A knock on the door made me jerk.

"Ness?" a deep voice called out.

Well, there went sticking my head in the sand. Sighing, I strode over to the door and opened it.

August was leaning against the wall, sporting a black beanie, a dark waffle-knit Henley, and fitted stonewashed jeans. His jaw was smooth from a fresh shave, and he smelled like he'd just stepped from his shower right onto my doormat.

Why oh why did he have to be so handsome?

His gaze trekked over my face. "You weren't answering your phone."

"I must have left the ringer off."

He pushed off the wall and rounded me. "Something's wrong," he said quietly.

The throbbing in my navel turned thunderous. I wasn't sure if I was feeling his stress or my own. "Why don't we sit down?"

He dropped down onto the couch and placed his forearms on his spread thighs.

I tugged on the hem of my crop top, trying to extend it beyond my navel, but the pale turquoise cotton just sprang right back up. I folded my knees beneath me and perched on the opposite side of the couch, hoping physical distance would make this easier.

"Something happened between you and Liam, didn't it?" There was a tremor in his gravelly voice.

"No." I shook my head, and my loose hair fluttered around my shoulders. "Nothing happened between us. When I was away, I . . ." I forced my eyes to stay locked on his, knowing that if I looked anywhere else, he would sense the lie before it even left my lips. "I didn't miss you, August. Not in *that* way."

Shadows rushed over his features. "Really?"

"I'm sorry for leading you on. I feel terrible right now. But I'm hoping we can move past this and stay friends?" My voice was so steady I sounded both convinced and convincing.

August didn't speak. He just stared as though waiting for me to say: *gotcha, didn't I?*

When I didn't utter those words, or any others for that matter, he got up. "Well, I . . ." He cleared his throat, gaze on the dining table and the open course catalogue. "I'll just show myself out." His tone was so heavy I almost leaped off the couch, but Evelyn's words held me in place.

He'd understand in time.

"Will you leave Boulder now?" I asked.

"I don't know." He glanced over his shoulder at me, eyebrows almost touching from how deeply his brow was furrowed. "You probably want me gone, don't you?"

"No," I replied so quickly his eyebrows jolted up. "Don't leave on my account, August." I gripped my bottom lip between my teeth. My heart was beating so fast I tasted metal.

He didn't move for a long moment, neither toward me nor toward the door. Did he sense my lie? Finally, his hand curled around the handle.

Before he stepped out, I said, "If you want me to return the money you put in my bank account, I'll—"

"Don't add insult to injury." Tendons strained against the bronzed skin of his neck.

My teeth elongated into fangs that sank into my lip, drawing blood. I swallowed down the salty taste of it, battling back my wolf before she could rise and take control of my human body.

August's nostrils flared. Could he scent my blood? Was he wondering why I'd lost control? Maybe he assumed I was anxious for him to get out of my house.

He shut his eyes and squeezed the bridge of his nose. "I guess I'll see you around." The tether that linked us swung like a jump rope. "Good luck with college," he added tonelessly.

"Thank you."

When he opened his eyes again, they shone as brightly as the bloated moon hanging over Boulder. He looked at me one last heartbreaking time, and then he left, the door snicking shut behind him. I held my breath as his heavy footfalls pounded the stairs, and then held it some more as his car engine rumbled.

Only when it petered out and the world turned silent did I unbolt my bloodied lips and let my pain pour out of me in great heaving sobs.

CHAPTER 19

I spent all of Tuesday in bed. I told Liam I'd suffered from food poisoning, and he let me take the day off. The following day, though, I got up and drove to the gym at the crack of dawn. When I reached the building, Liam, Lucas, and Greg were already there, waiting for me.

Lucas dragged his blue gaze up and then down my body. "What the fuck did you eat, Clark? You look like hell."

"Thanks, Lucas. Exactly what I rolled out of bed to hear."

Lucas smirked, but then his smirk vanished when he turned toward our Alpha. I didn't meet Liam's gaze, afraid he would see that it wasn't my stomach that had made me sick but my heart. I bet he knew—wouldn't be long before the entire pack knew. I just hoped he wouldn't see it as an overture to make a move on me.

Why couldn't I have stuck to my plan about not dating any man for at least a year?

"So the Sillin . . . How much am I taking, Greg? And how long before we can test the results?"

Greg handed me an insulated pouch containing two pill packs. "Take two pills every day at exactly the same time. From the minute you stop taking them, you'll need about ten hours for your werewolf gene to reactivate, give or take an hour. Oh, and store them in the fridge when you get home." He unzipped a leather satchel and took out a syringe. "I'm going to take some of your blood now, and then again in two weeks to check for traces of Sillin."

"Okay."

"Not afraid of needles, are you?"

"No." Still, as he took my wrist in his dry hand and brought the syringe to the inside of my arm, I looked away.

When the pointed tip slid beneath my skin, I cinched my eyes shut. The uncomfortable pinch soon subsided, and then it was done, and Greg said, "Call me if you notice any side effects. There shouldn't be any, but just in case, you can reach me at any time, day or night."

I nodded and took the business card he extended my way.

"I guess you won't be needing a bandage," he said.

Sure enough, my skin had already patched up. Only a bead of blood remained. I swiped it away with my thumb. "Should I take the Sillin now or after my torture session?"

"After," Liam said, shrugging off his black hoodie. He wore nothing underneath. "Since we won't have another opportunity to train in fur once you start taking those pills, we're fighting as wolves today."

As Greg left, the heavy door clanging shut behind him, I looked around for a place to change. The loft space didn't have locker rooms, but it did have a questionably clean bathroom stall.

As I started toward it, Liam called me back. "Ness, you'll be shifting out here. You need to get used to it."

I must have gone ghostly pale, because Lucas chuckled. "In the other packs, females and males shift together. Didn't Sarah tell you?"

"She did, but—"

"I'm not trying to make you uncomfortable," Liam added, hooking his thumbs in the elastic waistband of his sweatpants.

"I promise that on the day of the duel, I'll shed my clothes in front of everyone, but please don't ask me to do it today."

My desperation must've rang out loud and clear, because he relented. I scurried into the bathroom that stank of dried piss, leaving the door ajar so I could get out after the change. I kicked off my sneakers, yanked off my leggings and exercise top, and piled everything neatly on the sink top even though it wasn't much cleaner than the beige-tiled floor.

Once I'd morphed, I padded out into the gym on four legs. Liam was already in fur, three full hands taller than I was. Only Lucas remained in skin. He was sitting on a bench, curling massive dumbbells.

Justin's the one you're going to have to keep in your line of sight at all times, Liam said.

My ears perked up. *You think he'll attack me?*

He's not supposed to, but it's Justin we're talking about. He might attack you to distract me.

But that wouldn't be fair . . .

If you're expecting fairness, you signed up for the wrong duel.

But am I not allowed to stop the duel if he doesn't play by the rules?

By the time you manage to stop the duel, it might be too late.

What do you mean too late?

Cassandra will have delivered a blow I won't be able to recover from.

The skin beneath my fur broke out in goose bumps. *How do I stop the fight?*

You'd need to howl three times.

Liam, when we're out there, don't watch my back, okay? I can take care of myself.

He looked at me long and hard. *You're risking your life for mine, so don't think for a single moment that I'll let you out of my sight.*

Liam—

He cut my whine off with a sharp bark that made my muscles jam together.

We're going to work on your defensive game. I'm going to come at you from all angles, and you're going to have to get away. It'll teach you to think fast and act faster. Ready?

I said yes, but that was before I got my ass handed to me. If I'd known I would be trampled and shoved and flattened against the jockstrap-smelling mats, I probably would've said no.

Then again, I didn't want Liam to take it easy on me, because leniency wouldn't serve me.

TWO HOURS LATER, PANCAKED AGAINST THE GYM FLOOR, LIAM took pity on me and called it a day. Before leaving, I swallowed my first dose of Sillin, then entered a daily reminder into my phone.

"Dinner tomorrow night at Tracy's?" Liam asked just before I pushed through the doors.

Lucas looked at Liam, then at me.

Before the invitation was misconstrued as a date, I said, "Can I invite Sarah?"

"I'm not sure that's a great idea."

"She's not spying on us, Liam."

"That's not why. I just think it's not a great idea for her. I'm not sure the Creeks would appreciate one of theirs sitting at a table of Boulders."

"She's not a Creek."

Liam's jaw twitched. "At the present moment, she is."

"So, is that a no?" I asked.

He dragged his hand through his damp hair. "Fine. Bring her along." He looked over his shoulder at Lucas. "Free for dinner tomorrow night, Lucas?"

Lucas's frown grew. "Why are we all going to dinner?"

"Why, to bond obviously." I shot Lucas a taunting smile. "The paintball arena was already booked."

A corner of his lips sloped up. "I knew you'd enjoyed that activity."

"Yeah. Top ten best moments of my life."

That earned me a grin from Liam and a chuckle from Lucas.

"Who else will be at this dinner?" Lucas asked.

"Matt and Amanda." Liam turned back toward me, the smile gone from his lips. "Did you want to bring anyone besides Sarah?"

What he was really asking me was if I planned on inviting August. "No."

Liam's umber eyes glittered like topaz in the sunlight streaming through the loft windows set high enough that no one could look into the gym, a good thing considering our morning activity.

Not August? he asked through the mind-link.

Before he could get his hopes up, I said, "He's busy. Anyway, I need to go. Tomorrow, I'm running with Matt at six-thirty and then?"

"That's it for tomorrow. Wouldn't want to tire you too much before our big night out."

Snorting, I waved and unbolted the heavy doors. Before heading to my car, I made a pit stop at the drug store on the corner. I grabbed a basket and went aisle to aisle, tossing in energy bars and ultra-moisturizing conditioners and lotions, because my skin and hair felt brittle from all my shifting. As I turned a corner, I bumped into someone I hadn't seen in a long time.

Tamara let out a little *oomph,* and what she clutched fell on the ground. I crouched and picked it up. She snatched it from me, her cheeks going as red as her hair.

"It's not for me," she said.

I sniffed the air, remembering Sarah telling me shifters could scent pregnancies. My sense of smell was definitely not as sharp as Sarah's or Lucas's, and would probably dull further because of my Sillin intake, but over Tamara's flowery scent, I smelled something else—loamy earth. Since I wasn't standing in the gardening aisle of Home Depot, I assumed she was giving off that scent.

And there was this tiny fluttering vibration in the air between us.

A heartbeat?

Tamara was halfway down the aisle before I said, "It's going to be positive."

She froze and then slowly spun around, green feline eyes narrowing. "I told you, it's not for me."

As she whirled back around, wavy hair bouncing against her shoulders, the enormity of her news hit me. Even though I could be wrong—but I doubted it—Tamara was carrying a werewolf baby.

Liam's.

CHAPTER 20

After showering, I met Evelyn at The Silver Bowl where she was interviewing for the position of head cook. The establishment was extremely fancy, which intimidated Evelyn. Before she could choke herself from tightening the red silk scarf tied around her neck, I grabbed both her hands and towed them off the scarf Mom left her in the will she'd scrawled on a legal pad.

"You do realize you already have the job, don't you?"

"If I had the job, I would not be passing an interview."

I smiled. "This isn't an interview. It's a meeting to discuss your salary and hours."

"I should have made them my *polvorones*," she said, completely disregarding my comment. "Or my *taquitos*."

I squeezed her hands. "You don't need to woo them. They need to woo you."

Her black eyes bolted to mine. "*Bueno.*"

Feeling her composure strengthening, I let go of her hands. "Want me to come inside with you?"

"No. I will be all right."

"*Te quiero*, Evelyn." I rarely spoke Spanish but understood it perfectly.

Her eyes got all misty.

"Go." I tipped my head to the restaurant. "I'll wait out here."

As she hobbled to the door, dragging her bad leg, she checked over her shoulder a few times as though to make sure I was really staying put. And I'd planned to, but when fifteen minutes had gone by and the scent of charred coffee beans and chilled milk ribboned toward me, I headed toward the coffee house next door.

As I waited in line for my order, I kept my gaze on the entrance of the restaurant. Which was probably the reason I didn't see August until he stepped right into my line of vision.

"Hey."

I tipped my head up, my heart whipping into gear. "Hi."

His gaze was soft and bright, devoid of the darkness and tension from two nights ago. For some reason, that stumped me. Not that August needed to pine for me or harbor resentment, but he seemed almost . . . *happy* to see me. I mean, I was happy to see him too, but if the tables were turned and he'd done the breaking up, I'd probably not have been all too glad to run into him.

Which highlighted my lack of maturity.

Which highlighted his surplus of it.

His lips moved, and I'm pretty sure he uttered words, but I was so lost in thought I failed to hear them.

"What?" I asked.

"I was asking what you were doing?"

"Oh. Uh."

The barista called out my name.

"Buying coffee," I finally answered.

He smiled, and I swear it dimmed the noise level around me. "I can see you're buying coffee. I guess I was wondering why you were in this neighborhood."

"Oh." I really had a way with words today. "Um. I was—*Shoot!*" I peeked around him just as the door to the restaurant opened and Evelyn limped out.

Shoot. Shoot. Shoot.

Not only was I not where I promised I would be, but I was with August. "I'm sorry, but I have to go."

"Okay." He frowned. "See you around, Dimples."

The fact that he was calling me Dimples again made me feel like he didn't detest me.

Right before pushing my back into the door of the shop, I

asked him, "By the way, could I borrow some equipment from the warehouse? I wanted to sand down the floors of my old house."

He shook his head a little. "I'm offended you feel the need to ask me whether you can borrow stuff from me. What's mine is yours."

What was his wasn't mine, even if once upon a time, it had been my father's.

"I'm headed back to the warehouse after I deliver coffee to the crew. Stop by whenever you want," he said.

"Thanks?" I didn't mean for it come out as a question, but his genial attitude stumped me. Had he already gotten over me?

I turned away before he could spot my anguish and joined Evelyn on the sidewalk where she was chatting with a man who looked to be around Jeb's age. I pasted on my widest smile as I approached them.

"Sorry. Just went to grab us some coffees." I extended her cup, then shot out my hand to the man and smiled. "Hi, I'm Ness. Evelyn's granddaughter."

I didn't usually introduce myself this way, but seeing the breadth of Evelyn's smile, I decided I should start doing it more often.

"Nice to meet you, Ness. I'm Trent." His grip was firm and his expression friendly. "Grams told me we have you to thank for getting in touch with Evelyn," he said, letting go of my hand.

"Glad to have been at the right place at the right time. Is your wife feeling better?"

"She's feeling fine, thank you for asking. Anyway, I should get back to my accounting. I'll see you tomorrow, Evelyn."

"*Sí*. Tomorrow."

After Trent was gone, I squealed and hugged her. "Told you so."

She ran her enlarged knuckle down my cheek. "*Mi nieta*." My granddaughter.

"You think your *nieta* can get a free meal in your new restaurant?"

She smiled, but then her tender expression warped as her eyes settled on a spot over my shoulder.

"Hi, Mrs. Lopez." August was carrying two cardboard trays filled with iced beverages. "You're looking mighty lovely this morning."

"August." As she said his name—none too congenially—her gaze traveled to me.

She probably assumed I'd rendezvoused with him in the coffee house, disregarding her advice.

"I should get this to my guys. Have a pleasant afternoon, ladies."

Thankfully he didn't say, *see you later, Ness.* If he had, Evelyn wouldn't have believed our run-in had been random.

After he got into his car, I whispered, "Before you jump to any conclusions, there's nothing going on between us."

She took a sip of her milky beverage, wrinkles deepening around her eyes.

"You believe me, right?"

"I believe you." She offered me her arm. "Now come and walk with me. It is so beautiful out."

I hooked my arm through hers and, chatting about her new job, we walked slowly down the street, bypassing the playground where my parents used to bring me. I told her stories of Dad, whom she'd never gotten to meet, and life in Boulder before I was uprooted. August came up in many of my stories, which earned me repeated chary glances.

"He was a big part of my life," I said as we took a seat on a bench shaded by a glossy-leafed magnolia.

"Did he . . . ever behave indecently?"

Horror had me gasping, "No! Never."

She folded one leg over the other and massaged her bad calf— the one her ex-husband had put a bullet through.

Just as I thought of Aidan Michaels, a yellow Hummer drove down the street. I didn't have to squint through the tinted window at the boy sitting behind the wheel to grasp whom the car belonged to: Alex Morgan. Another detestable Creek.

A violent desire to slash his tires, and his chest while I was at it, animated me. I balled my fingers into fists.

As though he sensed my glare, Alex turned his face toward me. He had the audacity to toss me a wink before taking off, tires screeching.

"Who was that, *querida?*"

Evelyn's voice zapped me out of my violent musings. "A Creek."

She wrapped her fingers around my fists, easing my hands open.

"And what has he done to make you abhor him so? Besides being a *Creek*."

"He's the reason Everest is dead."

A long beat of silence passed between us.

Then, "Have many Creeks remained in Boulder?"

"Yes."

"Why?"

"Because of the—" I smacked my lips shut. Had I really been about to tell her about the duel? She *absolutely* couldn't know about it. She'd kidnap me and fly me out of Colorado. "Because of the inn. Because Aidan bought it, and Aidan's a Creek. So they feel at home here."

Nothing worked quite as well as burying a big truth under a smaller one.

She tapped my knuckles with her fingers. "*El diablo.*"

Another reason I needed to help Liam win this duel . . . so that nothing and no one stood in my way to send the devil to Hell.

CHAPTER 21

After dropping Evelyn off at Frank's, I drove over to the warehouse. I called Sarah on the way. I preluded my invitation to dine with a bunch of Boulders with a, "Are you busy tomorrow night?"

"You mean, am I deejaying at The Den?"

Right. It was Thursday night. "I meant earlier, for dinner."

"I'm free for dinner, and even afterward. I'm taking some time off deejaying."

I didn't ask why, but I suspected it was because she was still grieving for her uncle and for her pack's annexation.

"Meet me at Tracy's at eight?"

"Is it just the two of us?"

"Um. No."

"Who else will be there?"

"Some people."

"Which people?"

"Um. Liam, Lucas, Matt and his girlfriend."

Would Tamara come? If she did, the guys would surely pick up on her pregnancy . . . How would Liam react?

"Why are you having dinner with all these people?" Sarah asked.

"*We.* You said you were free."

"Not sure if I am anymore."

"*Please.*"

"What about August? Is he coming?"

I sighed. "What are you doing tonight, actually?"

"Hanging out with you to find out what the heck's going on in your life. Plus, I'm dying to know how your weekend went."

As I made plans to head to her place later, the warehouse materialized like an oasis, which made my pulse skip. I parked the van next to August's pickup, then made my way toward the wide-open loading dock. As I approached, the tether solidified like concrete. Standing beside Uncle Tom at one of the worktables, August looked up at me.

I tried to smile, but I was so jittery the simple process proved tremendously arduous. When I was close enough, I said, "Hi, Uncle Tom."

"Ness!" Tom grinned wide, which made his purplish-red cheeks rise and round, and the faint scent of cold whiskey clout my nose.

It was just after lunch, and yet he was hitting the bottle? I knew he needed the job, but I hoped August was monitoring him so he didn't hurt himself—or anyone else for that matter.

"We miss you around here!" Uncle Tom's strident voice made me glance worriedly at August.

"I miss it here too." And I did, even though the warehouse brought me equal parts pain and pleasure.

Pain, because it reminded me of Dad.

Pleasure, because it reminded me of Dad.

I could almost hear my five-year-old self squeal with delight when Dad would suggest a game of hide-and-seek in the stacks.

"Ness?" August tipped his head toward one of the aisles.

I snapped out of my daze. "Sorry. What?"

"The sanders are down there."

As I trailed after him, I whispered, "He's drunk, isn't he?"

After a beat, August nodded.

"Isn't it . . . dangerous?" I gestured to all the heavy-duty machinery around us.

"I got one of my guys keeping an eye on him."

"Is he often like this?"

"Liquored up? Yeah. But not usually while he's at work. Today's his wife's birthday. Every year, Dad tells him to take the day off, but he says it's easier to spend his day here than in his home where everything reminds him of her."

August's words made my heart hurt. "I'm not sure I could keep living if everyone I loved died."

"You'd find new people to love," he said.

"I don't love very easily."

One corner of his mouth tipped up. "You're telling me."

Realizing what he was saying, I added, "I still love you."

"It's okay."

"No, it's not. Not if you think otherwise."

"Ness . . ." He sighed.

Why couldn't I have returned to Boulder at twenty-one? I dragged my ponytail over my shoulder and toyed with the ends. "You're one of my two favorite people in Boulder."

A small groove appeared between his brows. "Who's the second one?"

"Evelyn."

As August watched my coiling blonde locks, I wondered where I stood in his favorites list. Had I been relegated to the bottom? Was I even still on the list?

Even though the warehouse was alive with noise, in the shade of the tall metal shelves, away from everyone else, it felt as though August and I were enclosed in our own little world, a world as fragile as a soap bubble.

He closed his eyes and took a step back, bursting the bubble. When he lifted his lids, he was staring at something behind me. He cleared his throat. "You'll need a big drum and an edging sander. And a vacuum."

"If I can borrow all of the above, it would be really helpful."

He nodded and stepped toward the rack, his arm brushing mine. Even though he seemed absolutely unaffected, I jerked from the contact. As he grabbed both tools, I thought of what he'd told me . . . that he never did anything by mistake. Which led me to wonder if he'd meant to touch me and test the durability of my nerves.

"The vacuum's at the end of the aisle." He canted his head in the direction.

As I spun, my sneakers' rubber soles squeaked on the concrete.

I hurried to grab the vacuum; then together, we walked out of the warehouse and back toward the van. I shifted my hold on the contraption in order to pop the trunk open, but August loaded everything in the bed of his pickup.

As he eased the vacuum from my arms, he said, "You need a generator, or do you have electricity?"

"Jeb said we have electricity."

"And windows?"

"And windows." I smiled at his observance and thoroughness, and then I gestured to his truck. "Why did you put the stuff in your car? It'll fit in the van."

"I was going to help you set up the equipment."

"Jeb's at the house."

"And he's familiar with sanders?"

"Probably not, but I sort of remember how to use them."

"I'll give you a refresher course."

"You surely have better things to do with your time . . ."

"It's my lunchbreak."

"Well then, eat lunch."

"Not hungry."

Okay . . . I started toward the driver's side of the van. "Remember the way?"

Sadness glinted in his eyes. "I remember."

He was probably wondering why I'd want to move back into a house filled with ghosts. Or maybe *I* was wondering this and just projecting my qualms on him. Should I have sold it and moved on?

I shook my head.

I'd make new memories in it.

Fill it with new laughter and new scratch marks.

Besides, this was a good project for my uncle, who would've gone stir-crazy sitting at home, plotting his revenge on Alex Morgan. It was keeping him sane and safe.

CHAPTER 22

J eb came out of the house when I drove up, white wifebeater stained and damp with sweat. "We should be done with the plumbing by next week," he said as I hopped out of the van.

The overhaul had gone fast. It helped that one the elders' sons was an electrician. It also helped that Jeb was so hands-on.

August parked next to me, then got out and went to gather the equipment. "Hey, Jeb."

As Jeb wiped his hands on a rag that looked dirtier than his palms, he narrowed his eyes. "We got everything under control here, August."

I frowned.

"Oh, I'm not here on behalf of Watt Enterprises," August said. "Just came to get Ness set up."

Jeb thought I'd hired August?

My uncle was still wiping his hands, arms a little tense, as though he felt threatened by August. I rolled my eyes. Even though Jeb wasn't in wolf form, he was acting mighty territorial.

"Ness, can I grab the car keys? I wanted to go get some supplies."

I dug them out of my bag and handed them over.

Once he'd driven away, I said, "Sorry about that."

"'Bout what?"

"Jeb's strange behavior."

August smiled as he lugged the sanders past the wisteria vines wrapped around the porch's beams. "I'm used to people reacting that way. They see us coming and think we're either going to steal their job or present them with a hefty bill."

We carried the tools into the house that looked larger now that the furniture had been disposed of—Jeb had gotten some Boulders together over the weekend to clear the space. He'd asked me what I wanted to keep, and I said nothing. Not that there had been much left over from Mom and Dad; the previous owners had stripped the house.

As August set everything down, he stared around the bare space. "Never thought I'd come back here."

"You and me both."

He turned his attention to me. "You sure you want to live here?"

"I'm not really sure of much these days, but I don't see myself staying in Jeb's apartment forever. Besides, I want the forest on my doorstep. I want to be able to shift and come home without running into any humans."

I gazed out at the woods cinching the property and at the grayed picnic table buried in overgrown grass. I could still picture the boisterous meals we'd shared, could still hear my mother debating the merits of medicinal plants with Isobel, and my dad discussing inventions that would revolutionize the timber industry with Nelson while I swung on the tire swing August had fashioned for me.

God . . . he really had been such an integral part of my life.

August touched my arm. "Dimples?"

I swallowed and pushed away the memory before it slicked my eyes. "When are you starting construction on *your* home?"

"When I have time."

"Do you have a design in mind?"

He lowered his eyes to a dark knot in a floorboard. "I did. I'm not sure of it anymore."

"If you need input, I'll gladly offer my consulting services."

He nodded as though filing my offer away in a drawer he was never planning on opening. I supposed he didn't need the input of a girl with no experience or skill.

"Ready for your Parquet 101 class?" he asked after a moment.

I smiled. "I am."

After quickly vacuuming a corner of the living room, he showed me how to work both sanders. Even though there shouldn't have been anything remotely sexy about sanders, watching him operate the machines was mesmerizing.

"How old is Sienna?" The question popped out of my mouth before I could think better of bringing up his ex.

He flicked the big drum sander off. "What made you think of her?"

"*You* made me think of her."

"I'd rather if I didn't make you think of her." He straightened and rubbed his palms against his jeans. "She turned twenty-one back in January. Why?"

I shrugged. "Just wondering."

He eyed me. "You're never just wondering anything." He came a little closer, still skimming his hands over his jeans. "Age is just a number, Ness. I know some thirty-year-olds who act like teenagers and some teenagers who act like adults. What you've lived through, it made you mature faster." In a voice so low goose bumps flourished on my bare arms, he added, "Not that it matters anymore, considering how you feel about me."

For a moment, he didn't move, and neither did I, but then his gaze dropped to my mouth, and he inclined his head, and I thought that if he bridged the distance, I'd toss Liam's ban and Evelyn's opinion to the wind and confess my lie.

A ringing erupted between us. He shut his eyes and took a step back.

Palming the nape of his neck, he slid his phone out of his pocket. "I'll be right back," he said, returning outside.

I glanced at him through the window, watched his tendons and muscles shift beneath his caramel skin, watched the perfect Vee of his back. If only I hadn't missed him when the link had faded.

Sighing, I crouched and checked the floorboards for nails that would need to be removed. As I pried one loose, August's heavy boots reappeared before me. I trailed my gaze up his legs that were set stiffly apart, at his knees that were locked as tight as his jaw.

"You told me nothing happened between you and Liam when

you were out in the Rivers' territory." There was a sharpness to his tone that made me rock back onto my heels. "You two shared a cabin. A *one*-bedroom cabin."

As I stood, I folded my arms. "Liam was worried about leaving me on my own in the enemy camp."

"The Rivers aren't our enemy," August said through gritted teeth.

"I figured as much when Ingrid's father asked Liam to arrange a wedding between you and his daughter."

His face jerked back. "What? What are you talking about?"

"Ingrid wants to marry you, August. If you remain a Boulder, that is. If Liam and I fail, and you become a Creek, the proposal will be off the table."

His eyebrows lost some of their slant.

"And I didn't tell you about sharing a cabin with Liam, because I knew it would annoy you."

"If nothing happened, why would it annoy me?"

"Nothing happened, and it's bothering you now. And we're not even . . . *together*."

Silence stretched out like the ocean that had separated us after he'd reenlisted.

"Will you consider it?"

His chest rose and fell bumpily. "Consider what?"

"Marrying her?"

"Of course not," he snapped.

It shouldn't have brought me any relief, but hearing him say this filled me with hope that he might just wait for me to grow up. "How did you find out anyway?"

"Same way I find out about everything . . ." He tossed me a hurt look as he stalked away. "Through other people."

His words sliced past my ribcage, cutting deep. What else had he found out about? Was he talking about the dinner tomorrow night?

"So you don't find out about this *through other people*, I'm going to dinner at Tracy's tomorrow with a couple Boulders and their girl-friends."

He paused on the threshold of the house. "Are you telling me or inviting me?

I folded my arms in front of me. "Do you want to come?"

He looked at me long and hard before saying, "No."

And then he was trampling the unkempt front yard and climbing into his car. I felt his anger agitate the tether long after he'd gone.

CHAPTER 23

"Hey, bitch," Sarah said, flinging her front door wide. "Hope you like Chinese food, 'cause we're having Chinese food."

"I like Chinese food," I mumbled as I entered her marble-and-stainless-steel palace.

"Do contain your enthusiasm."

"Sorry. I've just had a crappy few days."

"Crappy? Try my life right now. I had the pleasure of being convened to a Creek assembly yesterday. Lori, who's apparently her mother's spokesperson, commanded us to fraternize with our new packmates and learn the fifty or so rules of the Creek way of life."

"I broke up with August on Monday," I blurted out.

Sarah's brown eyes broadened. "Okay, your crappy trumps mine. But only by a fraction . . ." She followed me over to the couch and sat daintily while I just dropped onto the seat cushion. "Spill."

"Both Liam and Evelyn think I shouldn't date a guy who's a decade older."

"Liam's your ex, and Evelyn isn't a shifter."

I glanced at Sarah, at the wild blonde corkscrews framing her delicate face. "What does that have to do with anything?"

"*He's* totally biased, and *she* doesn't understand the importance of mating links."

"What she doesn't understand is what a twenty-seven-year-old man sees in an eighteen-year-old girl."

"Did you tell her about the link?"

"I did, but that's not why I'm with . . . *was* with August in the first place." *Ugh.*

"I know, but maybe you could've used it to convince her that you're incapable of *not* being with him."

I snorted. The sound reminded me of August, which made my heart feel black and blue. "Like she would ever have fallen for that."

"She's not a werewolf. She doesn't know how it works."

"I don't want her to think I'm with him because I'm incapable of being without him." I burrowed deeper into the couch. "Doesn't even matter. I got in a fight with him this afternoon because he found out I shared a cabin with Liam when I was out East, and he's convinced something happened."

"Did something happen?"

"No!"

She raised both her palms in the air. "I was just fact-checking. I like to get all my info before doling out advice."

I leaned back into the couch and threw one arm over my eyes a tad dramatically.

"Just explain something. If you broke up with him on Monday, why are you having a jealous row two days later?"

"Because something almost happened between us this afternoon."

"I think I might be more confused now than a couple seconds ago. Start from the beginning."

And so I did. I told her everything in such detail that when I was done, the food in the little white takeaway cartons was cold.

"You do realize *you're* ridiculous, and *he's* ridiculous. Just fucking call him and tell him you lied, and tell Evelyn that you love August, graying hair and all."

"His hair isn't graying."

She smirked. "Life's too short, hun. You know this better than anyone else. You're here today, but you might be gone tomorrow, so just focus on making yourself happy instead of pleasing everyone else around you." She toyed with a diamond ring that looked a lot like the one which used to grace her uncle's pinkie.

"But I don't want people to pass judgment on August."

"He's a big boy. I'm sure he can handle it. I'm sure he'll be *happy* to handle it if it means getting you back."

I wasn't so sure he wanted me back after this afternoon. "I asked him to dinner tomorrow night, and he said he wasn't interested." I didn't clarify that I told him about it before inviting him because that would've won me an eye-roll, and I didn't want an eye-roll.

I wanted a hug.

I settled on dumplings and fried rice.

A lot of dumplings and a lot of fried rice.

While I ate, we talked about the Creeks, because one, I was done talking about myself, and two, I was hoping Sarah had uncovered something we could use.

"Cassandra didn't run with us during the Full Moon."

Alphas always ran with their packs during the Full Moon. "Why not?"

"Lori said her mother was feeling under the weather."

"Did Aidan Michaels run?"

"Nope. I doubt he can even shift what with all that Sillin still in his system."

I stuck my chopsticks into the carton of rice. "Sillin changes a werewolf's smell, correct?"

"Yeah, in substantial quantities, it dims it."

"Does Sandra still smell like a wolf?"

Sarah frowned.

"I mean, Cassandra."

"I got who you meant. I'm trying to remember."

I stuck my wrist in her face. "Do I still smell like a wolf?"

She sniffed my skin, then pushed my arm away. "Yeah, you do. You'd have to be away from your pack and taking *a lot* of Sillin to stop smelling like a wolf, Ness."

I sighed. "Do you think we're wrong in considering Sillin's how she defeated Julian?"

"Gosh, if I had the answer to that question, you'd be the first to know."

"I bet her family knows. The day of the duel, when Liam said he wanted to fight her straight away, Alex didn't look concerned at all.

It was as though he knew his mother couldn't lose. Which is why I'm convinced it wasn't just skill and luck."

Sarah sat up a little straighter. "You just gave me a brilliant idea."

"I did?"

She nodded, her springy corkscrews popping out from behind her ears. "I'm going to flirt with Alex Morgan."

I hissed. "Sarah—no. He drove Everest off the road! He's insane."

She stared at the crystal chandelier dangling over her leather coffee table without really looking at it. I prayed she was reevaluating the soundness of her decision.

I leaned over and trapped her fingers. "Sarah, I'm serious. Don't do this."

"I'll be careful."

A smile, which I imagined was supposed to be reassuring, graced her mouth. "I can't go out to dinner with you tomorrow night, though. Alex will see right through me if I dine with a bunch of Boulders. And you and I can't hang out for the duration of my stint."

"Sarah—"

"Why didn't I think about this sooner?"

"Because it's crazy, not to mention dangerous."

"And fighting in a duel is *oh-so*-safe?" She pried my fingers off hers. "I'll be fine. I promise." She rose and walked over to the island to root through her handbag. She came up with a cell phone. "I'm going to tell him about your visit out East to win his trust. Don't tell Liam or Lucas or anyone else the reason I'm betraying your pack, though. It's better they all think I'm trying to be a good Creek."

"I hate this."

"Well, I hate your lack of style, but you don't see me making a fuss about it."

"My lack of style? Seriously?"

She raised a wolfish grin. "All you wear is denim and tank tops—in a variety of blues and whites and blacks. Granted your clothes are skintight, so they're not horribly unsexy, but you could have so much more fun gussying up your hot self." She tossed her phone on her bag, then went into her bedroom.

Doors slid on rails, metal hangers clinked, heavy things thumped.

She returned a couple minutes later, lugging a huge bag filled to the brim with clothes. "Since you and I won't be hanging out for a while, here's some stuff. Most of it's too small for me—"

"We're the same size."

"—on top. Or no longer my style."

"Sarah . . ."

"Stop saying my name all breathily. You sound blonde."

"I *am* blonde. And so are you. And the only reason I'm saying your name like that is because you're not letting me finish any of my sentences, and you're behaving like you just broke out of the loony bin."

"I want Cassandra Morgan dead, Ness. And so do you. And unless you want me to creep up on her in her sleep and murder her, which would just make her heart useless for the taking—if I even manage to make it stop beating—I'm going to seduce her son to help you guys." She forced the bag into my arms. "Now go. I need to fumigate my apartment to get rid of your smell."

I got up, clutching the bag. "Why would her heart be useless for the taking?"

"Because only Alphas can take another's heart." When I frowned, she added, "Their hearts are already open to connections."

"So Liam could sneak up on her and kill her in her sleep?"

"He could, but there'd be no honor in doing it. He'd just be considered a coward and a thief. No self-respecting Alpha would resort to murder in order to steal a foreign pack."

I mulled this over as I walked toward her front door. Before letting myself out, I said, "If Alex tries anything, you let me know straight away, and I'll get you out."

She nodded, but excitement glimmered in her eyes. I understood her desire to help—if the tables had been turned, I would've been the first to volunteer—but I feared what the Creeks would do to her if they discovered her duplicity. Even though Morgan claimed she wasn't out for blood, she'd punished her defectors— Everest, disloyal Aspens, the River Alpha's daughter—with murder.

CHAPTER 24

Matt decided to test my endurance and friendship the following morning. Instead of a one-hour trek, he took me on a two-hour tour of Boulder's rockiest mountain roads and most treacherous hiking trails.

"Heard we're all doing dinner tonight," he said as he hydrated in my kitchen, his big forehead flushed and sweaty.

At least the exercise hadn't been too easy on him either.

"Not sure I'll be able to peel myself out of bed after what you just made me do. Did Liam ask you to torture me, or was it all your idea?"

"All my idea, Little Wolf. Glad you enjoyed it."

I stuck out my tongue as I refilled my glass with cold tap water. "Not to pry, but what's going on between you and August?"

"Nothing's going on between us."

Matt cocked one of his very blond eyebrows. "He almost ripped me a new one for hammering the wrong baseboard into a wall yesterday when just last week he was discussing bonuses, so I don't buy that nothing's going on."

"I'm telling the truth. Nothing's going on between us. I broke up with him for good."

"What? Why?"

"Because."

"Because what?"

I set my glass down on the counter, then turned on the tap and scooped some water up to splash my face. "Because I didn't miss him when I was out there, which means our attraction is caused by the bond." I hoped that between the sound of running water and having my back turned, Matt wouldn't detect the glaring lie.

"For real?"

I let the water run a couple seconds more, then shut it off. It trailed down my neck and bled into my running bra, cooling down my warm body. When I turned around, Matt's entire forehead was pleated.

"That's brutal."

"He'll get over it."

"I remember you saying the exact same thing about Liam." Matt shook his head. "He didn't get over it."

"He's about to get over me, considering—" I snapped my lips shut. Had I really been about to blurt out Tamara's baby news to Matt?

"Considering what?"

"Considering something I'm not at liberty to discuss."

"Ness . . ."

"Can't tell you, Matt."

"Why not?"

"Because it doesn't involve me."

"Who does it involve?"

"Liam. I think."

"I got that, but—"

"Please, Matt. Forget I said anything."

He pushed away from my kitchen counter. "You do realize that's like telling my wolf to forget about a deer? Once I spot it, I want it."

"Look at that. It's eight o'clock."

"Don't change the subject."

"You're late for work."

"And you're being amazingly annoying, which is quite the feat for you."

I shot him a brazen smile. "I can't be *that* annoying. After all, you hang out with me when you don't need to."

That won me a big-ass grin. "I have a thing for annoying people."

"I won't tell Amanda."

He chuckled. "I wasn't talking about my girlfriend."

I winked at him as he opened the door.

"Take an ice bath, Little Wolf. It helps with sore muscles."

I didn't take an ice bath, but I did take a cold shower that felt like standing underneath falling needles, and then I headed to the house and worked on the floors until I'd scraped off every last speck of the past. My bedroom took the longest, but that was mostly because I spent a bunch of minutes staring at the loose floorboard. For a moment, I thought of nailing it shut so it could never again be used to conceal secrets, but finally decided to leave it be.

Before being a depository for stolen Sillin, it had been a place where I'd stowed away my treasures and dreams.

———————

THAT NIGHT, EXHAUSTED, I ALMOST BAILED ON DINNER BUT ended up going because I felt like I should make an effort to spend time with the pack outside of training.

When I got to Tracy's, Amanda and Matt were already seated at a table along the wall which was decorated with vintage movie posters in cheap frames that were smudged with greasy handprints. The former housekeeper in me cringed at the cleanliness of this place. I didn't even want to think about the state of the kitchen. Thankfully, I was endowed with a wolf stomach; in other words, I could digest questionable meat and not hurl.

As I sat in front of Amanda, Matt all but yelled over the music playing in the background and the continuous plink of cue sticks against pool balls, "You made it!"

"I almost didn't. Everywhere hurts."

"I heard my baby's been working you out," Amanda said, pushing her wavy, brown hair behind her ear.

"Torturing me's more like it."

Matt grinned, and so did Amanda, which was a nice change from her usual hot and cold attitude toward me.

She took a sip of her beer. "Heard you were starting at UCB. Did Matt tell you I'm going there too?"

"No!" Even though Amanda and I weren't besties, it was neat to know another person at UCB. Especially if I was to have no interaction with Sarah.

A waitress with heavy bangs came up behind me and asked what I wanted to drink. I recognized her right away: Kelly.

Another one of August's hookups . . .

"I'll have the same as them," I said. Thankfully, she didn't card me.

"Coming right up." She pushed her hair out of her eyes with her pinky finger, then poured me some iced water before leaving to grab my beer.

Amanda set her elbows on the table and steepled her fingers under her chin. "What are you thinking of majoring in?"

"Business."

Her already large eyes went a little larger. "Me too! So we'll probably be in all the same classes. Sienna and Matty already told me all the professors to stay away from and all the awesome ones."

"Liam's also filled me in."

"Yeah?" She cranked one eyebrow up and flicked her gaze to Matt as though to ask him what the deal was between Liam and me.

"Sorry we're late," Lucas chirped. "Liam had trouble deciding whether to wear his black T-shirt or his black T-shirt."

I turned and craned my neck in time to catch Liam smack Lucas's chest.

"Where's blondie?" Lucas asked, scanning the crowd by the pool tables. Why he thought Sarah would be playing pool instead of sitting with us was beyond me.

"She couldn't make it."

I caught Amanda mouthing *blondie* and Matt whispering Sarah Matz's name.

"So it's just the five of us?" Lucas asked.

"Seems like it," Liam said.

Lucas eyed the bar as though he were contemplating heading over there, but Liam must've spoken into Lucas's mind, because he cringed and dropped into a free chair. Unfortunately, not the one next to me. Liam took that one. And then he draped his arm over the top of my chair.

I leaned forward so that my shoulders didn't touch his arm.

Kelly came back with my drink and beers for the boys. She apparently knew them so well she'd preempted their order.

I bet she also knew what August drank.

After we'd ordered food, Liam said, "Heard Matt made you run twelve miles this morning."

"Twelve? Felt closer to forty."

Liam chuckled.

Even though the music was getting progressively louder, making conversation was surprisingly easy. This could've been due to the number of beers we'd put away. Kelly seemed way nicer toward the end of the meal. Especially when she delivered three extra orders of fries.

I probably overindulged, because my stomach was as hard as a pool ball. I caught Liam looking at the hand I held against my abdomen, before twisting around and scowling.

I turned.

It wasn't the hedonistic meal that was causing the stomach cramps.

Sitting at the bar with Cole was August.

And taking his order was Kelly, who suddenly didn't look especially pleasant anymore.

CHAPTER 25

"Hey, Cole's here!" Amanda bellowed loudly. She waved to get his attention.

I spun my almost empty beer bottle between my index and middle fingers, contemplating ordering another drink.

If they came over to the table, I'd definitely need another.

They didn't come over, but a couple minutes later, two girls showed up: Tamara and Sienna. Lucas grabbed some chairs from a neighboring table and scooted them around ours. Where Sienna smiled at me, Tamara didn't even glance my way.

I caught Lucas sniffing the air. Even though Tracy's was riddled with smells that ranged from bacon grease and tangy barbecue sauce, to perspiration and pungent perfumes, I felt like Lucas, who was a tracker, would detect the baby growing in Tamara's womb. When his black eyebrows jotted up and his gaze narrowed on Tamara's midsection, I took it he'd figured it out. He cast a glance in Liam's direction, but our Alpha was busy laughing at something Sienna was saying. I stared at Lucas steadily until his gaze met mine. Blinking, he shot to his feet and came around the table.

"We'll be right back," Lucas said as I got up.

We walked toward the pool tables where the noise level had grown almost deafening.

"What the fuck?" Lucas snapped.

"You're going to have to give me some more to go on, because I'm not sure how to answer that question. Was it even a question?"

He growled a little. "You knew?"

"I . . . *inadvertently* found out."

He scraped his hand through his chin-length black hair. "Fuck."

"We shouldn't be making a scene, Lucas."

"Not making a scene? She's fucking pregnant!" he whisper-hissed.

"Keep your voice down. Besides, maybe it's not his baby."

"Tamara hasn't *been* with anyone else."

I didn't ask how he knew that.

Concern, anger, and disbelief contorted all of his features. I wasn't sure what warranted the anger. "He's going to be furious."

He was speaking as though it was all Tamara's fault.

"It takes two people to make a baby, Lucas."

"No shit." Then in a low voice, he grumbled, "The last thing he needs or wants right now is to be a daddy."

I folded my arms in front of the leather tank top I'd dug out of Sarah's bag. It was pretty bad-ass and also pretty tight. "He should've thought about that before forgoing using a condom."

"He would never have forgotten to suit up. And why the fuck are we discussing Liam and condoms?" Lucas's jaw twitched. "He's about to fucking duel an Alpha . . . *Trust* me, he doesn't want to discuss diaper rashes and formula."

"Well, it's not like he has a choice." I glanced over Lucas's shoulder at our table. Thankfully, everyone was chatting again, even though the banter felt stilted.

Lucas grumbled something unintelligible, then looked over his shoulder at Liam. "I'm surprised he hasn't picked up on it yet."

Of course, the instant he said that, Liam's shoulders tensed. Had he heard our discussion or the stirring of life in Tamara's womb? He rocketed up so fast his chair skidded and toppled over. After setting it back on its legs, he looked toward us, froze, but then shook himself out of his stupor. Tamara's face paled as he leaned over and whispered something in her ear. Even though I stood at a distance from them, the tremors going through her body as she rose didn't elude me.

I chewed on my pinky's nail, worried he was angry, but from

what I could see of his face, it wasn't anger . . . more like shock. He placed his hand on her elbow and steered her through the rowdy bar and then out onto the street.

Lucas started going after them, but I clapped his forearm. "Let them be."

"But—" He looked at me, then at the glass door, then back at me.

"They need to talk. Let them talk."

Matt had gotten up now, too. Instead of traipsing after Liam, he came to us. "What the hell's happening?"

Since Lucas's mouth was gaping, but not moving otherwise, I said, "Tamara's pregnant."

Matt's green eyes rounded like frisbees. "No . . ."

"Yeah," I said.

"Was that your—"

"Big secret? Yeah."

"*Whoa.*"

"Yeah."

Cole made his way to us, but August didn't. As Matt filled in his brother, I weaved myself through the thickening crowd toward the shifter who had his back to me and climbed onto the barstool Cole had vacated.

"You're still angry with me, aren't you?" I asked.

August's gaze skimmed over my face, then over the black leather encasing my upper body, before returning to one of the TVs over the bar. Instead of answering my question, he asked, "Had a nice dinner?"

His tone made me smile. "You sound like you hope it was awful." This won me a piercing side-eye. "What about you?"

"We haven't had our food yet."

"I'm sure Kelly's working extra hard to fix that, or maybe she hasn't brought it over to extend your visit."

"What's that supposed to mean?"

I crossed my legs and spun on the barstool so that I was facing the TV too. "Didn't you have a fling with her?"

I felt his gaze trace my profile, linger on my chin . . . or was it my mouth? "I'm surprised this bothers you considering . . ."

"Considering?"

"Considering how you're not interested in me."

Ouch. I could've lied at that point, told him that it didn't bother me, that he could have flings with every girl in this bar for all I cared, but truth was, I did care and absolutely didn't want to drive him into the arms of another girl. "I finished sanding the floors. I'll bring all the equipment back tomorrow."

August watched me, then watched the boys who were still discussing the new development behind us, then moved his gaze back to the television displaying a live baseball game. He didn't ask me what all the excitement was about. Had he figured it out on his own, or was he simply uninterested?

"I was thinking of oiling the wood like Dad used to," I continued. "Which brand would you recommend?"

"The one we have at the warehouse. I'll put some aside for you tomorrow. You can grab it from the office when you drop off the sanders."

"I can also go to the store and buy it."

He angled himself fully toward me now, his broad chest eclipsing everyone behind him. "You could, but then you wouldn't get the quality stuff we stock."

I sighed. "Will you at least let me pay for it?"

Instead of answering me—or maybe his pointed look was the answer—he raised his hand to get the bartender's attention. "Hey, Tommy, can I get a Coors and another Michelob?"

The bartender nodded. Seconds later, two bottles appeared in front of us on the sticky bar.

August pushed the Coors my way. "That's what you were drinking, right?"

I wasn't sure why he was asking me, since he was well aware of the answer—August was the most attentive person in the Northern hemisphere.

I wasn't sure whether I should be drinking another beer. Then again, I was walking home, not driving, and I had a werewolf metabolism, so one more couldn't hurt. "I'll only drink it if I can pay for this round."

He smiled, as though amused. "Same way you're going to pay me for the hardwood finishing?"

"You do know I wasn't fake-offering, right?"

"I know."

"Then why won't you let me? I'd be using your money to pay anyway."

His smile vanished. "Stop thinking of it as my money. It isn't. It's money that was owed to your family—"

"Stop saying it was owed. Nothing was owed. You just gave me a handout because you pity me."

His eyebrows shot up. "That wasn't pity."

"I'm not mad; I'm just stating a fact."

"Don't state incorrect facts because that makes *me* mad." He lifted his bottle to his lips and drank a long, hard gulp that made his Adam's apple judder.

"I didn't come over here to fight with you."

His freckles darkened. "We're not fighting; we're talking."

"Well, let's talk about something else, then."

The spicy scent of his skin seemed to have gotten stronger. Perhaps because he was flushed from the heat of our *talk*. "What are you doing for your birthday next week?"

"Haven't planned anything. Probably just dinner with Evelyn after her shift at The Silver Bowl." Even though he hadn't asked, I explained why we'd been there the other day. "Actually, how about we all go to dinner there?"

He cocked up an eyebrow. "All?"

"Your parents, Jeb, Frank, you? We could go late so Evelyn can get out of the kitchen." I scrunched up my nose. Had I really just suggested his family join me? Just because they'd been to most of my birthdays, didn't mean they cared to sit through yet another one. Especially after everything that had transpired between me and their son. "Unless—unless you have other plans."

"I have no other plans."

"You really don't have to come if—"

"I'm honored to have been invited. And I can already tell you Mom and Dad will be there." A smile finally fractured his tension-filled face.

"Okay," I whispered.

He turned in his seat, and his knee knocked into mine. The contact made me jump, which in turn made him lay a big palm on my thigh. I wasn't sure if he was trying to pin me in place or calm me.

It wasn't calming in the least . . .

"Sorry about that. Not much room in between these barstools."

I wondered why he was passing it off as an accident when it was blatantly not. My gaze dropped to his hand, which he hadn't removed.

"You're not supposed to touch me," I said, my voice coming out a little choked.

"We're no longer dating, so I don't really see how I'm breaking Liam's rules."

August was so close that I could hear the steady cadence of his heart through his tight Henley, which meant he could hear the frenzied tempo of mine.

"Right?" he asked in a voice so rough it sounded like he'd used the big drum sander on his throat.

I swallowed, and I swear everyone in the bar heard my saliva go down. I grabbed the beer and chugged some down to cool off and calm down just as Kelly bustled over with August's and Cole's order. August slipped his hand off my leg and thanked her.

Before jetting off toward another table, she studied me, then August.

"I should probably give Cole his seat back." I started to get off the barstool when August caught the edge of the seat to cage me in. "He can find another seat."

"August . . ."

"He's not even back yet."

Cole stood with Matt and Lucas. Were those three still discussing Tamara and Liam? Hadn't they exhausted the subject yet?

As I turned my attention back toward the plate topped with ribs and barbecue sauce, my gaze stumbled on Sienna and Amanda, also huddled together.

Long feather earrings fluttered against Sienna's bare freckled shoulders, tangling with her pale, wispy hair. She was nibbling on her lip as though nervous. Were they also discussing Tamara? She must've sensed my stare, because she looked up. For a second, she froze, but then she offered me a tentative smile. Instead of reassuring me that I wasn't the most detestable person in Tracy's, it filled me with guilt.

Technically, I hadn't stolen August away; he'd broken up with her because he was reenlisting, which had nothing to do with me. But sitting next to him, letting him buy me a drink so publicly, letting him brand me with his hand . . .

How could she *not* hate me?

I thought of Tamara then and realized I didn't hate her because I was no longer hung up on Liam. Was that why Sienna wasn't sticking pins inside a voodoo doll version of me? Because she'd moved on?

"Ness?" August's voice made my attention jounce back to him.

"Did you say something?"

"Only your name a half dozen times." He placed his elbow on the bar and rubbed the back of his neck. "I'm sorry about yesterday. I had no right to be jealous or mad. I think I haven't gotten it through my head that I have no claim on you anymore." He sighed. "Might take me a while to accept it, so bear with me, okay?"

I bit down on my lip, thinking of my conversation with Sarah. I valued Evelyn's opinion, but I also cared deeply for the man sitting beside me. I glanced around the room, wondering if anyone was looking at the two of us in disgust.

No one was looking at us, period.

No one seemed to care.

I was drinking a beer so they probably assumed I was twenty-one. Maybe if they knew the truth, they'd gawk and wrinkle their noses.

"You have nothing to apologize for, August." I filched a fry and swirled it in the little heap of ketchup next to his burger. God only knew why I ate it since my stomach was jam-packed with food, beer, and nerves.

Cole returned then, blasting us with the charred scent of tobacco. "Just gonna grab my food. Don't want to interrupt anything."

I hopped down from the stool. "I was leaving."

Cole's blue-gray eyes zipped to August. "Don't leave on my account."

"I'm not." I smiled at both of them. "Matt made me run two hours this morning, so it's a miracle I even made it out."

"I heard about your little half-marathon. Apparently I'll be joining you two on Saturday. Matty's on my case about getting in better shape." Cole was already in amazing shape, so I wasn't sure how running could better it.

Werewolves had a couple advantages over humans—one of those being our metabolisms. Once the shifting process slowed though, around forty, shifter bodies didn't burn off calories as quickly, but even then, most remained in athletic form.

"I could use a run, too," August said. "If you don't mind the added company."

"Gosh, I'd love the added company. Especially Matt. After the third mile, I pretty much turn mute, whereas he can talk the whole way through."

Cole chuckled. "Sounds like Matty. Don't you know his full name?"

I cocked an eyebrow.

"Matty-the-Motormouth-Rogers."

I smiled. "I'm sure he loves that. Anyway, see you guys on Saturday." I went back to my table to grab my stuff. "I'm gonna head home."

"So soon?" Lucas asked. "The evening's young."

"If I'm expected at the gym tomorrow morning, I need to get myself to bed." I rooted around my bag for my wallet. "Am I expected tomorrow morning?"

His expression sobered. "I'll text you."

"Okay." I plucked out two twenties and put them on the table. "If I owe anymore, just tell me in the morning."

"Sure thing, Clark."

"It was nice seeing you, Amanda. And I guess we're going to be hanging out a lot more come Monday, huh?"

She bobbed her head, which she'd nestled in the crook of Matt's arms, and shot me a disarmingly nice smile. "Yep."

"What's happening on Monday?" Sienna asked in that silken voice of hers.

"Ness is starting UCB."

"Ooh, that's fantastic! You're going to love it." She smiled, and again, I wondered *why?* "I'll try to meet up with you two at lunch if we break at the same period. Can't believe I'm graduating in nine months. It went by so fast."

As she discussed the passage of time with Amanda, my mind stuck to the nine months part.

In nine months, she'd graduate and Tamara would have a baby.

I was so lost in thought that I bumped into someone by the entrance of the bar.

CHAPTER 26

"Well if it isn't my favorite Boulder bitch."

I glared at Justin, my knee itching to make contact with his crotch. "Get out of my way, Justin."

He grinned, nice and wide, putting all of his teeth on display. He looked like he had an abnormal amount of them, or maybe they were just all bigger than normal.

"Or what? You'll call all those boyfriends of yours to the rescue?"

"Do you have the shortest memory in the history of *shifter*kind, or are you missing a brain completely?"

He smirked.

"I don't need anyone to rescue me, asshole. Now get out of my way." I tried to shoulder my way past him, but he blocked me.

I shoved my elbow into his jaw, but he anticipated my move because he bent backward and swiped at my arm. A burn erupted over my skin. The bastard had clawed me!

"Gosh, dueling you's going to be so fun," he slurred.

Out of the corner of my eye, I caught a flurry of movement. Cole seized Justin's two buddies by the neck and clapped their heads together, and then Matt was jumping another large guy.

A hand dragged me back. Not a hand.

August yanked on the tether to get me out of the way, then stepped in front of me. "You just never learn," he growled right before delivering a mean right hook to Justin's ear that had the hateful Creek swaying a little.

Unfortunately, it didn't make him stumble or fall.

"Fucking mutt." Justin's lips flapped, and spittle hit August's forehead.

I drew my bleeding arm closer.

"What did you just call me?" August asked in a deadly whisper.

Lucas shoved past August, rubbing his palms together. "Justin, my man, I've been meaning to pay you a visit for some time now."

Justin rubbed his temple. "That reminds me . . . Taryn's no longer wrapped around my cock. But she's going around the Creeks. If you get my drift." He tossed Lucas a wink that made him pounce, but the shifter fell into a crouch, managing to get out of the way. When he lurched up, he headbutted Lucas in the chin.

I gasped at the sound of cracking. Lucas seemed stunned for a second, but then he narrowed his eyes and barreled into Justin so hard he backed him into the door of Tracy's and right out into the street. I stood frozen for a second, but then I moved, heading out onto the street after them.

August hooked his finger into one of my beltloops and held me back. "Lucas can handle him, sweetheart."

"But—"

"But nothing. You stay away from that asshole." He pulled me to the side, along the windowed façade and then farther down the sidewalk, but then he stopped walking and cinched my wrist, slowly tugging it away from my leather top. As he took in my wounds, his eyes flashed with bloodlust. "He did this?"

As he started to turn, I grabbed a handful of his T-shirt. "Don't bother."

He listened to me—even though it seemed to take everything in him to do so.

A car alarm made us both look back at the scene unfolding outside Tracy's. Lucas had tossed Justin onto the hood of a car, cracking the windshield. A police siren layered itself over the sound of the wrecked car. Matt and Cole gripped Lucas's shoulders and peeled him off Justin, and then they shoved Lucas down the street in the opposite direction from where I stood with August.

"We have to go. The cops in Boulder are all dirty," August hissed.

I remembered someone telling me they worked for Aidan Michaels. Did they know what he was? Would they still be loyal to him if they knew?

August gripped my fingers hard, as though afraid they'd slip out of his hold, and towed me down the road just as police strobe lights painted the pavement and the gathered crowd blue. Even though my arm hurt and my legs felt like a solid bruise, I lengthened my strides to match August's. In minutes, we'd reached my apartment.

I dug through my bag for my key, but my fingers shook from a mixture of adrenaline and fear. My bag toppled, and everything inside spilled onto the sidewalk.

August crouched to retrieve my things. When he noticed how hard I trembled, he stood and cupped my jaw. "Sweetheart, it's okay. You're okay. Everything's okay."

That miserable phrase again. All those words ever did was herald chaos into my life.

Sensing I wasn't reassured, he wrapped one hand around the base of my neck and pulled me to him. I let out a dismal whimper, because nothing was okay.

"I couldn't even . . . I didn't even manage—" My voice caught on a sob. "How am I supposed to . . . block Justin in fur when I can't even . . . do that in skin?"

"Seconds don't usually fight."

"He said . . . he said"—I pulled in a shuddering breath—"that dueling me . . . would be fun." I'd always suspected Justin was planning on doing more than standing guard over his new Alpha, but the realization that my suspicions might become true felt like salt in my veins.

August pressed me away and tipped my head up. "You think I'd let that happen?"

"You won't be in the ring," I murmured.

My navel pulsed and heated. And then my body slammed into August's, and it felt like hugging a rock, except this rock hugged back.

He dropped his mouth to my earlobe. "Of course, I'll be there," he whispered.

My navel thrummed again. He was talking about using the tether to cheat.

"They must know what we are, August, which means they'll keep you away from the fight."

His gaze crowded with shadows. I gathered he hadn't considered that.

"How about we discuss this off the street?" he asked.

Because my boots had become one with the sidewalk, he steered me up the stairs, and then he unlocked the door and pushed it open. After shutting it behind us, I dropped down in one of the dining room chairs while he went into the kitchen. He grabbed a dish cloth and wet it, then returned to tend to my arm. I tried not to wince, but failed.

August's jaw slackened and tensed, as though he were working out a kink in his cheek. "Why are you still bleeding?"

I stared at the grooves Justin had etched into my skin. "Probably because I'm taking Sillin."

August's green gaze jerked to my face. "Why are you taking Sillin?"

I pulled my bottom lip between my teeth before releasing it and sighing. "Because we're experimenting with it."

"Experimenting?"

"I volunteered to take Sillin to test its long-term effects."

"You what?" he choked out.

I was pretty certain he'd heard me.

His eyes gleamed with anger. "And Liam okayed this?"

I got those two had baggage, but that didn't give August a right to blame Liam for this. "I didn't give him a choice."

"He should've picked someone else to experiment on. You can't be taking Sillin and doing all that training!" He clapped the table, which made me jump. "You shouldn't even be doing all that training in the first place. You shouldn't have signed up for another duel!"

"Why don't you tell me how you really feel?" I muttered.

His nostrils pulsed. "I hate this. *All of this.*" He carved the air with his hand. "Ness, I lost you once before"—his voice shook with anger, but also with something else—"and I don't want to lose you again."

I leaned over and placed my hands over his. "That's why I'm

experimenting with the Sillin. We suspect Morgan's taking it, and *she* fought a duel."

"She's an Alpha, Ness. The way things affect her body isn't comparable to the way things affect yours."

I slid my hand off his and curled my fingers into my lap.

He leaned back in his chair, making the rungs creak, then looked toward my uncle's closed bedroom door. There was no other heartbeat in the apartment—Jeb wasn't home.

August crossed his arms. "Besides, she wouldn't have been able to shift if she were taking Sillin."

"I'm trying to see if a habituation to the drug modifies the body's response to it."

"Habituation? How long are you planning on taking it?"

I studied the bloodied tracks on my forearm. Unspoken words saturated the air between us. He wasn't pleased, but was it with me or with our theory? Or was it with something else altogether?

"Maybe the happy news will knock some sense into Liam and make him cancel the duel," he grumbled.

So he'd heard about Tamara.

I peeked up at him through my lashes. "You think Morgan would accept canceling the duel?"

August sighed. "She didn't seem overly keen on dueling the day Liam challenged her. And she *did* offer Liam a peace treaty. Maybe it's still on the table."

"That was to save her son. Alex is free now."

"He could become *un*free."

"You're not actually entertaining thoughts of kidnapping him?"

"If it saves your life, I'm entertaining many thoughts. Killing Justin's another. In case you were wondering."

I leaned forward and touched his arm. His tendons twitched under my fingertips. "It'll turn this town into a bloodbath."

"So it's okay if your blood's spilled, but no one else's?"

I'd signed up for this, so yes, I supposed it was. I refrained from pointing this out to August.

It dawned on me that instead of resolving this with violence, we could resolve it with words. Morgan was a smart woman. Surely wise, too. She'd understand that things had changed for our pack.

Besides, she'd told me to pay her a visit. I decided it was time I took her up on it.

The front door opened then, and Jeb walked in. He blinked as he took us in, bloodied towel and all.

"What the hell happened?" he asked.

While I was trying to decide what to tell my uncle, so as not to worry him, August said, "Bar brawl with some Creeks."

So much for not worrying Jeb. His light-blue eyes went as wide as doorknobs. "Creeks?"

I got up. "August will fill you in. I'm going to bed."

As I stepped past August, he caught my hand, then flipped my arm around and inspected the wound. "Still not healed."

"It'll heal during the night." I added a smile to reassure him, but it seemed to miss its mark, so I leaned over and placed a kiss on his forehead. "Don't frown so much. You'll get premature wrinkles."

His forehead didn't smooth out as I freed my hand from his grip and walked to my room. If anything, the grooves seemed to deepen. After washing my arm with soap and wrapping gauze around it, I pulled on my sleep shorts and a long sleeved tee to keep my bandage in place, then slid under the covers.

August and Jeb were still talking in the living room. I tried to stretch my hearing to grasp what they were saying, but however hard I tried, their words sounded like gibberish. Was the Sillin to blame for this too?

I pressed my hand against my abdomen. Would the tether also fade if I kept ingesting the drug?

My heart held still, then skittered, making my skin prickle from the release of rapid beats. I didn't want it to fade.

I pressed the pillow against my face and let out a muffled cry of frustration, because I was so damn confused about everything.

If only *one* thing made sense . . . If only *one* thing could go right . . .

Mom would tell me to count my blessings, so I did. Evelyn was alive and happy. August was sticking around Boulder. My house was almost in livable condition. I was starting college on Monday. I was turning eighteen on Friday. Isobel had beat cancer.

I counted my blessings until sleep zippered over me.

CHAPTER 27

Even though I'd dressed for the gym, Lucas texted me that there would be no working out this morning, which suited me perfectly. My arm had stopped bleeding but was in no shape to swing or block a punch. After a cup of bitter black coffee, I knuckled my uncle's door and asked if I could borrow the van.

"Sure." The word was garbled. He popped open his door, a toothbrush dangling from his mouth. "I'll get Eric to pick me up. He was planning on helping me out at the house this morning anyway."

"Thanks."

"How's the arm?"

"Still attached to my elbow, so there's that."

He took his toothbrush out, and pasty-foam dribbled out. "Is it still bleeding?"

"No." I pushed off the wall I'd been leaning on and displayed my knitted skin. "All healed. Anyway, I'll see you at the house later. I was going to oil the floors today."

"Eric and I can do that."

"You're already doing so much."

He let out a little snort. "Honey, I'm loving this project."

I smiled. "I'm glad."

As I headed for the front door, he asked, "Where *are* you going?"

"To campus. To pick up books I need for Monday."

He nodded. "I keep forgetting you're starting college. For some reason, I feel like you're so much older."

I felt way older too.

"Hey, it's your birthday next week!"

I jumped from the intensity of his voice.

"Eighteen." He wiped his mouth with the back of his hand. "That's . . . that's it. You won't need me anymore." Sadness mangled my uncle's tone.

"Aw, Jeb. Just because I'll no longer be a minor doesn't mean I won't need you."

His lips bent but then fell, and then his eyes became all glossy.

I strode back over and hugged him. "I'm not going anywhere. At least nowhere without you, okay?"

He didn't speak but squeezed me hard. When he released me, I repeated that I wasn't leaving, because he wore a look I recognized; it was the look of people who'd been repeatedly abandoned . . . who didn't believe people stuck around.

"Love you," he said right before I exited the house. I was pretty certain it was the first time he'd said those words to me.

"Love you too." I was pretty certain it was the first time I'd said them back.

As I drove down the roads I knew only-too-well, I itched to phone Sarah and find out how her evening had gone, but what if she was hanging out with the Creeks and they saw my name appear on her phone?

Maybe she'd be at the inn.

When I started up the sinuous drive, my heart grew weighty with dread and something else . . . anticipation? Call me crazy, but I was looking forward to speaking with Sandra. *Cas*sandra. I wondered why I hadn't gone sooner.

I parked in the far corner of the employee lot; then, fully alert, I walked up to the revolving doors. The land had once belonged to my family, but not anymore. Now I was in enemy territory. When I pushed through the glass doors, I expected shifters to pounce on me, but no one pounced. No one was even here. I had to remind myself that this was no longer a public inn.

Nothing had changed. Except the smell.

The air still carried the odor of wood smoke, but it was barely distinguishable under the aroma of damp fur and warm musk. It was as though the Creeks spent more time in fur than in skin. Perhaps they did. I realized I knew more about the Rivers than I did about the wolves in my own town.

Heartbeats pounded behind the wooden walls. I heard them above me, below me, in front of me.

"Hello?" I called out, not wanting to spook anyone.

The shuffle of rubber soles had me jerking my face toward the back office. Emmy, one of the women who worked at the inn before it was annexed, froze on the threshold.

"You're still here?"

I'd imagined she'd handed in her letter of resignation after the night the Creeks arrived.

She crossed her arms nice and tight. "Are you expected?" Her tone was so sharp that both my eyebrows jolted up.

"You're mad at me?"

"I'm mad at a lot of people and things right now." We stared at each other in silence for a long beat. Then, "Are you one, too?"

The desire to shake my head almost won over my desire to confess the truth. "Yes."

She shuddered, and the row of tiny silver hoops adorning the shell of one of her ears glittered.

I moved toward her, and her body seized. She even took a step back. She was afraid of *me*?

"Why are you still working here?"

"Because I signed a contract." Her gaze snapped to the entrance of the living room.

We were still alone.

"Emmy, you're not trapped, are you?"

Her eyes gleamed with unshed tears.

"Are you?" I repeated a little more insistently.

"Michaels offered me twice what your uncle and aunt were paying, so I signed on the dotted line. Skylar, she said the new management gave her the creeps, so she didn't renew her contract. After I found out—" Her voice cracked and then tapered off. "After I found out what you all were, I told Mr. Michaels I didn't feel comfortable working here anymore. I told him I wouldn't talk, but he said it was too late. He said I should've read the fine print better." She sniffed. "You know what the fine print says? It says that if I leave my place of employment or speak about my new employ-ers' nature, I would be taken into the woods. And *not* for a nature hike."

Without even realizing it, I'd moved closer to the bell desk, closer to her. "They threatened your life?"

She nodded. "Along with the lives of everyone I hold dear." She snorted. "Serves me right for not listening to my wife."

"Have they hurt you?"

"No. As long as I make up their rooms and clean their clothes and pick up their dirty dishes, no one bothers me."

I rounded the bell desk.

She uncrossed her arms and shot out her palm. "Don't come any closer."

"Emmy! I'm not like them. You don't have to be scared of me."

"You just said you were one of them."

"Just because I can shift doesn't mean I'm like them."

"That's exactly what it means."

I sensed there was no reasoning with her. "How many humans work here?"

"Four. But the other three are thrilled. I don't think they've gone home once since the *pack* arrived. You should hear them talk. They're all so freaking dazzled. Even your aunt. I swear. It's disgusting how attentive she is to her new employer."

"Emmy!" The snap of a familiar nasal voice had me whirling around. "If you're done gossiping, Linda could use some help setting out breakfast."

Emmy scurried past my aunt without a backward glance at me.

Lucy had slimmed down considerably, or perhaps it was an illu-sion cast by her choice of attire—a simple black sheath belted at the waist. As I kept staring at her, I realized it wasn't an illusion. Her milky-pale cheeks had lost their roundness, and her freckled arms seemed too narrow for her column of bangles. Even her eyes had gone through a transformation. They carried haunted shadows, as though grief had absorbed into the fragile skin of her lids and swelled her orbits.

"What are you doing here, Ness?" she asked.

"I came to see Mrs. Morgan."

"Mrs. Morgan doesn't care for visitors. *Especially* Boulders."

She spoke the word as though we were something glued to the bottom of her shoe. Granted, she wasn't a werewolf, but being the wife of a wolf and the mother of another had made her just as much of a Boulder as I was.

"She told me to stop by."

"I very much doubt that." I started advancing, but she blocked the entrance of the living room. "You are no longer welcomed here. *Leave.*"

I reined in my annoyance by tightening my hold on my bag's crossbody strap. "Lucy, I *have* to talk to her."

"I'll let her know you stopped by. Now, go."

"Lucy?" came another voice that always made my hackles rise.

Her hazel eyes widened, and she mouthed, "Go," again, but I didn't heed her command.

Surely Aidan would allow me to meet with his cousin. He appeared behind my aunt and then slowly brushed past her. "Miss Clark, to what do we owe the pleasure of your visit?"

"I came to see Sandra."

"Huh." His lips twitched, and then his fingers rose to his earlobe, and he rubbed it—one of his weird little ticks. He did it when he was nervous, but he also did it when he was intrigued. His stealthy smile told me it was the latter. "Right this way."

My aunt—former aunt—went as rigid as marble. "Aidan, I—I don't think it's a good idea. We don't know what her intentions are."

"My intentions?" I said. "You think I came to burn down the inn?"

Her nostrils flared.

"My rose"—Aidan ran a knuckle along the pillar that was Lucy's neck—"do not fear for our safety. You know we could snap her like a twig before she'd even have time to strike a match."

I let out a low hiss.

Leering at me, Aidan started toward the living room but stopped and patted his thigh. "Come along now."

"I'm not a dog," I snapped.

"Oh, I know. I'm fond of dogs; I'm not particularly fond of you."

The feeling was mutual.

Lucy didn't even blink as I passed by her, didn't even twitch, but I caught the spike of her pulse and the aroma of something cold and tinny wafting over her heavy rose-and-tobacco scent: fear. Was Lucy truly scared I'd set the inn on fire? My aunt had never been a very caring person—at least not toward me—but believing me capable of arson was a whole new level.

The leather couches in the living room had been arranged in a semi-circle around the massive stone fireplace blackened by a recent fire, and the Native-American patterned rugs had been dragged in the middle. They overlapped and were strewn with throw pillows as though the yellow-stuccoed living room had become a hippy campsite.

"You like our new décor?" Aidan asked.

I eyed him.

"I think it's much more convivial."

"Do the rest of your hotels look like this?"

"No. But this isn't a hotel. It's a family home."

From what I could see through the glass wall of windows separating the living room from the deck was that the Adirondacks and charming teak tables had been removed and replaced by plain picnic tables, the sort with attached benches. Dozens of them from the looks of it. They were lined up in two neat rows and topped with pitchers of drinks, thermoses of tea and coffee, and platters of breakfast offerings.

A handful of Creeks were already seated, digging into the food. As I stepped out, the loud chewing noises subsided and hunched backs straightened. And then heads perked up.

Only two were familiar—the Alpha's and her daughter's.

"Sandy, look who stopped by to see you," Aidan said.

CHAPTER 28

Cassandra's narrow jaw moved as she chewed on whatever was in her mouth. After swallowing, she wiped her lips with a napkin. "I was expectin' you sooner."

My heart began to stampede inside my chest. Was walking into this den of wolves alone a poor idea? Would I leave here alive and in one piece?

I lifted my chin a notch to show I wasn't scared, hoping they wouldn't associate the pounding behind my ribs with fear. What else would they associate it with, though?

"Can we speak in private, Sandra?"

She smiled at me. "You may call me Sandy. All my wolves do."

"I'm not your wolf."

Her smile strengthened, and although she didn't utter the word, *yet*, I could see its shape take form on her bluish lips. She rose and stepped over the bench. A shapeless tunic that seemed made of tarp dropped to just below her knees. "Would you like to take a stroll or sit in the living room?"

As she stepped closer, I cranked my face up. I didn't like how small she made me feel, even though being a full head taller than me wasn't her fault. She wasn't even wearing shoes. Her toenails, like her fingernails, were lacquered in dark polish, and her toes were stained with dried mud and crushed grass.

"I'm not a fan of shoes. I'm not much of a fan of clothes either, but I was told walkin' around these populated parts naked was frowned upon."

"Where you live in Beaver Creek is that remote?"

"Even more so than the Rivers' compound. Was your trip to their domain enjoyable?"

Sarah had shared the info I surmised. I found myself gaping up at the small balconies in front of each room, wondering if my friend was standing on one of them.

When Cassandra raised her head to study the log façade, I shot my gaze away. I couldn't have her wondering what or who I was looking for.

"A walk sounds good, but not in the woods. Right here in the clearing."

The Creek Alpha turned the full force of her blue gaze to me. "I got no plans on murderin' you, Candy."

"My name's not Candy."

"Sorry. Must've slipped my mind."

I doubted it had. As we walked side by side toward the stairs built into the porch, I heard footsteps behind us and glanced over my shoulder. "Tell your cousin not to follow us."

"Aidan. You heard the girl. Leave us be."

After a beat, I asked, "Where's the rest of your pack?"

"Some are runnin'. Some are sleepin'."

"They're all still here?"

"Not all of them, but most stayed. They like how fresh the air is here." She tipped her face toward the sun and inhaled slow breaths. "What's the nature of your visit, Ness?"

"I wanted to know if your offer to sign a peace treaty is still on the table."

She closed her eyes and pulled in another breath. "Is Liam gettin' cold feet?"

"Liam doesn't even know I'm here."

Her eyes opened and set on me again.

"But my uncle knows I'm here," I lied so she didn't do away with me. "So . . . is your offer still available?"

Her light-brown hair, which was cut within two inches of her scalp, appeared grayer in the sunlight. "Why didn't you become Alpha? Everest all but handed it to you."

"Handed it to me? How did he *all-but-hand* it to me?"

"Liam cares for you. He wouldn't have fought you."

"If we hadn't dueled, Lucas would've been Alpha, not me."

"What I meant was if you'd actually fought, Liam would've let you win."

I blinked as I understood what she was insinuating. "Winning would've meant killing him."

"Your pack's soft, Ness. They surely wouldn't have required death."

I didn't think the Boulders were soft. Unless by soft, she meant civilized, which hadn't been my first impression, but now that I'd met the Creeks . . .

"You don't know that," I ended up saying.

She clasped her hands behind her back. "Did it even cross your mind to fight for what you wanted?"

"I didn't want to become Alpha."

"Then why did you enter the trials?"

"Because I didn't want a Kolane to become Alpha."

"And yet a Kolane became Alpha."

"Look, I'm not here to discuss the past. I'm here to discuss the future. Is your offer still available?" I asked for the third time.

"We agreed to duel."

"Agreements change all the time."

"You're obviously not well-versed in pack politics."

Her condescension stung.

"When duels are agreed upon, they can no longer be annulled."

"Why not? No one's forcing you to fight another shifter to the death."

"I offered him peace, and he didn't want it, so—"

"That's why I'm here."

"Listen," she hissed, which made my wolf bristle. Not that she could get out from her Sillin-cage. "Alex is always cuttin' me off before I can finish explaining things."

"Don't compare me to your son."

"When an Alpha expresses a desire to kill another, it's never taken lightly. If Liam had accepted my treaty, I would've spent my life lookin' over my shoulder, which would not have been ideal, but would've been worth it, because it would've meant saving my son's hide and my own."

Niggling guilt filled me . . . We should've kept Alex locked away.

"It wouldn't have been the first threat I'd have had to learn to live with, but that's neither here nor there. Anyway, Liam wasn't content with my offer. Your Alpha thirsts for more, which is a dangerous trait in a leader."

"You thirsted for more. You took over the Aspens."

"You think the Aspens were innocent? They killed off most of my pack."

"No, they didn't. You're the one who walked into their camp and challenged their Alpha."

"Your truncated comprehension of my pack's history is alarming. I can't tell if you've been fed wrong information or if you're lacking information."

I bristled again. "Why don't you tell me your version?"

"My version?" Her tone turned a notch shriller. "You mean, the truth?"

Although we hadn't penetrated the forest, we were following the tree line fencing the great lawn from the wilderness beyond.

"Yes." There was no point debating whether her truth was the same as everyone else's.

"Something in the mountains made us sick, and when we came to the Aspens for Sillin, which is one of the only drugs that work on wolves—"

"I thought it only helped us if our blood came in contact with silver?"

Her eyes thinned a little. "It has lots more properties than voiding our magic."

"I didn't know."

"You don't seem to know much about werewolves."

I bristled. "That was uncalled for."

She didn't apologize. "Do you want to hear the rest of it?"

What I wanted was for her to stop disparaging me. Fearing how childish it would sound to voice this, I grumbled, "Go on."

Cassandra observed me a protracted instant before pursuing her tale. "When we went to the Aspens for help, they turned us away. They had stocks of Sillin yet wouldn't share a meager amount. We'd even offered to pay an exorbitant amount for the drug. A month went by, and so many of us died that my grandfather, who was Alpha at the time, attempted a new negotiation with the Aspen Alpha. Again, they told us we should've taken better care of our supplies and offered us nothing. My little sister and I, we snuck onto their property and into their stock. We took only what we needed. She was caught and executed instantly. I got away, and then we ran and hid. Only five of us survived. Well, six . . . Aidan never lived among us, so he wasn't subjected to the poisoning.

"Four years ago, when I took over the Aspen pack, Julian Matz visited the compound to meet with me. At least, he claimed that was the nature of his visit. My father, who was so sickly he could no longer shift, was found dead the following morning. The pack doctor said he'd stopped breathing. I believed he'd been asphyxiated, but for the sake of diplomacy, I let it go. I let *Julian* go . . ."

A chill skated over my skin, which had nothing to do with the tall shadows that stretched like fingers over Cassandra and me. "What poisoned you?"

She watched the loamy earth squish between her bare toes. "There was a toxic waste site on our land. It polluted our main water source." Her gaze scraped over my face with such intensity that her eyes felt like claws. "Do you understand now why Sillin is so near and dear to me? I liken it to my security blanket; I may never need it again, but I can no longer live without it. I learned the hard way what lack of foresight brings about, and I will not let this happen to my wolves."

I wasn't going about getting what I wanted from Sandra the right way. "Thank you for sharing your pack's history with me."

She dipped her chin into her swan-like neck and scrutinized me from underneath her stubby lashes.

"I've always felt you were smart, but now I see you're a sensible woman." The words burned on their way out. "So I have to wonder why you won't offer us the deal again. I swear I'd make Liam keep away from you."

Her lips twitched, and then a bark of laughter burst out. "You'd *make* him? Oh, honey," she tittered, "Liam may appreciate your looks, but he doesn't *respect* you. Men like him—so conceited and chauvinistic—they don't take advice from a gender they deem inferior."

"You have a skewed vision of Liam. He's nothing like his father. Besides, he listened to me when I told him not to duel you the day you killed Julian."

Her smile turned broader. "He listened to get you into his bed."

Heat splashed my face. Why did I have to go and blush now? "That's not true."

"Ness, let me tell you a little something about myself that very few people know. My sister, she was mute, so I learned to read lips at the same time I learned to talk." Her shoulders were pulled back as straight as a rake. "That day beside the pool, I saw what Liam asked you . . . to break up with your new boyfriend. August, correct?"

The shock of her revelation made my footing falter. Cassandra shot out her arm to steady me, and it felt like a wooden bat against my sternum.

"I also know y'all think I cheated to win and you're desperately tryin' to figure out what I did. One of the reasons for your trip to meet with the Rivers, if I'm not mistaken?"

I kept silent.

"Let me save you some time and headaches. I did not inject Julian Matz with any substance." She glanced at the deck where more Creeks had arrived. Although most were busy eating, many gawked at us. She returned her attention to me and canted her head to the side. "So, have you picked a date yet?"

"You didn't even want to fight before. Why so adamant about it now?"

"'Cause I want to go home, *and* you have nothin' I need or want anymore."

"We have Sillin. A lot of it." I had no clue if the amount we had constituted a lot.

"I have enough to tide me over for a couple years. Besides, if I beat Liam, I get your pack's stock, and the Pines', for that matter."

Icy fingers climbed up my spine. *She knows it's hidden . . .*

"So it's a win-win for me."

"If you lose, you get nothing."

"If I lose, my pack still gets the Sillin."

"You mean to tell me, you're doing this for your pack?"

"Everything I do is for my pack." Her gaze tightened on me. "I didn't ascend to the highest tier for a title; I did it to better the lives of shifters." She gestured to the terrace. "Please, be my guest, Ness. Go around and ask my people what they think of me."

I was most definitely not going to ask a bunch of shifters what they thought of their Alpha in front of said Alpha. No one would *ever* tell me the truth. I thought of the Rivers' contact then—Avery —about how he'd said many were rooting for Liam, which meant Cassandra was either delusional or lying.

"No one visits us for a week, and now two Boulders in a day."

Her voice made me follow her line of sight. Lucas was glaring at me while descending the stairs two at a time.

Shit. Shit. Shit.

"That one's particularly insufferable, isn't he?"

I didn't answer her, just started striding toward Lucas before he could cause a bigger scene than I had.

CHAPTER 29

"What the fuck are you doing here, Clark?" he spat out as I joined him in the middle of the lawn.

Cassandra was still standing in the shadows of the evergreens, and the rest of her pack had remained on the terrace.

I pursed my lips. "How did you even know where I was?"

"Liam wanted to speak with you, so we drove over to your house. Jeb said you were at the campus bookstore, but the campus bookstore doesn't open at the ass crack of dawn, so I'm not sure how he fell for that. He probably assumed you went to see your boyfriend."

"August isn't my boyfriend," I said, making sure my mouth was visible to Morgan. I wanted her to know this. Even though she hadn't threatened August, it couldn't hurt to get him off her radar. "And I'm here because I was trying to get her to put the peace treaty back on the table."

"You think Liam's changed his mind because of the—" I stepped on his foot so hard that he grumble-shouted, "What the hell's wrong with you?"

"I'm his Second. I should get to make these calls without being undermined by someone who has no rank in the pack."

His jaw unhinged.

"Now let's get out of here. We're making a scene. I bet Liam would hate that even more than his Second coming to negotiate on his behalf. And even though you didn't ask, the duel's still on."

I started walking around the inn. There was no need to go through the deck where more wolves had come out to eat breakfast.

Lucas fell in step beside me. "Wasn't sure if we'd get you back in one—" A soundless snarl contorted his lips.

I followed the direction of his stare. Sitting at one of the picnic tables was Sarah, and next to her was another blond: Alex Morgan.

"When did that fucking happen?" Lucas said through gritted teeth.

"Sarah eating breakfast with her pack?" I knew that wasn't what had gotten his boxers in a twist.

"He's playing with her fucking hair," he hissed.

Alex caught us looking his way and smiled wide, and inside, I cringed, but outside, I glared. Sarah said something that made the Creek in front of her chuckle, and that deepened Lucas's scowl.

I touched his arm that felt like steel rigging. "She's a Creek now. It's only normal that she tries to fit in."

"Fit in?" He sounded like he was choking.

I pulled him around the building, straight into the employee parking lot where I'd left the van.

"How come you're so chill about this, Clark? Isn't she your bestie?"

"She's nineteen. She knows what she's doing."

Lucas's lips curled in disgust.

I scanned the parking lot for Liam's car. When I didn't see it, I asked, "You have a ride or do you need one?"

Barely opening his lips, he said, "Liam dropped me off but was worried what he'd do if he stuck around."

To me or to Cassandra?

I beeped the doors open. "Well, get in then."

During the drive into town, he didn't say a word. Just simmered quietly. I almost confessed that Sarah was putting on an act, that she hadn't turned on us . . . on *him* . . . like Taryn had. But I clamped down on the truth. Lucas was trustworthy, sure, but the more incensed my pack seemed with Sarah, the more believable she'd be to the Creeks.

At a traffic light, I asked, "Where am I dropping you off?"

"The gym. But you're coming in with me."

"I thought we weren't working out."

"We aren't."

I raised an eyebrow.

When we arrived, Lucas texted Liam. A moment later, the heavy doors were unbolted. The vast space was as dark as a cave, and it took my eyes a moment to adjust.

Liam's face sheened with sweat, and his knuckles bled from pummeling the punching bag that still swayed in the back of the room. "Do you have a death wish, Ness?"

I squared my shoulders. "No more than you do."

"Do you know what they could've done to you?" Even though his voice was still loud, it had lost some of its venom.

The realization that he'd been afraid for me softened my stance. "I wanted to see if she'd agree to cancel the duel."

"Cancel the duel?" Liam sputtered. "What makes you think I'd want to cancel the duel?"

Had the thought *not* crossed his mind? "I thought that after—"

"Yesterday changes nothing!"

"You're going to be a father, Liam. Don't you want to be there for your kid?"

His eyebrows hugged closer to his eyes. "You know what the odds of shifter babies making it to the end of the first trimester in a human womb? Fifteen percent. But even if it were a hundred percent, it wouldn't change anything. I still want to destroy that woman, so you had no right to make this call without consulting me! I'm not interested in a treaty."

I crossed my arms. "She said no anyway."

His chest heaved. "Good."

"You could lose."

"I could also win."

A beat of silence echoed like an ominous drumroll between us. I was angry about his reaction. I glanced at Lucas, wishing he'd weigh in and tell Liam he was being a stubborn ass, but Lucas was too busy sulking and glaring at the weight rack.

"There are more important things in life than winning or losing, Liam."

"Not for an Alpha. Besides, I already have a family, Ness. The pack is my family. And I need to protect them." His voice had quieted. "You all think I'm doing this to prove something. I'm not. Sure, I could've taken that treaty, but once Cassandra gets replaced or dies, her successor would've challenged us. We'd only be pushing back the inevitable. I'm young now and in way better shape than she is; Julian was old and slow." His breathing deepened, his chest growing calmer with each passing minute.

Even though I was disappointed, a part of me also understood his reasoning.

"Did you learn anything interesting at least?"

Sighing, I let my arms fall back along my sides. "She can read lips."

"She can read lips?" Lucas asked, finally popping out of his daze.

"Yeah. Her sister was mute. So start watching what you say around her."

Liam dragged his fingers through his sweat-matted hair. "We don't need to watch what we say around her, because the next time we see her will be at the duel. Am I making myself clear?"

"Crystal," I said a tad frostily because I sensed that was directed only at me. "I also learned she took an extremely high dose of Sillin when she was younger to cure herself of toxic waste poisoning. Which might mean traces of Sillin remain in her body." I tucked a strand of hair behind my ear. "So maybe taking tiny doses of the stuff is pointless. Maybe I should take a huge dose and see what it does."

Liam went as still as the punching bag behind him.

"Morgan can still shift, so it wouldn't impair Ness's magic completely," Lucas said.

For a moment, I wondered if we'd be dueling Morgan if Liam and I had still been together. But then I wondered why I was even contemplating this and shook my head.

"I'll speak to Greg to see what a high dose would be," he finally said.

As he took out his cell phone, a twinge of panic crept up my spine . . . What if it irreparably impaired my werewolf gene? What if that was the reason she was often bedridden and healed slower? I swallowed back my panic, reminding myself that Morgan had still risen to the top of shifter hierarchy.

Liam disconnected the call I'd heard no word of. "He's going to figure out the dosage based on your weight and age, then phone you this afternoon to administer it intravenously." He flipped his phone over and over in his hand, shadows devouring his eyes. "Even though I want you to consult me in the future, it was good work."

"Thank you." I nibbled on my bottom lip. "Can I leave now?"

"You can leave."

I started to go, but before reaching the door, I glanced at him over my shoulder. "Are you happy at least? About Tamara?"

Although his lips didn't move, inside my head I heard, *I didn't want a kid, and I didn't want Tamara.*

Pain carved his forehead. I hoped it was the shock of the news and the worry of the first trimester that was to blame. Perhaps he'd never love Tamara, but I hoped he'd grow to want and love his child.

I hoped he'd be the man his father never was.

CHAPTER 30

I spent the rest of the morning buying college supplies and paint cans and brushes for the house. The only thing I ended up not buying was a laptop. I needed one, and technically, I could afford one, but the money on my account didn't feel like my own. Since August wasn't going to take it back, I'd decided to go speak with Nelson and Isobel about it. I was sort of dreading the conversation, especially if they didn't know about their son's generous donation.

After stopping by The Silver Bowl to check up on Evelyn, whose cheeks were high in color from the heat of all the simmering pots around her and the excitement of her new job, I went home fed and relaxed, ready for Greg to arrive.

He got to my place around four, a cooler swinging from his fingers. "Sorry I'm late. I went to check on Isobel."

My blood turned to ice. "Why? Is she—Is the cancer back?"

"The cancer's gone." Greg smiled. "Sorry. I didn't mean to worry you."

I nodded and watched as he set a syringe, a vial filled with clear liquid, and some gauze on the kitchen table.

Concern deepened the wrinkles bracketing his eyes and mouth. "Are you sure you want to do this?"

"Someone has to."

"But does that someone have to be you?"

I frowned. "There's no chance of it killing me, is there?"

He took a seat and scooted closer to the table. "No, but . . ."

Fear tiptoed into my veins and navel as I sat down beside him. "But what?"

"But I've never administered such a high dose, so I can't even tell you what the side effects might be. Besides not shifting, that is."

"How long will it block my wolf?"

"From my calculations, if all goes well, you should be back in fur before the next full moon."

Considering we had to fight Cassandra then, that was good.

I licked my chapped lips. "And if all *doesn't* go well?"

"The Sillin could stay in your system longer."

"Like another month?" I couldn't be Liam's Second if that happened . . . Someone else would have to be. Could another Boulder take my place? Were we allowed to switch Seconds? Perhaps Lucas—

"It could affect your magic forever," Greg said in such a low voice I almost missed his words.

"You mean, turn me into a *halfwolf?*"

He nodded.

"I thought that could only happen after prolonged use?"

Greg twirled the vial, squinting at the liquid sloshing inside as though seeking an answer within its clear depths. "I don't know. I've never administered so much Sillin." He fisted the vial before placing it carefully back on the table. "Your parents would be so angry with me right now."

I was certain they'd be mad at a whole bunch of people if they'd been alive, the first one being me, but they weren't here. Besides, if it meant saving Liam's life, I'd endure being a *halfwolf* for a while.

"I'm surprised Jeb's letting you do this," Greg added.

"Jeb doesn't know, and I'd like it to stay that way. He's got plenty enough to worry about."

Greg studied me for a beat. "Any way I can talk you out of this?"

I shook my head. "We need to understand."

"But why you? Why don't I call the River medic and see if his pack can test it out—"

"They might be our allies, Greg, but I don't trust the Rivers.

Besides, if this experiment could potentially harm one of their wolves, why would they agree?"

"Because they hate Morgan."

I worried the inside of my cheek. "They'll ask for something in return." Ingrid wanting to marry August came to mind. "Favors never come for free."

"You're right. Favors are never free." He sighed. "What about another Boulder?"

"I'd never forgive myself if this had a lasting effect on someone from my pack." I tapped my fingernail against the tabletop. "So just lay it all out there. How else do you think this injection can affect me?"

"It'll dim your senses. And, possibly, it'll affect your mating link."

I suddenly felt a lot warmer. I gathered my hair and rolled the strands up into a bun. "You know everything that goes on in the pack, huh?"

"Pretty much."

"How come you work with us?"

"Why wouldn't I work with you?"

"Because we're not . . . *human*."

He leaned back in the chair. "My father was the pack physician before me, and my grandfather before him. So I grew up right alongside the Boulders. They never treated me differently because of what I wasn't."

"Lucky you."

"I'm sorry they were hard on you, Ness."

"Not your fault."

Greg's gaze roamed over my face. "Do you know that Maggie was one of my favorite people?"

"My mother? Really?"

"We were in the same grade in school. And I was, well, a bit of a nerd, which got me bullied a lot. Maggie, she was always really quick at thinking up the best comebacks, and she was popular, so no one ever messed with her. Back in third grade and until the end of high school, she took it upon herself to be my protector."

I frowned. "I didn't know that." I dug through my memories for

Greg, but he didn't feature in any. "I don't remember you from before I left Boulder."

"Because I went to study in Boston and then practiced there until my father died. When Heath called and asked if I'd come home, you'd been gone a year with your mom." He steepled his fingers. "I was heartbroken when I heard . . . that she'd passed."

My throat felt like a drawbridge was being yanked shut. "Yeah." I whisked my lids closed a moment, breathed in slowly, then, when I felt like I'd gotten myself under control again, I opened my eyes. "Can we get this over with?"

"Yes. Of course. Sorry."

"Don't be sorry. I'm always glad to hear stories about her. To know that little pieces of her live on in other people's hearts and minds. It's the closest thing to getting her back." My voice cracked. "It gets easier, right?" I fit a smile onto my lips to make them stop quivering and to make Greg stop looking at me as though I were about to break apart.

"It does." He slid his hand over mine and squeezed my fingers before picking up the syringe. As he popped the solution into it, pounding that threatened to bring down my door had Greg turning.

I didn't turn because I knew who was behind the pounding. My navel had tightened like a fishing knot.

I got up to let August in. When his hands gripped my shoulders, I thought he was going to shake me, but he just stood there, gaze running over my body and nostrils flaring as though to pull in my scent . . . make sure I still had one.

"You didn't take it yet." He was so completely out of breath that I suspected he'd run from his house to mine. His crazed eyes scanned the apartment, landed on the paraphernalia laid out on the table. He removed his fingers from my shoulders so suddenly I almost stumbled. "Greg, you can put all of it away. Ness isn't *experimenting.*"

"August!" Surprise made me speak his name louder than intended.

"What?" he snapped.

"You can't just barge in here and make decisions for me."

He took a step nearer, even though not much distance separated us. "You are not injecting yourself with fucking poison to test out a theory."

I planted my hands on my hips. "Sillin isn't poison."

"It messes with our werewolf gene, Ness. It's poison! Ask Greg if you don't believe me."

"August is right," Greg said. "It's not lethal, but it's not *good* for you."

"I'm aware of the risks—"

"Are you?" August's tone was so sharp that it made me blink. "Because I'm not aware of them. And I doubt Greg's aware of them since no one's ever taken such a high dose."

"Morgan has, and she's still alive. *And* she became an Alpha."

A nerve ticked in his jaw. "What if she lied to you?"

"Lied to me?"

"So you'd poison yourself."

"She doesn't want me dead."

"How do you know that?"

"August, you're being completely irrational right now."

"Because I *care*! I care what happens to you even though no one else in this stupid pack seems to."

Silence settled as thickly as snow, making the air lose several degrees of warmth.

"Greg said the worst case scenario is impairing my gene for an undetermined length of time." I didn't want to be a *halfwolf*, but it beat Liam being a dead one, because even though no one was speaking about it, if Morgan had an unfair advantage over us, and we didn't figure out what it was, she'd win the duel.

"Not exactly, Ness. I said I didn't know. It could *irreparably* damage your gene, your senses, your mating link."

Pain streaked over August's face at that last part. He tried to disguise it by turning away from me, but I saw it.

"That *halfwolf* complication could become permanent," Greg added.

"I understand," I said at the same time as August said, "I'll do it." Then, "Is it the same dosage?"

My hands slipped off my hipbones. "August, no."

"Not exactly, but frankly," Greg said, "I'd rather give you this dose than her. It'll still affect you, but you should burn it off quicker."

"No!" When August started for the chair, I wrapped my fingers around his forearm. "I am *not* okay with this! I don't want you to experiment on yourself." My voice sounded so thin.

His lips flexed but didn't produce words for ten whole heartbeats. "Everyone has to do their part for the pack. This is me doing my part." He pried my fingers off his arm one at a time, then took a seat, pushed the sleeves of his sweat-stained navy Henley up, and laid his arm flat on the table.

"Ready?" Greg asked.

August looked at the window. "Hit me."

I crossed my arms to make them stop trembling. When that didn't work, I went to draw myself a glass of water. As I brought it up to my lips, water sloshed over the rim and trickled down my wrist.

There was a hollow suctioning noise—probably the cooler—and then chair legs scraped against the floor.

"Try to shift every day," Greg said. "Once you manage, call me, and I'll come and take a blood sample to see if any traces remain." I heard him walk to the door, but I kept my back to him. "It shouldn't give you any fever or seizures, but I'd feel better if someone was with you tonight. Maybe go sleep at your parents."

Chills zigzagged through my body, icing my already frigid limbs.

"And, Ness, I left you some salve for your arm. It'll help with the scars."

When the door snicked shut, more water spilled out of my glass. I set it down, then ripped paper towels off the roll to blot my skin, the countertop, and the floor.

"Ness—"

"I'm so mad at you," I hissed.

"I got that, but it's done now, and I didn't drop dead, so—"

"So that's supposed to make me feel better?" I yelled, spinning around. "Greg just mentioned seizures. Seizures!"

He snorted. "You do realize this could've been you?"

"I *do* realize!" I breathed hard. "But if this hurt me, it would've been my fault. If this hurts you . . ." My voice broke. "I'll never forgive myself if this hurts you."

"Shh. It'll be all right. I'll phone up Cole. Get him to spend the night at my place."

"No, I'll do it. There's no need to drag yet another person into my harebrained schemes." After the ice, I now felt filled with fire. I bet smoke was wafting from my nostrils.

"You don't have to—"

"After what you just did, you don't get to tell me what to do. I'm spending the night at your place or you'll spend the night at my place. Your choice."

One side of his mouth tipped up with a smile. "If I'd known that was all it took to get you to spend another night with me, I might've injected myself sooner."

I glared at him. Not because I was mad at what he'd just said, but because I was furious with what he'd just done.

His smile vanished. "Pack a bag. I'll call a cab."

CHAPTER 31

"Have you seen this movie?"

"What's the title?" Since leaving my apartment, I hadn't taken my eyes off August, not even to glance at his enormous television screen.

He sighed and set the remote control on the arm of the couch. We were sitting on either end of it—me with my legs curled beneath me, and him with his ankle perched on his opposite knee.

"Please stop looking at me as though you want to throttle me." His leg had been bobbing restlessly since he'd sat down. "It's done. Let it go."

"Let it go? Really?" I narrowed my eyes. "Until you shift—*fully* shift—I'm not going to let this go."

He wrapped his arm around the back of the couch. "You're going to stay mad at me for weeks?"

"Possibly even months."

He winced so suddenly that my heart all but stopped.

When his fingers came up to his temples, I sprang toward him, almost landing in his lap, and palmed his forehead. "What is it? What's wrong?"

His forehead smoothed out, and a smile overtook his lush lips. "You were sitting too far away."

I blinked, and then I smacked his chest hard. "That was *so* not funny, August Watt."

When I tried to crawl back to my side, he wrapped his fingers around my wrist and held me in place. His expression was gentle but serious. "I don't want you to be mad at me even another minute."

"I'm not mad. I'm scared."

"I know, Dimples, but put your anger on hold for a second and look at me. I'm fine."

I scanned him from forehead to chest. Even though I wasn't on his lap, I was close. The side of my bent leg was flush against his thigh, and I could see every single dab of green and sable in his irises, every freckle dotting his nose and cheekbones.

I was way too close.

Heat snaking up my neck, I averted my gaze and wriggled away. "I'm hungry. Are you hungry?" I asked, getting to my feet.

August stared at me fixedly, and then I felt a tug behind my navel that had my shins hitting the frame of the couch. I bent at the knees to absorb the listing.

"I wanted to check if it had affected the link," he said.

Relief surged within me, washing away the awkwardness that had made me shoot to my feet. "It hasn't!"

His eyebrows rose. "Why do you look happy about this? Don't you want it gone?"

I froze like a robber caught mid-theft. From the intensity with which he studied my face, I thought August was going to see right through me.

"I do," I lied, dragging my hair back, "but the fact that it's still there means the Sillin's not wreaking havoc on your system." I hoped the excuse sounded believable. "How's your sense of smell?"

Eyebrows still raised, he pulled in a lungful of air. "Still there, too."

"But is it as strong as before?"

He lowered his gaze to the pulse point in my neck. "It's hard to tell with you standing so close."

I didn't ask him why that was because I understood. I had the same "problem." When I was close to him, little else penetrated my senses over his woodsy, spicy scent, and the steady drumbeat of his heart, and the sight of his remarkable body.

I hadn't taken my dose of Sillin this morning, so my senses were sharpening again. Afraid my frenzied pulse would give away all I was feeling, I took a step back, then rounded the couch and ambled to the kitchen. "What do you feel like eating?"

August twisted around. "I'm not sure I have much back there."

"I found some dried pasta and a jar of tomato sauce."

"You don't have to cook. We can order in."

"Don't underestimate my water-boiling skills."

A smile ghosted over his lips.

"Why are you smiling?"

"Am I not allowed to smile now?"

"I was just wondering if it was a *she's-going-to-burn-down-my-kitchen* smile, or a polite *is-she-going-to-make-me-eat-undercooked-pasta* smile?"

He snorted, and my fingers itched to flick him. "It's an *I'm-relieved-she-doesn't-hate-my-guts* smile."

My hands faltered on the jar, and it dropped onto the wooden countertop. Thankfully, the glass didn't shatter. "I never hated your guts, August. I was scared. I still am. Because, like you, I care."

His eyes didn't turn a brighter shade of green like they usually did, but his gaze scraped across my face with an intensity that made me crouch and pull open one of his cupboards to get out of his line of sight.

"Now where do you keep your pots and pans?"

CHAPTER 32

I sat up so fast my head spun, and August's apartment swam out of focus. A coverlet slid off my shoulders and pooled onto the floor. I clicked my lids open and shut a few times to clear my eyesight, then looked around for August.

He wasn't on the couch. Maybe he was in his bed?

The sound of running water had me leaping to my feet, plodding to the bathroom, and knuckling the door. "August?"

"Be out in a minute!" His voice was strong and steady. He was all right.

Pulse decelerating, I dragged the heels of my hands into my eyes. Something buzzed. I shot my gaze to my bag which I'd set on one of his barstools. I plodded over and dug my cell phone out.

There was a message from Matt: *In front of your door. Ready?*

I checked the time, then mumbled, "Shoot, shoot, shoot," just as the door of the bathroom opened and steam billowed out, thickening the air with August's scent.

ME: *I'm not at my place. Can you pick me up at the warehouse? And it's NOT what you think.*

MATT: *I'll be right over. And the fact that you're telling me that it's not what I think means it's exactly what I think.*

ME: *Your logic is illogical.*

MATT: *Apparently that's what you told Cole last time he was over at August's place.*

MATT: *Be there in a sec. We like our coffees with lots of milk.*

"What's going on?" August asked.

"Matt and Cole are on their way over here. They think . . ." I set my phone down on the smooth slab of ruffled wood. "I'm sure you can guess what they think."

"Are you worried they're going to tell Liam?"

"No. Why—*oh!*" My eyes went wide. With everything going on, I'd completely forgotten about his ban. But then I reasoned that I hadn't broken any rules, because August and I weren't together, *together*.

"Might want to inform him so he doesn't schedule your duel for today."

I worried the inside of my mouth, surely deepening my dimples. "I'll call him later. Right now, I have to get ready. May I use the bathroom?"

"Go right ahead."

I carried my bag inside and quickly changed into my exercise bra and running shorts, then put yesterday's tank top on and brushed my teeth. Tying up my hair, I returned into the kitchen where August was brewing coffee. He'd pulled on a pair of mesh shorts and a short sleeved T-shirt.

"You're feeling up to running?" I asked, grabbing a glass and filling it with tap water.

"Yeah."

"Nothing hurts?"

"Just my neck." He rubbed the back of it. "But that's probably from falling asleep sitting up."

"Can't believe I slept. I'd suck as a nurse."

He smiled. "I'm sure plenty of bedridden men would disagree with you."

Leaning back against the island, I shook my head and drank my fill. "Thanks for trying to make me feel better about my lousy job."

"I survived the night. And I feel absolutely fine. I promise. You can stop worrying about me."

"Can you shift?"

He held out his arm and concentrated. When brown fur didn't sprout from his pores, he shook his head.

"Then I'm not done worrying."

The coffee maker behind him began to gurgle and dribble dark, sweetly charred liquid into the glass carafe.

"Dimples . . ."

"Don't Dimples-me, August Watt. You're my best friend. I'll worry if I want to worry."

His lips tightened as though he found my reasoning maddening. Or maybe it was my sticking him in the friend-zone which he found maddening. Little did he know that he featured in many more zones than that one.

Loud knocking redirected our attention toward the front door. A keypad beeped, but it wasn't followed by a click.

"You changed the code?" I asked as he strode over to open up for Matt and Cole.

"I did."

I clutched my glass of water tighter. Had August changed it for me? So that people—his parents and Cole—didn't walk in on us?

If there had been an *us* . . .

"Yo." Cole slugged August's shoulder.

Although Matt's brother was the same height as my mate, he wasn't half as ripped. August had been away from the Marines for over a month now and was still in formidable shape—slimmer than Matt but carved like a Greek God.

I really had to stop ogling August if I wanted to convince the two Rogers my sleepover had been platonic.

"Morning, Little Wolf," Matt belted out, moss-green eyes way too shiny.

I decided not to bother convincing him or his brother of anything. I didn't have anything to feel ashamed of. Besides—as I took a sip of my water, I sniffed my hand discreetly—I didn't think I smelled of August or of our mating link. Sure, I'd slept on his couch, but apart from when I'd all but jumped onto his lap to check if he had a fever, I'd kept my distance from him.

Giant smile pasted on his lips, Matt rubbed his hands together. "You got our coffees ready?"

I tipped my head toward the coffee machine, and he dug through the cupboard of mismatched mugs to grab two.

I wasn't sure why he was Mr. Smiley this morning. He was one of Liam's friends. Shouldn't Matt have been rooting against me and

August? Unless he thought my presence in August's life would get him work benefits.

"Milk?" Matt asked.

"In the fridge," August said.

I noticed he'd put on his sneakers while I was still barefoot. I curled my unpolished toes, feeling, however superficial, that a coat of nail polish might've made my feet more attractive. Not that anyone was staring at them. I set down my glass and grabbed a pair of socks from my bag. After lacing up my sneakers, I went back for some coffee.

"So . . .?" Matt started as I elbowed past him to grab the carafe.

"So . . .?" I volleyed back. I knew exactly what he was hunting for.

"You guys have something to tell us?" Cole asked.

I looked at August, who proceeded to rub his neck. I wasn't sure if he was still trying to get the kink out of it or if he was nervous.

Taking in a deep breath, I said, "August decided to get injected with a massive dose of Sillin so I wouldn't do it myself. I stayed over to make sure he didn't have a seizure during the night."

The brothers blinked at me, smiles fading.

I sipped my coffee, letting the information settle. "Let me guess . . . that wasn't where your minds had gone?"

"Nope. Not even close," Cole said.

"Why?" Matt asked, watching August as though to spot the effect of the drug.

"Morgan told me that when she was younger, she had to take a big dose of it to heal from a toxic waste poisoning. This led me to wonder if taking an enormous dose somehow left traces in our system—not enough to impair our magic, but enough to impair our enemies. Once August manages to shift, Greg will test his blood."

The atmosphere, which had bordered on lighthearted when the Rogers had arrived, turned downright somber.

"How long before we know the result?" Matt asked.

"Greg said it could take weeks before I can shift," August said, which skewered me with renewed guilt. August must've spotted the guilt, because he added, "But I feel good. Great, even."

I sensed he was overplaying how *great* he felt to reassure me, but I also sensed, through the link, that he wasn't in any pain.

"As you both can see, though, Dimples doesn't believe me."

I pursed my lips.

"You sure you feel up for a run, man?" Matt asked.

August shook his head. "Don't you start babying me too, Matty."

Cole smirked. "Ness's babying you, Auggie? I'm sure that's really awful."

August smacked his friend, which just made Cole chuckle.

I rolled my eyes. "If you guys are done acting like girls, can we go?"

"Acting like girls?" Cole howled a laugh. "I'll have you know, we Rogers are extremely manly. Watt, though—"

"Don't bother coming into work on Monday. You're fired."

"August!" I yelled.

"Don't worry, Ness. That's the twentieth time he's fake-fired me."

"Nothing fake about it this time," August grumbled.

"Temperature's supposed to be scorching today," Matt said, setting his mug in the sink. "We should head out soon."

CHAPTER 33

"Yo, Matty, can we stop?" Cole wheezed. "My lungs are on fire . . . and I feel like I'm gonna hurl." He was running beside me while Matt and August were ahead of us.

Way ahead of us.

Even though my lungs felt vacuum-packed, at least I didn't sound as though I was about to drop dead.

Matt whirled and jogged backward. "If you quit smoking, you'd feel a lot better."

August glanced over his shoulder at us. Like Matt, he'd barely broken a sweat. "Maybe we should take a breather. Don't want to have to explain to Kasie how she lost her oldest son to physical exertion."

Cole flipped him off before coming to a stop. He bent over and clutched his thighs, panting hard. "Why are we running . . . on a Saturday morning . . . again?"

"Because Ness needs endurance training," Matt said, finally halting too.

"Let me rephrase. Why am *I* running? Liam should be the one up here murdering his lungs."

A shadow crossed August's face at the mention of Liam.

"Liam's Alpha," Matt said. "He's magically in better shape than all of us put together. You know that."

I raised an eyebrow. "Magically?"

"The blood oath acts like natural steroids," August explained.

So why had he asked me to prep him for the duel when he didn't need any training?

My gaze snagged on August.

Of course . . .

Cole and Matt suddenly snapped their heads toward the ever-greens behind them. Glowing eyes stared back at us from the cover of the forest. I squinted to make out any distinctive markings on the wolves' pelts, but they stood at a distance. I sniffed the air. Sure enough, these wolves weren't Boulders. In case I hadn't come to this realization on my own, the sweaty T-shirt smacking my bare thigh followed by the sight of the two Rogers' naked backsides would've alerted me to the fact that we weren't in the presence of friends.

August stepped closer to me, the lines of his face and body as taut as the spines of the two giant blond wolves now standing guard next to us. The six Creeks trotted out of the shadows but kept their distance from us. One of them—a lemon-yellow wolf—whined. Matt barked.

How I wish my human ears could've grasped wolf speech . . .

The only thing I could tell from Matt's raised hackles was that they weren't exchanging pleasantries.

"Do you recognize any of them?" I whispered to August.

"No, but the yellow one with the violet eyes could be Alex." He tipped his chin up and smelled the air, and a rumble of frustration ripped up his corded throat. "I can't fucking smell anything."

A penny for his Mom's curse jar and a punch to my already guilt-ridden gut.

The yellow wolf—Alex?—craned his long neck and peered at us over one of his companion's pelts. Had they picked up on what August had just said?

I sidled closer until my hipbone hit the side of August's thigh, feeling my wolf scratching against my envelope of skin, desirous to come out. I bridled her back, because one, I didn't want to get naked—yes, I know . . . incredibly silly—and two, because I wanted to offer August some solidarity. His anger at not being able to morph agitated the tether.

The Creeks made more whiny noises. When one took a step

closer, Cole charged her, bumping her back a couple steps with his shoulder. The brown wolf yelped and stuck her tail between her legs.

The fair-colored wolf growled at Cole but didn't attack. Even though Matt's fangs were bared, he didn't lunge forward.

Cole gnashed his pointy teeth, and the wolf in front of him soared back. The yellow wolf emitted a shrill howl, which got the attention of the five others. He swung around and sprinted into the copse of trees, and his packmates followed.

Matt and Cole waited a good five minutes before shifting back into skin. Once their fur had receded, they straightened, eyes wild with energy and ferocity.

Keeping my gaze on their torsos, I asked, "What did they want?"

"They said we were trespassing on their property!" Cole exclaimed.

"Put your clothes on." August plucked dark mesh from the grass and lobbed it at Cole, before stepping in front of me.

"You do know I have to get used to nudity?" I whispered against his shoulder blades that were pulled in like metal wings.

He grunted, so I flicked the base of his spine. He tossed me a hooded glance over his shoulder.

"What?" I asked all innocently.

He didn't say anything, just slowly returned his attention to the Rogers.

After a few seconds, I walked around my muscular blockade. "*Were* we trespassing?"

"No. This is neutral territory," Cole said, spearing his arms through his muscle tee. "The Boulders and the Pines signed an agreement a long time ago about boundaries. This part of the forest belongs to no one."

If the land was for sale, Aidan Michaels would surely snatch it up with a briefcase of cash.

"Who was here?" August asked.

"Alex Morgan, his sister Lori . . . She's the one Cole knocked back. The other four were Creeks I'm not familiar with."

"Why did you leap at her?" I asked Cole.

"'Cause she was trying to sniff you guys."

My head jerked back. "Sniff us?"

"She said you had an odd smell."

"The mating link," August murmured, barely shifting his lips.

I twisted toward him so fast my ponytail flogged my cheek. "You think they don't know about it?"

"If they didn't, they probably do now," Matt said.

"Or not," Cole said, straightening up. "It's pretty faint."

"It is?" I asked. "You think that's because of the Sillin?"

"Either that, or it's because you've been keeping your hands off each other. You have, right?"

My cheeks burned. "Yes," I hissed.

Cole raised his palms in the air. "Don't bite my head off."

"We should head back," Matt said, studying the woods as though expecting more wolves to show up.

"Did they say anything else?" I asked.

Matt flicked his gaze to the grass at my feet. "Nothing worth repeating."

I folded my arms. "What else did they say?"

The Rogers exchanged a look.

"What. Else?"

"Alex said something about Sarah." Cole spoke really fast, as though speed might lessen the sting. "About how *fun* she was and asked if you'd be interested in a threesome."

My navel pulsed so hard I half expected it to pop right off my abdomen. August hadn't said a word nor let out a sound, but his already rigid body became as still as the trunks of the evergreens in front of us.

"Classy," I said.

"*Classy?*" Matt raised a blond eyebrow. "That's what you got from that?"

"What else was I supposed to get from that?"

"Your best friend's screwing him," Cole said. "Doesn't that repulse you?"

My forearms tightened in front of my chest. "It does, but I'm not her keeper."

Cole exchanged another look with his brother, and then both of them looked at me again, and for a second, I thought they would see the truth behind Sarah's actions, but then they shook their heads, and Matt said, "I hope you didn't share too much sensitive information with her, because if she's willing to screw them, she's probably willing to screw you over."

"She doesn't know anything damning."

"She knows we're mates," August said.

"But she won't tell them." I said this way too quickly and confidently.

"How do you know that?" Matt asked.

In truth, I didn't know. I'd never told her it was a secret. I could only hope she would keep it to herself. "What'll it change if she does tell them?"

"They'll keep me away during the duel," August said softly.

I stared up into the hazel depths of his eyes.

"Yeah," Cole said. "They're always worried about the reaction of mates. Some turn feral if their partners get hurt."

"Eric told me," Matt spoke slowly, "that some mates—when both are wolves—can control the other's body. Apparently, that ability's linked to how much they crave the other as a mate."

Whoa . . . I averted my gaze and rubbed my palms against my running shorts.

"Can you guys do that?" he asked.

"No," August said.

I frowned at him, then at the grass, wondering why he was lying. Was he afraid Matt and Cole would tell others about our ability, or was he embarrassed by it? But then it hit me . . . it wasn't *our* ability.

It was *his*.

I wasn't able to move his body. We'd assumed it was because he was so much bigger than me, but the true reason had nothing to do with size.

He backed away from me, his large sneakers crushing the earth beneath him. "We should get back. I promised my parents I was going to have lunch at their place."

I sensed his desire to get down from the mountain had nothing to do with being on time for his meal and everything to do with what Matt had just told us. Was August ashamed by how much he wanted me, or was he angry by how little he thought I wanted him?

I hadn't tried to pull on the tether since the night I'd slept in his bed, but considering how my feelings for him had grown and solidi-fied, I was pretty certain I could drag him all the way down the mountain if I tried.

I didn't try, though, because if I moved his body, it would destroy all the work I'd put into keeping my hands off it.

Off him.

CHAPTER 34

I sent August several text messages during the weekend to ask how he was feeling. His answer to all of them was the four-letter word: *Fine*. He wasn't fine, but I didn't think that had to do with the Sillin.

Throughout Sunday night dinner at Frank's, Evelyn kept asking me what was wrong, and I kept telling her I was nervous about starting college. While Jeb told stories about his college days, especially about what a formidable running back he'd been, Frank kept casting glances my way. He probably thought my mood was sullen because of the imminent duel.

During the ride back to the apartment, Jeb was acting so uncharacteristically giddy that I worried something could be wrong. My uncle wasn't a giddy person.

"Are you all right, Jeb?" I asked after he'd parked the van on our street and we'd gotten out.

He grinned so wide his teeth gleamed in his gray-blond beard. There was definitely something up with him.

"I know your birthday isn't until Friday"—he dug into his pocket—"but I'm going to give you your present early."

"You don't need to give me any presents."

He *tsk*ed and plucked my hand from my side, then dropped a car key into it. "The payment for the inn came in, so I got you something. It's not brand new, but it doesn't have lots of mileage."

"You got me"—my voice caught—"a car?" I finished quietly.

He pointed at a compact silver SUV with a big red bow on the back fender. "Here she is."

I let out a breath that sounded a lot like a whimper, and Jeb grinned, eyes all glittery. I flung my arms around his neck and hugged him tight.

"Thank you thank you," I whispered.

"You're very welcome." He patted my back. "How about we take it out for a spin?"

"Yes! Absolutely yes!" I detached myself from my uncle and strode over to the car, running my fingertips along its shiny, smooth body.

Mine.

It was mine.

Jeb was still grinning. "Let's get ice-cream. I noticed our freezer was depressingly empty."

I didn't think I could eat anything more after Evelyn's meal, but I nodded excitedly. I climbed behind the wheel and adjusted the seat and the mirrors, my heart feeling exactly like my stomach— close to bursting.

THE FOLLOWING MORNING, PUMPED UP ON CAFFEINE AND excitement, I slipped into my car and turned up the music to match my mood.

I rolled down the window and took my time getting to the campus, relishing the purr of the engine and the feel of the warm breeze twisting my hair. After I parked in the student lot, I took a map of the campus and my schedule out from my college packet. I studied both a moment before setting out toward my Introduction to Statistics course.

I dragged my hand through my snarled hair, realizing I hadn't even checked my reflection in the rearview mirror. I hoped I didn't look like I had an addiction to hairspray. I arrived in the lecture hall with a few minutes to spare and sat up front. As I dug out my note-book, the scent of apricot flecked the air, overpowering the smell of chalky deodorant, milky coffees, and synthetic perfumes.

"Hey, Amanda," I said without even looking up.

She flounced into the seat next to mine. "Did you sleep last night? I didn't. I couldn't. I just drank my weight in coffee."

I smiled at her exuberance.

She peered at me through her thick lashes, brown eyes narrowed. "This might be one of the first times I've seen you smile since you got to Boulder."

My smiled faltered.

"It's a nice change. Makes you more . . . *approachable*."

An older man walked in then, plaid shirt neatly tucked into pressed pants. He set a leather briefcase down on the desk up front.

What Amanda said troubled me. I'd never realized that not being a high-spirited person made me aloof.

In a low voice, I said, "I thought you girls didn't like me because I was . . . *you know* . . . different."

"Ness, we never *disliked* you, per se. You're just very reserved and a little prickly. But I think we'd all be if we were in your position."

"Tamara and Taryn definitely don't like me."

She pursed her lips. "Taryn's a ho, so whatever. As for Tamara, you sort of stole her boyfriend."

"He said they weren't dating," I whispered a little louder.

She gave me a look that said: *and you believed that?*

"I didn't know."

For a long while, Amanda studied my expression. A couple minutes into the lecture, she said, "She'd really like to sort things out with him." Even though she didn't add, *stay away*, I heard her warning loud and clear.

"What about Sienna?"

"What about her?"

"Does *she* hate me?"

Propping her mouth to my ear so no one else overheard our conversation, she said, "Sienna had a tough time right after the breakup, but the girl's got the biggest heart in the world. Plus, like she told me, there's no point in trying to keep a man who's in love with someone else." She pulled away to inspect my face. "This isn't news to you, right?"

My heart began to batter my ribs so loudly I thought Amanda's human ears might hear it. Hell, I thought our professor, who was busy singling out students and asking them what they hoped to learn during the semester, would hear it.

"I know you're not together because of Liam—Matt told me—but if you ask me, maybe you should get with August. That way, Liam would go back to Tammy."

My spine drew straight.

"What?" Amanda asked.

I didn't know much about dating but sensed entering a relationship to better someone else's wasn't smart. "Tamara shouldn't be Liam's backup plan; she should be his only plan."

Amanda puckered her lips.

"As for August, he's my friend."

"I thought . . . never mind."

"What did you think?"

"That you and him already crossed that line," she said, just as the professor called upon her to introduce herself.

I was surprised that Amanda, a notoriously critical person, didn't seem disgusted by the age gap. If anything, she seemed confused as to why we weren't together anymore. Or perhaps, she was acting cool as a cucumber in the hopes of driving Liam back into Tamara's arms.

CHAPTER 35

T he first week was almost over before I crossed paths with Sarah. She was standing with two guys from her pack beside the entrance of the Roser Atlas Center. I almost waved when I spotted her—a kneejerk reaction—but thankfully, I stuffed my hands in the back pocket of my shorts.

She didn't acknowledge me either. It had been more than a week since we'd started acting like strangers, and it had left a huge gap in my life which I'd been filling up with work on my house and learning new fighting techniques from Lucas. Liam had stopped by the gym only once since the day he'd yelled at me for going to visit Cassandra alone. Lucas was vague as to our Alpha's whereabouts. I hoped he was off learning something we could use during the duel, but maybe he was spending time getting reacquainted with Tamara.

This afternoon was no different; Lucas trained me. We fought in fur, and although I felt like I was getting better, he wasn't doling out any compliments. Honestly, I didn't need praise, but getting some verbal encouragement would've been nice. Not that Lucas had seemed in any mood to be overly kind. Since the inn episode, he'd been acting downright testy.

I imagined his crabby mood was due to Sarah but didn't broach the subject, because one, I didn't want to meddle, and two, I was afraid I might let the truth slip out to comfort him.

As I left the gym, he called out, "Happy birthday, Clark. Hope you have a fun evening planned." He raised a smile that didn't reach his eyes.

I paused with my fingers on the heavy door. "Thanks." I almost invited him to come, but it would be a little weird. Lucas and I weren't really friends.

If Sarah had come, though . . . I let that thought drift away before it could bum me out. Soon, I'd get my friend back.

"You did good today," Lucas said.

I blinked. "Did you just compliment me?"

His plastic smile turned into a real smirk. "Only because it's your birthday."

"Uh-huh." I winked at him and turned to go, but before heading home, I patted the door and said, "Sometimes, things aren't what they seem, Lucas."

His black eyebrows listed toward his nose.

Hoping I hadn't said too much, I left him to ponder my cryptic declaration.

When I got home, there was a shopping bag on the kitchen counter with crinkly pink silk paper spilling over the top like cotton candy.

"Came for you after you left this morning," Jeb said, flipping through channels. He was already dressed for dinner in a crisp linen button-down and khaki pants.

I opened the little card tied around the fabric handles. It wasn't signed, but it said: *So you don't wear sneakers to your b-day dinner. Miss you. XX*

I grinned. Only one person had an issue with my sneakers, and that person was Sarah.

I pulled the paper out and extricated a shoe box. Inside was a pair of sky-high nude heels. I stared at the shoes before kicking off my sneakers to try my gift on.

"Who got you shoes?" Jeb asked.

"A friend."

"Which friend?"

"Just a friend." My left foot jammed against a piece of balled paper. I removed the shoe and fished the paper out.

"A *boy*-friend?"

I looked at my uncle. "I don't have a boyfriend, Jeb."

"You don't?"

I shook my head, still clutching the piece of paper.

"What about Liam?"

"Liam?" I almost choked on his name. "He and I broke up a while ago."

The day your son died . . . Like paddles, the memory of Everest delivered an electrical jab inside my chest.

I slid my feet out of the pretty heels and tossed the piece of paper in the box, but lines of black ink caught my eye. I picked it back up and smoothed it out. As I read the words on it, my breath snagged.

Hoping my face didn't betray my emotions, I said, "I should get ready." I hurried to my bedroom, already dialing Liam. The second he answered, I blurted out, "Liam, the Creeks are coming after the Pines' stash of Sillin. They know where you hid it."

"How do you know that?" His voice was hushed, as though he was somewhere he couldn't talk.

"I can't tell you, but you have to move it."

He was so silent I thought the line went dead. "Okay. I'll call Lucas." I was about to say bye, when he added, "Happy birthday, by the way."

"Thank you."

Hinges groaned, and then air rushed through the receiver. "Got any plans?" he asked, louder this time.

"Just dinner with Evelyn, Frank, and Jeb." I didn't mention the Watts would be there.

There was another beat of silence. Was he waiting for me to invite him?

He sighed and said, "I'll call you later," before hanging up.

I thought Tamara's pregnancy would lessen his feelings for me, but what if it hadn't? Perhaps it was a matter of time. Or perhaps it was a matter of me being single.

Maybe Amanda was right. Maybe if I was in a relationship, Liam would stop seeing me as an option.

FRANK, NELSON, AND ISOBEL WERE ALREADY SEATED AT A TABLE in the back of the restaurant when I arrived with Jeb. All three got up. Where Frank and Nelson offered me one-armed hugs and whispered happy birthdays, Isobel kissed my cheeks and then held me in a hug that was almost as fierce as my mother's used to be.

As my heart pinched, I was dragged into a set of new arms.

"*Feliz cumpleaños, querida.*" Evelyn pecked my forehead. "You are sitting here. Next to me."

After lowering herself into her seat, which Frank gallantly held out for her, she leaned over and scrubbed her thumb over my forehead. "I am always leaving marks on you."

I didn't mind the marks she left on me. I let her wipe away the kiss, even though I was certain I'd get more before the evening was over.

The vacant seat at the end of the table had me glancing at Isobel. "Is August coming?"

"He said he was on his way. You look beautiful tonight. Doesn't she, Evelyn?"

"She always looks beautiful," Evelyn answered, her tone a little gruff.

Isobel's lips flexed into a wide smile as she leaned over and whispered, "Remind me never to get on her bad side."

Trent, The Silver Bowl's owner, arrived then, and I got up to shake his hand and thank him for hosting us. "It's my pleasure." He uncorked a bottle of champagne from my year of birth. Which meant he knew I was underage, and yet he filled the champagne flute on the table. He winked at me. "A little gift from my wife and myself. Enjoy."

Just as he was finishing pouring champagne into everyone's flutes, the door of the restaurant opened. I didn't have to look up to know who'd arrived, but I looked anyway, because the tether thrummed. August smiled at the hostess at the door, who smiled right back. He spoke a couple words to her, and she tittered, fingers dropping to the V-collar of her dress. Was she trying to drag August's eyes down to her breasts?

Subtle.

Finally, she turned sideways and pointed to our table. His eyes locked with mine as she led the way toward us. I should've probably looked away, and I sort of did. I looked down, first at his white dress shirt which he'd left unbuttoned at the top, and then lower, at his dark-gray slacks that hugged his long, muscular legs.

I realized I was being as unsubtle as the hostess, so I finally tore my gaze off him and set it on the champagne popping in the glass I'd unconsciously plucked off the table.

"Sorry I'm late." Before taking his seat, he kissed his mother's cheek, then his hand gripped my shoulder gently, and my heart jumped high, as though trying to reach his palm. "Happy birthday, Dimples." He handed me a little pouch.

Heart still suspended, I set my champagne down. "You didn't have to get me anything."

"It's nothing really." He smiled, and I sensed we were okay again. It had just taken him a week of one-word text messages to come around.

I undid the ties on the pouch, then dipped my fingers inside the velvet until I came away with something warm and smooth: an intricate carving of a palm tree on a metal keyring. A grin broke over my lips as I stroked the perfect little piece of wood.

"I heard you got a car. I thought you might need something to put your new key on."

"Is that a palm tree?" Isobel asked, leaning in closer to look at it.

I nodded, the hair I'd blow-dried straight fluttering over one of the dresses from Sarah's reject pile. The frock was as red as Evelyn's lipstick and draped off one of my shoulders before tapering at the waist and flaring out. It had this vintage flair that made me think of something a Hollywood star would wear.

"They're my favorite trees," I explained, then added, "Apparently."

"Apparently?" Isobel quirked a painted-on eyebrow. Like her hair, which was covered by a wig, her real eyebrows were growing back, but the process was slow.

"Apparently I sketched my dream house when I was a kid, and it had a palm tree in the middle. August reminded me of it."

"Can I see the carving?" Jeb asked.

I handed it over, and he *ooh*ed and *aah*ed at the detail before passing it along to Frank.

I mouthed a *thank you* to August, and it won me a devastating smile, which made my navel tingle behind my cinched waistband.

Nelson lifted his champagne. "Before the food arrives, we wanted to say a little something. Ness, you're like a daughter to Isobel and me, and although we know we can never replace Maggie and Callum, I hope you know you can come to us with anything you might need."

My bottom lip wobbled.

"We will always be here for you, sweet girl," Isobel said, making my attempt at keeping it together worse.

"Nelson, you just stole my entire toast," Jeb chided, humor lilting his tone. Directing his attention on me, he said, "Ness, I know you're eighteen now, and *legally* not mine to keep, but I hope you'll choose to stay with me a couple more years. I really enjoy having someone to take care of, even though"—his Adam's apple bobbed underneath his gray-blond scruff—"even though you take better care of me than—" He stopped talking abruptly, his eyes growing red and shiny with emotion.

As Frank patted my uncle's back, tears trickled down my cheeks. I palmed them away, hoping they weren't dragging down the mascara I'd applied.

"I'm not going anywhere, Jeb," I managed to whisper. "At least not without you."

He smiled, and my heart squeezed because in that moment, he looked so much like Dad. He didn't have his dimples, but he had the same smile.

"Six years ago, I met a sweet little girl with blonde pigtails who would not let me into her apartment," Evelyn said, "and yet, the same little girl ended up letting me into her heart. *Querida*, I never had the chance to become a mother, so I never imagined I would have the chance to become a grandmother, but you made this dream of mine come true."

So much for staying stoic and well made-up. I lifted my napkin from my lap and blotted the corners of my eyes, leaving behind little black smudges on the pale linen.

"I do not know if I am any good at it, though." She lowered her gaze to her ornate plate and added quietly, "I want what is best for you, but maybe I have been wrong about what is best for you."

A beat of silence descended upon the table.

I nibbled on my lip, my heart accelerating. I prayed I was the only one who knew what she was referring to.

Whom she was referring to.

"I'm happy your father didn't take well to the pledge drink, Ness," Frank blurted out, which made Evelyn's gaze jerk off her plate.

I laughed, which was a nice change from all the crying.

"What about you, son?" Nelson said.

"I'm still thinking," August said, but something in the intensity with which he stared at my face told me he knew exactly what he wanted to say but didn't want to utter it in front of everyone. Which was fine by me, because I was also certain that whatever he'd say would be heartfelt and make me cry . . . *again*. "But don't let my thinking keep you from your drinking." He raised his glass. "To you, Ness."

Without breaking eye contact, he took a long sip of champagne.

CHAPTER 36

We had three incredible courses followed by the most decadent flourless chocolate birthday cake. When it was brought out, ablaze with candles, everyone in the restaurant sang and clapped. By the time coffees and teas were served, the waistband of my dress felt like steel wire.

I was listening to one of Evelyn's kitchen nightmare stories when I caught Nelson asking August at what time he was flying out to Tennessee to meet with the Rivers.

He was going to meet the Rivers?

I was so disconcerted by the news of his impending trip that I didn't realize I'd spoken out loud until both Watts turned toward me.

"They want us to build them an indoor recreation center for the winter months." Nelson beamed proudly.

"That's . . . that's"—I flipped the tiny spoon on my teacup saucer over and over—"*wonderful.*"

It wasn't, though. Not in the least. Even though I knew first-hand that the Rivers genuinely liked what August and Nelson had crafted, I also knew the River Alpha's daughter had a thing—more than a thing . . . *ugh*—for August. And if he went, the distance would cancel out our bond, and since he assumed my feelings for him were entirely platonic, nothing would stand in his way to hook up with her again. Trying to rein in my glumness, I swallowed the tepid and over-infused dregs of my tea that tasted way better than the jealousy basting my palate.

At the end of dinner, after everyone had thanked Trent and filed out of the restaurant, Nelson said, "We have a birthday present for you. It's for your new house. Let me know when you're done redoing it, and I'll bring it over."

"You didn't have to—"

"Will you just let us spoil you without putting up a fight?" Isobel asked, flicking the tip of my nose.

"Okay."

Nelson pulled open her car door, and she climbed into the passenger seat. Before shutting the door, she said, "Thank you for sharing your special night, sweet girl," and then she blew me another kiss.

They couldn't replace Mom and Dad—no one could—but I was fortunate to have them in my life. Whoever August ended up with would be one lucky girl.

That thought just crushed me. Where had it even come from?

Evelyn hugged me tight and told me she loved me a great many times before finally letting Frank tug her away. Only Jeb, August, and I remained on the glittery pavement.

Digging the van's key out of his jacket pocket, my uncle congratulated August on landing another deal with the Rivers, then to me, he said, "I'll bring the car around."

We hadn't parked far, but I was glad not to have to walk in the heels that were so high I was only half a head shorter than August.

Keeping my gaze on the stubble coating his jaw, I said, "Thanks for my palm tree."

"You're welcome."

His scent and heat eddied in the air between us, tempting me to step in closer. "I love it."

His lips arched. "I'm glad."

I inhaled a long breath that just tortured my heart. "How are you feeling?"

"I still can't shift. But otherwise, I feel good."

For a moment, neither of us spoke, and then we both spoke at the same time.

He said, "How was your first week of school?" while I asked, "When are you leaving?"

"You first," he said.

"My first week was really good."

"It's a big milestone. We should celebrate. If you have time next week, we could go for ice-cream at the Creamery."

His suggestion had me wincing. I loved that parlor and I loved the idea of going with him, but it was a place he'd bring me to when I was a kid, and that made me feel so young, like I'd blown out thirteen candles instead of eighteen.

"Sure," I said, just as the van turned the corner. I started heading toward it, but paused. "You didn't answer *my* question."

"I'm leaving tomorrow morning."

I clenched the pouch that held my little palm tree. "For how long?"

"Two nights."

I swallowed and eased my grip before I could break the creation like I'd broken us. "Huh," I ended up saying. Not very eloquent, but it beat the wounded sound forming at the back of my throat.

As I staggered the few feet that separated me from the van, I attempted not to topple from the weight of the war raging within me. I paused by the car door, the desire to admit my lie burning on my tongue. I glanced over my shoulder. August was reading something on his phone's screen.

Something that made him smile.

Had the River Alpha's daughter sent him a text message?

"Ness?" My uncle's voice made me jump. "I'm holding up traffic, sweetie."

"Sorry," I mumbled, getting into the car.

I didn't look at August as we drove away, afraid he was still smiling at his phone.

CHAPTER 37

"Last coat of paint goes on tomorrow," Jeb said before heading into his bedroom. "If we start early, we could be done with everything by nightfall and move in on Sunday."

"Only if you take the bigger room."

"Ness—"

"Please, Jeb. I can't live in their room." Already moving into my old home, however different it would look with fresh paint and new furniture, was going to be difficult.

"You're sure?"

"Two hundred percent."

He looked at me a long time before saying, "Okay," then drummed his fingers against the doorframe. "Have a good night, sweetie. And again, happy birthday."

Once his door clicked shut, I reached for my zipper and started easing it down, but then the memory of August smiling at his phone had me tugging it back up and grabbing my keys.

Maybe it hadn't been the River Alpha's daughter on the other end of his *pleasant* conversation, but either way, I wasn't letting him leave without understanding my reasons for shutting him out.

I wrote Jeb a note that I was going over to a friend's house and left the paper on the dining table. Ten minutes later, I was standing in front of August's front door. I lifted my finger to the ringer, but before I could press it, the door opened.

August stood on the threshold, shirt flapping open, as though I'd caught him in the middle of undressing.

"How—how did you know I was here?" My voice tripped in time with my pulse.

He tapped his bare midriff. "I have this nifty, built-in mate-detector. I believe you possess the same one."

My stomach was tied in too many knots to sense much over my heightened nerves. "Can I . . . can I come in?"

He drew the door wider.

My heels clicked on the gray floorboards, echoing through the dimly lit loft. A slowly moving image of our planet seen from space ebbed on his TV screen, splashing one end of the apartment in a rich-blue glow. The only other source of light came from the glass fixture suspended over the kitchen island, dimmed to its lowest setting.

I closed my eyes to center myself and silence the voice of reason that was telling me to get back into my car and drive away. When I lifted my lids, August was standing before me.

"Don't—" I swallowed thickly.

"Don't what?"

"Don't go tomorrow."

He frowned. "Why?"

"Because . . ." I tucked a lock of hair behind my ear. I was being selfish; I had no right to ask this of him.

"Because what, Dimples?"

"Because I don't want to lose you."

His gaze turned so dusky his bright irises became barely distinguishable from his pupils. "Why would you lose me?"

"Because"—I wet my lips—"the Alpha's daughter. She wants to marry you. And the link—"

"You think I'm going there to get engaged to Ingrid?"

Ingrid . . . I'd conveniently forgotten her name, but August hadn't.

He never forgot anything.

"It's just work." He tilted his face to the side. "But I do have to wonder why it would bother you since you don't have feelings for me."

Evelyn's warning beat against my temples, but then the words she'd spoken tonight trickled over them, blurring the line between right and wrong.

I steeled my spine. "August, I lied."

A beat of silence passed before he said, "I know."

"When I was away, I—wait. What do you mean, *you know?*"

His expression gentled but stayed guarded. "Frank called me a couple nights ago."

"Frank?" I frowned. "I don't understand."

"He overheard you and Evelyn talk the day you came back from your trip. He didn't want to get involved, but you know Frank, and how sacred he finds mating links."

My eyes widened.

"And he might've mentioned that you looked miserable and that I was obtuse if I actually believed you didn't want me."

I didn't think my eyes could get wider, but my lids stretched higher.

August raised his hand to the nape of his neck and cradled it. "What is it you want from me?" His voice was so raw it had me shivering. "To wait a couple years for you to grow *readier?*"

"No."

His brow furrowed. "Then what?"

"I want you to forgive me."

"For what?"

"For lying. I know I hurt you, and I hate myself for it."

He let his hand drop back to his side. "You think I can stay mad at you?"

"Not staying mad at me and forgiving me are two separate things."

His jaw tensed. And then, in a voice that scattered goose bumps over my skin, he said, "I forgive you."

My heart was pounding so hard the fabric of my red dress vibrated. The tether too, probably. For a second, I considered tugging it to pull August toward me, but what if . . . what if it *didn't* work?

Or what if he didn't want me like that anymore?

My arms started shaking, so I clutched my elbows. "I'd understand if you say no, but would you give me a second chance?"

He didn't answer me for so long that I wondered if I'd spoken too quietly, but then he took a tentative step toward me and crooked my chin up on his finger. "Only if you promise not to let anyone, and I mean *anyone*—not Evelyn, not Liam—come between us again, because I'm not interested in our Alpha's rules or societal propriety. It's *you* and *me*. No one else. And even though I could never hate you, if you break my heart again—"

"When I break yours, it breaks mine," I whispered in a tenuous voice. I hadn't realized I'd started crying until his thumbs swiped my cheeks. And here I thought I'd exhausted my tear ducts earlier, but apparently they were bottomless. "I'm so sorry, August."

He pressed his mouth to mine and stroked away my apology with his tongue. And then his hands trailed down my arms, loosening them, before lacing around my waist.

His scent would be all over me, but I no longer cared. Besides, I was pretty confident that Tamara's pregnancy would make Liam think twice before jumping into a duel now.

I pushed up on my tiptoes and gripped the back of August's neck to deepen the kiss and to erase any remaining space between our bodies. His mouth slid off mine but didn't leave my body. It traveled across my jaw and down my neck, traced the slope of my shoulder, tracking wet heat over my sensitive skin.

I shivered. Shuddered. Shook.

When he lifted his head to look at me, I thumbed the back of his neck. "As far as birthday presents go, that kiss might've beat the palm tree. Which is a feat, considering how much I love that palm tree."

He smiled quietly, his fingertips sketching unhurried circles at the base of my spine. "Ness, I have to ask, what made you change your mind?"

I worried the inside of my cheek. "I didn't want you going somewhere the link didn't work thinking I wasn't attracted to you." I dragged my hand through my straightened hair. "I'm really jealous of Ingrid. Of pretty much every girl you've dated."

"You have nothing to be jealous about."

"Are you kidding? They're all still hung up on you. And they're all older, and way more experienced, and—"

He kissed me before saying, "And none of them are you."

"Are *you* sure it's not just the link that makes you want me?"

He pulled away, the tendons in his neck pinching beneath my fingertips. "When you went off to Tennessee with Liam, I considered boarding a plane and coming after you, but Mom told me the best way to scare a girl off was to do just that, so I stayed here and sulked and imagined the worst things. And then when you came back and said you hadn't missed me"—he grimaced—"it felt like I'd taken a bullet to the heart."

"I'm sorry," I said again.

"I'm just sorry we lost all this time, sweetheart." He nudged my nose with his before kissing me so tenderly it made my toes curl. After a deliciously long while, he said, "I have a confession of my own."

"You do?"

"I went to speak with Evelyn this week."

I blanched.

"I told her about my intentions toward you."

I stared at him in mute horror. "Your intentions?"

"I told her that when I returned from my trip, I would ask you out. On a proper date."

"Did she threaten to murder you?"

His lips quirked. "No. She thanked me for my honesty and then she left the room." His mouth straightened into a contemplative expression. "I didn't mean to upset her; I only meant to show her that I was serious about you. I hope that, in time, she'll accept me."

"I think she's already starting to."

He stared so intently into my eyes that I shivered again.

"What *are* your intentions toward me?"

He leaned in to nuzzle the base of my neck again. "Long term, making you mine, but you already know that."

My heartbeat detonated.

"Short term, showing you how right we are for each other." He licked a line up to my earlobe, making a fierce wave of desire break against my skin. "How well we *fit* together."

The word *fitting* had my mind concocting all sorts of scenarios that involved a lot less clothes. None at all for that matter. "If we use protection, we can have sex without consolidating the mating link," I blurted out, before slapping my hand over my mouth.

Had I really said this out loud?

He pulled away from me, eyebrows writhing in amusement.

"I learned that in Tennessee," I mumbled, cheeks flaming.

He studied me a long beat before dragging my hand off my mouth. "Is that what you want?"

My throat went dry so fast I had to swallow several times before I could speak again. "Isn't it what you want?"

"What I want is you." He crooked my face up. "And I'm not going to lie . . . I most definitely want to make love to you, but I don't want to rush into something you're not ready for."

"I'm ready."

His gaze turned hooded.

"I don't want to feel like a kid anymore, August."

He frowned. "You're not." His hands tracked up my ribcage and cupped my breasts. "I'm not sure why you don't seem to believe this, but you're already very much a woman."

"Maybe I feel this way because I'm still a virgin." I strained against his palms. "Please?"

Letting out a husky growl, he dropped his hands to my ass and lifted me up. I gasped, my legs reflexively coming around his waist. He carried me over to the kitchen island and sat me down on the satiny wood, the dim glow over our heads casting luminous ripples over his face.

As he stood between my legs, he said, "I won't have sex with you to make you feel like more of a woman."

My heart stumbled around in my chest. Everything about his body echoed my own desire. Had I read him wrong?

He traced the contour of my lips with his fingertip. "I'll have sex with you to show you that you already are."

He dipped his finger down my neck, then kissed the hollow at the base of my neck where his finger had been, before trawling his tongue lower. His hands came around my back and eased my zipper open.

Air rushed out of my mouth at the sensation of the fabric falling away from my skin, baring my upper body.

He straightened and drank me in. "God, you're beautiful."

I wanted to roll my eyes or say, *have you looked in a mirror?* Instead, I forced his already open shirt off his shoulders and rolled it down his arms. I knew this wasn't a comparison, but my upper body had nothing on his. I trailed my fingers over his copper skin, over his dark nipples, over the perfect grid of his abs, stilling on the sharp indents at his waist.

Looking back into his eyes that flashed with the same lust heating my blood, I lowered my hands to the button of his pants and popped it open, then got off the island so that my dress pooled around my feet.

August's pupils swelled, blotting out all the green around them, and then his calloused hands grazed my skin. After an agonizingly quiet moment, his face slanted to one of my breasts. He tugged me into his mouth, licking the pebbling skin. As he moved to the other, he raked his deft hands down my spine, hooking the waist-band of my black thong and sliding it down my legs.

He lifted me back to the island, his breathing growing so ragged that the mere sound of him exhaling on me sent daggers of heat into my core. When he took a step back, I squeezed my thighs together and covered my breasts.

"Please don't hide yourself from me, sweetheart."

Biting my lip, I whispered, "Can you also—I don't want to be the only one . . . naked." I felt silly asking him to take off his clothes, but the weight of his stare made me terribly self-conscious.

He pushed his pants and briefs down in one swift stroke. The sight of him springing out, thick and ready, made my entire body blaze warmer. I inched my hand closer to his silky flesh, closed my fingers around him, then dragged them up to the tip.

He cuffed my wrist and towed it off his body.

"You have a . . . condom?"

A corner of his mouth tipped up. "I do, but we won't be needing one for a while still." He eased me onto my back until my spine was flush against the cool wood, and then he parted my legs and draped them over his shoulders.

When his tongue flicked against me, I picked my head off and gasped, "August! You don't have to do that."

I could only see his eyes, and they glowed with amusement and with a bunch of other things, but mostly amusement.

"Don't have to do that?" He spoke the words so close to my delicate flesh that I shivered and writhed. He clamped his hands around my thighs to pin them to his shoulders. "Oh, I've been wanting to do this"—he gave me a long, slow lick—"since the day you walked back into my life." He skated a kiss over my pulsing center. "Fuck, you taste so good," he growled.

He was relentless and made me shatter so many times that my body felt made of clouds and stars instead of flesh and blood.

At some point, he came up for air, lips swollen and slick. He scooped my boneless body up, grabbed his wallet, then carried me over to the couch. He laid me out before pulling a condom from his wallet. The casing crinkled as he tore it open. With unabashed curiosity, I watched him roll it on.

"Ness," he whispered raucously, climbing over me and bracing himself on his arms as his length settled against my abdomen, "condoms . . . they can break. It's never happened to me before, but they can. Are you sure you want to do this?"

I traced the shape of Cassiopeia on his cheek, connecting each freckle to the next. "I have never wanted anything more."

"But you understand the risks?"

"I understand the risks." When he still hadn't moved, I said, "Are you going to make me sign a disclaimer?"

A laugh burst from him. "Maybe I should." He moved down my body to position himself at my entrance. "Next time."

Next time . . . My heart felt like it had melted and little pieces of it were beating everywhere in me.

His hips shifted, and then he was stretching me open, and a gasp tore up my throat. When he pulled out, eyes stained with concern, I clamped my hands on his backside, over his scar, and pressed him back in.

Pleasure warred with pain. Neither sensation won. They battled till the very end, till his body stilled and shuddered over mine . . . *into* mine.

Stroking his scar, I whispered, "You had a toast ready for me tonight, didn't you?"

A smile touched his mouth that smelled like a mix of him and me. "I did."

"Can I hear it?"

"You can." He nosed my jaw.

When he didn't say anything more for a prolonged stretch of time, I asked, "Tonight?"

He lifted his head, tucked a lock of hair behind my ear, and then in that raw-honeyed voice of his, he said, "I may not have been your first choice for a mate, but I hope I'll be your last."

Emotion gripped my throat so hard I couldn't respond with words, so instead, I picked my neck off the couch pillow and aligned my lips and heartbeats with his.

CHAPTER 38

I woke up to the scent of coffee.

As I stretched, every second of our love-making replayed in my mind. I twisted around, but August was no longer on the couch next to me. Last night, he removed the back pillows to make room for our two bodies, and then he dragged me against his chest, and we fell asleep skin to skin.

"August?" I called out.

When he didn't answer me, I sat up but regretted the sudden movement that awakened a dull throbbing between my legs.

Pale sunlight fanned over the loft, tinting everything lavender and gray.

"August?" I repeated, my throat feeling as raw as the rest of me. Had he left for Tennessee?

I pushed my senses out, trying to pick up on another heartbeat, but only mine resounded.

He left.

He'd gone and left, and he hadn't even woken me to say good-bye. The most overwhelming devastation crushed my lungs, made it impossible to breathe. Hands shaking, I took the cover and wrapped it around myself, then struggled to a standing position that intensified the throbbing.

The front door snicked open, and my heart all but short-circuited.

I clutched the cover tighter.

August walked in, a brown paper bag dangling from his fingers. When he caught sight of my expression, he kicked the door shut, tossed the paper bag on the kitchen island, and rushed over. "What is it?"

My bottom lip wobbled. "I thought you . . . I thought you'd left."

His forehead puckered, but then he smiled, cupped both my cheeks, and tipped my face up. "Just to get breakfast."

When had I become this needy girl ready to cry for having been left alone? I averted my gaze from his. "I feel so stupid right now."

"Why?"

"For flipping out."

"I like that you flipped out." He pushed a lock of tangled hair off my face. "I was worried you might have regrets and run away from me again."

I looked up at him. "Run away? It was the best night of my life."

His hazel eyes blazed. "That's a dangerous thing to say."

"Why?"

"Because I want to hear you say that every morning you wake up"—his hands settled on the base of my spine and pressed me against him—"which means I'll have to outdo myself each and every night." He bumped his nose into mine.

My pulse fluttered against my neck and then lower, until it had all but soothed the shallow ache and replaced it with fierce want.

"I'm on board with that," I murmured.

His eyes twinkled a tad wickedly. "On a scale of one to ten, how much pain are you in right now?"

"Pain?"

"Down there."

"Not much."

"Not much isn't a number."

"Two."

His brows slanted. "Really?"

"Okay, maybe three. And a half." My body was supposed to heal fast. Why was I even still in pain?

Yes, he was *big*, but—

"When you get to zero, you let me know." And then he walked

back to the kitchen, pulled a bread basket from a cupboard, and poured out the flaky pastries that smelled like warmed butter and spicy cinnamon. My stomach clenched and let out an embarrassingly loud rumble.

"Someone's hungry," he said, smiling.

"Ravenous." Still mummified in the cover, I shuffled over to the island. "Aren't you?"

He ran his palm over the wood that had absorbed the waves of my pleasure. "Oh, I'm starving."

Sandwiching my face between two hot irons would probably have scorched my cheeks less.

"Did I just make you blush?" he asked, smirking.

I broke off a piece from the cinnamon roll and lobbed it at him.

"How very mature, Dimples. I thought you were a real woman, now."

"Shut up," I muttered, breaking off another piece of the sweet pastry, but this time to eat it.

August came around the island and sat on the stool beside mine. Still laughing, he leaned over and kissed me. It started out as a peck but escalated quickly.

"Two," I whispered against his mouth.

"What?" he asked, voice all raspy.

"On a scale of one to ten, I'm down to a two. Kiss me again, and I might get to zero faster."

He sucked in a ragged breath before clearing his throat. "Your body needs to heal."

"My body needs yours."

"It's all yours."

"But you're leaving in a couple hours."

His eyes, which encompassed every color of the forest beyond these walls, turned very serious. "Ness, I'm not going anywhere."

"You canceled your trip?"

"Dad's gonna go."

The silliest relief filled me. Even though I'd rather have gnawed off my own leg than let him go into River territory, I said, "If you need to go with him, you can."

"The only place I need to be is here with you."

And here I'd up and gone on my trip without considering how my absence would make *him* feel. "I don't deserve you."

"What are you talking about?"

My eyes heated. Oh my God, was I about to cry? *Again?* What was wrong with me? Was I getting my period?

"Hey, hey, hey." He kissed my lids.

"I don't know what's happening to me," I whispered. "I've never been like this."

"Like what?"

"So needy."

He stroked the edge of my face.

Had we somehow consolidated the bond, and now I couldn't physically be away from him? "You think the condom broke?" It would explain—

"The condom didn't break."

Then how come I felt like I couldn't breathe if he wasn't around?

How come I wanted to duct-tape my body to his?

"You look a little pale," he said.

I lifted my hair and twisted it into a rope. "However clingy I get, don't run from me, okay?"

He leaned over again and gripped the back of my neck. "Why would I run from the one thing I want?"

As he kissed me, the tether between us solidified into a thick and shiny rope, which I itched to pluck but still feared to touch. In the end, I set the temptation aside for another time, a time when August would be so certain of my feelings for him that he wouldn't worry if I couldn't move his body with my mind.

CHAPTER 39

I was glad it was Saturday. At least none of August's employees would witness my walk of shame.

August flicked his gaze toward me as we ambled hand-in-hand toward my car. "I know some very capable house painters who work weekends."

I powered open my car doors. "I'm sure you do."

"Let me call—"

I kissed his still moving mouth, then pulled away and said, "I like painting walls."

"If memory serves me, you also like what I did to you last night . . ."

Heat smacked my cheeks. "I did also like that."

"And swimming in lakes." He gestured to the sky. "I mean, look at this weather. It's perfect for what I had planned."

Maybe I could let Jeb—*No.* I needed to help out. Especially if we wanted to move in tomorrow.

"You know what I also really like?" I asked. "Sunset swims. Less people around."

His eyes flashed. "You make a convincing argument. What time should I pick you up?"

"Six. At the apartment, so I have time to change."

He looked up at the sky before returning his gaze to my face. "That's in too many hours."

I smiled. "Want to bring us lunch?"

His lips curved. "I can most definitely do that." As he leaned in for a kiss, my phone vibrated inside my bag. I disregarded the call, giving August's addictive mouth my full attention.

A while later, he drew open my car door, and I settled behind the wheel. And then he backed away and watched me leave, the rope between us stretching like spun sugar. At a traffic light, I dug my phone out of my bag to call Sarah, but then remembered I couldn't make contact with her.

My disappointment was quickly superseded by apprehension when I noticed Liam's three missed calls.

Bracing myself, I dialed him back.

It was Lucas who answered. "We're waiting for you in the gym."

"I thought you said I had the day off."

He sighed, then dropped his voice, "Just get here quick, Clark."

"Did the Creeks—"

"Not over the phone."

"Okay. I'll be there in twenty." Pulse skittering like claws on pavement, I tightened my grip on the steering wheel and tore down the streets toward my apartment.

SHOWERED AND CHANGED, I BANGED ON THE GYM DOORS. I hadn't been convened to train, so I'd donned a plain crop top and a pair of overalls I'd purchased to work on the house. A small part of me was hoping the burned-plastic smell of the paint primer dappling the denim would conceal August's scent.

But I quieted that small part of me.

I wasn't here to hide what I'd done; I was here to defend my actions. If this meeting was even about August.

Lucas opened the door, and I strode in, muttering a quick hello, but then I did a doubletake when I caught sight of a bruise purpling his jaw.

"What happened to your face?" I asked. "Did you get in a fight?"

His blue eyes shone like lapis. "No. I walked into Alex Morgan's fist for the fun of it."

I stiffened. "Alex Morgan?" My gaze jumped to Liam to see if he, too, had gotten hit. His face was shiny with sweat but unblemished.

As he set down the weights he'd been curling, he speared me with a look that had my heart banging harder. "Thanks to your little message, the Creeks followed Lucas and Matt to where we'd stashed the Sillin, and ambushed them."

I gasped. "Ambushed?"

"It was a fucking set-up, Ness! They had no clue where we'd hidden it," Lucas hissed.

"Sarah sent you the message, didn't she?" Liam asked.

My lips trembled too hard to answer.

He rose from the weight bench and strode over to me, his gait so brutal I took a step back. "I told you she was using us, and you *didn't* listen."

"Sarah wouldn't have done that . . ." I whispered.

"How can you still defend her?" Liam hollered.

I pressed my palms against my ears. "I can hear you fine. Don't shout."

"You didn't hear me fine the first time I said it. Maybe this time, if I say it loud enough, you'll listen!" Spittle smacked my nose.

I gritted my teeth. "Stop it, Liam!"

Would Sarah have set me up to gain the Creeks' trust? I couldn't imagine her doing such a thing.

I prayed she hadn't.

"I trust Sarah. She wouldn't have betrayed us, not willingly anyway. Maybe *they* set her up. Maybe—"

Liam's eyes flashed like hammered copper. "Funny you should mention trust."

I sucked in a breath. "What's that supposed to mean?"

"You broke your promise." His voice was chillingly flat, but his expression wasn't. His expression was a medley of sharp angles. "I can smell him all over you."

My lungs contracted, but then I crossed my arms. "Don't you think we have more important—"

"We had a deal," he snapped.

"That deal went both ways." Underneath the hot musk and fresh mint of Liam lay another scent, a feminine one. "I'm not the only one who spent the night with someone, so don't you dare tell me off. You don't get to tell me off!"

His Adam's apple jostled in his throat. He hadn't shaved in days, which made him look older, more severe.

"How's Matt?" I asked, his wellbeing mattering more than this stupid feud over who we'd spent our night with.

"What?" Liam blinked.

I turned toward Lucas. "How is he? Did he also get banged up?"

"He looks better than I do. Fucking Alex Morgan. I was this close"—his index finger hovered a breath away from his thumb—"to killing him. This. Close."

"I'm really sorry you guys got jumped," I said, "but I stand by my conviction. Sarah cozied up to Alex Morgan to get *us* information. Not to give them any."

Lucas narrowed his eyes at first, but then he shook his head, tossing his shaggy black hair. "I don't buy that, Clark. She's a Creek through and through."

Tension whirred as loud as the AC vents blowing cold air into the high-ceilinged room. It was interrupted by the ringing of a cell phone.

Lucas pulled it out of the pocket of his black mesh shorts. "It's Frank."

"Pick it up," Liam said, "and tell him what happened."

"He probably wants to speak with y—"

"Just take the call, Lucas. And tell him I'll call him back when I'm done here."

Meaning, when he was done hauling me over the coals.

Once Lucas had walked to the other end of the gym, busy recounting the Creeks' trap, Liam said, "You didn't tell me the Watts would be at your birthday dinner."

"Why are we still talking about that, Liam? And how do you know?"

"After Lucas and Matt got jumped, you weren't answering your phone, so I tracked you through the blood-link to tell you what happened. Led me straight to that fancy restaurant."

"I didn't see you," I said.

"I didn't go inside. I thought better of interrupting your cozy celebration." After a beat, he added, "You've found another family, and there's no place in it for me."

And here I thought he was about to admonish me again. My throat squeezed tight.

"I hate how it ended, Ness. I hate that August came back. I hate that you and him have all this history. I hate that whatever fucking God up there decided to link the two of you! Why not *us*? Why the hell not us?" he whispered hoarsely.

After the heat of his anger, Liam's anguished outburst softened my stance. "I didn't choose him because of a magical link."

"You chose him because I failed you."

Like my throat, my heart tightened. "Your distrust broke me . . . broke *us* . . . but it didn't drive me into someone else's arms."

"Then what did?"

"When you slept with Tamara—"

"It was a mistake."

"Don't say that," I said gently but firmly. "She's the mother of your baby, Liam. Besides, she's not a random girl you picked up in a club. You guys have history, just like August and me."

Pain crinkled Liam's face. "If I could go back—"

"But you can't." A beat of silence filled the cavernous space, disrupted only by Lucas's animated conversation. "We have to learn to live with our choices. And in the end, even if your intention was to test my affection, maybe what happened is a blessing in disguise. You're an Alpha, Liam. An Alpha with a strong, *strong* personality." I made my tone light to sweeten my assertion. "You need a woman who's willing to bend without breaking. I'm not that woman. When someone bends me too hard, I splinter."

He snorted. "You obviously haven't spent much time with Tamara. She's not submissive."

I smiled. "Perhaps not, but from what I've seen, she worships you."

He loosed a ragged sigh. "The night I found out, I lost it. I asked her if she'd done it on purpose. To trap me."

"Liam!"

"I know. Not my finest hour, but I was scared, Ness. A baby? Do you see me with a baby? I can barely take care of a pack of grown men. *And* a woman." He added that last part with a wry smile that dismantled some more of the tension between us. "Know what she said? She said that if I didn't want the baby, then she would raise him on her own, that she wouldn't even ask me for handouts, that she wouldn't ask me for anything until our son reached puberty and would need to be brought into the pack. And even then, she would turn to Matt or someone else if I didn't want to be involved." He shook his head. "Can you imagine that she thought I'd want nothing to do with my own son?"

"I don't think she thought you wanted nothing to do with your son. I think she was giving you a way out." Cornering a man, who was part wild animal, was never a good idea, and Tamara knew this. "Which leads me to think she'll make a good mother."

"I know."

"And you'll make a good father."

He let out a brusque exhale. "I'm not so sure about that."

"Well, I'm sure for the both of us. You're protective and gener-ous, but you do have to work on your fuse. It's a little short."

A streak of sunlight cut across his face, illuminating his brown eyes, making them glow more amber than brown. "I can't believe we just had a heart-to-heart."

"That's what friends do," I said.

"Is that what we are?"

"I think we're getting there." My lips flexed into a smile that he returned. "You're not going to phone up Cassandra and schedule the duel for tomorrow, are you?"

"I'm not."

"Good. Now about that Sillin. They took their stock. But we still have ours, right?"

His features hardened again. "We stored it in the same place."

"Shit." The word popped out of my mouth.

"Yeah." He stabbed his fingers through his hair. "Not my brightest decision."

"Well, I still have some." In truth, I hadn't checked, but since I hadn't spotted any breaking-and-entering, I assumed as much. "Thirty-two pills."

Liam nodded. "Can you shift yet?"

I frowned but then realized he was talking about the injection. "Greg didn't tell you?"

"Tell me what?"

"I'm not the one he inoculated."

Liam's eyebrows tipped toward his nose.

"August volunteered. And no, he can't shift yet."

My news thinned Liam's mouth. "You should've run this by me."

"August didn't give me a choice. Besides, I didn't want to bother you. I knew you had other stuff to deal with."

"The pack always comes first, Ness. No matter what."

I felt a twinge of regret for Tamara, because she would always come second to the pack. Perhaps it would be enough for her, but for me, it would never have been enough. And this made me appreciate August more, because I knew with complete certainty that he'd always put me first.

CHAPTER 40

s promised, August arrived with lunch. But he didn't leave afterward. He rolled up his sleeves and stayed through the afternoon, lending the walls of our house his time and expertise and sneaking me kisses when my uncle wasn't looking.

While I painted my bedroom, the ambush ran on a loop inside my mind. I wanted to discuss it with August; I wanted to get his opinion on the matter but was worried about what it might be. What if he aligned with Lucas and Liam and insisted Sarah was a traitor?

Could someone else have sent me the message?

No, it had been her handwriting.

Had they forced her to write the message? My fingers itched to call her, but what if they'd forced her to con us? Then getting a message from me would only seal her fate . . .

Dusk was falling when I emerged from my bedroom, dizzy with worry and paint fumes. "I'm done."

August glanced away from the baseboard to which he was adding a final coat of white paint. "I'm almost finished here."

"Me too," Jeb said, dragging the lambs-wool roller over the ceiling in the hallway. Paint dribbled down his arm and onto the plastic tarp blanketing our lustrous floors. "How does Chinese takeout sound to you guys? I could go get some while this last coat dries."

August caught my eye.

"Um." I bit my lip. "I, uh . . . already have plans."

Jeb nodded even though disappointment was written all over his face.

August rose from his crouch and dunked the brush into the almost empty paint bucket. "Maybe you could change your plans, Ness?"

I tipped my gaze up to meet his and mouthed a *thank you.* "Yeah. Maybe I could meet my friend *after* dinner."

"Or maybe your friend can join you for dinner," August said, and my heart performed a little backbend because inviting said friend would reveal who said friend was.

"It's okay, Ness," Jeb said. "Derek's always up for getting out of his house. Let me call him."

"You sure?"

"Yeah." He rolled the brush one last time before setting it down and going to grab his phone from the kitchen counter that was also covered in plastic. He dialed Derek, exchanged a couple words, then gave me a thumbs up. After they disconnected, Jeb grabbed his car keys. "I'll be back in an hour. Don't lock up, okay?"

"'Kay."

As soon as the van vanished down the short driveway, August came at me with a predatorial gleam in his eyes that made him look more wolf than man. "You have some paint"—he dipped his fingers inside a bucket, then raked them down my side, over the patch of bare skin beneath my crop top—"right here."

Goose bumps rose beneath the white paint dripping down my ribs. "Huh. Clumsy me. I must've brushed up against a wall."

He smiled, then brought that smile closer to my mouth.

"A very big one," I added.

"Very big," he echoed. "We should clean you up, and I know just the place."

I rolled my eyes but smiled nonetheless, and it dispersed some of my clinging stress.

When car beams splashed the window, I sprang away from August.

Jeb blustered back in, face so white it looked as though he'd dunked it in the bucket of paint. "Ness! Ness, you . . . she . . . Lucy . . ."

My spine snapped into alignment. "Lucy what? What happened, Jeb?"

"Lucy is . . . at Aidan's." He was breathing so hard I had trouble understanding the next words out of his mouth. I caught the last, though. "Dead."

"*Dead?* Lucy's dead?" I asked.

My uncle shook his head from side to side. "No. Maybe Aidan. She doesn't know."

Color leached from August's skin. "What do you mean, she doesn't know?"

"Aidan's house. I need to get to Aidan's house," Jeb whispered.

My skin bristled, and white fur spouted from my pores. I was shifting. I pushed my wolf back before she could rip through my clothes and race across the forest toward the hateful Creek's estate.

"Give me your car key," August said, taking charge. "I'll drive."

"August, you can't shift. I'll go with Jeb—"

He shot me a glare that shut me up. "Like hell I'm letting you go without me. Get in the van."

We all sprinted outside and into the car. My uncle was muttering to himself. I tried to make out what he was saying, but his words were all garbled.

I leaned between the front seats and said, "We should call Liam."

August's gaze was narrowed on the road he was hurtling down at breakneck speed. "I texted Cole."

When, I wondered? I hadn't even seen him use his phone.

He tore his gaze off the road to look at me. "When we get there—"

"Don't tell me to stay in the car."

He slammed his gaze back on the windshield and took a turn so fast I had to dig my nails into his headrest to stay upright. He veered again and then the van lurched up the long driveway toward Aidan's glass and wood mansion. My aunt stood on the threshold, shivering like a strip of cut-out paper dolls.

Jeb flung open the passenger door and leaped out before the car had come to a full stop. He ran to his ex-wife and hugged her.

August spun around in his seat. "Ness—"

"Together. We go in together." I jumped into the passenger seat and out the door that was still open.

August rounded the front bumper, long strides devouring the flagstones.

Amidst chest-wracking sobs, my aunt said, "He's downstairs. With a knife in his throat."

"Lucy!" Jeb said, gaping at her in terror.

"He helped Alex murder our son, Jeb. I heard them joking about it. *Joking.*"

My uncle made a pained sound as he gathered his ex-wife against him again.

"I went to the police," she said. "They asked me for proof. I told them Aidan put a tracking device in the Jeep. They called me back saying they'd gone to the impound lot and checked the car. They told me they didn't find anything."

"Oh, Lucy," Jeb said. "The police . . . they're corrupt. You should've come to us."

"You hate me." Her voice trembled. "You all hate me."

"Lucy . . ." He squeezed her tighter to him.

"Stay out here with her," August told my uncle whose face had gone as pale as his beard.

I started toward the door when Lucy called out my name.

Her lids were so puffy her eyes were mere pinholes. "I'm sorry for . . . for everything." Tears ran down her cheeks, mixing with the blood splatter. "Everest, he was my baby. He could do no wrong."

My uncle's lips wobbled.

"But he did do a lot of wrong." Lucy's body shook anew, jangling all her bracelets. "And I helped him. And now he's gone."

My aunt's apology was so unexpected that it rooted me in place.

"Ness . . ." The urgency in August's voice broke the spell.

"Get her out of here, Jeb," I said. "In case—"

"We'll wait for you."

"Jeb, if she killed him, the Creeks will hunt her down."

Lucy released a whimper that had my uncle's face contorting with indecision.

"Go!" I hissed.

He jolted, then latched onto her arm and guided his ex-wife to the car. After he shut the door, he sprinted back toward me and crushed me against his chest.

In a rushed whisper, he said, "I'll come back for you. I promise."

I nodded. "Just keep her safe. Keep *yourself* safe."

He broke away and jogged to the car. As the van rumbled to life, I sent a silent prayer up into the heavens that someone would watch over them so they didn't end up in a ditch like their son.

I watched the car turn before drifting into the house behind August. As soon as I stepped into the foyer, I pushed out my senses for sounds other than my gunning pulse. A faint thump hit my eardrums.

"Did you hear that?" I whispered.

August nodded, narrowed gaze sweeping the house.

Canine whines and scratches ensued.

"Just his dogs," August murmured, but he nonetheless raised the umbrella he'd grabbed from beside the front door, positioning it over his head like a baseball bat, before stalking toward an open doorway.

When I realized he was following a trail of bloody footprints, my stomach contracted.

"Stay behind me, Ness," he said as we crept through the kitchen that was white and black like a checkered board, and glaringly bright.

The only color in the room was an abstract neon-yellow painting on the far wall and crimson droplets on the shiny floor. As we passed the knife rack, I grabbed a small paring blade that almost slipped out of my clammy fingers. The damp scent of blood wafted through the air, made my lungs cramp.

August was calm, his pulse barely speeding, a person used to the sight of carnage, a person used to storming into homes and seeking out criminals and corpses. He tipped his head toward a door smeared with red handprints, gaping like an open wound.

Were those Lucy's handprints?

Nausea made monochromatic dots dance in front of my eyes. I'd wanted the man dead, yet the idea of finding him swimming in a pool of blood had my stomach roiling. I flung my hand out to clutch the black marble island before I blacked out. The knife clattered from my fingers, and I heaved, but nothing came out.

August hissed my name.

"I'm okay," I murmured, blinking to clear my eyesight.

His concerned and lengthy gaze told me he didn't believe me.

"I promise," I added.

Another long second passed before he raised his hand to the door and drew it open. The hinges creaked like in a horror movie. He touched his ear, and I understood he was asking me to listen. I closed my eyes and concentrated.

A faint but steady thud had my eyes flying open.

Either there was someone else in the house or Aidan Michaels wasn't dead.

August nodded once in understanding, and then he started down the stairs just as an arm hooked my throat. I screamed as I was hauled backward.

August spun and lunged back up the stairs but froze on the landing.

A wet voice rasped against my temple, "I called Sandy . . . She's on her way." Aidan's speech was slurred, as though he were gurgling on mouthwash. "So you go on . . . and leave now, Watt."

Something sharp prodded the skin on my neck. Without moving a muscle, I glanced down and caught sight of a glinting blade soaked in blood. I thought of my own knife and flexed my fingers, but then remembered I'd dropped it.

"Let Ness go, and we'll leave," August said calmly.

Aidan didn't let me go. The blade even nicked my skin.

For a brief second, I wondered if Lucy had set us up, but the pain in her eyes . . . her apology . . . *No,* she'd really tried to put an end to this man's life.

"Who do you . . . take me for?" Aidan's voice was jagged and slow. "The village idiot? Ness will be staying with me . . . until my pack arrives . . . to make sure no other . . . Boulder attacks me."

Something hot dripped down my neck, over my collarbone.

I needed to get out of Aidan's chokehold. I concentrated hard, trying to force magic into my extremities to sprout claws and fangs. As my neck thickened and lined with fur, the knife burrowed deeper into my flesh, and I yelped.

"Don't you shift," Aidan warned, his tinny breath reeking of death.

Howls sounded outside, and Aidan flicked his gaze to the doorway.

If his pack was here . . .

I stared at August, my eyes misting with tears.

If the Creeks were here . . . they would . . .

I shuddered, unable to bring myself to envision what they might do to us.

CHAPTER 41

"This is your last chance, Michaels. Let her go or die." My navel pulsed with August's barely contained fury.

When claws clicked in the foyer, Aidan pulled me back, tightening his hold on my neck that was long and thin again, delicate . . . human.

Three furred beasts erupted into the kitchen, eyes aglow, thick bodies tensed, tails horizontal.

Boulders. Not Creeks!

The black wolf's lambent yellow eyes met mine, and relief careened up my spine.

Our wolves had come. Not Aidan's.

I used the distraction to my advantage.

Willing my nails to transform into claws, I shifted my hips to the side and swiped my paw between Aidan's legs. When my sharp claws pierced the fabric of his pants and met skin, he let out a shrill shriek, and the knife popped away from my skin. I whirled, and remembering what Liam had taught me, shoved Aidan's flailing limb under my armpit, clamping down on his elbow with both my palms to immobilize him.

Aidan's face had become a patchwork of whites and reds glossed over by sweat. He puffed out his cheeks and agitated his wrist. The blade scraped my shoulder before clattering onto the floor.

Suddenly, his body was torn out of my grip and airlifted. Even though he was still in skin, August snarled as loudly as the wolves circling us. He flipped Aidan around, squashed him against his chest, then wound his arm around the Creek's shoulder and cupped his chin.

Aidan's eyes bulged behind his glasses that sat askew on the bridge of his nose.

Our Alpha barked and then shouted into our minds: *STOP! Don't kill him!*

August stared fixedly at Liam, and then at my neck, absorbed the cut that must've been deep because it was still dribbling blood. With a flick of his wrist, my mate snapped Aidan's neck.

NO! Liam's voice exploded inside my skull.

August unwrapped his bicep from around Aidan's shoulders, and the limp body of the man who'd destroyed my family crumpled, his cheek smacking the floor like a dead fish, his glasses tinkling against the stone like a Christmas ornament.

I squinted at his chest to see if it still rose and fell. Weren't we more difficult to kill?

In a croaky whisper that barely carried over Liam's barking, I asked, "Is he . . .?"

Ignoring our Alpha, August stepped over the prostrate body. And then his arms were around me and his face burrowed into my hair. "Yes. He's gone. He can never hurt you again. He's gone."

Both my neck and navel burned, one with blood and the other with fear and fury. The dregs of adrenaline made me shiver so hard my teeth rattled. All of my bones felt as though they were rattling.

"Are you sure?" I murmured.

"Sweetheart, I severed his windpipe. Even we can't—" A guttural *oomph* surged out of August as we rocketed forward, hitting the yellow painting on the wall. He cushioned the back of my skull with his palm, his knuckles getting the brunt of the blow.

What the? I peeked over his shoulder and found Liam back in skin, his incendiary gaze burning a hole into August's back.

"Liam!" I gasped at the same time August wheeled around, muscles twisting beneath his skin.

Our Alpha punched August in the jaw. "What part of *no* didn't you understand, Watt?"

August growled, "Aidan was a threat to the pack, and to Ness. He didn't deserve to live. He should've been killed six years ago!"

Liam snarled. "You don't realize what you've just done, do you?"

"I neutralized a threat."

"Neutralized a threat?" Liam snorted. "This isn't the fucking Marines, Watt!"

"Liam, calm down," I said

"*Calm down?*" He yanked on the roots of his hair as though trying to tear it off his scalp. "Do you not remember what we promised Morgan, Ness?"

What we'd promised Morgan?

What *had* we promised Morgan?

Oh . . .

Realization hit me as hard as a kick to the gut.

"Yeah." Liam bobbed his head a tad maniacally. "I hope you're ready to duel, because now, it'll be on their terms."

"What are you talking about?" August asked.

"I'm talking about the fact that we promised Morgan no harm would come to her son or her cousin until after the duel! I'm talking about the fact that if one of them died at our hands, then the choice of time reverted back to them! That's what I'm talking about!" Spittle flew out of Liam's mouth and smacked August's grinding jaw.

"Lucy . . ." I whispered, my fingers coming up to my neck. Wetness slicked my shaky fingertips. "She's the one who attacked him. She's not a Boulder. We can pin the murder on her."

Liam's nostrils pulsed, and his shoulders still heaved, but his heart rate was slowing. I could feel the echo of it in my own chest. "Our smells are all over Aidan."

"We could burn him and his house down." The new voice had me peering past August's rigid arm.

Cole was crouched over Aidan's lifeless form, fully clothed, which told me he'd come by car. Matt and Lucas, though, prowled beside him, both in fur.

"Aidan said he called the Creeks," I said. "That they were on their way."

"He was bluffing." August's voice was alarmingly flat.

"How do you know?" I stepped around August whose temper had bled into his eyes, stamping out their natural brilliance.

"I've been around enough people like him."

The tether trembled between us as he hunted my expression. I realized he was trying to gauge my reaction to the chain of events Aidan's death would set in motion. I was scared—we weren't ready to face the Creeks—but I was also grateful that justice had finally been served. I caught the balled fist resting against his thigh and spread his stiff fingers with my own.

"August is right. They'd already be here if he'd called them," Cole added.

Liam backed away. "Burn the place down," he said before shifting back into fur.

He craned his neck and watched me through his yellow eyes. *Let's hope they'll believe Lucy did all this on her own. Cole, phone Rodrigo. Tell him to stall the firetrucks as long as he can.* He swung around. *Keep your phone on, Ness. I'm going to try and do some damage control. In case I can't . . .*

He let his voice trail off, but I heard all the absent words.

In case he couldn't talk sense into the Creeks, we'd be at their mercy.

CHAPTER 42

I tugged on August's hand, trying to dislodge him from where he stood beside Cole, watching the fire devour Aidan's mansion. They'd splashed a variety of chemicals throughout the house, over the expensive drapes framing his large windows, over the wooden furniture. The flames skipped around the trails of flammable liquids, growing rabid.

I heard Aidan's hounds howl. I'd broken the window of the study in which he or Lucy had locked them, hoping they'd find their way out. I hadn't dared open the door, afraid their master had trained them to scent Boulder blood and attack.

"We need to go," Cole said, heading to his navy sedan.

August got in the back with me, his arm wound tight around my shoulders.

"I'm glad he's dead," I whispered so he'd stop torturing himself.

"It was the right call," Cole said as he sped down the darkened roads toward the warehouse.

Grunting, August set his attention on the moonless sky. Even the stars seemed darker tonight. At some point, he squeezed the bridge of his nose and closed his eyes, so I cupped his jaw.

"Look at me," I said.

He did.

"My aunt fled. After cozying up to him, she fled. They'll connect the dots and blame her."

"What if they don't, Dimples? What if they don't?"

"We were going to duel them anyway. It was a matter of days."

He made a low growly sound in the back of his throat and punched the headrest of the empty passenger seat. "We don't even know the outcome of the Sillin injection. What if that's not Morgan's *trick*?"

"Maybe Sarah found out something."

"Sarah?" Cole asked. "I thought she'd turned to the dark side."

Of course he'd think this. "I know that's what Liam and Lucas think, but I don't."

Cole's gaze flashed to mine in the rearview mirror. "She set us up to help her new pack steal the Sillin."

When August frowned, I recapped all that had happened, from the concealed missive inside my birthday present to the theft.

"Why didn't you tell me before?" he asked.

"Because I didn't want to worry you," I mumbled.

He twisted around on the seat to peer down at me. "It wouldn't have worried me. What worries me is you carrying the weight of this on your own." He pushed a lock of hair off my face. "I'm here for you."

He'd always been there for me.

I attempted a smile but failed miserably. He settled back against the seat and pulled me into him.

"Cole, can you get in touch with her?" I asked, my voice cracking around each word, as though the knife had damaged my vocal cords.

He scrutinized me a long minute before offering, "I can message her from a remote number when I get home. What do you want to know?"

"If she's all right." I wish I'd thought of asking Lucy.

I took my phone out of my pocket and dialed Jeb. His phone didn't even ring, which made me think he'd turned it off. Or maybe he'd tossed it so he couldn't be tracked.

"And if maybe"—I flipped my phone around, then flipped it again—"if maybe she found out how they're planning on using the Sillin."

He nodded.

Everything had gone from bad to shit so quickly, and yet, I feared we hadn't reached rock bottom.

Soon, Cole was pulling in next to the warehouse. "I'll call you if I get news."

"Okay," I said, scooting out after August. As Cole drove off, August wrapped his arm around my waist, and together, we walked toward his front door.

He punched in his code, and the door beeped open. After he entered, he let go of me and paced while I turned the lights on.

"Let's go away. You and me," he said suddenly. "We can leave tonight."

"August, I can't leave."

"So you want to see Liam die?"

I swallowed. "Liam won't die."

"Ness—"

"He won't. He's stronger than you give him credit for."

"Strength won't help him if she's cheating!"

"Don't yell, August."

He dropped into his armchair and cradled his head between his large, blood-soaked hands. "I'm sorry," he whispered. "I'm sorry."

I went over to him and placed my palm on his hunched spine. He sighed, long and hard, and then he pulled me into his lap and hugged me, burying his face against my collarbone. After several quiet minutes, he pulled away and leveled his gaze on my injured neck. I probably looked like I'd escaped from the set of a slasher film.

"Bet this wasn't quite how you pictured our romantic lakeside evening going," I said, curling my fingers around the nape of his neck.

He grunted, and I flicked him. Although it brought a little light to his eyes, it wasn't nearly enough to disperse the shadows teeming in them.

I stood up and extended my hand. "Come on. Let's go wash away all this blood."

Exhaling raggedly, he took my hand and rose. On the way to the bathroom, he said, "We need to burn our clothes."

Right. Aidan's blood was all over them.

August yanked off his shirt, jeans, and briefs, and dumped everything in the kitchen sink. While I unclipped my overalls and pulled off my crop top, he walked over to the wall and used a pole to open two of the hopper windows.

Even though it was probably not the time to appreciate his naked body, I couldn't help myself from taking him in.

"Your underwear too," he said, coming back toward me.

"My underwear?"

"It'll smell like smoke."

Nibbling my lip, I lowered my thong to the ground, then scooped it up and added it to the soiled pile. He grabbed a bottle of vodka from his freezer, doused the fabric, then struck a match and tossed it in. Flames burst to life and spread, consuming the last pieces of the terrible night.

"Go," he said. "I'll keep an eye on the fire until it burns out."

Hoping the spectacle would rid him of his lingering anguish, I went into the bathroom and stepped inside the enormous shower.

Hot water spurted out of the rain-shower nozzle, raced down my hair and over my skin, dragging away the blood and smoke. I closed my eyes and didn't move for a long moment. How had we gone from playing with paint to arson?

I touched my sides, felt the white paint that had dried there. Large fingers pressed mine away and curved around my ribs. I opened my eyes but didn't turn. August reached around me for a bar of green soap that he dragged over my body. He worked the woodsy sandalwood into a lather over my collarbone and shoulders. When his palm coasted up my neck, I cringed, and he gentled his touch. Without saying a single word, he dragged the slick bar over my breasts, then over my stomach, and circled his calloused palm over my soapy skin.

When his hands drifted lower, I rested my cheek against his shoulder and closed my eyes again. Sensations rose like steam, curling through my veins, warming my blood, billowing through my stomach, and expanding in my chest. I relaxed against August's solid chest, my breathing slowing as his fingers moved against me. When his mouth nipped mine, I dragged my heavy lids up and crooked my neck.

The sable and green eddied as he stared at me, watching . . . waiting.

Pressure built and swelled everywhere, and then I was soaring over a cliff into a lake full of moon and stars, the wondrous sensation buffing away the horror of my strange world.

As my body softened, as my moans quieted, he spun me in his arms, my wet skin sliding like silk against his. I hooked my hands around his bent neck and pushed onto my tiptoes, guiding his mouth to mine.

Our kiss was gentle at first, but soon his lips crushed mine, devouring me the same way the flames had devoured one monstrous Creek.

CHAPTER 43

The shower had rid August of a layer of stress, which wasn't to say he was calm. He was anything but. His upheaval worsened when my phone rang, and Liam's name appeared on the screen.

I answered the call on speakerphone and sat down on the couch. August wound his arm around me and pulled me close.

There was rustling, as though Liam were taking off his jacket. "I just came back from the inn."

"And?" I asked.

"And the duel will take place tomorrow evening."

August's fingers flexed on my waist. "She didn't believe it was Lucy?"

For a moment, Liam didn't answer, as though he hadn't expected me to have company. "Oh, no. She believed it, Watt. Apparently Lori repeatedly warned her mom that Lucy was ill-intentioned."

I blinked. "Then why are we fighting them tomorrow?"

"Because she asked me to call Jeb so he would bring Lucy in, and I refused to sacrifice your aunt."

I didn't say anything.

Something thumped on his end of the line. A shoe, maybe. "Would you rather I make Jeb bring her in?"

"No." Lucy was far from my favorite person, but her courage to

248

avenge her son had changed my opinion of her. Besides, I couldn't do that to Jeb. A divorce surely hadn't erased years of tenderness and love.

Liam sighed. "That's what I thought. Come over in the morning so we can figure out how to win this damn fight."

"Want me to come over now?" Trepidation distorted the sound of my voice.

"No. I need to think."

"Try to sleep," I whispered.

"You, too."

I didn't think I could sleep. I didn't think Liam could either.

"I'm sorry it took so long for your dad to be avenged, Ness," Liam said. "I'm sorry I was too much of a coward to do it myself."

I swallowed down the ball of emotion rising in my throat. "You're not a coward."

He let out a rattling breath.

"Liam, when you were at the inn, did you see Sarah?" I asked.

"No."

Worry suspended my breaths for a few heartbeats. "Did you ask them about our Sillin?"

"I did. They said they took what was theirs."

"They took more—"

"I was in no position to negotiate!"

His tone made guilt well up inside me.

"I'll see you tomorrow," he said, a tad less gruffly, and then he hung up.

August pressed his mouth against my temple. Then, suddenly, he rose and pulled me up. "Go into the kitchen."

I frowned. "What? Why?"

"Because I have an idea."

I sniffled. "Okay."

While I walked toward one end of the apartment, he went to stand by the other.

"I'm going to test my reach," he said.

My eyebrows jolted up, and then I gasped as my body jerked forward. I caught myself on the island. "That was really . . . *strong*."

His eyes gleamed as he strode toward the front door and extended his hand. "Let's try it in the warehouse."

The T-shirt I'd borrowed from his closet twisted against the tops of my bare thighs as I followed him into the night and into the cavernous building that smelled of sawdust and wood varnish and home.

After turning on a row of industrial lights, he said, "Stay here," then padded down one of the aisles. When he reached the farthest shelving unit, he turned and concentrated on me.

A moment later, I felt a hard tug that had my bare feet shuffling over the cool concrete. Unlike in the apartment, he didn't let go of his hold. He reeled me in.

"Dig your heels in, Ness. I want to see how much strength I can exert."

"I *am* digging my heels in," I called out.

He pulled my body halfway across the warehouse before slackening his magical grip, and then he strode toward me, a new spring in his step.

"At least I can keep you safe tomorrow." He locked his arms around my waist and rested his forehead against mine. "This way, you can concentrate on keeping Liam safe."

My thundering pulse beat against the delicate, knitted skin of my neck as his hope enveloped me.

"Good thing I desire you so much, huh?" Even though his tone was light and no blame limned his words, I couldn't help but sense his underlying sadness.

He still believed I didn't reciprocate the intensity of his feelings.

After the duel . . . once my mind was clear and my heart didn't beat with trepidation . . . I'd show him just how much *I* desired him.

CHAPTER 44

August and I spent the night lying in his bed, talking about the past, about the present, but not about the future. Whenever he'd venture into the unknown territory of the days ahead, I'd steer the conversation back to the here and now.

I feared what the next few hours would bring.

I feared all it might change.

At some point, I drifted, but a nightmare had me springing awake with a gasp.

August's heavy arm anchored me to the warm mattress. When I shivered, he pulled me closer and whispered, "You're safe, Dimples."

Dimples . . . I no longer minded when he called me by his favorite nickname. Perhaps it was the alluring tone with which he spoke the word, or perhaps it was because I no longer doubted how deeply he craved me.

I turned in his arms. "I should get up. I need clothes. And my car."

August combed a lock of hair off my forehead.

"Your truck's at my house, too." *Shoot.*

"How about you relax here while I go get one of our cars?"

"*Relax?*" I snorted.

He flicked the tip of my nose.

"Hey," I chided him.

Smiling, he kissed the spot he'd flicked. "You grunted."

"You did just tell me to relax."

Meaning to be reassuring, he said, "It'll be over soon."

It was the absolute opposite of comforting. His words made my stomach writhe with more nerves; they made my heart thump with more anguish.

"We should really get going," I said, scooting out from underneath his arm to crawl off the bed and down the ladder. "Can I borrow a pair of boxers? I feel a little naked."

He climbed down the ladder slowly, every muscle in his back roiling alluringly. I'd put on muscle in the past two and a half weeks, but I had nothing on August. Not that I wanted his body. Well, I did, just not—What was I rambling on about?

I added a pair of boxers underneath the T-shirt that tented around my body, then gathered my phone and bag while he got dressed in his fatigues and an oatmeal Henley that hugged his upper body.

He leaned over and kissed me. I savored the sweet interlude, sensing that once I walked out August's front door, there would be no more sweetness to this day.

He called a cab, which took us back to my house. As the cab bumped up my cracked driveway, I thought about how I needed to get the road fixed, and then I stopped thinking about asphalt and seized up. I must've gasped because August's attention jerked off the wad of cash he'd taken out of his pocket to pay for our ride. He trailed my line of sight, his jaw hardening when he saw what I was looking at.

"Whoa. Wild party?" the cabby asked.

Stuffing a bill into the driver's hand, August kicked the door open and got out. "Yeah," he answered gruffly.

When I still hadn't moved, he leaned over to pluck the fingers I'd balled into a hard fist and towed me out. I stumbled, because my joints had locked as tight as my knuckles.

Last night, in our haste, we'd left the front door wide open, and someone—more than one person from the looks of it—had let themselves in.

Anger fired through me. I ripped my hand from August's and stalked inside my home. Smells assaulted me—sweet metal, charred dust, sour urine. The white walls had been smeared in blood—deer blood, from the loamy odor of it—and acrid black ash. Puddles of ochre piss glistened on the plastic tarp and browned the baseboards August had so painstakingly painted.

This was payback for Aidan's death. The Creeks must've seen my uncle working on the house and assumed it was his and Lucy's.

"I will *kill* whoever did this," I whispered.

I started down the hallway to inspect the extent of the destruction, but August caught my arm and held me back. "Let's go."

"I want to see—"

"You've seen enough. Let's go." When I didn't move, he added, "Now."

Gritting my teeth, I turned around and headed back out of my stinking kingdom.

How. Dare. They.

"I'll follow you in my—" He froze by the truck's bed.

Two eviscerated deer carcasses haloed by black flies had been heaped inside. A slew of words that would make his mother's curse jar overflow spewed from his mouth. He unlatched the tailgate, then seized the hooves of one creature and yanked hard. The animal landed on the grass with an awful thud. As he wrenched the second one out, I peered through the windows of his car.

"August!" I gasped.

Something viscous oozed down the backrest and dripped on the seat that was covered in animal intestines.

His eyes turned a murderous shade of black. "Check your car," he said, his voice as sharp as the knife blade Aidan had held against my throat yesterday.

I sprang toward my silver SUV. Thankfully the doors were all locked, and the vandals hadn't shattered any windows, but they'd raked their claws through the silver paint, leaving grooves *everywhere.*

"Those fucking Creeks," August growled from behind me.

We stared at the destruction a moment longer, and then he snatched my palm tree keychain and opened the passenger door for me.

He didn't say anything as he drove too quickly down the quiet

Boulder streets toward my apartment. Fear that it, too, had been defaced made me wring the life out of the grab handle.

The second I stepped over the threshold, I exhaled the breath I'd been holding since leaving my house. August walked to the sink and lathered his hands with dish detergent, scrubbing his skin until it turned pink. After almost a minute, he shut the water off and tore the dish cloth hanging on the oven handle.

"I'll fix your house." His eyes were animated with the same ferocity I'd spied last night when Aidan held me hostage.

I wanted to tell August he didn't need to do that, that I'd do it myself, but nausea roiled in my stomach at the memory of the blood and piss, so I clamped my lips shut. As he lifted his cell phone to his ear, I went to change into shorts, a tank top, and my black hoodie. I took off my necklace and buried it in my underwear drawer, then stuffed my feet inside my scuffed boots. Even though we'd sprayed our shoes with air freshener last night to camouflage any lingering smells, I thought it safer to wear some that hadn't been in contact with blood and smoke.

Suddenly, a horrific thought speared my mind, and I sprinted out of my bedroom. "August!"

He dropped the phone, and it clattered against the floor but didn't break. "What?"

"You need to get out of Boulder!"

His eyes, which had widened with panic, now crimped with confusion.

"They sabotaged your pickup, which means they know you were involved." The words rushed out of my mouth.

His eyebrows pinched closer together, darkening his already murky gaze. "I don't care."

"What if they try to hurt you during the duel? Or after the duel? Or—"

"Sweetheart"—he gripped the back of my neck—"I'm angry but I'm not scared. If anyone should be scared, it should be the people who did this, because, mark my words, I'll find out who was involved." His fingers were hot and unyielding. "Besides, how can you even think I'd run away without you?"

I bit my lip. "Fine, but tonight, during the duel, you need to look out for yourself, or I'm not letting you come."

Smirking, he chucked me under the chin.

"What?" I asked.

"Not letting me come . . ." He *tsk*ed and shook his head. "I respect the hell out of you, Dimples, and I know you're strong, but don't *ever* ask me to stay away or flee. It's insulting."

I crossed my arms. "I didn't mean it as an insult."

He nodded, smirk gone. "I know."

"I'm scared, August."

"I know." Sighing, he pried my arms out of their tight knot. "But don't worry about me. I'll be fine. Everything will be—"

"*Don't!*" My heart jolted into my throat and beat there. "Don't finish that sentence!"

He frowned.

"It never comes true."

Dipping his chin into his neck, he gathered my stiff body in his arms and held me.

Just held me.

And I held him.

Until my heart settled back behind my ribs. Until my pulse quieted. Until my temper appeased and my muscles stopped spasming. Until I was ready to take on the outside world again.

CHAPTER 45

Before going over to Liam's, I called Evelyn because I wanted to see her.

I *needed* to see her.

She told me she was already at the restaurant, prepping for their popular Sunday brunch, so we drove there. While August parked the car, I went inside and straight into the kitchen. I hugged her before even saying *hi*, which wasn't smart of me. Instantly, her pleasure at my visit wilted into concern.

Her all-seeing eyes skipped over all my haggard features. I hadn't bothered improving my appearance with makeup this morning, so I knew I looked part ghost, part zombie, possibly worse than when I'd gone "rock-climbing" on my own, which had been the story fed to Evelyn when I'd been returned to her after the first Alpha trial.

"*Querida*, what is wrong?"

I shrugged. "I didn't sleep well. That's all."

She hunted my face some more, seeking the truth I was holding back.

Did she know about Aidan? Did she know that my uncle was gone? Did she know there would be a duel tonight?

"You do not fool me, Ness Clark. That is *not* all."

From the worry tightening her crimson lips, I guessed Frank hadn't imparted any of those things. I was glad he'd protected her. I hoped he would shield her from the world for the rest of her life in case I wasn't there to do it myself.

The thought made my heart drop to somewhere below my ankles.

Seconds rarely engage, I reminded myself, but then I also reminded myself that I would be facing Justin.

Justin delighted in hurting people.

"It is. I promise." I smiled but then followed the arc of her gaze as it moved to a place above my shoulder.

I glanced over my shoulder. Biting my lip, I turned back toward Evelyn. I hadn't even considered how it would look arriving with August so early on a Sunday morning.

On any morning, for that matter.

I hesitated to lie and tell her we were on our way to work on my house, but I didn't want to risk her coming there after her shift.

"Morning, Mrs. Lopez." He didn't touch me, but his body heated my taut spine.

Without taking her eyes off mine, she said, "Good morning, August."

Her sous-chef glanced our way, a giant knife rocking rhythmically against a white onion, dicing the slimy flesh into tiny little squares that flecked the air with stinging fumes.

Even though Evelyn had given me her blessing two nights ago, I sensed it would take her a little more time to accept August and me together. "There is a waitlist for the brunch, but I am sure I could find you two a table."

I smiled. "We can't do brunch today. I just came by to say hi."

Her thin eyebrows writhed a few times. "Dinner then? Tonight. At the house. I would like"—she fixed her eyes on August again—"I would like to get to know the man my baby girl has decided to let into her heart."

God only knew in what state we'd be tonight. I slipped my pinky's fingernail between my lips and chewed on the edge of it. "Tomorrow would be better. The restaurant's closed on Monday nights too, right?"

She nodded. "Before you leave, Trent's wife wanted very much to meet you. She is in the dining room. Will you go out there and introduce yourself, please?"

I took my pinky out of my mouth. "Sure." I kissed her cheek and then turned to leave.

When August started after me, Evelyn called him back. "Can I speak to you a moment longer, August?"

I cringed, but August squeezed my arm in reassurance. I mouthed, *good luck*, which kicked up one side of his mouth.

There were three women in the dining room. One of them had served us the night of my birthday, so I assumed she wasn't Trent's wife.

"Hi, I'm looking for—" I racked my brain for the family name but wasn't sure if I even knew it, so I went with: "Trent's wife?"

The waitress tipped her head toward a woman clipping the stems of poppies on the mirrored bar.

"Thank you," I whispered as I traipsed toward the blonde with a sharp bob cut. "Hi. I'm Ness. Evelyn's granddaughter."

The woman twirled away from her flowery spread and extended her hand. "Ness!"

I blinked as she smiled at me.

When I still hadn't taken her outstretched hand—because shock had made me forget my manners—she said, "It's not contagious. I promise."

I jolted my hand into hers and shook it. "I'm sorry. It's not— What, *um* . . . how come . . .?"

"My lips are blue and my nails purple?" Her smile was still intact. "I have something called Argyria, which is sort of ironic considering the name of my restaurant."

I slipped my hand out of hers and gripped the crossbody strap of my bag.

"Anyway, it's my dentist's fault. He put all these silver fillings in my molars . . . I won't bore you with the details, but know that it looks way worse than it is. I'm Molly, by the way."

I tried to snap my jaw shut, but it wouldn't close. "*I'msorryI'm-staring*," I said in a single breath.

"It's okay, honey. A lot of people do. Besides, if it truly bothered me, I'd wear makeup."

"I know this woman who has the same thing," I blurted out. "At least, I think it's the same thing. She told me it was a birthmark."

"Yeah, some people are a little embarrassed by the condition."

She fingered one of the poppies' fuzzy stems. "Tell her that if she needs someone to talk to, she can find me here most days. Especially now that the kids are back in school." She gave me one last smile. "I should get these flowers into water before they wilt. It was a pleasure to make your acquaintance, and thank you again for lending us your grandmother. She is a godsend."

"Thank *you*," I said. And I didn't mean for employing Evelyn— even though I *was* grateful for that—but for giving me the answer to a question which had tormented me for the past two and a half weeks.

My speculations were accurate—Cassandra Morgan *had* poisoned Julian. But not with Sillin. With silver! I wasn't sure yet how her blood could contain the toxic metal without killing her, but it didn't matter.

We could call the duel off now that I had proof she was cheating.

As Molly turned back toward her flowers, August came out of the kitchen.

I rushed to him and threw my arms around his neck, waves of relief coursing through me, breaking the stress that had devoured me since Liam's phone call.

"Were you worried I wouldn't survive?" August asked, a lilt to his voice. "It *was* a close call."

Smiling, I pressed away from him, crooked my head up, and whispered, "I know how she did it."

A groove appeared between his eyebrows. "We're not talking about Evelyn now, are we?"

I shook my head. "I'll explain everything on the drive over to Liam's."

CHAPTER 46

A ugust whipped his eyes off the road to stare at me. "Silver? In her blood?"

"It's called Argyria." I gasped as a memory collided into my brain. "Trent's mother told me about it. The day I met her in the bank."

To think I'd known all along...

I watched the dashboard without seeing it. Thank God I wasn't at the wheel of the car; I would've been incapable of staying on the road.

"How can she have silver in her blood, yet still be alive?" he asked.

Something niggled at me. What was it?

I spun toward him as my synapses fired off a hypothesis. "After Dad was shot, I was given Sillin because I'd licked his gunshot wound." Bile rose in the back of my throat. "What if that's why she needs Sillin? To neutralize the silver."

His brows rose. "Still doesn't explain how she can shift."

"Does silver impair shifting?"

"No, but Sillin does."

"You don't think that she's somehow figured out a dose that cancels each substance out?"

"We'd have to ask Greg. Although I'm not sure he'd even know."

I rested my head back and expelled a sigh, which made August reach over the center console and pluck my restless fingers off the latch on my bag.

To think of something else for a short while, I asked, "What did Evelyn want?"

"She asked me the real reason you'd stopped by."

"You didn't tell her, did you?"

"No. I told her you came to check whether she was truly okay with *us* being together."

"I'm sorry you had to lie."

He squeezed my fingers. "Some lies are kinder than some truths."

As we turned down Liam's driveway, I asked, "Is your dad home?"

"Not yet. He's coming back today."

Through the picture window, I spotted Liam sitting on his couch. Cole, Matt, and Lucas were there too. I was glad Liam wasn't alone. I didn't hear any human heartbeats, so I guessed Tamara wasn't around.

I started to disengage my fingers from August's, but he held on to them.

I smiled at him. "Can't get out of the car if I'm holding your hand."

"I'm worried what'll happen once I let go."

"Once you let go?"

His gaze shifted toward Liam.

Oh. "I'm yours, August."

"Say it again," he whispered, his tone an octave deeper.

"I'm yours." I leaned over and kissed him, sensing several sets of eyes on us.

My promise combined with the kiss loosened his fingers but didn't do much to ease the tension in his shoulders.

Liam's front door was open. As I strutted inside, all eyes turned to me. Probably because I was giving off *way-too-cheery* vibes.

Lucas's scarred eyebrow hiked up. "How many bowls of Lucky Charms did you ingest this morning?"

I rolled my eyes and then announced, "I know how Cassandra killed Julian!" I said it so loudly Morgan herself probably heard me all the way back at the inn.

Liam, who'd been sitting a little hunched, straightened.

"She's been poisoning herself with silver."

The silence that ensued was deafening.

"Forget the Lucky Charms, what the fuck have you been smoking?" Lucas asked.

I shot him a genial scowl. "What she has on her mouth isn't a birthmark. Silver poisoning causes lips and nails to turn blue." They all stared at me as though I'd morphed into a squirrel.

"That's impossible, Clark," Lucas said. "Silver kills us."

"Not if you take Sillin to balance it out," I countered, feeling more and more certain about my theory.

"If she's ingesting Sillin, then there's no way she can shift," Cole said.

Their mood was seriously starting to put a damper on mine. "Liam, remember her story about the toxic waste poisoning? What if the toxin was silver? What if she somehow built an immunity to it? Would that be possible?"

"What toxic waste poisoning?" August asked. The first words he'd uttered since stepping inside Liam's house. He was leaning against a wall, long sleeves pushed up to his elbows, arms crossed in front of his chest.

Lucas tipped his head in my direction. "The day she went to have tea at the inn with Morgan—"

August's expression darkened. "You went to the inn?"

"Yes, but not for a tea party." This time, there was nothing amiable about the scowl I shot Lucas. "I went to talk to her about canceling the duel, which she refused. And then she filled me in on her pack's history. She told me that what decimated the original Creeks was their water source. Apparently, it was polluted." I perked up again as an idea materialized. "Is there a way to see the topography of their old territory? Maybe there's a mine, or a news article."

"Cole?" Liam said. "Can you look it up?"

Cole nodded and went to take a seat at the game table where a laptop was already powered on. As he clicked away on the keypad, I walked over to him.

"Can you shift?" Liam's voice was taut and low.

I glanced over my shoulder.

"No," August said.

"When did you do the injection again?"

"Nine days ago."

"Have you tried shifting this morning?"

"Yes. It didn't work."

"Show me."

"Why?" Tendons writhed beneath the skin of his forearms. "You think I'm lying?"

A nerve ticked in Liam's jaw. "Greg will be over soon. He can test your blood to see how much Sillin's left."

Wishing those two could bury the hatchet, I sighed and returned my attention to Cole's computer screen.

"So . . . anything?" Matt asked, slinking toward me as though to move as far away as possible from Liam and August.

Windows were popping open on the computer, one over the other, and then a map appeared. Cole zoomed in, then clicked on something that turned the flat map 3-dimensional.

He squinted at the screen before leaning back in his chair and clucking his tongue. "So Ness is a little genius."

My skin prickled. "There's a mine?"

"There's a mine. A silver mine. And a bunch of class action suits filed to have it shut down by a certain Henry Morgan."

"Was that Cassandra's father?"

"Uncle." Liam's breath burst against my temple.

So concentrated on the screen, I hadn't heard him come up behind me.

"He was the Creek Alpha at the time," Lucas explained.

I turned toward my Alpha, goose bumps scattering over my arms from the thrill of our discovery. "Liam, you realize this means we can call the duel off?"

His eyes gleamed as brightly as his teeth, which were on full display.

His smile unsettled me. "What?"

"Babe, we're not calling it off. Thanks to you, we now know how to defeat her."

My stomach hardened like a fist. "Thanks to me, we know how she cheated. We have no clue how to beat her."

"Of course we do. By not getting any of her silver-tainted

blood in us." Liam backed up and started pacing the cowhide rug. "Julian bit her. That was the beginning of his end. I won't bite her."

I gasped, not okay at all with the turn of events. "How are you going to kill her if you don't bite her?"

"Claws. I'll use my claws."

"What if she wounds you and rubs her blood into your wound?"

"I heal fast."

"You said wounds inflicted by Alphas take longer to heal," I sputtered.

"I'll make sure to keep away until my skin seals shut. Besides, you saw her. She's slow and not particularly strong." He stopped pacing, beelined toward me, and then scooped me up and spun me. "Fuck, Ness, we got this."

When he set me down, my head spun, but not only from the sudden movement. It spun from dread. There were still so many risks . . . And then, because having a headache wasn't bad enough, my navel began to burn as though someone were jabbing it with a fiery poker.

August pushed off the wall and shot toward Liam. "You're a selfish prick, Kolane."

Liam wrenched his shoulders back and got into August's face. "A selfish prick?"

"You think you got this, but what if you don't? You won't be the only one in that ring tonight."

"Seconds don't engage," Liam spat out.

"Have you fucking met Morgan's Second?" August snapped.

I squeezed myself between both males and pushed them away from each other. "Stop it. Both of you."

"August is right, Liam," Matt said. "Justin's a sick fuck."

"We know what their edge is," Liam exclaimed. "We're going to beat them at their own game."

I slid my hands off their battering chests and whirled to face Liam. "Stop calling it a game. It's not!"

His excitement dimmed. *Finally!*

"It was a manner of speaking, Ness."

"Was it? Because if memory serves me, you called it a game the day we signed up."

His voice lowered, and more light left his eyes. "I hadn't been referring to the duel then."

August's chest brushed up against my shoulder blades.

I stared long and hard at Liam. "None of it was ever a game to me, all right?"

"I'll take her place," August said. "I'll be your Second."

"No!" I spun around.

"Don't believe she can hold her own out there, Watt?" Liam asked.

August's gaze sharpened on Liam. "This has nothing to do with what I think of Ness," he said in a chillingly low voice, "and everything to do with what I think of Justin."

"*I* signed up for this. *I'll* see it through." I turned back around. "If I have to," I added. "I still think we should call them up on their cheating and chase them off our land."

"They own the inn and all the Pine territory," Liam said, eyes locked on August's, "so chasing them off our land won't get them out of Boulder."

Pine territory! "Cole, did you get in touch with Sarah?"

"No, but Liam received a message from Avery."

"Avery?" I asked.

"The Rivers' contact," Cole said.

"I remember who he is," I said. "I meant, why did he send us a message?"

"Because he heard Alex Morgan talk about *having put the two-timing Pine bitch in her place*, and he believes Alex is talking about Sarah since he's seen them together," Liam said.

Dread curled through me. "In her place?"

"I don't know what that means," Liam said. "He doesn't either, but he's trying to find out."

Fear for Sarah superseded everything else in that moment. I pressed a fist against my mouth. "Oh my God."

Lucas careened toward the door. "I can track her smell."

"No," Liam said. "We stay put. Avery's there. He said he's working on it, and I trust he is."

My head jerked back. "He didn't even want to get involved, yet you trust he's helping us?"

"People change their minds all the time." When his eyes lifted to August, I wondered if Liam was talking about Avery or about me.

A thought struck me. However much I wanted to call this duel off, I couldn't abandon Sarah to the Morgans. But Liam couldn't turn the Creeks into Boulders without ingesting Cassandra's heart. "Let's say we go through with the duel, and you win—"

"I will win."

His conviction made me purse my lips. It also made August's pulse spike and hammer my tight spine.

"Have a little faith in me, Ness."

"Okay. Fine. What happens after you win? How exactly are you planning on eating her heart?"

A corner of his mouth curled. "With my teeth."

I rolled my eyes. "Don't be dense. If her blood's full of silver, then her heart is too."

"Little Wolf's right," Matt said.

"I'll have it injected with Sillin. Or I'll inject myself with Sillin. Greg would know. You brought it?"

I pulled the tablets out of my bag just as the front door opened and Greg stepped in.

Liam smirked. "Look at that. I speak his name and he appears. We were just talking about you."

Surprise crinkled the fine lines around the doctor's eyes. Or maybe it was concern. "And what were you discussing?"

"We were discussing how you're going to purge a heart of silver without purging it of blood. You know, so I can eat it."

CHAPTER 47

Greg scrutinized the screen of the portable device in which he'd just inserted a drop of August's blood. "Down by a little more than a half. You should be Sillin-free by the next full moon."

Considering the duel was tonight, it was a good thing I hadn't been the guinea-pig in the experiment.

"Can you shift at all?" Greg asked, putting away the handheld machine.

August, who was sitting at the game table between Cole and the doctor, palmed his cropped hair. "No."

"Can you get your claws to come out?"

Studying the ball of cotton he held to the puncture wound on the inside of his elbow, he said, "No."

"Did it affect the mating link?"

August raised his gaze to me. "No."

I was standing by the windowed wall, alternately watching the males behind me and the ones on the other side of the glass. Ever since Greg told Liam that injecting him with a hefty dose of Sillin at the end of the duel—not as hefty as what he'd given August, because we didn't have enough pills left for that—would counteract the silver in Cassandra's blood, Liam was mentally and physically psyching himself up for the duel.

Both he and Matt had shed their clothes and morphed into fur.

For the past half hour, they'd been battling relentlessly. Liam wasn't immune to Matt's blows—he tumbled and winced—but he'd hop back on his paws and give as good as he got.

Better.

But then, they were play-acting.

However violent the fight, it wasn't real.

I lifted my gaze to the miles of swaying pines that separated Liam's property from the Inn, wondering what the Creeks were doing at this exact moment. Vandalizing more of our homes, burying Aidan's ashes, or preparing to face-off with us?

As Lucas came to stand next to me, I hugged my torso. "Sarah got with Alex to help us. She hates him."

He watched Matt catch Liam's hind leg and flip him onto his back.

"How do you feel, by the way?" I asked.

"Fucking relieved."

I couldn't help smiling a little at his answer. "Not about Sarah."

"Oh." A blush streaked his cheeks.

"I meant, since you ran into Alex Morgan's fist."

"Murderous, but otherwise, good."

"For what he did to you or what he might've done to her?"

His eyebrows slanted behind his shaggy, black hair. "Both."

We went back to our silent but companionable observation of Liam and Matt.

At some point, Lucas said, "I know you're worried, but Liam's skilled and quick. Have you ever noticed how fast he moves? Like those vampires in the shows chicks love to watch."

I side-eyed him. "I'm not sure I'm familiar with those shows. Why don't you tell me more about them?"

He started to walk me through the plot of one, but then he caught my dimples excavating my cheeks and stopped.

"Don't worry. I won't tell Sarah about your secret obsession with vampires."

A brighter blush slashed his cheeks. "You're a real pain in my furry ass."

"But surprisingly endearing, right?"

He shot me a look, which was probably supposed to be scathing, if it weren't for his crooked smile. "Surprisingly so."

I knocked my shoulder into his, and his mouth curved a little more.

"You know what's crazy?" I asked after a while.

"I think you should rephrase your question to: do you know what *isn't* crazy?"

"Probably." I bobbed my head. "Anyway, if we win tonight, I'll go from being the only female in my pack to being one of many females."

"Oh, the horror."

I shoved him again. "Watch it, Mason."

He chuckled quietly.

Ness, get out here and shift.

I jumped at Liam's command.

And no getting naked behind closed doors. When I still hadn't moved, he pawed the ground. ***Now.***

Heat spiraled through my body.

"What?" Lucas asked.

"Liam wants me to"—I uncrossed my arms, because coupled with the hoodie and Liam's order, I was getting hot—"join them."

Lucas frowned. "Can't hurt to train a little more."

"That's not—*um* . . ." I pulled on the collar of the hoodie but still couldn't get myself to peel it off.

The black wolf barked, which made me jump, and then he pawed the earth again.

"Go on," Lucas said.

Pressing my palms, which were thankfully a little cold, against my neck, I unglued my soles from the hardwood floors and stalked out the front door. "I said I'd do it tonight, and I will."

Now.

My body felt as though it were impaled on a spit hung over an open fire. "Why?"

The shimmering blue rope that connected me to August tightened as he stepped out of the house, Lucas at his side. At least Cole and Greg hadn't come to watch, not that they couldn't see me through the window.

"Please, Liam—"

You're a werewolf, Ness. Act like one.

I bristled. "Fine." I pulled off the hoodie and tossed it on the ground, then unlaced my boots and kicked them off.

When I reached for the hem of my tank top, August trampled the grass until he stood in front of me. "What are you doing?"

"Acting like a werewolf, apparently," I gritted out, yanking off the top, exposing my bare chest.

August's nostrils flared, and he snapped his head toward Liam. "If I want to stand in front of her, I'll stand in front of her." I guessed Liam had told August to move through the mind-link. "I get that tonight she'll be on her own." He returned his attention to me, his chest all but squashing my bare breasts.

I'd rather have been waxed from muzzle to paw than strip in front of an audience, but Liam was right, I was a shifter, and nudity wasn't taboo in our circle. It was a way of life.

I sighed and splayed my palms on August's pecs to press him away, but it was like trying to displace a block of cement.

"I can do this," I told him.

The green around his irises seemed to glow brighter, as though his wolf was somehow rising to the surface in spite of the Sillin.

I took a step back as I popped the button of my shorts and dropped them. When my thumbs hooked into my underwear, August turned his attention to the others and stared them all down until they looked away.

I shut my eyes, willing the transformation to come quick, realizing full well that tonight I would be expected to stand out there—wherever out there was—in the buff way longer than mere seconds.

It was silly, but when I dropped onto my paws, I felt a little braver by what I'd just accomplished.

A little more ready to face off against Justin.

I trotted toward August and rubbed my cheek on his stiff thigh before glancing into his human face, finding that his features had softened. His fingers slid through my white fur. Once I sensed he was calm, I darted toward my Alpha.

"Nice ass," Lucas said, tossing me a wink. "A little on the skinny side for my taste, but—"

August cast Lucas such a barbed glare that he shut up and raised his palms.

"Calm down there, Watt. No one's stealing your girl. I mean, with that temper . . . *yeesh*. She's all yours."

I smiled on the inside because my rubbery lupine lips weren't engineered for smiles. But then I gasped as I was knocked onto my ass.

Hey, I growled at Liam. *Was that really necessary?*

The minute you're in fur, your attention needs to be on me, Justin, and Morgan. Not on your mate.

My attention wasn't on my mate. It was on Lucas.

Get up, Liam barked.

Huffing, I stood. *You want me to attack you? Or—*

My body skidded sideways as though my black pads had sprouted tiny wheels.

What the hell? Matt yelped, sliding right past me. *How'd you do that, Little Wolf?*

For a moment, both wolves observed me in silence, and then Matt craned his long neck and peered over his shoulder at August who was still planted on the lawn, fingers tapping his thighs.

Fuck . . . Matt said at the same time as Liam asked, *Can one of you please enlighten me as to what just happened?*

As Matt filled Liam in on the mysterious mechanism of mating links, August tugged on the tether again, but not to move my body, just to remind me he was there, watching over me.

That he had my back.

The shimmery blue rope tautened between us. I wrapped an invisible hand around it and prepared to pull back to prove to August it went both ways, but then Liam barked.

I jumped, losing sight of the elusive rope.

How far is his reach? he asked.

Far.

How far?

As long as I'm in his line of sight.

Good. Although his massive body was coiled tight, he sounded genuinely pleased by what he'd just learned.

He must've spoken through the mind-link, because August nodded before returning to the open front door and sidling in next to Lucas.

He's not going to help you out until tonight, Liam said. *In case anyone's watching . . .*

Heart skidding to a halt, my gaze swept over the wooded expanse surrounding us, seeking lambent eyes in the shadows of the great evergreens. I saw none, but did it mean they weren't watching?

Where will the fight take place? I asked Liam, skirting his lunge.

On the lawn of the former Pines' headquarters.

In the maze?

Not in the maze, but next to it.

I didn't like the idea of fighting next to a maze. There was no telling what could leap from the dense shrubs.

Liam pounced on top of my back. *Concentrate, Ness.*

I shoved him off.

As he circled me, surely calculating at which angle to come at me, he added through the mind-link: ***Don't ever rely on another person to keep you safe.***

Was he insinuating that I wouldn't be able to keep him safe or that August wouldn't be able to keep me safe?

I'll try to keep track of you the entire time, but I might not be able to.

His words stilled me. *I* was supposed to keep track of him, not the other way around.

Of course, Matt took advantage of my lapse of attention to barrel straight into me, and none too gently. He apologized, but the impact still stung.

As I straightened and wrung myself out, I pinned Liam with an inflexible stare. *Don't you dare take your eyes off Morgan tonight. Not for a second.*

His yellow irises seemed to ignite at my concern, but then he chuffed and wheeled around. *Matt, again!*

CHAPTER 48

We spent the remainder of the afternoon sitting around Liam's house, discussing everything but the duel. Even Greg stayed. Under Matt's curious gaze, the pack doctor distilled Sillin into three little vials, then aligned and realigned them in his cooler.

After I'd shifted back into skin, Liam made me take a shower in his house, and then he told me to stay away from August. "In case the Creeks aren't aware he's your mate."

When he suggested August leave and meet us at the former Pine HQ, my mate glared and muttered, "Like hell."

So he'd stayed too, alternately clutching the armrest of the couch, glowering at the woods outside, and pacing the lawn while barking on his phone.

About an hour before we had to leave, Liam got a message that made him speak my name very loudly even though I was sitting a couple feet away from him. "Avery."

He pushed his phone into my hands.

AVERY: *Sarah just arrived at her family's former HQ with Alex Morgan. I haven't been able to get her alone, but thought you'd want to know she was here. She looks a little spooked. Hope Alex hasn't hurt her.*

Spooked? Sarah wasn't the type of girl who spooked easily, so Avery stating this had my hackles rising. "She's alive," I said, handing the phone to Lucas who'd stiffened at the mention of Avery's name, "but if you don't kill Alex Morgan tonight, I will."

Either Lucas read the message slowly, or he read it a few times, because he scrutinized the screen a long time.

My hatred fueled my mounting adrenaline. By the time Liam rose from the couch and announced that it was time, I was extremely ready to get out there.

"Ready when you are, boss," Lucas said, jingling Liam's car keys.

Liam nodded to his black SUV. "Ness, you ride with us."

I didn't care who I rode with as long as they got me there fast so I could ascertain that my friend was truly all right. I opened the door to the backseat and got in. Instead of getting in the front, Liam climbed in the back with me.

When August opened the passenger side door, Liam said, "Not a good idea, Watt."

"I won't touch her."

Liam narrowed his eyes. "Do you want the Creeks to make you leave the dueling ring?"

Heat erupted behind my navel as August's gaze found mine. Even though it seemed to take everything within him to back away, he heeded Liam's words and headed to Cole's car with Greg.

Matt hopped up front, and then Lucas careened down the driveway. I watched the dark world unfurl past my window. At some point, I asked Matt to shut off the AC. My bones were so cold I thought they might not thaw out in time for the duel.

"Did you speak to Tamara today?" I asked Liam as a beat-heavy song came to an end and another began.

He glanced away from his window. "I sent her a message."

"Does she know what's happening tonight?"

"I told her I'd call her later. And that if I didn't, the pack would take care of her."

My breathing stuttered.

Liam leaned over and patted my knee. "I'll be calling her later."

I tried to return his smile but couldn't. I went back to staring at the stars blooming like baby's-breath in the purpling sky. I wondered if my parents were somewhere among them, watching over me, but that line of thinking turned even more painful than contemplating the duel.

As we drove, Liam went through the rules again. They'd been drilled so many times inside my skull that I knew them by heart. Still, I paid attention.

"Your main purpose is to referee the fight, not to get involved. When you inspect Cassandra tonight, don't linger on her lips or nails. We're not looking at calling her out on foul play. If Justin attacks you *or* me, you're allowed to strike back."

"And if Cassandra attacks me?"

His expression became more cutting than a knife point. "If Cassandra attacks you, she'll regret it for the rest of her very short life."

"I'm serious. What happens if she does? Can I kill her, or does it have to be you?"

"If she attacks first, then you're allowed to retaliate." He reached across the backseat, collected my hand, and squeezed it reassuringly. "But it won't come to that."

For three entire songs, he was quiet. We were all quiet.

When the ten-foot metal fence that screened off the Pines' former property came into view, I shivered. And then I shivered harder when Lucas slid the car through the open gate. The white stone headquarters appeared like a mirage at the end of the cedar-lined alley, its staircase darkened by bodies. It seemed like every man and boy in our pack had come.

My heart began to beat a rhythm more hectic than the one blaring out of the SUV's speakers.

Liam squeezed my hand to garner my attention. "Ness, if I fall tonight, you are not to challenge her, understood?"

I blinked as emotion rushed into my eyes. And then I squeezed his fingers back. "The day I signed up to be your Second, you said you wanted my admiration. Well, you'll get it, but not if you don't get back up."

A gentle smile settled over his lips, and then he squeezed my hand one last time before letting go and exiting the car. The pack swarmed him, whispering words of encouragement. I hopped out after Liam, and Matt and Lucas came to stand at my sides like two giant bookends.

I looked for August, but Cole's car hadn't pulled up yet. Hadn't they been right behind us? Had they stopped at a red light? Or missed a turn?

"You look a bit green, Little Wolf."

I tried to feel out the distance using the tether, but my stomach was in shambles. "Can you call your brother, Matt?"

I wasn't looking to stress him out, but my quiet plea had him craning his neck toward the long driveway.

He all but tore the seams off his shorts pocket in search of his phone as we climbed up the stairs and entered the buffed stone atrium. "He's not answering."

"I'll try August," Lucas said, taking out his own phone. "Matt, call Greg."

As we descended the staircase, I watched the crowd milling beyond the French doors along the sharp hedges of the maze. The slender moon crescent cast an eerie glow over the land and the dueling ring that stretched from the maze to the stone terrace.

"Did you reach them?" I asked, returning my gaze to Matt.

He shook his head.

Liam had gone down the terrace steps, but one look at my pallid cheeks had him lumbering back up. "What's going on?"

"We can't reach Greg, Cole, *or* August," Lucas said quietly, darting a glance at the assembled Creeks below who were all—and I mean, *all*—staring at us.

"Can you sense them?" I asked Liam hopefully.

He closed his eyes. After a while, he said, "They're a couple miles out but approaching fast."

A breath whispered through my lips just as someone spoke my name. I turned around to find Frank.

He hugged me, cinching my rigid body. "You go on out there and show them what Boulder females are made of, okay?" He rubbed his bristly jaw against my temple, marking me with his scent in a show of affection.

Heels resonated in the quiet headquarters. I pulled away and peered past Frank, praying I'd see August or Sarah, but found my friend's mother and sister-in-law instead. They strode toward the terrace, arms locked together.

"We believe," Margaux whispered.

They believed what? In us? That we'd win?

No other footfalls disrupted the silence; no car tires crunched the pebbled driveway.

"Boulders, it's mighty impolite to keep your hosts waitin'." Cassandra's voice bellowed from the center of the torch-lit field.

Liam lifted his gaze to mine. *They're coming, Ness.*

I hoped he was saying this because he felt them approach through the blood-link and not as some inane reassurance.

He tipped his head toward the garden. In perfect synchronicity, we walked down the stairs. Memories of another time flashed through my mind—Liam, lip bleeding, yelling for me to come home with him while two Pines shackled his wrists.

I didn't like that memory. There'd been too much hurt in Liam's eyes that night, hurt I'd put there.

I realized then that what had broken Liam and me wasn't Tamara or my mating link. What had broken us was that we'd spent more time fighting each other than fighting alongside one another.

They're getting closer.

The words whispered into my mind made my skin buzz with renewed hope. I became acutely aware of the tether which swelled and effervesced with something dark and sour.

"Something's wrong," I whispered to Liam.

Liam frowned, zeroing in on the ring of shifters and then on Cassandra, whose blue lips twitched with a smile.

Remembering her confession, I placed my palm in front of my mouth before murmuring, "With August. He's angry. Really angry."

A mane of wild blonde curls caught my attention in the first line of shifters. Sarah stood directly ahead of us, her hand clutched in Alex's, her eyes glistening as though she were crying. Was he hurting her, or were her tears for us? Had she found out something else but not found a way to relay the information?

Suddenly, she gasped, and her eyes rounded as they set on a spot over my head.

I whirled around.

August, Cole, and Greg burst through the open veranda doors, sweat glossing their flushed cheeks and bruises marbling their jaws. Blood had seeped into the collar of Cole's gray T-shirt and speckled the oatmeal fabric of August's torn Henley.

I started in their direction, but Liam clapped his hand over my forearm.

Don't. They're fine. They're here.

"They're not fine," I growled. Then to Cassandra, I yelled, "What did you do to them?"

"Me? I'm a werewolf, honey, not a magician. I've been here waitin' the whole time. I didn't do nothin' to these men."

But someone had.

I caught Justin exchanging a loaded glance with Alex Morgan. *Of course . . .*

I searched my intended's gaze for a hint of what had happened, but all of his features were ironed too tight to read anything besides absolute fury.

I noticed Greg's empty fingers balling and uncurling at his sides at the same time as Liam.

They took our Sillin, his voice sputtered inside my skull.

That was why they'd been attacked . . . Not to keep August away, but to keep the drug away.

Doesn't matter.

Didn't it? Could he eat her heart without a Sillin injection?

"For the love of the Wolf God, could we please begin?" Cassandra asked.

"By all means"—Liam yanked off his black V-neck and tossed it to the ground—"let's get this over with."

CHAPTER 49

Liam and Cassandra stood naked, shoulders squared, spines taut, muscles twitching. Justin had already shed his clothes, but I hadn't. I'd take them off at the last minute.

As I circled the giant Creek Alpha, pretending to inspect her body, she said, "You're a ruthless little thing, aren't you?"

"Wanting what's right doesn't make me ruthless."

"*What's right?*" Her glacial blue eyes, mere slits behind her gummy lids, thinned even more. "Righteous people possess virtue. You lost yours this weekend."

Alarm straightened my vertebrae. Had she spied on August and me? Or could she smell him—

"And don't you bother convincin' me it was all your aunt's doing. I know she had help, and who better than a girl famished for revenge?"

She was talking about Aidan, not August. I tried not to let my relief show, repressing it as best I could.

"Or maybe it was my cousin's ex-wife who aided your aunt?"

That snapped something in me. "Evelyn had *nothing* to do with Aidan's death."

"And how would you know, since you weren't *there?*"

She's trying to get under your skin. The intensity of Liam's voice had me flinching. ***Finish the inspection and return to me.***

Cassandra raised a stealthy smile. "I believe it's her night off from that fancy new job of hers . . . Too bad Frank decided to attend the duel."

My breaths congealed inside my lungs. "Are you trying to get me to kill you before the duel begins?"

Ness!

I started to turn, but spun right back to face the black-hearted woman. "The first time I heard about the female Alpha who brought the largest pack to their knees, I was awestruck. Proud that a woman had risen so high. But now that I've met you and understand how you got to the top, I'm ashamed."

Her blue lips writhed as though she were chewing on something particularly unsavory. Even though I wasn't the only one who'd fallen for her birthmark lie, it incensed me to have been so naïve.

"How I got to the top? You mean by fightin'? We all got our techniques, but seducin' men to get to the top wasn't for me." Her eyes glinted maliciously. "To each her own."

Anger bolted my bones. What man had I seduced? Was she talking about when she'd sent me to Heath, posing as an escort? Or did her barb have to do with Liam? Did she think he and I were—

"Ness!" This time, Liam roared my name out loud.

I jerked around. "She passes my inspection," I muttered, my voice crackling through the starlit expanse.

"And Kolane passes my inspection," Justin said, crossing back over toward his Alpha, leering at me. "Time to take those clothes off, Ness."

I glowered at Justin as I stalked to the perimeter of the ring, yanking off my hoodie and lobbing it at Matt. He caught it.

As I closed in on him, fingers trembling on the bottom of my tank top, I whispered, "Tell Frank to go home."

Matt's pale eyebrows pinched together.

"Evelyn . . ." Her name came out hushed but clear.

As I handed him my top, he nodded. "I'll tell him."

A howl pierced the night. I looked over my shoulder to find Cassandra's light-brown wolf edged in pale moonlight.

"I'll take care of it. Now, go on out there, Little Wolf, and crush them, 'cause that's what Boulders do. We roll and we crush."

I could feel the sting of eyes on my spine as I dropped my shorts and underwear, but I didn't care. I was too infuriated to care.

I kicked both beyond the dueling ring, then padded back out toward Liam, who was still in skin and waiting for me.

Behind me, Matt repeated, "Roll and crush."

"Ready?" Liam asked.

I nodded without hesitation. I'd never been this ready for anything.

CHAPTER 50

When Liam released a howl to signal the beginning of the duel, everything and everyone outside the ring melted into the darkness.

My breaths were loud in my ears, like the whoosh of waves on sand, frothing into my veins, slowly filling them with grit.

Unless I call you, Ness, you stay as far back as you can, you hear me?

I hear you. But just because I'd heard him didn't mean I'd heed his command. If I felt I could help, I would.

Justin was larger than I remembered, more bulky than tall. I estimated he weighed twice what I did and bet he planned on using those extra pounds on me if push came to shove.

His golden eyes slid from Liam to me, lighting up with a smirk.

I wasn't scrawny, but I was small.

Unimpressive.

Easily overlooked, like the River Alpha said after Liam and I slayed the bear.

A breeze picked up, blowing clouds over the sliver of moon and smattering of stars, darkening the already dusky expanse. My lupine eyesight sharpened, adjusting to the dim luminosity. Cassandra was waiting for Liam to make the first move, the same way she'd waited for Julian to attack.

Exactly like he'd predicted.

Now! His word cracked like a whip against my hide

I took off alongside him as he raced toward Cassandra.

She waited and waited, and then, just as his hind legs bent in preparation to fling himself upward, she pressed her belly low to the ground, limbs coiled tight against her long body. She didn't move, expecting him to pounce on her, but he arched high, overtaking her flattened form.

She blinked, ears perked up in surprise that he hadn't landed on her. His front paws hit the earth with a thud that shook the ground. When his hind paws crushed the blades of grass, Cassandra lurched back onto all fours and swung around.

Liam turned fluidly and then held still, fixing the Creek Alpha with his yellow eyes.

For a moment, neither moved. And then she lurched forward.

Liam hopped back, his big body stirring with a grace that shouldn't have belonged to a creature so colossal. She stopped her attack, which wasn't so much an attack as a taunt. She wanted him to sink his fangs into her. Not into her neck of course, or into her chest where dwelled that soft organ that had miraculously kept her alive all these years, but in a chunk of flesh irrigated by her silver-tainted blood.

Justin, who was standing opposite me, jerked, and then his muzzle scrunched up as though Cassandra had assaulted his skull with silent words. She snarled and launched herself at Liam, and he crouched and opened his maw wide.

Which was exactly what Cassandra wanted.

Her speed decreased, and she stumbled, her performance impeccable. If I'd been standing on the sidelines, I would've assumed she'd tripped.

I wouldn't have seen the eagerness to feed the waiting wolf flare in her blue eyes.

A heartbeat before she landed on Liam, he flipped over and scraped his claws into her belly, yanking a shrill whine from the Creek Alpha. Blood sprayed out of her wound. Liam twisted his face, shutting his eyes and mouth so that none of the crimson liquid landed in him. Droplets dotted his fur though, wetting the black mass.

Just as Cassandra toppled, he sprang onto his paws and

pounced, swiping her withers with his claws, slicing her flesh. A sound between a yowl and a snarl pitched out of her.

If Liam could've bitten her, this would already have been the end of the duel.

He had her on the ground, neck exposed. But claws, however sharp, didn't have the impact of teeth, and paws didn't have the pressure of jaws.

She tried to rise, but he slammed his two front legs into her spine, and she sprawled back onto her belly. Low growl rumbling out of her, she bared her teeth and wrenched her neck to nip at his pastern.

She must've sunk her fangs in, because Liam jolted off her body. Even though licking his wound would've made it heal faster, the injury was too near his claws that were wet with her blood.

As Cassandra heaved herself up, pale fur mottled by maroon patches, her eyes burned with murder and fury.

Did she understand that we'd figured out her technique for eliminating the greatest Alphas?

A flutter erupted deep in my belly, not strong enough to move me, more of a quiet reminder that August was watching. A shadow crept into my peripheral vision, and then the oily musk scent of Justin snaked into my nose. I skipped away, never taking my gaze off Liam who remained still as a boulder while his leg healed.

Cassandra snarled, ripping the heavy silence. She took off running, her strokes slow but powerful. Liam dashed, sketching a wide arc around the dueling ring, making her run after him, making her expend precious energy.

When I noticed he was favoring his left leg, worry enveloped me. Was her saliva laced with silver the same way as her blood?

Justin bumped into me, and I staggered but stayed upright and growled at him.

Didn't see you there, bitch.

My white fur made me stand out in pitch blackness . . . I practically glowed.

I growled at him before snapping my attention back toward Liam. He was still running but had slowed down considerably. Again, I worried it was from pain, but then I noticed Cassandra had stopped chasing him and imagined he was evaluating her next move.

I liked what you did to your new house, but you gotta admit, it was a little . . . sterile.

My skin prickled at Justin's implied admission. Of course he'd been among the Creeks who'd vandalized my home. He'd probably led the whole damn team.

After this duel, I'll kill you, Justin, I muttered between clenched teeth.

He made a noise that sounded like a chuckle. *'Cause you think Cassandra will let you out of this ring alive? She knows you're a bitch that can't be tamed. Which makes you a liability. She doesn't keep liabilities.*

Good thing she's not going to win this fight.

Oh . . . she's not gonna lose. She can't *lose.*

As the clouds shuffled off the moon, I could see every twitching muscle in my Alpha's body, every sweep of eyelashes, every pulse of air. He lifted his tail high in the air.

Get away from Justin, Ness. Liam spoke into my mind without breaking eye contact with Cassandra.

I loped off toward the other side of the ring.

Cassandra dipped her muzzle, and then she burst toward Liam. His muscles coiled like springs as he exploded forward, running straight at her. Just before their bodies connected, he executed the sharpest turn I'd ever seen a wolf make.

Cassandra dug her claws into the ground, spraying the faces of the shifters on the cusp of the dueling ring with grass and dirt. Flicking her ears, she turned and dashed after Liam, neck extended, snout inches from Liam's tail. Jaw wide, she seized it. Liam growled, and then his back paw came up and scraped Cassandra's cheek, shoving her face away, inflicting another deep gash.

She grunted as she released his tail and hacked up black fur, cheek weeping blood. How was he going to end her with just his claws? None of her injuries had healed yet, and if he added any more, not making contact with her blood would become near impossible.

Stashing his tail between his legs, Liam pranced away. I didn't know how deep she'd chomped down, but he would need several minutes for his skin to zipper shut.

Cassandra's nostrils flared, and then her head canted toward me. For numerous heartbeats, she stared my way, blue eyes thin and calculating.

My navel heated up to scorching as something wet bumped my rump. I whipped around and growled. *Did you just sniff me, you prick?*

What if I did? What are you going to do?

Justin was looking for me to attack, because if I made the first move, I'd become fair game for Cassandra to kill.

The dark-brown wolf leered at me. *You smell awfully sweet for something that isn't.*

You touch me again, and I will rip your testicles off and toss them to the coyotes. My breaths came in violent spurts. *And then I'll kill you.*

Will you be ripping them off with your mouth? 'Cause I've been fantasizing about your head between my legs.

A shrill bark erupted from the field, and I spun to find Liam standing over Cassandra. He swiped at her neck, and she swiped back, the dark tips of her claws sinking into his belly.

He let out a cry that had me pitching toward him, but before I could get close, Justin planted teeth that felt like twin saws into my hip and dragged me to the ground. I spun and batted him away, the pain so violent it blanched my eyesight.

Up . . . I needed to get up.

I needed to get to Liam.

CHAPTER 51

A fter managing to dislodge Justin's jaw with my kicks, I crawled away, belly to the ground, limbs trembling like the tiny leaves of Julian Matz's hedges.

Suddenly, my body skidded several feet to the side.

What the fuck? Justin growled, standing at the exact spot I'd been.

Using his astonishment to my advantage, I hoisted myself up, my backside ablaze from his bite.

Ness? Are you okay? Liam's voice pinged inside my skull.

I nodded, backing away from Justin when he started advancing. Thankfully, he moved slowly as though afraid that if he progressed any faster, I'd slip away from him again.

A black form materialized between us: Liam. *You stay the fuck away from her, Justin.*

She attacked me first, Justin said.

I did not! I bellowed, the pain in my rump forgotten.

Cassandra stepped in next to Justin. *Seems like our referees can't agree.*

I saw what happened. Justin bit her; Ness did nothing, Liam growled.

He wouldn't have bitten her if she'd done nothin'. Besides, you aren't a referee, Kolane. Cassandra peered at me behind Liam. *Good thing you prepared her so well, 'cause rules are rules.* She licked the blood coating her rubbery lips.

This fight stays between you and me, Liam barked.

Too late for that.

Liam's body seemed to expand like an afternoon shadow, blackening the overwrought air. ***Ness, can you run?***

Yes, I answered out loud because he had his back to me.

Remember our bear hunt?

My ears peaked. Was Liam about to shift back into skin to distract the Creeks?

I'm going to create a diversion.

The Creek Alpha's furry brow wrinkled. *What are you two cookin' up?*

Energy crackled through my body.

Our audience should be told what's happening, Liam said.

They'll understand, Morgan said.

I'd rather explain it. I'll switch into skin. And since we're sticking so closely to the rule book, unless you get into skin, you can't attack me until I'm back in fur. Right, Morgan?

Her blue gaze glowed like a flame atop a wick. *Right.*

Even though the air was rife with rapid heartbeats, I caught the pace of hers accelerating. Was that excitement?

Don't keep us waitin' too long, Morgan said, her voice syrupy, borderline gleeful.

I backed up a few paces, agitated by the intensity of her focus.

Keeping his back to me, Liam said through the mind-link, ***She thinks I've forgotten that you're fair game to attack since you're in fur.***

I jerked to a stop.

They're going to go after you. Just keep running, and don't stop. Run in circles; run around the ring. August will adjust your trajectory. Got it?

I didn't say anything, afraid of spoiling our plan, and afraid Liam would hear the tremor building inside me at the idea of being chased by not one, but *two* giant wolves.

Like he'd done in the Smoky Mountains, Liam slid into skin. His muscled form was outlined in moonlight. He turned a little, and I blinked at the amount of blood coating his stomach. Scabs and seeping gashes crisscrossed all over his abdomen. "Shifters, Justin attacked my Second."

People frowned. I didn't think it was in surprise—after all, they'd seen it happen—but in confusion—they probably didn't understand why Liam felt the need to interrupt the show to explain it to them.

The tether tautened . . . I glanced over my shoulder at August. His green eyes were steady, his arms crossed in front of his chest, his shoulders pulled in a line. He was ready and concentrated.

As I twisted around, my gaze collided into Alex's. His hand was no longer wrapped around Sarah's, but she still stood next to him, concern glittering in her dark eyes.

"Ness! Watch out!" she screamed.

Just as Liam predicted, Cassandra and Justin raced in opposite directions, drawing a V around my Alpha, a V that converged on me. I took off at breakneck speed along the edge of the ring, thanking Matt when my lungs didn't explode and my muscles didn't give out. Then again, I couldn't feel any of my limbs, only the wind brushing my fur, whooshing inside my ears. In that moment, I became more bird than wolf.

Suddenly, my body was hauled almost to the center of the ring, blades of grass ripping beneath my claws, the only things keeping me from toppling over. I whipped my neck toward where I'd stood, and found Cassandra shaking Justin off of her. They must've collided, which might've amused me had her gaze not locked like a double-barreled shotgun on me.

She must've yelled through the mind-link, because Justin squirmed and then vaulted in my direction.

I took off again, my back paws almost reaching my ears as I ran. A roar sounded at my left, and then a shadow shot out from behind me. Was it Cassandra? I pushed myself harder, sprinting faster than when the rocks rained down the mountain during the first trial. Bodies crashed behind me, and then snarls. Without decreasing my pace, I swung my head toward the ruckus, found a mountain of black fur atop a mountain of dark brown.

A sharp wince punctured the night, followed by a wet rip.

I was so shocked by the sight of Justin's blood dripping from Liam's muzzle that I didn't see the shape arrowing for me.

Ness! he screeched into my skull.

I froze. A heartbeat before Cassandra crashed into me, August yanked on the tether. This time, I fell as he drew my body toward the center of the ring, mere feet away from Justin's slack form.

Cassandra yowled in frustration.

My pulse seemed to have penetrated my eyes, because the world beat and bobbed.

Liam trotted out in front of me, head and tail held high, shoulders relaxed, a wall of pure, unadulterated confidence.

She's cheatin'! Morgan yelled.

Too bad your referee's no longer alive to call the duel off, Liam barked.

Wheezing, I climbed back onto my paws, ribs feeling bruised and displaced. The smell of warm blood and wet earth penetrated my nostrils. I kept expecting Justin to twitch, but only his fur rustled.

He was gone.

I could hardly believe how rapidly his life had been snuffed out.

There one minute and gone the next.

A disturbance in the ring of shifters behind Justin had my gaze springing up. Alex Morgan was elbowing his way toward my pack. I let out a shrill bark, but my mate's attention didn't veer off me. I barked again, and still he didn't look around him, but a groove appeared between his eyebrows. Did no one see Alex approach? He wasn't freaking transparent!

Then again, he hadn't breeched the first line of Boulders yet.

A snarl had my attention jumping back to the ring where Cassandra was hurtling toward Liam.

I needed to focus on Liam.

Someone in my pack would surely spot Alex and bar his path.

I tried to keep my eyes on the two Alphas, but I peeked past their bodies. Alex had disappeared, but August was still there.

Where had Alex gone?

A burst of yellow materialized in the darkness behind the thin row of Boulders.

Alex had shifted.

I barked.

Still, August didn't understand. The groove simply deepened.

No Boulder looked over their shoulder. All of them too focused on what was happening in the dueling ring.

The yellow shape loomed larger so terrifyingly fast that I locked my gaze on the shimmery blue cord that connected me to August and pulled so hard my belly button almost burst open.

August jerked.

His arms fell out of their bind and extended to steady his teetering body.

I'd moved him, but only by inches.

August finally looked away from me, but only to stare at his abdomen.

Over your shoulder, I barked. *Behind you!*

When he looked back at me, wonder lit up his entire demeanor. He didn't understand.

I raced toward him, hoping Liam had Cassandra under control, hoping that by choosing one wolf, I wasn't sacrificing the other.

When Alex dropped into a crouch, I was still too far away.

I don't know if it was the panic lighting up my pupils or my mad dash toward him, but August finally spun around.

Too late.

Too late.

Alex was already airborne.

CHAPTER 52

I clutched the blue rope with my mind and poured all of my hatred for the boy who'd driven my cousin off the road and into his grave into my grip.

August lurched forward, several feet this time. He fell, hands smacking the ground before his head could make contact. Alex's lids hitched up as he landed on grass instead of flesh, and the shock made him stumble.

As he righted himself, his narrowed violet gaze locked on August's kneeling form. Before my mate could stand, Alex galloped toward him. The rope escaped my invisible grip and swung so chaotically it blurred, thwarting my attempt to latch onto it.

I came to a screeching halt, and the rope stabilized some. I clutched it, and this time, closed my ghostly fingers hard around it. I pulled just as another wolf barreled out from behind the blockade of human legs and jumped on top of Alex. At first, I thought it was a Boulder, but the wolf was small and slender, not male. And its fur was wavy.

Sarah.

Alex flung her off, and her small body arched through the air, slamming hard into the ground.

Alex growled and darted toward her just as another wolf appeared, this one gray and large.

Larger than Alex.

Lucas.

Snarling like a wild animal, my packmate sank his fangs into Alex's spine. I watched in morbid fascination as Lucas's muzzle and teeth came away drenched in blood.

Ness.

The thin sound of my Alpha calling my name jerked my attention off the sidelines.

I pitched around so fast my vision swam, but then it honed in on the heap of fur at the far side of the ring. Cassandra was standing over Liam, front paws on his shoulders.

He wrung his body to shake her off, but her paws stayed put as though welded to his fur. When he heaved a cry that detonated against my eardrums and echoed in my chest, I understood it wasn't her weight keeping her anchored to him but her purple claws.

As her mouth lowered to his neck, I shot forward, adrenaline zipping through my bones and electrifying my muscles.

He twisted sideways, and her mouth missed its mark, but she remained fastened to him. When another violent holler hit my ears, I sensed her claws had cleaved open more of his back.

I was almost there.

Almost beside them.

Cassandra snarled, and her moonlit fangs approached the mound of thrashing black fur beneath her.

I'd sworn to protect him, but I'd gone off and left him on his own.

I'd let my mate distract me.

I'd failed Liam.

He bucked, interrupting Cassandra's momentum but failing to dislodge her.

Another blood-curdling yowl erupted from my Alpha just as I slammed into Morgan's side. It was like hitting a brick wall, but the wall toppled. Her claws popping out plucked another guttural moan from Liam.

Runnels of split flesh wept blood onto his black fur, but his heart still beat.

It still beat . . .

Praying she hadn't bled into him, I hopped over him, creating a shield with my scrawny body.

Before Cassandra was fully upright, I jumped on top of her and forced her back down. She landed on her spine, teeth flashing. I batted her face with my paws, but all that served was to anger her further.

Like the punching bag Liam had obliged me to train on until my knuckles bled, I hit her, over and over and over, dragging my claws across her cheek, across her forehead, across any pliant surface I could make contact with. Howling and snarling, she smacked my cheek, trailing fire over my temple, my left eye, my muzzle.

I blinked wildly, but I couldn't clear my vision. And then I was yanked off her.

NO! I cried as August pulled on the tether, reeling me in.

I dug my claws into the ground, my muscles screaming, my bones spasming. I fought against the invisible bit hauling me away from Cassandra and Liam.

Liam who still hadn't gotten up but whose chest continued to rise and fall.

As Cassandra bounded onto all fours, I crawled toward her, stretching the tether so tight it almost snapped. And then, praying that for once I'd be stronger than August, I vaulted onto the Creek Alpha's back and did the only thing I could think of to save Liam's life.

I sank my teeth into her neck. As the taste of metal and salt filled my mouth, I worked on not swallowing a drop of it.

"No!" I heard someone scream. I couldn't tell if the voice was inside my head or outside.

I whipped my face from side to side to tear through her sinews and veins, and didn't stop until her body slackened . . . until her giant body collapsed beneath mine.

CHAPTER 53

I gagged on the mouthful of Morgan's blood. Forcing my throat closed so that none of her tainted fluids entered my throat, I spit and heaved. A jet of vomit spurted out of me and sprayed Cassandra's blotchy fur, which was already receding into her pores.

I blinked as my eyes filled with heat and more slickness. My vision became even blurrier, but not blurry enough to miss her slipping back into skin for the very last time.

Cassandra was dead, and I was still alive.

We did it, Liam, I whispered.

I inched closer to my Alpha, reveling in the sound of his heart pounding against his injured flesh. If her poison had penetrated him, his heart would've already stopped. His neck lifted, and his luminous yellow gaze fell over me.

We did it, I said again, swiping my paw over my cheek, trying to see through the sticky veil of blood.

His entire body moved this time. He rose like a billow of smoke, darkening the sapphire air and the emerald grass, advancing in slow-motion toward me.

The ground trembled, rife with footfalls. I tried to turn my head, but it felt so heavy, as though Lucas had attached a set of those enormous dumbbells he so enjoyed curling when he watched me train.

The world blurred, colors and sounds swimming and blending like murky watercolors.

When I blinked, I found myself staring at a sheet of brilliant stars.

Even though I was a creature made for land, I loved the sky, the beauty of its forever shifting colors, of its distant luminaries that had inspired so many of my father's stories, of its clouds that drifted like windblown dandelion florets, of its brilliant moon that had found me worthy of its magic.

A face as magnificent as the sky loomed over me, obscuring the sight of constellations and yet presenting me with another made of freckles instead of stars.

The low, raspy timbre of August's voice soothed the sting streaking through my veins and drew my lids down. How many times had I fallen asleep listening to that rough silken voice?

My chin dropped against my collarbone and then lolled backward.

The earth shook again, or perhaps it was the arms clasped around me that quaked.

"Dimples!"

I heaved my heavy lids up, caught a glint of green and gold, like sunlight threading through the leaves of the tree August had taught me to climb.

My heart jerked as though hit by a shot of pure adrenaline, and my skin bristled, my muscles seizing and my bones clinking as they realigned.

Large fingers swept over my cheek, through my hair, curled around my human neck, lifting my limp form, cradling it.

The world spun, as though toppling off its axis, and the green and gold melted into black, then gray, and then pure white as though the night had been shot through with fireworks.

Had August lit up the sky for me again?

I so loved fireworks.

I looked for him, but he'd gone.

All was quiet.

All was bright.

CHAPTER 54

F ire singed my veins.

CHAPTER 55

Noise crashed against my eardrums.

CHAPTER 56

Heat charred my skin, and then a chill slid down my throat, and my lungs expanded like bellows, ripping a cry that reverberated against my palate and pulsed my cheeks, awakening a ferocious ache.

Thump.

Thump.

CHAPTER 57

Metal clinked.
Wild battering inside my chest.
Strips of glaring light.
Flashes of blinding pain.
Smears of color.
Light blue.
Peach.
Green.
Brown.
Then white.
So much white.

CHAPTER 58

B eep . . . *Beep* . . . *Beep.*
   "She died but she came back, Mom."
   Who'd died? *Sandra?*
"Wait. I have to—I'll call you back."
A loud, shrill scrape.
Then five dots of heat on my cheek.
And green.
Two green orbs.
Not orbs.
Eyes.
"Dimples?"
The green blurred, faded.
Not into white but into black.

CHAPTER 59

Beep . . . *Beep* . . . *Beep*.
The warm scent of skin.
Spice and sawdust.
The steady beat of a heart against my spine.
Ba-bump . . . *Ba-bump* . . . *Ba-bump* . . .
Rhythmic and solid.

The sharp spike of beeps echoing around me jolted the body cocooning mine.

"Dimples?"

Beep. Beep. Beep.

I blinked, but everything was dark. So dark.

"I want . . ."

"What do you want, sweetheart?"

"Colors."

Something clicked, and then hands gently eased me onto my back.

Against the cream ceiling, green, sable, and gold churned. Heat stung my eyes; then something wet rolled along my cheek: a tear.

The beats of my heart lengthened. Slowed. *Beep* . . . *Beep* . . . *Beep* . .

"What is it?" the deep voice trembled in the air between our faces.

I lifted my hand to touch August's jaw. He turned his face until his lips connected with my palm. "It was so dark and then so white," I murmured. "What happened to me?"

His breaths faltered.

"What?" I asked as I lifted my other hand to push the hair obscuring my left eye.

Found it wasn't hair but gauze.

Thick gauze.

I prodded it until I found the edge and then started peeling it away when August caught my fingers. "Don't take it off."

"Why not? Am I bleeding?"

"No. Maybe. Just don't take it off yet. Greg said he'd be here in the morning. He'll do it."

"O-okay." Something about his expression had my heart thump a little quicker, which filled the hospital room with nippy, harsh *beeps*. "Is Cassandra . . . is she . . .?"

"Dead? Yes. She's dead. You killed her. Which killed you." His voice broke. "It . . . killed . . . you."

I ran my palm along his jaw, pressing a little harder to make sure he was real, and that I was too. "I died?"

The quiet white void had been death.

"How . . . how did I come back?"

His lids swept down over his eyes as though to clear them of the memory. "I bit you."

I frowned. "You bit—*oh* . . ." My unbandaged eye widened. "Like in the legend?"

He nodded, his dense stubble scraping my palm.

"You brought me back to life," I said in wonder. As I remembered who told me the story, his name burst through my lips. "*Liam!* What about Liam? Is he alive?"

"He's alive."

Beep. Beep. Beep.

"We won then?"

August closed his eyes. "Oh . . . Ness."

"What? We didn't win?"

"No. We won. But—"

"But what?"

He removed his cheek from my hand and laced his fingers

through mine, careful not to shift the heart monitor clamped to the tip of my index.

"What is it, August?"

His silence intensified my pulse. The beeps pinged against my eardrums, against the fawn-colored walls, against the closed hospital door. He lowered our twined hands to my abdomen.

"It's gone," he whispered raucously.

My brow furrowed. "What is?"

"The link," he murmured. "It's gone."

And that was when I felt it.

Or rather . . . when I didn't feel it. "Oh."

He watched my face as the revelation settled like silt on the bottom of a river.

"Death severed it," I said matter-of-factly.

He pressed his forehead against my collarbone, his body heaving, first with ragged breaths and then with quiet sobs.

Was he mourning its absence, or had its absence made him realize that the link was the reason he'd been attracted to me?

Probably the latter.

He wouldn't be crying over a broken link.

Not if it hadn't altered his feelings toward me.

He was probably worried confessing his change of heart would send me into a tailspin of intractable pain. Or back into the white void.

I shuddered just remembering.

I lifted my free hand to his hunched spine and stroked the hard knobs of his vertebrae. "It's okay," I whispered, trying to act strong even though I felt the loss inside the marrow of my very bones. "You don't need to feel guilty, August. I won't break, I promise."

I was too broken to break, right?

"Wh-what?" He picked his head off my chest and dug the heel of his palm into his reddened eyes.

"We'll go back to being . . ." I shrugged to buy myself time to clear my throat. "Friends." I tried to smile, but my lips wobbled too much for it to stick.

His strong brow grooved. "What are you talking about?"

"I . . . you . . . I thought . . ." My eyebrows pulled together. "Why *are* you crying?"

"Because I lost you." He said this with an anger that made me shrink deeper into the tough pillow propping my head up. "Because when Liam told me to bite you, I thought it was some sick joke, that he'd gone soft in the head. Ness, you died in my arms. And then for the past week, you've been in and out of consciousness. I apologize for being emotional, but until a few minutes ago, I was terrified you might never wake up. Or that when you did, you wouldn't remember my name. Or that you might not want me now that nothing binds us."

"The past week?" I whispered. "The duel was last week?"

He nodded carefully, as though waiting for me to touch upon the rest of what he'd said.

"You think I forgot you?" I dragged my thumb across his palm. "How could I forget the boy who picked me up from school to buy me ice-cream? Who taught me to climb my first tree and who sat by my bed to make sure all the monsters stayed underneath it?" I kept stroking his palm. "I remember everything about you, August. I remember when you came to talk to me the day of the pack gathering, when you shot Lucas at the paintball arena, when you collected me in the woods the night Liam called me a traitor. I remember our swim in the lake when you tried to tickle me, and the feel of your palm on my skin. It was the day I realized my feelings for you weren't all that platonic." While I kept caressing his palm with my thumb, I raised my other hand to touch the faint white line where I'd carved his cheek the night I'd had a nightmare, and he'd woken me up. "I remember giving you this scar, and then licking the blood away."

A full-body shiver went through him.

"I remember our first kiss. Each one of our kisses, for that matter. I remember my birthday dinner and all that happened after."

His lips parted a little, as though he were trying to catch his breath.

"I remember you, August." I cupped his chiseled jaw.

Those glorious emerald eyes bore down on mine.

"And concerning the link, it's not the first time the bond between us has been absent, now is it?"

His eyes seemed to shine a little harder.

"What about you?" I asked.

"What about me, what?"

"Have your feelings for me *changed*? I know you love me, but do you still"—I shrugged—"*want* me?"

Shaking his head, he captured my wrist and brought it up to his lips. "Want is a mighty feeble word for what I feel for you, Ness Clark."

When he kissed the delicate skin, the room filled with the melody of my heartbeats.

He peppered the inside of my arm with kisses before carefully laying my hand down on the twisted sheets, wrapping his fingers around the back rung of the bed to keep his weight off me, and leaning over until his mouth was parallel to mine. I tried to reach around his back, but the cord of the heart monitor fumbled my first attempt.

"Can you turn off that machine so I can get my finger back? I don't want to remove the clip and give all the nurses strokes when they hear me flatline."

Would it still alert them? Probably . . .

August winced.

I wrinkled my nose. "I didn't mean to remind you."

"I don't think it's something I'll ever be able to forget, sweetheart. Those were the worst minutes of my life. On par with crashing in the helicopter and having a heart-to-heart with Evelyn."

"Evelyn! Does she know?" I asked as he studied the machine monitoring my heartbeats to figure out how to turn it off.

In the end, he simply unplugged it.

"She knows." He slipped the clamp off my fingertip. "The first two days, she didn't leave the chair next to your bed, but then Frank forced her to go home at night so she could rest. She made me swear not to leave your side, then muttered a couple things in Spanish, but I didn't quite catch their meaning. She was probably hexing me."

I grinned, but it tugged on my injured cheek, so I uncurled my lips.

As I raised my hand to feel what was underneath the gauze, August caught my fingers and towed them away. "Tomorrow. You'll get the bandage off tomorrow. Now, where were we again? Right . . .

I was just about to do this." He kissed me gently, and it made me forget all about my injury.

It made me forget about a lot of things . . .

Suddenly, a lightbulb went off in my head, and I skated my mouth off his. "You could've died!"

"What?" His voice was all raspy.

"When you bit me! I had silver in my blood. You could've died. How come you didn't?"

"That Sillin injection Greg gave me counteracted the silver I ingested. Counteracted the metal in your blood, too."

I was about to go off on him when the door of my room flew open and a nurse burst in, cheeks puffing and red.

"You . . . the machine . . ." She couldn't seem to catch her breath.

"Sorry. We unplugged it," I said. "But I'm fine." When she started bustling toward me, I raised my palm to stop her. "I promise."

"I'm going to have to call your doctor."

"Sure." I doubted he'd ask her to clip me back onto the monitor. Once the door shut, I focused on August again. "Liam should *never* have told you about—"

He pressed a finger against my lips. "When I bit you, I understood the risks, and I would take them a thousand times over to get you back."

Tears welled up.

"Oh, sweetheart. Don't cry. There's been too much crying around here."

I inhaled a breath, trying to rein in my emotions.

"Between Mom, Evelyn, Matt, Sarah—"

I smiled, even though my cheek turned wet. "Sarah cried?" I scrubbed the tears away with the back of my hand. I could believe Matt had gotten teary-eyed; he had the gentlest heart. But Sarah?

"Don't tell her I told you. She swore me to secrecy." August tucked a piece of hair behind my ear. "You're the most popular girl in this hospital. Every single Boulder has come to visit you, to the greatest pleasure of the nurses."

I laughed, and again it tugged on whatever awaited me behind the gauze.

"I have more questions."

He sighed. "Let me get comfortable." He scooted me to the side of the narrow bed so he could lie down beside me.

"I know Evelyn visited me here, so I imagine she's okay, but did Cassandra—did she send someone?"

"Are you sure you want to know everything tonight?"

I nodded.

He splayed his hand against my ribcage. "After you warned Matt, Frank left with Derek. They found Morgan's daughter lurking on his property."

I blanched.

"Little J.—Frank made him stay behind—he managed to put a bullet in her leg with his dad's old shotgun."

Dread creeped up my veins. "He's only fourteen."

August smiled. "Stood his ground like a grown man."

"What about the girls? Were they okay?"

"The girls?"

"Tamara, Amanda . . ." I didn't add Sienna's name to the list, since, to my knowledge, she wasn't dating a Boulder, which meant she probably wouldn't have been targeted.

"Liam ordered two of our guys to stay with them before the fight began. They're all fine."

I was glad to hear Liam had guarded Tamara.

"Any more questions?"

I nibbled on my bottom lip. "Do you think they'll discharge me tomorrow?"

"Greg will decide. If it was up to me, you'd be recuperating at my place."

His place . . . Thankfully, I was no longer connected to the machine, because I was pretty certain my heart rate had just shot through the roof.

"Is that where I'm going after this?"

His freckles darkened. "I'd like that, but I'd understand if that's too much for you. Your new house is also ready."

The memory of the blood and urine made the walls of my hospital room squeeze in around me. "It was Justin. He confessed to the vandalism. He probably had help, though."

August's head dipped. "Don't worry. I already took care of it."

It being my house or the rest of the perpetrators? I didn't ask. "What about Alex? What happened to him?"

"He's gone too."

"Gone?"

"Dead. Lucas."

"And Lori? Did Frank kill her when he got to his house?"

"No. She's in captivity back at HQ. Liam wanted to keep her for questioning. He's trying to find out who Morgan's biggest supporters are."

A yawn popped out of my mouth.

August's eyes softened. "You need to rest."

"I've been sleeping for a week."

"You've been *mending* for a week. You had three cracked ribs and several other . . . *injuries*."

I inhaled deeply. Nothing hurt, which told me my ribs must have already set.

"Nothing feels broken anymore," I said. Except my face.

"I'm relieved to hear that."

"Did Liam . . . Did he"—I wrinkled my nose—"*eat* Morgan's heart?"

"He did."

"How? Did your blood also—"

"Remember how Dad was with the Rivers? The afternoon of the duel, Greg was worried about how little Sillin we had left, so I told Dad to purchase some from the Rivers. They ended up giving it to us for free."

"Oh. That's . . . *kind* of them." Since nothing was ever free in this world, I assumed it was given in the hopes of getting something in return. Was August that something?

"They arrived at the duel right after . . ." He shuddered.

"Right after?"

"Right after you made it back to us." His words lingered in the air. "But he got the whole story, which made his hair go a lot grayer."

"He must hate me for having put you at risk."

August's body went a tad rigid. "*Hate you?* First off, Dimples, my dad loves you. Both my parents do. Secondly, you didn't put me at risk, so don't ever say that again. Don't even think it, all right?"

I said, "All right," even though I knew I would always think it. How could I not? When August reached over me to click off the light shining over the bed, I said, "Can you leave it on?"

"Of course."

He played with my hair, and the gentle movement lulled me.

"I didn't see them," I murmured.

"Didn't see who, sweetheart?"

"Mom and Dad." My throat narrowed. "When I died, I didn't see them." A beat passed. "You think I wasn't dead long enough, or do you think there's nothing waiting for us *after*?"

Although his chest rose and fell steadily, his pulse picked up speed. "I don't know."

I appreciated his honesty, even though it made my throat close up some more. "Thank you."

"For what?"

"For bringing me back." At least people had waited for me on this side.

He dropped my hair and tucked me closer, stamping a kiss on my temple, which I felt even through the gauze. "I'll always bring you back."

And I knew he would. Every time I'd gotten lost, he'd been the one to bring me back.

CHAPTER 60

I woke up to a brightness so white I snapped my lids up—*lid*. The other one was still mummified by the gauze. The tan wall came into focus first. I'd never been particularly fond of that color, but as I gazed at it, I thought it was quite marvelous.

The low drone of voices outside my hospital room made me turn onto my other side. Chair legs scraped, and a tremulous whispered, "*Querida*," rose in time with Evelyn.

With trembling hands, she cupped my cheeks, careful not to apply too much pressure to my bandaged one, and then pressed her uncharacteristically pale lips to my forehead, then to my nose, and then to my forehead again. "I will not make old bones if you keep doing things like this to me."

"I'm sorry, Evelyn."

Moisture clumped her black lashes together. "Oh, *querida*. Please, no more danger. Please."

"I promise I'm done with duels and contests for the rest of my life."

"*Bueno*. Now tell me, how do you feel? Frank said you heal fast, but I worry."

When did she not? "I feel fine."

Her dark eyes inspected my covered face, making me wonder if the gauze was soaked in blood. As I raised my fingers to feel it, there was a knock on the door.

"Can we come in?" Frank called.

Evelyn looked over her shoulder, then back at me.

"Who's we?" I asked her quietly.

"The men you call the elders."

"All five of them?"

She nodded.

I hoisted myself into a sitting position and finger-combed my hair. Not that they'd notice my rat's nest when half my face was swathed up. "C-come in!"

The door opened, and they entered, one after the other, August closing ranks.

Last night, I hadn't noticed the violet shadows beneath his eyes or his ashen complexion. I wanted to tell him to go home and rest, but Eric stepped in front of him and started speaking to me, saying what a spectacular fight Liam and I had led, and then Derek mentioned how I'd go down in the Hall of Fame of Boulder Wolves, which made me wonder if my pack had an actual Hall of Fame. And then Frank, placing his hand on Evelyn's shoulder, said that my courage changed the course of pack history.

Even though tears were probably out of character for the warrior they were painting me as, emotion rose and overflowed.

Evelyn knitted her warm fingers through my chilled ones.

"We are so proud of you, Ness. You will forever have our gratitude," Frank added.

I swiped my palm against my wet cheek just as another knock sounded. The person didn't ask to be allowed inside.

He just barged in.

This was so like Liam that it made me smile. He walked over to my bed, winding through the picket fence of elders. For a moment, he didn't say anything, neither out loud nor in my mind.

Could he still speak into my mind, or was that bond broken too?

He cleared his throat. "Could you all give me a moment with the girl who saved my life?"

The girl who'd saved his life . . . "I didn't save your life, Liam."

He didn't answer, but his jaw worked.

The elders patted my arm before leaving. Frank kissed my cheek, and then he tugged on Evelyn's hand.

"I will be back this afternoon. Or earlier if you need me," she said.

After she left, Liam said, "You too, Watt."

August stiffened. Even though no tether connected us anymore, I could feel his reticence at leaving me alone in a room with my ex.

"I'll go get us some coffees," he finally said.

I nodded. "I'd like that."

Rigidly, he walked to the door.

When the door snicked shut, Liam said, "I can't believe you bit her!"

I winced from the shrillness of his voice but then squared my shoulders. "It got you what you wanted."

"You died, Ness! You. Died!"

"I know. I was there," I said drily.

He shook his head, not appreciating my morbid humor. His shoulders seemed broader, his arms ropier. Even his height seemed to have changed. Although his face was unscathed, I couldn't help but wonder what his abdomen looked like. Had he healed, or was his stomach crisscrossed with scars?

After heaving a sigh, he dropped onto the foot of my bed and ran his hands through his hair. A wayward lock fell into his amber eyes. He shoved it away, but it just tumbled back down.

"How are you doing?" I asked.

He grunted. "How do you think I'm doing? You died," he repeated. The morning sun slanting through the blinds made his eyes seem shinier, as though he were about to cry.

I captured the hand with which he was wringing the scratchy bedsheet. "You didn't think I'd let you become the only living legend?" I fit a smile onto my lips and winked. "Way neater than being a dead one."

He grunted, but his fingers softened in my grip.

My smile grew, but so did the ache in my face, so I leveled my lips. "I'm getting inducted into the Boulder Hall of Fame apparently."

"Didn't know we had one of those . . ."

"And you call yourself Alpha?" I rolled my eyes—well, my *eye*. I hoped Greg would come soon . . . "Aren't Alphas supposed to be all-knowing?"

Something I said destroyed Liam's fragile tranquility. "About that."

I frowned.

"I ate Morgan's heart."

I wrinkled my nose. "I heard. Did it taste black and bitter?"

"I'd rather not recall what it tasted like. The point is, if I hadn't ingested it right after the duel, I wouldn't have been able to connect our two packs."

"Okay . . ."

"But it wasn't mine for the taking."

I cocked my unbandaged eyebrow up.

"Ness, *you* defeated Morgan. That heart belonged to *you*. Our pack . . . it belongs to *you*."

"What? What are you talking about?"

"You deserve to be Alpha, and I'm here to make that happen."

I dropped his hand as though the mere contact of his fingers could somehow transfer the link. "Um. No." I clasped my fingers in my lap. "I most definitely don't want to be Alpha."

"Why not?"

"Because that was never my ambition. I signed up to be your Second to help you. Now that that's done, I want to go back to college and"—I shrugged—"*live*. Like, really live. Without having to scheme and run half-marathons and watch over my shoulder."

He glanced at me through his long lashes. "Are you certain?"

"I've never been more certain of anything."

"I owe you. So much. I owe you *everything*."

"You owe me nothing, Liam."

"I do. Money, for starters."

"I don't need any money."

He raised a quizzical brow.

"At least, not right now." Maybe once I spoke to Isobel and Nelson to return what their crazy son had given me.

"You tell me as soon as that changes, all right?"

"I will."

"And if you need anything else—and I mean, *anything*—come to me, and I'll make it happen."

I nodded.

"I mean it, Ness."

"I know you do."

A beat of companionable silence ensued.

"Feels strange," I finally said.

"What does?"

"That it's over."

"Over? It's just beginning. The pack's so big now. Speaking of"—his eyes practically glowed—"I'm going to need Betas. Would you consider being one of them?"

"Me?" I squeaked. "Why? Did Lucas turn you down?"

The smirk was slow to come, but it made an appearance on Liam's hard-edged face. "Haven't asked him yet."

"Well, you should."

"I'm going to need at least two or three."

"I'm no politician, Liam, but maybe you shouldn't designate only Original Boulders for the job."

"I was thinking of making Sarah a Beta."

I smiled. "She'll make a great Beta. And so would Lucas. Now you just need a Creek, and you'll have a holy trinity."

His expression gentled. "You're right. So wise, Miss Clark."

"Why thank you, Mr. Kolane."

We smiled at each other a moment, and then his gaze dropped to my abdomen.

Worried he might mention the tether, I said, "Morgan mentioned they were six. Well, five, because Aidan wasn't living with his pack back then."

He raised his gaze back to my face. "Huh?"

"Original Creeks." When he frowned, I added, "Did the others have tainted blood too, or was she the only one?"

"Oh." His nostrils flared. "Funny you should ask. I just had a long chat with Lori about that."

"You trust her?"

"I trust she wants to live." He rubbed his palms against his thighs. "One of them was Cassandra's father—the one supposedly murdered by Julian. The other was her grandmother; she died of old age two years back. And then there was Lori and Alex, but they were never exposed to the toxic spring since they were born years later. However"—he rested his hands on the bed—"they were exposed to something else."

I frowned.

"The heavy dose of Sillin Cassandra ingested after the poisoning, it transferred to them during the pregnancy, which gave them a very high tolerance to silver."

How interesting... "Like a new and improved race of shifters."

"Exactly."

"So the only OC left is Lori?" I asked.

"Yes."

"And you're sure she has no silver in her blood?"

"I had Greg run tests on her. No silver showed up. Besides, Lucas killed Alex, and his blood didn't poison him, so it's safe to assume Lori's silver-free."

I chewed on my bottom lip. "How did Cassandra survive when the rest of her pack died?"

"Because she was the Alpha's niece. He reserved the highest doses for his surviving relatives. Him and his mother never shifted again, but Cassandra somehow managed to tap into her werewolf magic. Took her years, according to Lori."

"So it *is* possible to shift with Sillin in our blood?"

"Lori thinks it was the combination of silver and Sillin. Cassandra never got rid of either."

I frowned. "It stayed in her system? So she wasn't still taking it?"

"No."

"Then why did they steal our Sillin?"

"Because they didn't want *us* to have it."

My frown deepened.

"As long as we had it, we could heal from her silver blood."

My eyebrows shot up so fast it tugged on my left cheek.

"Cassandra's plan was to annex us because we had a good foothold in the region. That's why she had Everest take our stock."

"So she didn't come in peace?"

"No."

I stared a long minute at Liam, trying to arrange all this information inside my slow-firing brain. I didn't know if it was the medication they'd given me or my week-long coma, but my head felt wadded up with cotton. "Why did they go after ours instead of the Pines?"

"Apparently it was next up on their to-do list. Lori said her mother wanted to start with ours because we were more dissipated, and therefore, *easier* to take over."

I fingered a crease in my bedsheet, trying desperately to smooth it out. To think I'd once longed to meet this woman. To think I'd once been impressed with her. I'd sink my fangs into her neck all over again if I had to.

Liam reached over and trapped my hand in his. "I can't do this without you, Ness."

"*This?*"

"Reorganize three packs and make them one."

"Of course you can."

"I don't *want* to do it without you."

"I'm not going anywhere," I promised him, easing my fingers out of his grip.

He made a fist, his knuckles turning paler then redder as he tightened and released them. "I heard the mating link's gone."

My heart stilled a moment. After several breaths, I said softly, "Doesn't change how I feel about August, though."

He shut his eyes. "Maybe, in time, it will."

"Liam," I whispered, "you have a pack to take care of, a son on the way, a woman who adores you, friends who would do anything for you. You don't need me."

His lids flew up, and his amber gaze flared. "You're wrong!"

I let the intensity of the emotions rolling off him settle before adding, "Guilt and gratitude are coloring the way you think of me."

"Guilt and gratitude?" he scoffed.

"Yes. Guilt because, for some reason, you feel like you took this position from me. And gratitude for saving your ass. 'Cause I sort of did save it, didn't I?" A corner of my mouth tugged up, in turn yanking on my injured cheek. "Could you call Greg? I'd really like to get this bandage off."

Adam's apple bobbing, Liam stood to extract his phone from the pocket of his jeans. As he phoned the doctor, the door to my room flew open.

CHAPTER 61

"**N**ess!" Sarah raced to me. Her arms went around my shoulders and pulled me into the fiercest hug. After a couple long seconds, she pressed me away. "I'll have you know, I'm really pissed at you! You can't go playing hero and dying on me like that."

"Says the girl who dated Alex Morgan to gather info." I inspected what I could see of her body. "Did he hurt you? Are you okay?"

"I'm fine, hun." She shuddered as she said this, which made me sit up straighter.

"What happened?"

"I'll tell you everything some other time. I think you have enough to deal with right now."

"I have nothing to deal with right now besides getting this bandage off."

"Greg's on his way," Liam said.

"Thank you, Liam." Then to Sarah, I said, "I hope he's going to take this thing off. And discharge me."

Sarah and Liam exchanged a glance that made my stomach tighten. Had they seen what lay beneath the bandage?

"Did I lose my eye or something?" I thought I still felt its presence, but perhaps it was like a phantom limb.

"Your eye's still there," Liam said.

"Then why does everyone keep blanching when I bring it up?"

"The reason I sent you that message in the shoe is because I overheard Alex and Justin talk about how they'd found out the location of the Sillin stash." Even though I was glad for an explanation, I sensed Sarah was feeding it to me to evade my question. "I was honestly certain they knew where it was. I didn't think they were using me to find it."

I flicked my gaze up to Liam. "I'm very tempted to say *I told you so*."

He flashed me a pained smile. "Go ahead. Say it."

Lucas sauntered in then, shaggy-haired and shiny-eyed. "Back from the dead so soon, Clark?"

I shook my head in amusement. "Would you rather I have haunted your ass, Lucas?"

"Did you just . . . did you just"—he slapped a palm against his chest—"*swear?*"

While Sarah rolled her eyes, I snorted. "I'm happy to see you, too."

"You gave us quite the scare last week." A genuine smile now graced Lucas's lips.

"Wasn't my intent."

"Can you tell Matt it was? 'Cause I sort of have a bet going with him that you did all that for the attention."

I gawked at him.

He smirked. "Kidding."

"So I got you something," Sarah interjected, digging into her enormous Mary-Poppins handbag. "I got *us* something."

She pulled out a firetruck-red silk bomber jacket.

"Wow that's really . . . *red*."

"Wait for it." She flipped the jacket around. On the back, in flowy white embroidery, was written Boulder Babe. "I have a matching one for myself. Obvs."

My eyes—or rather eye—dampened again.

"I suggested Boulder Bitch, which would've been species-accurate, but this one"—Lucas pointed to Sarah—"vetoed my proposal."

Sarah gave him the stink-eye, which made laughter burst out of me. I never thought I'd laugh about anything containing the word bitch, but hey, I hadn't thought I'd die and come back to tell the tale.

"Do you love it?" Sarah asked, her wild curls glinting in the sunlight.

"I love it."

"Good."

The sound of someone knocking had all of us turning toward the open door.

Why was Ingrid Burley standing on the threshold of my hospital room? When August walked in behind her, I realized they must've bumped into each other in the cafeteria, because they were holding matching takeaway coffee cups.

"Hey," she said, watching him bring me one of the coffees. "I'm sorry for bargin' in here, but I heard you were finally awake."

I wrapped my fingers around the warmed paper cup, unsure as to why she was in Boulder in the first place.

"Ingrid's the reason I managed to unite the packs," Liam said, as though he'd heard my thoughts. When I frowned, he added, "She brought us the Sillin."

Ingrid shrugged. "That's what allies are for." She drew her fingers through her long, glossy strands, working out a tangle. "I'm just glad we made it in time."

Perhaps I should've been thankful the Rivers had aided us, but it nagged me that she'd used it as an excuse to fly out here with Nelson. More importantly, though, why was she still in Boulder a week after the duel? Was she still holding out hope for August to change his mind?

"Congratulations," she said.

"Thank you." I offered her a stiff smile.

"Are you heading back to Tennessee today, Ingrid?" Sarah asked.

"Not sure yet." She took a sip of her coffee, glancing over the rim at Liam. "Might stick around a few more days."

I squeezed my lips shut to prevent myself from asking why.

"Liam, can you and I talk a sec?" she asked.

Liam nodded, then cupped the nape of my neck and rested his cheek on my forehead. *I wish I had been the one to deserve you.*

My heart jounced at the sound of his voice in my mind. Unlike the link connecting me to August, the one connecting me to Liam hadn't shattered.

I ducked my head out from underneath his. "I heard you," I whispered, remembering another time when I'd spoken the same words to him with the same amount of wonder.

He frowned. "Why wouldn't you have heard me? You're my wolf."

"I just thought . . ." I glanced up at August who stood so rigidly he looked carved out of wood. "I just thought that link might've been gone too."

There's nothing more powerful than a bond to an Alpha.

I craned my neck to look at Liam.

Nothing, he repeated, gaze leveled on August.

I felt like a fly caught in a web belonging to two equally big and possessive spiders. But it wasn't my life or my heart I feared for; it was theirs. I couldn't split myself in half, and even though I loved them both, I loved them differently.

I set my untouched coffee down on my bedside table and wrapped my hand around the one August had fisted at his side, prying his fingers open until they relaxed and twined with mine.

"See you later, Liam." I smiled at him, but all I got in return was a sharp nod.

He backed away.

As Ingrid trailed after him, I called out, "In case I don't see you again, Ingrid, have a safe trip back, and say hi to your family from me."

She looked over her shoulder at me, then at August, then at our hands. "I will," she said, offering me a weak smile.

Once the door was closed, Sarah loosed a breath. "Well, that was a little awkward."

"And this is why I advocate polygamy," Lucas said brightly. "And orgies. Everyone gets what they want, or rather, *whom*."

Sarah smacked his thigh.

"*Ow.* What was that for? I'm allowed my opinion," he muttered. "It's my constitutional right."

"When you're going to say stupid shit, use your inside voice," Sarah said.

"*Stupid shit?* How was that stupid?"

"It was unhelpful," she said, gaze pinging between August and me.

Greg blustered into the room then. "Got here as fast as I could."

I'd never been so happy to see the pack doctor. One, because I was anxious to get my bandage off, and two, because I didn't want to talk about our tangled love lives anymore. I sensed Lucas had been trying to lighten the atmosphere, but his quip had the adverse effect. August's grip had become bruising, as though my former mate was afraid that if he let go, I would venture away.

I'd moved him the night of the duel. Perhaps if the link still connected us, August wouldn't have felt so threatened, but now that it was gone . . .

"Glad to see you awake, kid." Greg squirted some disinfectant into his palms and rubbed them as he approached my bedside.

I tried to smile, but a bolt of nervousness shot through me.

"So, I'm going to take a look under the bandage."

Take a look underneath it? "Is there a chance it's not coming off?"

As his fingers inched up to the gauze, he seemed to realize we weren't alone. "You mind giving Ness and me some room?"

"Sure, doc," Lucas said.

Sarah rose from the bed reluctantly. "I'll be right outside."

"Want August to stay, Ness?" Greg asked.

My heart started pounding double-time. "I-I . . ."

August's motionless body finally came alive. "I'd like to stay." He dipped his chin into his neck to peer down at me. "If that's okay with you?"

Greg waited until I acquiesced before proceeding to remove the bandage. As the strips fell away, and cool air touched my newly exposed skin, I shivered.

August let go of my hand and skated his palm across my back to drive warmth into my chilled skin.

Greg gathered the fallen gauze and chucked it in the garbage. He lifted his fingers to my face again, I assumed to remove the last of the bandages, but he simply prodded my cheek.

"You're not going to remove everything?" I finally asked.

His hand arced down slowly. "I did, Ness."

He must not have, though, because something was still obstructing my sight. I raised my hand to do it myself. When my fingertips bumped against my lashes and the slick surface of my eye, I turned to marble.

CHAPTER 62

The weight of my surprise made my numb fingers glide down a hardened ridge that tapered off into smooth skin.

Greg was saying something, but his words banged into my eardrums without penetrating. I flung the sheet off my legs and got out of bed. When the balls of my feet hit the cold linoleum, my head spun. Two sets of hands wrapped around my upper arms to steady me—Greg's and August's.

The tan-colored wall swam in and out of focus. I shrugged their hands away, then padded into the bathroom in my hospital gown.

Cold air snuck through the papery fabric, wrapping around my bare skin, bringing more goose bumps to the surface.

I flicked the switch on the wall, or thought I did, but my fingers whispered through air, missing their mark. My second attempt, though, was successful.

Light flooded the tiled space that had been scrubbed with so much antibacterial soap my nose twitched. I stepped in front of the mirror, wiped my right eye to clear it of the blur. As my vision sharpened on my reflection, a breath stumbled through my parted lips.

I raised my fingers to my face and traced the two centipede-like violet scars that started at my left temple and curved over my lid and cheek, arcing toward my ear. But the scars were hardly the most alarming thing about my face. No, what truly distressed me was the paleness of my blue iris and black pupil.

I swallowed back the lump rising in my throat. Crying over my appearance and loss of vision felt so silly considering everything.

I caught movement and turned to find August leaning against the door. I palmed the left side of my face to hide my disfigurement.

"Dimples . . ."

The pity coating his tone had me bristling.

I sidestepped him and returned to Greg. "Will my eyesight come back?" I asked, my voice surprisingly firm.

Eyes crinkling with grief, he shook his head. "Your scarring, in time, will become fainter—Liam's has already improved, but he's Alpha so you can't really compare your healing capacities—however, your eye won't improve. The corneal abrasion was too deep and drops of Morgan's blood came in contact with your aqueous humor."

Humor . . . What a strange term for something that was decidedly not funny.

"Do you see anything at all?" he asked.

"No."

He nodded.

Heat glazed my cold spine. Instead of leaning into August, I took a step forward, bumping my shins into the gray base of my hospital bed.

Greg shot out a hand to steady me. "It'll impact your depth perception. You're going to have to relearn how to move your body in space. It'll probably take some time, time during which you shouldn't drive and should exert extra caution on stairs."

My heart pumped blood that felt like sludge through my veins. "How long?"

"Weeks. Months."

Air pulsed through my nose as I thought of my new car. With my hand still covering half my face, I sat on the firm mattress. "Can I still shift?"

"I pumped you with quite a lot of Sillin, so you might not be able to for a while still." He tipped his head toward August. "Shouldn't be too long, though. August can already shift again."

"Completely?" I asked, watching August's jean-clad knees.

"Yes." August's voice was as tight as his locked joints.

After a beat, I asked, "Can I go home?"

"Yes." Greg rose from the bed. "I'll go get all the paperwork in order." His hand dropped to my shoulder and squeezed lightly. "If you have any questions for me, you have my number."

Lowering my gaze to the shiny linoleum, I nodded.

Once Greg left, August crouched in front of me to capture the attention I was withholding from him. His hands coasted over my kneecaps that were wedged together, the bones grinding into one another. I hadn't yet seen the rest of my body but sensed I'd lost too much weight.

"Dimples . . ."

"Is Jeb back?"

August sighed, probably not wanting to discuss my uncle right now. "He's at the inn with Lucy, putting it in order. Liam gave it back to them." August tried to tow my hand off my face, but I resisted. "You don't have to hide from me."

I didn't say anything . . . I couldn't. The lump had grown too much to speak around it.

"Ness . . ."

I turned my face away and stared at the dancing boughs of the oak tree, trying to settle my churning thoughts.

August's knees clicked as he rose. For a long moment, neither of us spoke.

Then, "Can you ask Sarah to come back in here? Just Sarah. No one else."

A moment later, his footfalls petered out. While I waited for her, I wondered if she'd already glimpsed my face without the bandage.

When her lavender-and-silk perfume replaced August's heavy, heady scent, I turned. Making sure no one else was in the room and that the door was shut, I lowered my hand and exposed my ruined face.

Her gaze didn't waver in surprise, didn't widen in horror. It remained steady on mine. I guessed she'd known what to expect.

"You know what's insane?" she finally said, blowing a puff of air out of the corner of her mouth. "It's how ridiculously pretty you still are in spite of your battle scars. Here I thought I'd finally have a chance to outshine you."

Tears tracked down both my cheeks. My left eye was inept at capturing images but not at producing tears.

"Oh, sweetie." Sarah dropped down on the mattress, making it bounce a little, and then she wrapped her arms around my neck and hugged me close.

"I know it's stupid to be angry about this, seeing as I could be dead, but it sucks," I whispered.

Sarah pressed away. "It's not stupid. You're allowed to be angry. I don't think it would be healthy if you weren't." She combed a lock of hair behind my ear, exposing more of the horror.

"Everyone's going to stare."

"Everyone already did."

"But not for the same reasons."

"You're right. Most people are probably going to wonder how you got your scars. Better come up with a good story that doesn't involve a duel with a massive wolf. You don't want to frighten the townspeople." She smiled, but it didn't reach her eyes.

Her perfect eyes and her smooth skin.

"I can't drive. Not for a while. Depth perception," I added glumly.

"Good thing I'm an exceptionally great chauffeur *and* we go to the same school."

"Sarah . . ." I pressed my trembling lips together. Tears circled around them and dripped down my chin, plopping onto my hospital gown.

"What?"

"You're not going to spend your days driving me around."

"Why not? I love driving, and surprisingly enough, I love spending time with you. It's a win-win for me."

A knock on the door had me quickly wiping the tears on my sleeves and finger-combing my hair to shroud half my face.

"Ness?"

Jeb . . .

"Should I let him in?" Sarah asked quietly.

I nodded. "But just him." I didn't want to see Lucy. If she'd even come.

Sarah hugged me again before getting up and letting Jeb inside. "Do you want me to stay, Ness?"

"No. I'll call you when I get home."

"I meant in the room. I'll be out in the hallway. It's a real party out there."

I grimaced. "Can you get everyone to leave? I don't—"

"Say no more. Your wish is my command. Bye, BB."

"BB?"

"Short for Boulder Babe." She winked before pulling the door open.

I eyed the red jacket. If I hadn't been scarred, it might've amused me to wear it, but now . . . now people would surely laugh if I donned it.

"Ness!" My uncle barreled past Sarah and reached my bed before she'd even closed the door. He hugged me so tight it squeezed an *oomph* from my lungs. "I think I've aged a decade in the past week. Between you and Lucy." He didn't mention Everest, but I sensed my cousin was never far from Jeb's mind.

"I heard you got the inn back."

"Thanks to you." He let me go, but then his hand moved to my stringy hair. I let him tuck it behind my ear and inspect the mutilation. His lips pressed so tight they vanished completely in his thick beard. "If Liam hadn't burned her body, I'd—I'd . . ."

"He burned her body?"

"Yes. So she could rot in hell next to Aidan."

Had that been his reasoning, or had Liam worried the silver in her blood would contaminate the soil? For whatever reason he'd done it, I was glad she was well and truly gone.

"I saw Greg signing the discharge papers. Ready to come home?"

I nodded, but then asked, "Which home, though?"

He smiled gently, skating his palm over the side of my face that wasn't injured. "Whichever one you want? You have many now. I kept the apartment. August got a team together to clean and repaint your house, so it's ready too. And the inn, there's always a room with your name on it. It's completely up to you, honey."

"Where are you staying?"

"Wherever you'll be."

I smiled at him. "You don't need to take care of me anymore, Jeb."

"Who's going to take care of me?"

"I'm half-blind." My voice was a cracked whisper.

"You're half-sighted." He combed another lock of hair behind my ear. "And the best way of taking care of a person is to spend time with them and love them. You're really good at that."

"You have Lucy now."

"And what? I can't have *two* women in my life?"

"I know she apologized, but I'm not ready to live with her."

"Then you won't. She'll stay at the inn. And I'll stay wherever you want to live." He stood, extended his hand, palm face up, and waited for me to latch onto it. When I did, he said, "So where shall we go?"

"The apartment," I said without hesitation.

It had been a safe haven, unlike the inn, unlike my parents' house. "I might need some clothes though . . ." I tipped my head to my bare legs poking out of the hospital gown.

"Of course. Let me run back and get you some. Give me a half hour."

After Jeb left, August let himself in again. Draping my hair over the ugly wound, I sank down on the bed and gathered my hands between my knees.

"Everyone's gone," he said, coming to sit next to me.

"Except you."

I felt his body stiffen. "Did you want me to leave?"

"You don't have to stay."

He crooked a finger under my chin and lifted my face. I slid my chin off its perch and dipped it back against my neck. "Why won't you look at me?"

"It's not that I don't want to look at you," I whispered. "It's that I don't want you to look at me."

He sighed, a deep, rattling lungful that softened the line of his body, and then one of his arms hooked my knees and the other curved under my arms. He scooped me up and deposited me with the utmost gentleness onto his lap.

"I don't want you to stay with me because you feel pity, August," I said, nestling my head in the crook of his neck.

He snorted, sliding his hand through the back of the gown and running his fingers delicately over my spine. I felt something stiff press against my thigh.

"Because that's the reason I'm staying with you," he said softly.

"How can you still desire me? My face is—it's . . ." Tears crept down my scars and pooled in the corner of my mouth.

"It's the face I want to wake up to every morning and fall asleep watching every night." August's hand settled on the small of my back. "Besides, I'll remind you that I'm scarred too."

"Not your face."

"No, not my face." He tucked me a little closer still, locking both his arms around my juddering ribs. "Your scars are a piece of you now, and I love all the pieces of you, Ness Clark."

A loud sob scraped up my throat as I burrowed deeper into this man who'd always tried to keep me safe, and who, when he'd failed because I'd pushed him away, had risked his life so I could get mine back.

"You're the love of my entire life, August Watt," I whispered against his neck that smelled of wood and spice . . . that smelled of home.

EPILOGUE

The sunset dripped through the evergreen needles, showering the forest with a crimson glow that turned the rough trunks tawnier. I was still in Colorado, but miles away from Boulder.

When Sarah had caught me crying into my pillow after I'd failed, for the fourth morning in a row, to make myself a cup of coffee—I'd poured the scorching liquid all over the countertop and down my legs instead of inside my mug—she'd booted my butt out of bed and taken me on a road trip to a cabin that belonged to her father, but which he apparently rarely used.

We'd told next no one we'd left—just Liam, Jeb, and Evelyn. Evelyn because her heart would've given out if she thought I'd run away, Jeb so he knew I was safe, and Liam because he could track us, and I didn't want him to give my location away to August.

Sarah believed I'd taken her up on the trip to regain my footing in this new world, but that wasn't the reason I'd gone with her.

I'd gone because I was ashamed.

The morning I spilled the coffee on myself, August had cleaned up my mess. He'd cleaned up most of my messes since I'd been home. And although he never once complained, it wasn't fair to him. Which had been the second reason that propelled me out of Boulder . . . out of his life.

He had everything going for him. He didn't need to be saddled with a girl who couldn't manage to fill a glass, who knocked into furniture, who tripped because she constantly miscalculated the distance between her feet and the raised threshold of a doorway. Perhaps, one day, my brain would catch up with my two-dimensional vision, but until that day came, I didn't want to be anyone's ball-and-chain.

As I rocked in the hammock hooked between two great spruce trees, I twirled an aspen daisy between my fingers, marveling at the petals' lilac shade. I'd picked it with Sarah before she'd headed into town for some fresh produce.

Even though I could never hate you, if you break my heart again—
When I break yours, it breaks mine.

We'd been gone three days, and I'd spent all of them thinking about August, reliving tender moments we'd shared, but then I'd close my eyes to force the memories away, because the pain of being without him made my broken heart hurt more than my broken face.

A car engine rumbled up the long, dusty drive. I imagined Sarah was back. I got down from the hammock to help her with the groceries, but froze when I saw it wasn't a red Mini that had pulled up but a gleaming navy pickup.

Was her father visiting?

When the driver got out and slapped the door shut, the daisy tumbled from my fingers.

In spite of the sunset burning behind the man, darkening his body, there was no mistaking my visitor.

I supposed I would recognize August in the darkest of nights, his shape as familiar to me as my own.

He eyed me a long moment before opening the backseat of his new car and lifting a duffel bag. "You can run, but you can't hide, Ness Clark. Not from me," he said, his back still to me.

Words stuck in my throat as he turned. I wanted to ask him how he'd found me, but did it matter? I dropped my gaze to the bag clutched in his fingers, then looked at the road, wondering if my friend's car was about to make an appearance.

"Sarah will be back in the morning," he said, reading my

thoughts. "Unless you were looking at that road to assess how fast you could get away."

I snapped my attention back to him.

"We need to talk, so don't run. I *will* chase you, but I'd rather not have to do it after the last three days I've had."

As he drew the door of the house open, I finally found my voice, "You said that if I broke your heart again, you'd stay away from me."

He paused on the threshold. "Apparently, I can't."

I winced when the door banged shut behind him.

I DIDN'T GO INSIDE RIGHT AWAY.

I let him settle.

I let his anger settle.

Even though nothing tied me to him, I could sense his irritability seeping through the grayed plank walls of the cabin.

Pulling down the sleeves of my red silk bomber jacket, I waited for the sun to dip completely and lacquer the woods in darkness before heading inside. The air held a chill that made goose bumps spring across my skin. Granted I was only wearing a bikini under the jacket, having spent most of my afternoon drifting around the infinity pool on an inflatable pizza slice, trying to make sense of my life, of what I wanted to do with it now that I had it back.

A single lightbulb burned in the loft-style living area—the copper pendant over the granite dining table. August was bent in front of the fireplace, coaxing a fire to life. He didn't acknowledge me when I came in. Didn't glance over his shoulder as I took a seat on the couch behind him.

He poked the blackening logs. "When you disappeared with Sarah, I told myself you'd left because I couldn't give you what you needed, but then, when *no one* would tell me where you'd gone, I realized you'd left to get away from me." He finally straightened and turned around. "What did I do to make you run?"

"You didn't do anything." Slipping my hands between my knees, I tucked my chin into my neck, hoping the barrage of hair blocked the sight of me. "I left so you could get your life back."

"My life back?" His voice was so shrill it made me look up.

"You don't need to take care of me, okay? Nothing binds us anymore."

His green eyes flared.

"Ingrid—"

"I don't want Ingrid, Ness!"

I recoiled from the harshness of his voice.

"I'm sorry." He spoke quietly this time.

Heat snaked under my lids, blurred the crackling fire.

He came to stand right in front of me. "Thank you for giving me a choice. I didn't realize that was your intention."

I swallowed.

He crouched so his face was level with mine and stole my clammy hands from between my knees, cocooning them in his warm ones. "But, Dimples, I don't want anyone else. I want you. Just *you*."

Sobs stumbled inside my chest. "You say this now, but in a couple years"—my voice broke—"when I still can't fill a cup or drive a car—"

"I'll just say it again."

I bit my wobbly lip.

"Besides, I have no doubt that you're going to be back behind the wheel of a car soon."

"You don't know that," I murmured.

"I do." He hunted my face with his emerald eyes. "You're much too willful to give up hope, or your independence, for that matter." He raised one of his hands to my face to push back my long blonde strands.

I let him look his fill. Maybe if he looked long enough, he'd realize he didn't want to wake up to this face.

When he leaned over and kissed my spoiled cheek, my wet lashes swept down, stayed down. A part of me still didn't understand how he could stand the texture of my scars, much less the sight of them.

"I'm not sure what I have to do to convince you that I can't live without you, Ness." His words pulsed against the tip of my nose. "Bringing you back from the dead would've been enough for most girls."

My lips twitched. I opened my eyes to find his agonizingly gentle ones set on mine.

"Is it because I can't give you any daughters? Is that why you're pushing me away?"

A chuckle burst through my trembling lips. "I love boys too, you know."

He smiled, but then he grew so serious that my laughter wilted. He unfurled his long body, tugging me up in the process. "Will you come home with me? Not tonight. But tomorrow? Or the day after?"

Pressing my lips together to stop their shaking, I nodded.

"Good. Because I have this piece of land."

"By a lake?"

"That's the one. And the only thing standing on it right now is a palm tree."

My head jerked back a little. "You planted a palm tree?"

"Had to have something to build our house around."

Our house? Had this man ever envisioned his life without me?

"I'm starting to have a surplus of houses," I whispered raucously.

"As long as you only have one home."

A fresh wave of emotion slicked my eyes. "Oh, August," I croaked, throwing my arms around his neck.

His calloused hands slipped under the silk fabric of my jacket and pulled me close, pressing my body against his as though to seal me into his skin and erase the distance I'd put between us. Moment after moment passed in this quiet communion.

As the logs crackled in the fireplace, I filled my lungs with his familiar scent and my ears with his heartbeats. How I ever thought I could give up this man was beyond me.

The tendons in his neck flexed under my fingertips. I lifted my head off his chest and craned my neck as his mouth arced toward mine. He kissed me long and deep.

When he started on my neck, I rasped, "Want to go for a swim?" Between what he was doing to me and the fire, I was dangerously close to overheating.

I felt the curve of his smile on my skin. "I didn't bring any swim trunks. Hope it won't be a problem."

I had to clear my throat before I could answer him. "No problem at all."

Keeping his eyes on mine, he unbuttoned his flannel shirt and chucked it on the couch, revealing a torso honed to such incredible perfection that my hands trembled as I removed my jacket and draped it over the arm of the couch. As he lowered the zipper of his jeans, I walked toward the sliding glass doors and dragged them open, then crossed the stone deck and dove into the dusky pool to cool down.

After I broke the surface, I pushed my hair off my face and stared up at the moon that was brilliant and full, illuminating the dark world surrounding us. A moment later, arms wrapped around my stomach and pulled my back against a rock-hard chest.

A rock-hard *everything*.

"You're missing the pack run," I said.

"I'm here with you. Beats any pack run." He rested his chin in the crook of my neck and inhaled me slowly. "God, I've missed you so much."

"I can tell. That thing's going to end up bruising my spine."

"That thing?" He snorted.

I turned around to flick him.

He smiled roguishly at my fingers before backing me against the tiled wall and scooping me up. "To avoid any bruising."

He was no longer my mate, and yet I desired him just as much as when he had been. Locking my eyes on his, I rocked against him slowly.

He gripped my thighs to steady me. "Careful, sweetheart."

I tilted my face to the side to study his expression. "Why? We're no longer mates . . ."

Hurt darkened his freckles. "You're my mate in all the ways that count, Ness Clark."

"I didn't mean—" I held on to his shoulders, my pale fingers crimping his brown skin. "It came out wrong." I linked my arms around his neck. "I love you," I whispered. "Never doubt that."

Keeping one hand underneath me, he brought his other up to tuck a wet lock behind my ear. "I didn't doubt it until you left."

Raindrops began to fall from a dark strip of cloud that moved across the bloated moon, the droplets glittering as they plinked against the glassy surface of the pool.

"I'm so sorry," I whispered.

He cupped my jaw and kissed me. And for a long, *long* moment, that was all we did. And it was perfect and beautiful, but I wanted more. I craved more. So I moved against him again.

He ripped his mouth off mine.

Before he could speak, I said, "I'm not in heat." Sarah had taught me to use my sense of smell to determine my cycle since oral contraceptives didn't work all that well on werewolves.

A vein in August's neck began to throb faster.

I shrugged. "In case you wanted—you know . . ."

"In case I wanted to make love to you in this pool?"

Heat crept up my neck. "Yeah." *So much for using the pool to cool off . . .*

He shifted his hold on me until we were lined up, then his thumb brushed my skimpy bikini bottom aside before settling against my pulsing flesh. As he waited for me to make the next move, he swiped his finger over me.

Heart pounding like my wolf's when she scented her prey, I slid him in, inch by slow inch.

His thumb stilled against me, and a shudder went through him. He closed his eyes. When he opened them again, they glittered as wildly as the stars rioting around the storm cloud.

"I moved your body," I said. "We never talked about it, but I moved you."

"I know, sweetheart. Almost got me killed." He glided himself out and then dipped back in.

I shot him a sheepish smile. "Seems like I'm almost getting you killed a lot. Are you sure you're not better off without me? You'd surely live a much longer life."

August's expression became edged with so much fury and pain that I caressed his jaw.

"I didn't mean to make you angry."

"There is *no* version of me without you, okay?"

"Okay."

"It's you and me, Dimples. Always has been and always will be."

Between the feel of his thick, silky flesh, the scent of spice and rain lifting from his skin, and the timbre of his voice, my heart thundered in my chest. He dragged my body away, then thrust into me, causing the pounding to travel lower. As the rain fell harder, it created a cacophony that drowned out everything but the sound of our hearts.

His lips claimed mine with such violence that our teeth knocked together. My legs clenched around him as a thrill began to build in my core, and then a moan tumbled from my mouth straight into his as the sensation overrode my entire system. He pumped harder, and I clawed at his back, the orgasm exploding inside me, striking my veins and muscles, battering my sinews and bones, scorching my skin.

He deepened the kiss, his teeth catching on my bottom lip. As the taste of warmed copper coated my palate, a new wave of pleasure clapped against my thighs and rushed through my limbs, making me gasp his name.

His rhythm turned brisker, more urgent, rough grunts scraping the walls of his throat, causing the flutter behind my belly button to transform into full-on drumming.

"Sweetheart," he rasped a second before my body undid his.

The water around us rippled, and then it began to glitter as though it were drizzling stars instead of raindrops. It was so beautiful. Everything about that moment was so beautiful. I wanted to immortalize it in my mind for all the years to come.

Still surfing on the wake of my orgasms, I stroked the nape of his neck, watching his features crinkle and smooth as he poured himself inside of me.

Our first time had been special, but this time . . . this time had been spectacular. I hoped it had also been good for August. Maybe he'd had better. I grimaced at the thought.

"I have never had better," he whispered huskily. *"Never."*

The blood drained from my face. Had I spoken out loud?

August blinked. And then color leached from his skin as he looked down at the water that still glittered wildly around us. ***Oh . . . shit.***

I blinked, because his mouth hadn't moved to form the words, and yet somehow, I'd heard them. "Did I—did you—"

My navel pulsed harder than my core and heart put together.

Was the link back?

I think . . . I think . . . His voice surged inside my mind.

"I can hear you. Why can I hear you?" I asked, barely louder than the plinking raindrops. "Did we just . . . did we just *consolidate* the link?"

Sadness furrowed his brow. "I think—God, I'm so sorry. I know you didn't want this." He pressed his forehead against mine, his fingers digging into my thighs. "I'm so sorry," he repeated.

For a moment, I held perfectly still, absorbing the significance of what had just transpired. Then, without using sound or breath, I said, *I'm not.*

He lifted his face off mine.

"Are you actually sorry, August?"

"No." His forehead had smoothed. "But I've wanted this . . . Well, I've wanted this since the tether snapped into place." He shot me a sheepish smile that made him look more boy than man, but then he shifted a little, and I felt him harden inside me again, reminding me that he was all man.

My man.

His smile turned devilish as he tugged on the tether, reeling my body in until he was fully sheathed inside. *That's right, sweetheart.* Your *man.*

I laughed. "I can't decide if I like this new skill of ours or fear it."

"Why would you fear it?"

"Because I'll have no more secrets."

"Planning on keeping things from me now, are you?" He grunted, so I flicked him, which just intensified his amusement.

"How am I supposed to surprise you with anything if you can read my mind?"

I'll act surprised.

I rolled my eyes but grinned.

For a moment, neither of us spoke, neither out loud, nor through the new connection that had opened between our minds. We simply contemplated each other.

Then, "You look happy tonight, Dimples. Are you?"

I cupped his jaw, roughened by stubble and years, and even

though I didn't need to sound the word, I spoke it out loud for the moonlit land to hear. "Terribly."

READY FOR LIAM'S STANDALONE?
DIVE RIGHT INTO A PACK OF STORMS AND STARS.

Want to find out what happens to your favorite Alpha, Liam Kolane? Get the first spinoff here:

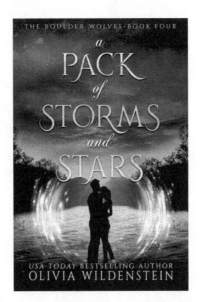

Be sure to sign up for my newsletter to stay up to date on all of my future releases:
Sign up on www.oliviawildenstein.com

WANT MORE PARANORMAL ROMANCE?

Discover my completed LOST CLAN series that readers have compared to *The Vampire Diaries,* but with faeries.
Start the adventure with **ROSE PETAL GRAVES**.

In a witchy, slow-burn romance mood? Travel to the coldest and mistiest town in France with a ragtag crew tasked with bringing magic back to the world in **OF WICKED BLOOD.**

Or head over to the City of Lights with my angels in **FEATHER** for a modern and darkly romantic *Romeo & Juliet* retelling.

ACKNOWLEDGMENTS

This book has been one of the hardest books I've written in my career.

The first reason being that it's the last chapter in my trilogy, which means I'm indefinitely parting with my characters. (There might be a spinoff at some point, but I won't promise anything until I'm certain I can deliver.)

The second reason it was bittersweet to pen is because of the love triangle. You might not believe this, but it wasn't my intention to write one. Originally, *The Boulder Wolves* was supposed to be a duology (Ha! Like I could ever fit all my twists and turns inside two books . . .) and Liam was supposed to die at the start of book 2.

Well, I loved him too much to kill him off, so I adapted my storyline to fit him inside.

And that's how I ended up with a love triangle.

Anyway, all this to say that I didn't mean to do this to Ness, or to you.

I hope you've enjoyed this series. Thank you for running along with my wolves, for your heartfelt messages and kind reviews. I hope you'll join me on my next adventures.

Up next, angels: **FEATHER**!

Thank you to my own true mate for putting up with me. For making my life sweet and beautiful, each and every day. For taking me on adventures even when I want to stay home with my computer.

Thank you to my children for inspiring me and for filling my life with your shrill voices and contagious laughter.

Thank you to my family for buying my books. Even if you never get around to reading them, I appreciate your support.

Thank you to my kick-ass beta readers—Katie, Astrid, and Theresea. I love you girls so darn much.

Thank you to my publisher, to my fabulous editor, Krystal, who never fails to challenge me, to my hawk-eyed proofreader, Janelle (there were *a lot* of backs . . .), and to Monika for another gorgeous cover.

But most of all, thank *you*.

ALSO BY OLIVIA WILDENSTEIN

YA PARANORMAL ROMANCE

The Lost Clan series
ROSE PETAL GRAVES
ROWAN WOOD LEGENDS
RISING SILVER MIST
RAGING RIVAL HEARTS
RECKLESS CRUEL HEIRS

The Boulder Wolves series
A PACK OF BLOOD AND LIES
A PACK OF VOWS AND TEARS
A PACK OF LOVE AND HATE
A PACK OF STORMS AND STARS

Angels of Elysium series
FEATHER
CELESTIAL
STARLIGHT

The Quatrefoil Chronicles series
OF WICKED BLOOD
OF TAINTED HEART

YA ROMANTIC SUSPENSE

Masterful series
THE MASTERKEY

THE MASTERPIECERS
THE MASTERMINDS

YA ROMANCE STANDALONES

GHOSTBOY, CHAMELEON & THE DUKE OF GRAFFITI
NOT ANOTHER LOVE SONG